EMMET AND ME

With best wishes,

Sara Gethin

honno

Gwasg Menywod Cymru
Welsh Women's Press

Also by Sara Gethin and available from Honno Press

Not Thomas

EMMET AND ME

Sara Gethin

HONNO MODERN FICTION

First published in 2021 by Honno Press, Ailsa Craig, Heol y Cawl, Dinas Powys, Vale of Glamorgan, Wales, CF64 4AH

1 2 3 4 5 6 7 8 9 10

A catalogue record for this book is available from the British Library.

Published with the financial support of the Books Council of Wales.

ISBN Paperback: 978-1-912905-33-1
ISBN Ebook: 978-1-912905-34-8

Cover design and illustration: Ruth Rowland
Cover images: © Shutterstock/Elzbieta Sekgwska/Dima Aslanian
Text design: Elaine Sharples
Printed in Great Britain by 4edge Limited

In memory of PT
and for S, R and J, as always

Acknowledgements

Thank you to everyone who helped make this book a reality. To Lucy Irvine, my wonderful agent at PFD, for seeing potential in the very early manuscript, and for wise guidance throughout. To the whole team at Honno Welsh Women's Press, especially my editor, Caroline Oakley, and also Helena and Janet, for being such a fantastic outfit and a true pleasure to work with. To lettering artist, Ruth Rowland, for another beautiful cover design. To my writing group friends and to Hay Writers at Work, for their thought-provoking feedback and for being such inspiring writers. To the readers of my debut novel, *Not Thomas*, for whose support I am extremely grateful, and to the amazing network of book bloggers that have reviewed my writing, for their dedication to promoting books and reading, and for giving so generously of their time. To Matthew Taylor and team, for insightful advice very early on, for setting me on the right path and giving me the confidence to keep going. To my early readers, Frank Phelan, Mairéad Cullen, Becca Jay, Lisa Kuhl, Jon David and Carole Ann Smith, for their very thoughtful comments, all of which have been invaluable. And to my wonderful family and friends, for their unfailing support, encouragement and love.

Special gratitude to the late Diarmuid Whelan who made possible the collection of Peter Tyrrell's memoirs, *Founded on Fear*, which provided much food for thought and sparked the idea for *Emmet and Me*.

I once had a forbidden friend. He was funny and brave, had scabbed knees and grubby shorts, a gleeful grin and fathomless eyes. My co-conspirator and hero. He called himself Emmet.

A Note from the Narrator

It was my brother who asked me to write this story. He'd reminded me that, since childhood, I'd imagined myself a writer. Now, he'd coaxed, was my chance to realise that dream. He wasn't simply indulging me. On those rare occasions when we'd meet up at weddings and funerals, I could tell he was frustrated to hear his family discuss the summer of '66, while he had so little to add himself.

What he didn't realise was that I'd already written it. A few years previously, I'd committed to a file on my computer a record of what happened during those months because, while he had barely a recollection of that summer, those times burned fiercely in my own memory. The child I was in the sixties, I'd realised, was still somehow trapped inside me, displaced and floundering. I shouldn't have been surprised. That was the decade my family imploded. I'd hoped to purge myself of the memories by transferring them into the written word – it was supposed to do the trick, it had done that before... So I began to type, believing that at the very least I was creating a family history, something future generations might find enlightening, and hoping it might banish some demons too.

But as I wrote, I discovered there weren't so many demons waiting to be dispelled as truths to be faced up to, and the story became less my family's and more my own – or to be exact, mine and Emmet's. Because, although my brothers and wider family played a huge part in that summer, it was Emmet who shaped the rest of my life.

Claire O'Connell
April 2016

Chapter 1

We were extremely annoying children. Our mother made that clear enough, though most of her Welsh curses were mercifully beyond our grasp of the language. It was only years later that I recalled the words she used to say, and realised their cruelty.

On the very first Saturday of the summer holidays, in the year I turned ten, we reached peak nuisance. I had wanted to cook my own tea – scrambled eggs, no less. Will had mentioned at least once he'd like to go to the reference library, and poor Louis had accidentally soiled his pants. We knew our mother had cracked when she started flinging the second-best plates at the wall above the cooker. When she picked up the good ones, we realised we'd broken her. We hid, trembling, under the kitchen table as Dad pleaded with her to calm herself. He'd been out for cigarettes and had come home three hours later with a smudge of something on his collar that Mother called 'Chanel Red'. Despite his pleas, she didn't calm down and he herded us to the hallway, shielding us from shattering china with a much too flimsy tea tray. 'Run!' he ordered and we charged up the stairs and into the bathroom where we locked the door and waited for reinforcements.

Help eventually came in the form of our uncle. Mother had given up on smashing things by the time he arrived from the pub but we could still hear her yelling. 'I bought her that lipstick. My *bridesmaid*. How could you? How could she? *Yr ast*!'

'Hi, kiddos.' It was Jack calling through the bathroom door. 'It's safe to come out now and I need a pee.'

We were relieved to hear his voice. Nothing serious happened when Jack was around. With him it was all jokes, ice cream and trips in Dad's Cortina belting out our favourite song – 'The Wild Rover', because we loved the 'no, nay, never' bit. Having Jack with us made everything all right. Will and I had laughed when our mother threw her first plate – actually laughed because it was so ridiculous, an adult throwing a plate. And Louis had laughed too, because he always copied what Will and I did. But while we were locked in the bathroom, what was happening downstairs was a terribly scary thing, and Louis had cried and cried. Jack was here now, though, and everything would be fine.

'Grab your pyjamas, Claire ... Will,' he told us as we burst out of the bathroom and he dashed past us for the toilet. 'You're coming to stay with me for tonight.'

Will and I looked at each other in amazement. Staying with Jack? Our dreams had come true. We'd never been to Jack's place before. We ran to get our things and I found Louis something to sleep in and his teddy. I was good at being a big sister when I had to be.

'Ready!' Will and I sang, as Jack emerged from the bathroom zipping up his flies.

'Grand,' he said. He cocked his head so he could better hear the voices downstairs. 'I think there's a lull in the war. Come on, out of here while we still can.' And we ran for our lives to the car with 'I've been a wild rover' ready on our lips.

* * *

Jack parked the Cortina on a terraced street. One or two of the houses had rubbish around their gates but most of them had tidy front gardens. 'Less likely to get your dad's tyres robbed here,' he told us. 'And it's not too far to the docks.'

We walked for ten minutes then stopped outside a pub. Jack said he was very sorry but children weren't allowed inside, so Will and I sat with Louis on a little wall near the door. The salty smell of the sea was all around and gulls flew over our heads. They perched on the rooftops, arguing noisily. I tried to spy a beach nearby but I couldn't spot even a glimpse of one between the houses, they were too tightly packed together. We waited on that wall for a long time and I was sorry I hadn't brought *Black Beauty*. I was reading it for the second time and I knew there was an exciting bit coming up. I'd been looking forward to spending the whole day with Beauty until Mother ruined my plans. How typical of her. I slipped from the wall and lifted Louis down after me.

'Giddy up,' I said, shaking his blue reins, and my little brother set off along the pavement. It was one of our favourite games. I loved the way the leather felt in my hands and if I closed my eyes a fraction, I could imagine Louis's blond head belonged to my imaginary pony. I'd named it Star. Mother said I should want a black pony named Beauty since I loved her old book so much but, as she often reminded me, I simply *had* to be different. After we'd cantered up and down the pavement enough times to wear us out, I pulled Louis to a halt with an 'Easy there, boy,' and Will rolled his eyes. I ignored him, as usual, and gave Louis's head a pat.

A lady came out of the pub, wobbling on high heels. She reminded me of a film star on a poster at the cinema, the one that was framed and hanging behind the sweet counter. The actress on it was wearing a black dress and had red lips, and the film was called *Some Like It Hot*. The wobbly woman was a lot older and nowhere near as pretty as the actress, but she did have blonde hair and thick red lipstick. Film stars were always very beautiful. People said Mother was just like Natalie Wood from *West Side Story*. I'd never seen the film but I guessed it must have a lot of shouting in it. The woman coming out of the pub was clutching onto the arm of a man with greased hair. When she saw my little brother, she bent down and gave his cheeks a squeeze.

'Handsome child,' she said, the words all running into each other. 'Whass 'is name?'

I didn't like the way she was leaning over us, and her powdery make-up had somehow climbed right up my nose, but I gave Louis a nudge. 'Tell the lady.'

He took a big breath. 'Lou-eee,' he announced, and the woman squealed and pinched his cheeks even harder. She wobbled so much, I thought she might fall headfirst into the gutter.

The man with the greasy hair turned to Will. 'Not interested in the World Cup then?' Will shrugged and the man shook his head. 'It's a lousy match anyway,' he said, just as a shock of yells burst from the pub.

'Charlton scored,' someone called when the man asked what was going on. 'From way out.'

I looked behind the couple through the open door to the crowd of men inside the pub. There was football on the telly and most people were bunched around the set. I searched the faces for Jack, and then I spotted him, with his elbow resting on the bar and a full glass in his other hand. He was talking for all he was worth to a man wiping glasses. I tried to catch his eye to remind him we were waiting outside but he was enjoying himself far too much to take any notice of my frantic waving.

After what felt like hours, he brought us a packet of crisps to share. He said he had a pint to finish and he wouldn't be long. Will and I took turns keeping Louis entertained by feeding him tiny corners of crisps. We kept the big pieces for ourselves. We finished the packet in five minutes flat and then we were bored again. The sounds of the football match finally faded and loud music started playing instead. Will said they must have a juke box in there. I'd heard the song before – 'What's New Pussycat?' by a singer Mother called 'her kind of Welshman' – and I tried to get Louis to join in with the 'whoa-whoa-whoa-oh's but he was too grumpy. He kept twisting around and around on his reins, tangling himself up and trapping my fingers. We were all glad when Jack finally reappeared and led us the rest of the way to his home.

* * *

'Sure, it's not the most salubrious of places,' he said, as we followed him between two rows of tall gloomy houses, 'but it'll do for the night.' The air in his street was thick with the smell of seawater, and

4

it was mixed with something else. It reminded me of the black paint Dad used on our garden fence. I couldn't decide if that smell was disgusting or delicious, but here it seemed to fill my lungs and I definitely didn't like that. I was glad when Jack led us up some steps and opened the front door of a very thin house. We followed him along a dark hallway and climbed some narrow stairs.

'Can we put a light on?' Will asked. I'd handed Louis over to him, not trusting myself to keep hold of his wriggly body. Will had sighed as he took him from me. He didn't like being in charge of Louis. He said it was woman's work.

'No electric,' Jack told him, flicking the light switch at the top of the stairs up and down to prove it. 'Not far to go now, though.'

After a few more steps, he stopped and pulled a key from his pocket. 'Ta-da!' he announced, flinging open the door.

'Shut up, will you?' a gruff voice shouted. It seemed to be coming from near the ceiling, but in the dim light it was impossible to make out what was what. The lack of lighting didn't stop the smell reaching us, though – boiled onions and sweaty feet.

'That's Ezekiel,' Jack whispered. 'The Preacher. He works nights. Takes the bed up there during the day. He'll be warming it up nicely for us.'

My eyes were slowly adjusting to the light coming in from the small window. It had a corner missing from one of the panes and the sound of the seagulls outside was as loud as if they had been in the room with us. I could spot a few shapes of furniture. There was a small table with a bowl and jug on it, and two chairs covered in clothes. Towering over the table and chairs, and cutting the height at the back of the room in half, was a wooden frame and platform with a ladder going up to it. I could just make out a bearded face peering over the edge.

'What are you doing bringing children to this God-forsaken house, Jack?' the face asked.

''Tis only for the night, preacher man,' Jack answered. 'Nothing for you to worry about. You'll be off in an hour or two in any case.'

'I was hoping for some more sleep,' the man muttered, but he was plodding down the ladder anyway, his braces dangling at his knees. He grabbed his shirt from the nearest chair. 'Don't touch my things,' he told us. Even in the bad light I could see the threatening look in his eyes.

Will and I shook our heads and Louis hid behind my legs.

'The kiddies are great, so,' Jack said. 'They'll be no bother.'

'They better not be here when I get back,' the man said, and slammed the door taking some of the revolting smell with him but leaving more than enough behind.

'Don't mind him,' Jack told us. He lit a candle stump on a saucer. 'He's fine enough with a few pints in him. Now, who's going to sleep where?'

It was a question I'd been asking myself ever since my eyes had got used to the light in the room. The platform seemed to be the only bed and I didn't like the idea of Louis sleeping up so high. I could clearly imagine him dropping head-first over the edge. And I certainly didn't like the idea of that horrible old man warming the bed for us.

'There's room for four men up there,' Jack said, 'top to tail like, so we'll fit no problem.' He saw the look on my face and added quickly, 'Or we can put my coat on the floor, if you're not keen on sleeping up high.'

'Do you really live here?' I asked, and my voice must have given away my disgust as Will shot me a look that said I'd thoroughly overstepped the mark.

'It's all some of us can afford,' Jack said, quite happily. 'You can thank your lucky stars your mother has an allowance from her parents or you'd be in a hole like this on your father's wages too. Thank God for fraud, eh?' He laughed, then he turned serious for a moment. 'Don't be telling your parents I said that, though.'

Jack was always talking about 'Fraud'. My best friend Karen had an Aunty Maud, so I'd decided a long time ago that Fraud must be an aunt on my mother's side that nobody except Jack talked about. There seemed to be quite a few people in our family only Jack talked about.

I couldn't bear the thought of him coming home to this horrible place every evening. 'Why don't you live with us? You could have the parlour and keep Dad company when he's listening to music.' But I wasn't sure Dad wanted company in the parlour. Will and I weren't allowed in there whenever our father played his records. We had to make do with listening through the door.

'Ah now, that's very kind of you, Claire, but I'm not sure your mother would be wanting me living in her house.' He shook out his coat and placed it on the floor by the table.

I realised he was right. Mother wouldn't want Jack living with us. She said he led our father into temptation. I knew that had something to do with the prayer we said every morning in school but what it actually meant I could only guess. I expected that it might mean Jack was leading Dad into pubs he wouldn't otherwise go into. Mother didn't like that at all.

'Now,' Jack said, pointing to the coat on the floor, 'if you and Louis sleep there, Will and I can take the bed. I know the floor won't be very comfy, but believe me, the bed's as bad.'

Will was already halfway up the ladder. 'This bed stinks,' he called down, pulling a face.

Jack gave a short laugh. 'That'll be the preacher leaving us a wet patch, no doubt. Ah sure, we'll sleep either side of it.'

I was glad I hadn't brought my precious *Black Beauty* to such a smelly dump of a room. We didn't get changed. It seemed pointless. Instead I wrapped my pyjamas and Will's around Louis and me for warmth, and put Louis's sleep suit under my head and his teddy under his. Normally, if he had to sleep anywhere other than his cot, he'd have made grumbly sounds – half-Welsh half-English not-quite-words – but he was too worn out by what Will called 'the great plate-flinging episode' to complain. I must have been exhausted too, because just as I was thinking I'd never be able to sleep in such an awful place, I woke up to find light streaming through a flimsy curtain and the preacher man standing over me with a string of onions in his hand.

7

* * *

'She'll never agree,' Dad said. He was in the kitchen talking to Jack. Will and I had been sent to play in our bedroom, but we were sitting on the landing instead, our ears straining for all they were worth. Every now and then, we had to shush Louis. We'd solved the problem of keeping him in our room by bribing him with Will's model farm – he was never normally allowed anywhere near it, even though Will was far too old to play with it anymore – but we'd accidentally caused the problem of his animal sound effects. He really wasn't interested in our shushing, so we only caught snatches of what Dad and Jack were talking about.

'My place isn't fit for the kids.'

Jack was right about that. After I'd stopped screaming at the preacher man and his onions, I realised I was covered in bites – horrible itchy ones. Louis had them too and so did Will. Jack said he was immune to fleas by now and the bites would stop itching if we didn't scratch them. Didn't scratch them? How on earth could we not scratch them?

Dad had found the calamine lotion as soon as we got home, and after we'd put our clothes in a bucket outside the back door and had a bath, he'd plastered us in the pink ointment. The relief was wonderful, although I didn't like the feel of cotton wool on my skin. It always made me gag, as if it had somehow climbed into my mouth when I wasn't looking and stuck to the back of my throat. One day, when I'd caught my finger in the spokes of Will's bike, I tried to explain to Mother why I hated cotton wool so much. She just shook her head, said I was a strange child and kept dabbing away at my cut with a clump of the stuff soaked in Dettol. I didn't mention my horror of it again the next time I got an injury, but I was annoyed at my mother for not caring about my feelings and for calling me a strange child, whether it was true or not.

'What do you think the place is like now?' That was Dad's voice.

It had barely a trace of Irishness. Mother often teased him that he sounded more like a man from Cardiff than Connemara.

'Sure, I don't expect a thing's changed around there in the last twenty years,' Jack laughed. 'Except electrification – she's just been connected.'

'It's 1966 and she's only just got electricity in the cottage?' Dad said.

'Well, a few years back, anyhow,' Jack told him. 'The Lynches out on the big boreen were difficult, you know, wouldn't agree to the line.'

'Makes a change from *her* being the difficult one.' I had to listen hard to hear Dad over the baaa-ing coming from Louis's direction. 'What's she like now?'

'She doesn't drink anymore,' Jack said.

'So she *says.*'

Louis had found the tractor. 'Shush,' I pleaded, as he started up his revving sounds.

Will tapped my arm. 'Jack just said, "We'd better leave for the ferry soon." I think they're talking about Ireland.'

'Ireland? Are we going to Granny Connemara's?' We'd never once been to our Irish grandmother's home and she wasn't mentioned in ours, although we knew Jack spoke to her on our telephone every month. She would call on the second Sunday – three rings to let Dad know it was her. He never answered but Jack would pick up the phone when it rang again and he would chat away. It seemed a lot of bother to go to, all that ringing and not picking up, but it wasn't something we could ask Dad about. I'd tried once and the look my father had given me had made me want to bite my tongue off. Mother simply said that Granny Connemara was a dragon, as if that explained it all. When I'd asked Jack, he'd given me an answer that confused me even more. He said Dad and Granny had fallen out a long time ago. But when I asked what they'd fallen out *of*, he'd almost laughed. Then he'd frowned. Then he'd sighed. 'Don't go asking your father that,' he'd said. 'Promise me, Claire.' So I never got to the bottom of why Dad didn't answer the phone himself. He never talked about Ireland at all, but Jack told us tales of our Irish family when we were out with him in the car.

He had three stories – one about his great-great-grandmother who could heal sick people, another about a great-great-uncle who let a tramp live in his big old shed, and my favourite about his great-great-grandfather who could talk to wild animals. They told him when storms were coming. I wished I could talk to animals, like Johnny Morris from *Animal Magic*. I quite often tried to talk to squirrels in the park without much success, although I had an inkling they knew exactly what I was saying and were simply refusing to reply. After every story Jack would say, 'Now don't be telling your father I told you that.' They weren't very entertaining stories really, but Jack could make anything sound amusing.

'Do you think they're going to send us to Granny's?' I asked Will.

'Shush,' he told me sharply. 'Just listen.'

'Can we trust her?' we heard Dad say.

'Do you have a better plan, now Eleri's run off to her sister?'

'So Mother's gone to Aunty Rhian's,' I said. The only aunty whose existence we knew of for certain shared a flat with two of her friends. She'd been fifteen, so Mother said, when she'd packed her bags in Carmarthen and made a dash for London – a year younger than Mother had been when she'd run away to Cardiff. Our mother said her sister just had to go one better, but she'd soon find out in the big city that she wasn't quite the jet setter she'd always imagined she was. Now Mother had run away to London, too, like a jet setter herself.

'Be quiet,' Will hissed as I sighed loudly.

'You can't look after the kids,' Jack said. 'And neither can I. They'll have to—'

'Moooo,' Louis announced loudly, as he crawled out onto the landing. '*Buwch. Buwch.*' He tried to hand me a plastic cow.

'Shut up, Louis,' I said, but I'd already missed the end of Jack's sentence. 'What did he say, Will?'

My brother looked at me with a mixture of surprise and fear. 'He said, "They'll have to go to Ma's today." Can you believe it?'

I groaned. 'But I'm supposed to be going to see *Mary Poppins* tomorrow.' I'd nagged and nagged to be allowed to go with Karen. She said Julie Andrews made a much better nanny than a nun, which I was glad about – I'd nodded off in *The Sound of Music*. Karen had already seen *Mary Poppins* twice and knew all the words to every song. Her 'Feed the Birds' brought tears to my eyes.

'Right kiddos!' Jack shouted, as he burst from the kitchen, sending us scampering off the landing and into our bedroom. 'It's time to get your stuff. Grab enough for a few weeks. You're going on holiday, so.'

We poked our heads out of the bedroom door as Jack bounded up the stairs. Will was casually holding a comic. My prop was my hairbrush. It was covered in a dark brown tangle.

'Where are we going?' Will asked innocently.

'Somewhere nice,' Jack said. 'Now get packing.'

A holiday was a holiday after all, I told myself, and I rushed off to find my new summer dress with the little lace collar and my pink Start-rite sandals. I'd persuaded Mother to buy the exact same outfit that Karen's father had bought for her. She looked so pretty in it, and I hoped the dress and shoes would make me look pretty, too, even if I didn't have blonde hair and blue eyes. Karen and I had been planning to wear our matching outfits to the cinema, but now, if I was going to Ireland, I might as well make the most of it. Maybe I'd get to see *Mary Poppins* there. I added two T-shirts and some jeans to the pile, and a cardigan and jumper. Will plonked his clothes on the bed too, grumbling into my ear that no matter what Jack said, we certainly weren't going anywhere 'nice'. Finally, I packed my books. Most of my favourites were in the library and I was sorry now I hadn't had a chance to borrow the best ones to read on holiday. But I could take my treasured *Black Beauty* with me. I carefully tucked it into my folded cardigan, along with the compendium of pony stories Aunty Rhian had given me for my

11

birthday. I hadn't started reading that book yet, but every evening I held it to my face and breathed in its bookshop smell. I imagined all the brilliant words and exciting stories inside, and my stomach flipped with joy. I topped the stack with my *Concise Oxford Dictionary*. Mother had thought it an odd request for a birthday present, but I'd been desperate for my own copy. Will was very mean with his, and there were just so many words I longed to look up.

We probably weren't the best packers, and in the end Dad got down the old trunk from the attic. He threw in everything from the bed and emptied our wardrobe and drawers too. I rescued my books, pushing them quickly into the sides of the trunk, making sure the pages weren't bent. Then Will and I climbed onto the lid to squash it shut while Dad did up the catches. Jack bumped it down the stairs and dragged it out to the boot of the car. I grabbed my Sindy doll, torch and my notebook, and followed Dad, Louis and Will outside.

'Bye my babies,' Dad said. He put his arms around Will and me, trapping Louis in the middle of us. He kissed us twice on our heads. 'Now, be good for your granny, won't you?'

'Granny Costa Del?' I asked, my fingers tightly crossed. Our mother's mother wore colourful clothes that Mother said were 'the height of fashion', and when she walked she jangled on account of her golden jewellery. She and our grandfather had lived in Spain for a couple of years but we'd never visited them there. In Carmarthen, they'd had a very big house with a long drive and two garages. But we'd heard that in Spain they had a swimming pool. An actual swimming pool! I was desperate to see if it was true. *Oh, please let Will have got it wrong*, I begged the bearded God I imagined sitting on a cloud and fiddling with a harp somewhere above me. *Please don't let us be going to Granny Connemara*. But I was afraid our fate would be much, much worse than a trip to Spain. We had, after all, just the day before absolutely ruined our mother.

Dad shook his head. 'No, not there. You're off to Ireland with Jack. And if he's wrong about this,' he added with a sharp look at our uncle, 'there'll be hell to pay.'

'When are we coming back?' Will asked.

'Soon,' Dad promised.

'Is Jack staying too?' I could hear the hope in Will's voice.

'For a few days,' Jack said. 'Come on now, will you? Get in or we won't make the boat.'

Dad helped Louis into the back of the car while Will and I fought over the front seat. 'Age before beauty, Claire,' Dad said, picking me up. 'Pretend you know how to behave, will you?' Then he fired me head first onto the back seat. 'See you all soon.'

It was the last thing he said to us for a very long time.

Chapter 2

Had I known that Wales would become a distant memory, I might have paid more attention to my last moments on Welsh soil. Instead I was totally absorbed by the thought of crossing the sea to Ireland.

* * *

The boat we boarded was nothing like I'd expected. It was huge, for a start, and we could walk around it. Louis and I could run around it, too, but even Jack got tired of us doing that and told us to sit down quietly. I imagined it would be like the ferry we took once when we were on holiday in England. Dad had driven onto it and we'd all stayed in the car and watched as the other side of the river got closer and closer. But this ferry was nothing like that – we'd had to leave the car downstairs, for a start.

After half an hour, Will and I went onto the deck and tried to spot Ireland, but it was getting dark and there was nothing to see, just Great Britain behind us and water for miles and miles ahead. I couldn't swim yet, but my class was signed up for a course of lessons when school started again. Will was great at swimming. Dad always said it was very important to know how to swim, even though he never went near the pool himself.

It took ages to get to Ireland. Louis slept most of the way but when he woke up, all he did was cry. Even Jack couldn't get him to stop.

'He'll be missing your mother,' he said, bouncing Louis on his knee for all he was worth.

Will was so embarrassed by all the noise, he took himself off to a quiet corner to study his maps.

'What's Granny Connemara like?' I asked as I settled down next to Jack. It was past midnight, and after all the running around I suddenly felt exhausted. I'd been thinking about how Mother had said many, many times that our Irish granny was a dragon. Mother usually muttered the Welsh word '*ast*' when she talked about Dad's mother, but *ast* wasn't a word Will and I were supposed to use about anyone. I wasn't really sure what *ast* meant, but still it was very unfair that only Mother was allowed to use a word you could say with a hiss.

'Your granny? Well,' he paused for a moment. 'Sure, she's quite a woman.' He scratched his head and frowned. 'But she's friendly enough,' he added quickly, turning to look at me. 'Won't you have a grand time with her.'

'Are we going to stay in the house you and Dad grew up in?' I knew nothing about my father and uncle's childhood.

'That's the one,' Jack said.

'Is Granny's house in a street like our street?' I hoped it was. The council had just built a new park at the end of ours. It had a witch's hat climbing frame that spun around fast. Wayne from my class had already flung himself off it and broken his arm.

'No, Granny's cottage is in the country.' Jack shifted Louis around on his lap. He'd fallen asleep sitting upright and Jack moved him carefully, gently resting Louis's head against his chest.

'Was it fun growing up there?' I asked. I wasn't certain anyone could have much fun in the countryside. Mother had grown up surrounded by fields, so she said, and she'd escaped to the city as soon as she could. Jack was quiet for so long I thought he might have nodded off. I glanced up at my uncle and found him gazing out of the window. I looked too and saw nothing but blackness. 'Was it?' I said.

'Ah, sure it was,' he told me quietly, and he brushed a hand over Louis's hair. 'It was a great laugh, so.'

* * *

15

Eventually, we piled back into the car and men with rugged faces waved us off the ferry and into the light of dawn. The roads in Ireland wound round and around and it didn't take long before Louis stretched out on the back seat with his head on my lap, worn out by all the howling, and fell asleep again. Jack gave Will the atlas so he could navigate.

'Don't you remember the way, Jack?' I asked, annoyed that Will had an important job and I didn't.

'Ah sure, it's all changed around these parts since I was last home.'

But it didn't look as though anything had changed for at least a thousand years. The roads were narrow and bumpy, and in the half-light the hedges that hunched over them seemed to threaten us, like wizards shaking angry fists. I pressed myself into the seat. The summer before, I'd been mad on library books about witches and wizards. Now I wished with all my heart I hadn't borrowed so many stories about magic. I was relieved when the sun finally got higher, and the wizard hedges became no more than branches and leaves. At last I could enjoy the view. The colour of the fields in the morning light amazed me. It was a kind of green I'd never seen before – too green for real grass. It looked like the plastic stuff in the butcher's window. There was nothing much else to look at, though, except hills and cows, and so, after a while, I fell asleep.

I was jolted awake as the car suddenly stopped. 'Toilet break,' Jack said. 'All out.' He swung Louis from the back seat and onto his hip then strode up the steps of a little teashop. It had grey net curtains in the window and peeling paint on the door, but I was glad we'd stopped because now he'd come to mention it, I needed a wee very badly.

I hopped out of the car and ran up the steps too.

'Hello, how are you?' Jack said to a woman who was wiping down the tables. The café was clearly not very popular because, apart from the woman with the cloth, there was only one other person there – an old woman in a headscarf and buttoned-up coat, drinking tea. She stared at us as we walked in.

'How are you yourself?' the woman with the cloth said without looking at us. She didn't sound very friendly. Then she lifted her head and saw Jack, and her face lit up because it was hard not to smile at Jack's cheerful face. 'Is it breakfast you're after?'

'Now breakfast would be grand,' Jack said in the strongest Irish accent I'd ever heard him use, 'but first, would you have a toilet for the kiddies? We've been on the road a desperate long while and they're bursting.'

The word 'bursting' made me suddenly clutch my crotch.

'They're out back, so,' the woman said, frowning at me worriedly. It looked like she'd only just mopped the floor and she very clearly didn't want to have to do it again. She pointed across the yard and I dashed off followed by the others. 'You'll be wanting tea,' she called after us, 'and maybe some eggs and a few rashers?'

I charged across the yard and lifted the latch on the door to the outside toilet. There was only one and I was already pulling up my skirt when Jack elbowed me out of the way.

'Quick, let me get your brother on the pot first,' he said. Louis's face was red and he was squirming in Jack's arms. We knew what that meant. I clutched myself again and let him get to the toilet, but sadly there were just too many buttons on the fly of Louis's shorts, and not enough time to undo them.

* * *

'What brings you to these parts?' the café woman asked. She'd told us her name was Nuala and she kept topping up our tea cups.

'We're on our way to Galway,' Jack said. 'I'm bringing these three to stay with their grandmother for the summer.'

'Galway, is it?' the old woman on the next table said. She'd been chipping in like this since we'd sat down.

Nuala ignored her. 'You and your wife will be getting some peace then.' She smiled at Jack and her eyes sparkled.

'Oh no, they're not mine,' he laughed, nodding in our direction.

17

'I'm their uncle.' He winked at Will and me as we stuffed ourselves with bacon, eggs and soda bread. 'I'm a bachelor myself.'

'A bachelor,' the old woman said, raising her eyebrows at Nuala.

Louis was dancing between the tables, swaying the flowery tea towel Nuala had tucked around his waist – 'For decency's sake,' she'd told us.

'So you're not living in Galway yourself?' she asked Jack.

'I live in Cardiff,' he said, wiping his plate with the last of the bread. 'My brother, too. There's plenty of work there at the minute for us. We go where we can to earn a crust, you know how it is.'

'I do.' Nuala sighed. 'Don't I have three brothers in England and no sign of them coming home.'

'Three brothers,' the old woman repeated, shaking her head at us sadly. 'All of them away.'

We'd eaten and drunk fit to burst so we had another turn on the toilet just to be on the safe side. Jack settled the bill with Nuala and we waited at the door, ready to head out to the car. The weather had turned and we didn't want to stand in the rain any longer than we needed. 'Well, thank you for your great hospitality,' Jack said, giving Nuala a wide smile.

'It's been a pleasure,' she said. 'It's quiet enough these days. Goodbye to you, Claire.' She'd learnt our names as she sat watching us eat. 'I'm sure you'll be a great help to your grandmother.' Then her eyes landed on Will tucking the atlas back under his arm and Louis swishing his makeshift skirt. 'Don't yous boys go terrorising your granny, now.'

'It'll be Cash Hill for you,' the old woman said sternly, 'if you do.'

Jack looked sharply at the woman and frowned. 'Cash Hill?'

'Don't go scaring them with the bad boys' school, Ma,' Nuala said, and flicked the chunk of string vest she was using as a cloth at the woman. 'These are good boys, aren't you?' She gave Louis a squeeze and managed to ruffle Will's hair before he could duck away.

Jack suddenly remembered his cheerful nature. 'Ah, the bad boys' school. You're messing with us, so.' He laughed then nodded towards Louis. 'You'll be wanting your tea towel back, Nuala.'

'Ah sure, keep it,' she said, waving him off with her cloth. 'Hasn't it got a hole in it, anyway.'

And we saw exactly what she meant as Louis ran ahead of us to the car.

* * *

Granny Connemara's cottage was tiny and white with a grey roof and a lake right next to it. It was very far away from any other houses, although Jack said there was another cottage up the lane and around the corner. From Granny's garden, you could see the mountains that seemed to follow you everywhere you went. I'd never seen mountains like them. They looked as if they'd been painted on the sky. It must have taken someone years and years with a massive paint brush, but they definitely did not look real. Jack swore blind they were actual mountains you could climb if you had a mind to.

'No one can believe how beautiful the Bens are when they see them the first time,' he told us. And he sighed as if he were lovesick.

I'd regretted asking Jack about Granny when we were on the boat – his answer had worried me. So, while we'd been driving along, I decided to ignore what he'd said and write a story in my head where my grandmother was a beautiful queen who would welcome us warmly to her wondrous castle. In her magical kingdom, Jack would entertain us with endless songs and ice cream. It would feel like home but it would be better because Mother wouldn't be there spoiling it by shouting every two minutes and throwing plates. I was good at inventing stories – as good as Will was at reading maps.

But now my brother had successfully helped Jack find the way to Granny's cottage, I had a sneaking suspicion I'd let my imagination run away with me. Grown-ups were always warning me about that. Granny Connemara, I discovered, was definitely not a queen, but she wasn't a dragon, as Mother insisted, either – even if she did appear to be in a cloud of smoke as we drove down the lane towards her. Granny was a normal woman with a lined face, and brown and

19

grey hair that was tied in a loose knot. She seemed to be squinting into the rain as she came to meet us at the car. I realised after a while that this must be her way of smiling. I squashed my arms against my sides and waited for a crushing hug and slobbering kiss, like the sort Mother's mother gave us whenever we met her at the airport. She was as tanned as Granny Connemara, but Granny Costa Del had sparkly eyeshadow and blonde hair you could see right through, piled up high on her head. Our Irish granny was nothing like her, and Will and I were glad to discover she didn't want hugs or kisses. In fact, apart from the squinting, she took no notice of us children at all.

'Well, Jack,' she said, dropping her cigarette and stamping it into the gravel. 'Would you look at you now? A right handsome lad you've turned out. It's good to see you in the flesh, instead of imagining you down the telephone line.'

Jack seemed to have completely forgotten how to speak. He kicked at the stones around the car. 'You're looking well yourself, Mammy,' he eventually managed, though how he would know I couldn't tell. His eyes hadn't moved from the ground. Granny seemed to be studying the top of his head.

'I am well, son,' she said. 'Much better these days.'

'Good,' Jack said, nodding. 'Glad to hear it.' He still hadn't looked up.

Louis clambered out of the car and tugged at Jack's leg, and Jack swung him onto his hip.

'So, these are Conor's poor divils,' Granny said finally, screwing up her eyes at each of us in turn. 'Sure, the girl is just as I remember her father at that age. All wild, dark hair.' I squirmed under her gaze. 'Claire, isn't it?' I managed a nod. It was true I hadn't used a comb in two days, but still, 'wild' seemed a very unkind way to describe my ponytail. I did my best not to glare at my grandmother. 'She has his dark eyes, too,' Granny muttered. She turned to Will. 'You've the red hair of your father's father, then.'

Will held out his hand as if he hadn't heard. 'Pleased to meet you, Granny Connemara. I'm Will.'

20

'Will?' Granny said, ignoring his hand. 'William?' Her squint had turned into a scowl. 'I thought he was Patrick.'

'I'm Patrick William O'Connell,' Will said, rather bravely, I thought, as Granny's face had turned as dark as the water in the lake behind her. He tucked his hand back into his pocket. 'Everyone calls me Will.'

'Well, everyone will call you Patrick here,' Granny said.

Jack had moved himself between Will and my grandmother. 'Now don't be starting on the children already,' he said. He was finally looking Granny in the eyes. 'William is named after Eleri's father, you know that.'

'And a fine rogue that man is too. There'll be no William under my roof and that's an end to it.' She strode off in the direction of the door.

Will stared after her. 'What's she talking about?'

'She has a long memory,' Jack whispered. 'Battle of the Boyne, and all that. I'll tell you later.' Then he called to Granny, 'This is Louis.' He jiggled our little brother until he chuckled.

Granny was leaning against the door frame. 'Is that a name from Eleri's family too?'

I saw my chance to shine and I grabbed it. 'No,' I said. 'Mother told Dad he could choose, for once, so he named Louis after a song.' And I threw back my shoulders, like I always did when someone asked how my little brother got his name. My wrist flopped as I held out my arm, and I showed off the imaginary jewels on my hand. 'Saint Louis woman,' I sang, shuffling my shoulders and my voice cracking, 'with her diamond rings, pulls tha—' But my performance was ruined when Jack shoved himself between me and Granny. I hadn't even reached the part where the man got pulled around by his girlfriend's apron strings.

Granny had a puzzled look on her face. 'What's the child doing?' she asked, and I realised, too late, my grandmother wasn't the sort to be impressed by party pieces.

'Being Claire,' Will muttered from behind me. I could practically hear his eyes rolling.

I kicked at the gravel in embarrassment. 'I was singing Dad's favourite song,' I informed her. '"Saint Louis Blues".' I scowled at my brother and uncle. 'Louis Armstrong sings it. Louis is named after him, as well as the song.'

Granny nodded. 'Conor likes music, then.'

Jack shrugged. 'Well, sad music anyway.'

'It's supposed to be sad,' I said. 'It's the Blues.' That's what Dad always told me whenever I complained that his favourite music was miserable.

But Granny only sighed. 'Oh, well then. Come on in Louis, Claire and Patrick. You're very welcome in Connemara.'

And we traipsed behind our grandmother into her cottage, already missing home and feeling not very welcome at all.

* * *

'Right Patrick, you can start by putting more turf on that fire,' Granny said, when we'd all crammed into her kitchen. It was a dark room with just one tiny window above the sink overlooking the lake. It was cosy enough, though, and the rich smell from the open fire was very welcoming, even if Granny herself wasn't. Jack nodded in the direction of a pile of brown stuff next to the hearth. Will took a lump and tried to balance it on top of the flames in the fireplace while avoiding getting his fingers scorched.

Jack rushed to rescue him when the lump of turf began toppling off the fire. 'Would you give them a minute to get their bearings, Mammy,' he said, shaking his head, 'before they burn their fingers right off.'

'If they're staying with me for the summer,' Granny said, 'and that's *if*, mind you, then they can't be sitting around all day. They'll have to help.'

'Grand,' Jack said, 'only don't go killing any of them.'

Granny turned to him sharply, her face full of fury. 'What's that you're saying now?'

22

Jack jutted his chin towards her and I saw anger flash in his eyes too. Then it vanished. 'Just a turn of phrase,' he said. 'I'll show Will – I mean, *Patrick* – how to tend the fire safely. But don't go asking Claire, unless it's burning down the cottage you want.' He ruffled my hair to show he was just making a joke, but he couldn't get around me that easily. It wasn't fair that Will got to play with fire and I didn't, even if I did tend to be accident prone.

'You could teach me to do it properly, Jack,' I said, with my sweetest smile. 'Then I wouldn't burn anything down.'

'Looking after the fire is a man's job,' Will said, in his most annoying voice.

'And if that were true,' Granny said, 'I'd have frozen to death years ago. Don't you go bringing your superior ways here, boy. There's no reason why your sister can't tend that fire too. Show them both, Jack, and we'll see if it's only boys that are special, won't we, Claire?' And I thought my grandmother might be a queen of sorts after all.

Once our fire-tending lesson was over, and I'd proved beyond all doubt that girls could place a piece of turf as precisely as a boy, even if I did singe the sleeve of my jumper, it was time for tea. After Granny's disappointing welcome, I was surprised to see she'd prepared a delicious spread for us. There was ham, thickly buttered bread, huge ripe tomatoes and a boiled egg each, and for afters, cold rice pudding sliced like a loaf and dolloped with red jelly. I'd never tasted a pudding so wonderful. After every helping – I had three – I thanked Granny Connemara and congratulated her on her amazing cooking skills. Mother mostly made us beans on toast or fish fingers for tea. Dad sometimes cooked us egg and chips on a Saturday, if he wasn't working. The cigarette would dangle from his lip and ash would spill into the frying pan and the oil would spit at him for all it was worth. Those dinner times were my favourite, but if this first meal at Granny's was the sort of food we'd get to eat in Ireland, then maybe staying for a few weeks wasn't such a bad idea after all.

'Now,' she said, hiding the last of the pudding and jelly in the larder in case I made myself sick, 'I'll have no more of this Granny

Connemara.' Will and I looked at our grandmother in amazement. Who was she, if not our Granny Connemara? 'You're to call me Grandma from now on. You don't have another one for miles and miles so just Grandma, plain and simple, will do.'

I tried it out in my head. Grandma. Grandma. But try as I might I couldn't stop myself adding on the Connemara bit, and it simply didn't sound right. Grandma Connemara. There were far too many 'n's and 'm's and they got all muddled in my mind. What with Will being Patrick now and Granny being Grandma, I was beginning to worry I ought to keep a list. I was sure I'd have forgotten it all by the morning.

'And Jack should be Uncle Jack to you children. Or by rights, Uncle John.'

Jack jumped to his feet and the chair he'd been sitting on almost fell over. 'Stop your messing now, Mammy. I've always been plain Jack to the kids and I'll never go back to being John – that's what the Brothers made everyone call me. You can't decide what my name is now. It's not up to you anymore.' He grabbed his cigarettes from the mantelpiece and marched towards the door. 'You gave away your right to decide anything,' he said over his shoulder, 'when you let us go. Remember?'

And he slammed the door behind him, leaving Will and me trembling at the thought that now Jack was outside, we had Granny Connemara – *Grandma* – all to ourselves.

* * *

Granny seemed sad after Jack left the kitchen. She looked very old, too. 'We'll clear this table and then I'll show you where you'll be sleeping,' she said, pushing herself up from her chair awkwardly.

Louis was curled in the armchair and he was sucking hard on his thumb.

'He's a quiet little lamb,' Granny said, reaching out to stroke his head then stopping short.

24

'He's missing Mother,' I said, realising guiltily that I hadn't missed her once since we'd left home. I had wondered about Dad, and how he'd be eating his dinner without any plates, but it was only Louis who was still fond of our mother. She was good with him because he was too young to answer back. 'He mostly speaks Welsh,' I told Granny. 'She used to speak Welsh to Will and me, too, when we were Louis's age.'

'Ah well, there's a thing,' she said. 'I've great respect for your mother for keeping her language going. That's something she's good for, anyhows.' She lifted her chin towards Will. 'You've not got a lot to say for yourself either, young man.' She was right. Will had been quiet since the fire incident. 'Do you speak Welsh mostly too, Patrick?'

'No,' Will said, and that was all he did say.

'Well, you can help with the washing up,' Granny told him. 'You don't need your tongue for that.' She took the kettle from the fire and filled a bowl in the sink.

I strolled around the little kitchen, glad Will had been cornered to do what was normally my job. I was 'familiarising myself with the new surroundings' – it was one of Will's favourite phrases. He always used it when he was talking about the camping trips he and Graham were going to have. They'd planned to camp at Barry Island over the summer holidays but I doubted that would happen now. Graham would probably be pitching his tent with somebody else.

This kitchen was much smaller than ours at home. I ran one hand over the bumpy wood of Granny's draining board and the other along the smoothness of her chair backs. I could touch both at the same time, they were that close. Louis could scoot his dog-on-wheels right around the table in Cardiff and not hit a thing. Here he'd be flattening everyone's feet, so it was just as well we'd left his ride-on dog at home. In fact, I realised with a heavy heart, I hadn't packed any toys for Louis at all, only the teddy he slept with. I hoped Granny had an old saucepan and wooden spoon he could borrow. He loved banging a pan.

The window in Granny's kitchen looked out onto the little yard, towards a small brick shed that was an awful lot like the outside toilet we had back home. No one used that, only Dad, each morning, which Mother said was a blessing to us all. I was glad we had a toilet *in* our house, too, because I was certain a huge brown spider lived under the toilet seat outside. I didn't mind spiders, really – I liked to catch them and let them run over my fingers. But I didn't want one biting my backside or falling on my head when I was having a wee.

While Granny's kitchen had only the one window with a view of the brick building and the lake behind, it had four doors. There was the door to the yard we'd come in through, and a door opposite that. Annoyingly, it was closed. There was the door to the pantry – I'd made a special note of that because it was where Granny kept her jelly and rice pudding – and next to it, at right angles to the back door, was one that was open and led to a bedroom. I was about to go in when I stopped myself. I realised just in time that the room wasn't one I could slip into without Granny's permission, and I was pretty certain I wasn't about to be given that. I'd only met her a couple of hours ago, but already I knew her well enough to be certain anything Granny gave me would be hard won. So I satisfied myself with leaning against the door frame.

The room was dark, with just a small window to my left above the neatly made bed. Out of the window I caught a glimpse of the rickety metal barn where Jack had parked the Cortina. A curl of smoke wafted past the glass. Jack was enjoying some peace and quiet with only a cigarette for company. In the bedroom there was a low, heavy-looking chest of drawers against one wall with a wooden hairbrush on it. The room was very tidy and the walls were bare apart from a photograph hanging next to the door. It had a dark, wooden frame. A necklace of beads that matched the colour of the frame was hung over one corner. The photograph was faded in parts but I could make out two women and the smiling faces of four children. Three of them had longish hair even though, judging by their shirts and rolled up trousers, they were boys. The smallest one had curly hair like Louis. In fact, I would have sworn it *was* Louis if the boy in the photo hadn't been a bit older. And the photo had obviously been taken outside Granny's cottage – I could see the little brick shed and the lake behind. One of the two women in the photo was crinkling up her eyes just like Granny had when we'd arrived with Jack, except the woman in the photo was a lot younger than our grandmother and almost pretty, too.

I turned back to the kitchen. It had been silent a long time, with only the slosh of water and clink of china as Granny washed the dishes and Will wiped them dry.

'Who are these children?' I asked. I reached out my fingers to touch the photograph.

Granny looked up sharply. 'Don't touch that.' She put down the dishcloth and wiped her hands on her apron. Then she squeezed past Will and reached out for the door handle. 'That's my room,' she said, shutting the door. 'Louis can sleep with me.' She turned and stood looking into the yard. Her shoulders sagged. 'I can keep an eye on him in my bedroom.'

I followed her gaze to the lake. The water reminded me of something. 'Granny,' I said, 'where's the bathroom?'

With that, Jack appeared round the corner. 'Bathroom, did you say?' He gave a short laugh. 'You see how used to their luxuries Conor's children are, Mammy?' He patted the top of my head. 'There's no bathroom. There's a tin bath in front of the fire on Sundays.'

'Oh,' I said, and I thought I couldn't imagine anything worse. But I was wrong because when I asked where the toilet was, Jack pointed to the little building across the yard, and my imagination did itself proud.

'Are there spiders?' I asked nervously. I desperately needed to use the toilet. It was a long time since I'd had a wee at the café and I'd drunk two cups of tea since then.

'I swept them all out yesterday,' Granny told me, 'but bring the

27

broom with you and give it another sweep while you're there.' And she handed me the brush from behind the door. 'If you're emptying your bowels, use the scoop to sprinkle sawdust.' I had no idea what she meant about the scoop – or bowels, either – but I nodded, anyway.

Half way down the yard I looked back to see Granny staring after me. Jack was grinning. How cruel of him to find this so funny. 'Is there paper?' I asked hopefully. I wasn't sure what I would do if the answer was no.

'There is, but you're to use only one square,' Granny said firmly.

One square seemed terribly mean. I wondered if Granny had counted them. I wouldn't have put it past her.

'And don't go using all of Michael's sawdust,' she added. 'He's not made of it.'

'Who's Michael?' I asked. I was half afraid he might be in the toilet. Who knew what weird things went on in this strange place?

Granny looked at me oddly. 'Michael from up the boreen,' she said, as though that answered my question.

A little spark of hope suddenly fluttered in my chest. There was a boy called Michael in my class in Cardiff. Karen and I sometimes persuaded him to play catch with us. I suspected there'd be very little to do at Granny's, and I certainly wasn't silly enough to think Will would want to play games with me. But maybe Michael from up the boreen would be more of a sport.

'He's a sheep farmer,' Jack said, dashing my hopes. I doubted a sheep farmer would have time for playing catch.

'Sure, he keeps a few cows too, you know,' Granny threw in, as if that made any difference.

To my relief, Michael wasn't in the toilet, but the privy itself was a shock. The toilet seat was a wooden plank with a hole cut out of it and it was balanced on bricks. I glimpsed a pit beneath the seat but I didn't dare look down into it. I perched myself carefully on the plank, shuddering at the thought of what was below me and all the creatures that might live in such a horrible place. I relieved

28

myself as quickly as I could and used only one square of paper, folding it over and over until I'd mopped up most of the dampness. My knickers would have to deal with the rest. I didn't touch the scoop or Michael's sawdust. And I didn't see a spider, although I kept the brush handy, just in case.

Chapter 3

I sometimes wonder whether I seem to my own grandchildren as Granny seemed to Will and me back then – ancient, remote and scary. I hope not. I do try to be the opposite, probably with too much vigour. But perhaps my own style of smile is as unwelcoming to them as our grandmother's was to us.

* * *

'Patrick ... Claire.' She grimaced at us. 'This will be your bedroom.' I was washing my hands at the kitchen sink. There was only one tap, and the water spurted out of it, brown and cold. Granny's green soap was so huge, I couldn't turn it between my hands, so I just left it at the side of the tap and rubbed my fingers on it. But no matter how hard I tried, I couldn't make any bubbles.

I glanced over my shoulder to see her opening the door at the back of the kitchen.

'Where did those bunks come from?' Jack asked. He was blocking my view of the room and I wished he'd get out of the way. I rinsed my hands quickly and dried them on the towel Granny had put on the draining board for me. The roughness of the towel brought some life back into my fingers – they'd been thoroughly chilled by the water in the tap.

'They're Michael's. The ones I had in there for you and Conor had worm in them.'

I squeezed past Jack and looked in through the bedroom door. The room was tiny, smaller even than Granny's, and the window was filled with frosted glass. The bunks had a blue metal ladder and frame, and they took up nearly all the floor space. Next to the bed,

Granny had put a wooden crate and on it was a candle, stuck to a saucer. I had to share a bedroom with Will at home, too, so that Louis could have his own, and the only thing that made it bearable was knowing Will hated sharing even more than I did. Sharing this tiny room would be a whole new experience for us, and one Will would thoroughly despise.

'What about Michael's grandchildren?' Jack said. 'Don't they use the bunks?'

'There's only the one,' Granny told him. 'But anyway, Rónán and his family don't visit. Michael and him fell out years ago.'

'That's a shame.' Jack ran a hand over his hair.

''Tis,' Granny said. 'And we know all about that, don't we? Mind you, he'd have a job having them to stay. Remember how house-proud Mairead was when she was alive? The house is a terrible mess now, and no one wants to stay in a pigsty.'

I was glad we weren't staying in a pigsty and that Granny was still alive to keep her house tidy. I was glad, too, that Michael had spare beds. What would we have done otherwise? Maybe we'd have had to sleep on the floor like at Jack's place. I shuddered at the memory.

'Go get their things from the car, and we'll have these children settled,' Granny told Jack.

He tapped Will on the shoulder. 'Come and give me a hand with the trunk.'

Will got up slowly. He hadn't even looked into the bedroom – he'd just been sitting at the table staring into the fire. Louis was still curled up in the armchair, fast asleep. He stirred a little as Will's chair legs scraped against the floor, and then he went back to sucking his thumb.

Will and Jack brought in the trunk and dumped it on the bottom bunk. I'd already climbed the ladder and was getting used to being near the ceiling.

'You're not sleeping there,' Will said. 'I'm thirteen, so I get to sleep on the top bunk.'

'You're not thirteen 'til November, and anyway you're too late –

'I bagsied it.' I showed him my tongue in a way that would have got me into a lot of hot water at home.

'Bagsy doesn't work when you're too young to sleep on the top bunk. She is too young, isn't she Jack?'

'Well, I'd say it would be safer for Will to sleep up there to start with,' Jack said. 'We don't want any accidents, do we?'

'But I'll be perfectly safe,' I argued.

Jack held up his arms to me. 'You sleepwalk, Claire,' he said, 'so I don't think it would be a good idea.'

I sighed and let him lift me down. I had walked in my sleep once and no one would let me forget it. I wasn't even entirely sure I hadn't *pretended* to sleep walk. I'd seen something on *Blue Peter* about it and thought it was fascinating that anyone could walk around without realising what they were doing. I very much suspected I'd been play acting, but it was too late to suggest that now. The damage was done.

'Can I have a turn one night?' I asked. I knew my voice was whiny.

'We'll see,' Jack said.

Thinking of *Blue Peter* had reminded me of something else. 'Where's Granny's television?' I asked. I'd seen into all three rooms in the cottage now, and I hadn't spotted it anywhere.

Jack laughed out loud. 'Television? Why would your grandmother be having a television in a house with only one socket for electricity? The cooker's plugged into that. What would you prefer – hot meals or *Jackanory*?'

I was very tempted to choose *Jackanory* but I knew it was the foolish answer. I looked at the walls in our bedroom. There were no switches anywhere, and there wasn't a light hanging from the ceiling either. The only light bulb I'd seen was in the kitchen. 'But if she hasn't got a television,' I said, 'how am I going to watch *Champion the Wonder Horse*?' It had been my favourite programme until it got changed, just in time for the school holidays, for a silly cartoon, but I'd been hoping Ricky and Champ would be galloping back very soon. Now if they did, I'd miss all the action. I gave a heartfelt sigh.

Jack rubbed the top of my head. 'Put your things away in the press and don't be starting with your whingeing.' He chuckled. 'Television!'

The press was a tiny cupboard on the opposite wall to our bed. There was hardly room to open the door and very little space for both Will's stuff and mine. We got around this by shoving all our clothes into it in one big heap. There was no room on the crate for my books, so I stacked them on the floor beside the bed with my notebook, then I sat Sindy and my torch on top. Jack took the trunk back out to the car, freeing up the bottom bunk for me to bounce on.

'Don't do that, Claire,' Will shouted. He'd climbed onto the top bunk with an armful of atlases. 'The whole thing's going to fall apart.'

It was making a rather peculiar creaking sound. 'Why are you being so quiet, Will?' I asked.

'Quiet? I was just yelling at you, wasn't I?'

'Not just now. I mean in the kitchen, with Granny Connemara.'

'We're not allowed to call her that, don't you remember?'

'I know. I won't call her that to her face.' Although actually, I had a terrible fear I would. She didn't seem like a person you called 'Grandma'. Surely a grandma was a sweet old lady in a rocking chair with a bagful of barley sugar and a cat snoring on her lap.

'And you're not allowed to call me Will, either. From now on I'm Patrick, or so *Grandma* says.'

'Mmm.' I sucked on my bottom lip. 'I don't like all these new rules, do you?'

'No. So do you really have to ask why I was quiet at teatime? How would you like it if you had to have a new name all of a sudden? And we haven't even got a telly.'

'It's not a *new* name,' I reminded him.

'It's a name everyone in school makes fun of and I hate it. They call me Paddy. It's not fair for Granny to say I can't be Will anymore.'

33

And I thought I heard his voice crack. I didn't like my big brother to be weak. Not when I needed him to help me stand up to Granny.

'You could tell her you don't want to be Patrick.'

'Oh yeah. That'll help a lot.'

We weren't allowed to say 'yeah' at home. It was a word Mother got very angry about, but I didn't point that out to Will. He had enough problems for the time being.

'Well, I'm still going to call you Will,' I promised, 'at least when we're not with Granny.'

'You mean Grandma.'

'Oh yes, Grandma.' I sighed. This summer holiday was going to be a real challenge.

And as I picked at the flaking white paint on the bedroom wall, I couldn't help mouthing with a snarl Mother's favourite bad word – *ast*.

* * *

Will and I were shocked when we opened the door to the kitchen the next morning, hungry for our breakfast, to see Jack already in his coat and cap.

'Time for me to say cheerio,' he said brightly, although his eyes dipped downwards guiltily. He'd obviously been trying to sneak away before we were up.

I ran to him and flung my arms around his waist. 'No, Jack, don't go.' I couldn't bear the thought of being left alone with Granny. There'd be no one to stand up for us if Jack left. We were only children and everyone knew children didn't have any power over grown-ups. 'You said you'd stay for a while.'

'Didn't I warn you no good would come of leaving before they were up?' Granny said. She lifted the kettle from the fire.

'Sorry, kiddo,' Jack said, unwinding my arms and ignoring his mother. 'I have to get back to the yard. I'm after losing two days' wages already.'

34

'Just tell them you're on holiday,' I said. 'Gruff the Foreman will understand.' Gruff's granddaughter, Sioned, was in my class and from what she said he was a lovely man with toffees in his pockets and pennies magically hidden behind his ears. But by the way Dad and Jack talked about him, you could swear Gruff was a complete demon.

'He will *not* understand,' Jack said with half a smile. 'He'll just give me the sack and we can't afford that, can we?' He looked at Granny as he said those words and I saw her cheeks colour. 'Anyway, the boat's not going to wait for me so one last hug, Claire, and you too, Will.' Will was leaning against the frame of our bedroom door. He didn't move.

'Ah well, it looks like I'm not your favourite person.' Jack shook his head.

'And who can blame him?' Granny said.

'When are you coming back for us?' I asked, squeezing Jack as tightly as I could.

'When your ma's feeling better,' he said. 'When she's had enough of a rest with your aunty in London.'

'Next week?'

'No, Claire.' He freed himself from my hug and held me at arm's length so he could look me in the eyes. 'She's going to be there a while longer yet. You'll be staying here for the summer holidays. But lookit, you and Will can explore all this.' And he opened the door.

I looked outside and gasped in horror. 'Where's the lake gone?' Most of the water had disappeared, leaving behind huge, drab, seaweed-covered rocks.

Jack laughed. 'It isn't really a lake. It's full of seawater.'

'Seawater?'

'It's a bay,' Will said. 'The Atlantic's just over there but you can't see it because it's around the corner. I've looked at this area in my atlas.' He was using his most annoying know-it-all voice. 'The tide's out, that's why the water's low at the moment.'

'That's right,' Jack said. 'It's changing every minute, so won't you

35

and Will, I mean Patrick, have fun watching it?' It certainly didn't seem like fun to me. He smiled. 'The weeks will fly by and I'll be bringing you home again in no time at all.'

Then he patted Louis's head, kissed my hand, gave Will and Granny a nod and was gone.

* * *

We got used, in a way, to being at Granny's. The evening before he'd fled back home, Jack had fenced off the area of garden that edged the lake, using rolls of chicken wire that Michael from up the boreen had going spare. We weren't allowed to go anywhere near the water but as it was mainly rainy and cold, despite it being July, I didn't mind too much. Will had said one morning, when the sun unexpectedly stole from behind a cloud, 'A rowing boat would be fun. Or swimming. I'm a good swimmer.' Granny had given him a sharp look. 'I'm glad your father saw fit to teach you to swim,' she said, 'but you'll not set a toe in that water, do you hear me?' And her tone of voice made him quickly change the subject.

We'd followed Granny's order to call her Grandma but I still couldn't think of her as that. She was always Granny Connemara in my head and when I spoke about her to Will. And I only called Will 'Patrick' in front of Granny. It was tricky to start with, and I got it wrong often enough, but she seemed hard of hearing most of the time. Either that or she just plain ignored me.

A few weeks into our holiday, she took us to Roundmore, a town an hour's drive from the cottage. I was very excited at the thought of a change of scene – we'd been stuck at the lake for what felt like ages.

'Calm down, child,' Granny said while I tap-danced beside her as she shut the cottage door. 'You'd swear I was bringing you to America.'

We bounced along the rough tracks in Granny's van, with Will, Louis and me perched on the long bench of a front seat, and

Michael from up the boreen riding in the back. He'd offered to drive us there in his Bedford, but Granny had scowled. 'Do you think I'm a fool? I'm not letting Conor's children into a van driven by a person with the use of only one arm,' she told him, and Michael had replied, 'It's amazing what you can do with one hand and your knees.' Granny had snorted, 'Not turning corners safely in a motor vehicle, that's for sure.'

Roundmore looked a small place to me – I was used to shopping in Cardiff with Mother, and that was huge – but Granny said the Connemara town was the biggest for miles and miles. Everyone seemed to know her, and people called 'Hello, how are you?' from the other side of the street. Although she raised her hand politely, she stopped to talk to no one, and we found ourselves scurrying behind her as she went about her shopping.

After half an hour, she'd been to every shop on her list except the post office. 'Come in with me,' she said, 'but don't touch a thing. I'll just be getting the money from your grandparents in Spain.' And we waited in the queue for what felt like hours while Granny stood silently, like an island in a sea of old people complaining about their rheumatism and bad gums.

Last of all she had to ring Jack from the public telephone in the hallway of Grogan's bar. We could take Louis into the newsagent next door, she said, and look at the comics. We looked at the sweets too, but we hadn't been given pocket money since we'd come to Ireland, so sadly, we couldn't buy any.

After twenty minutes, the newsagent got tired of us drooling over the gobstoppers and creasing the pages of his comics and he sent us off. We hung around on the pavement outside the pub, waiting for Granny to reappear, and being stared at by every child that passed. My face burned with each new inspection. Why were they staring at me? Tracey Hopkins, the meanest girl in my school, often called me ugly. She called Karen ugly, too, but that was ridiculous because Karen was easily the prettiest girl in class. I realised I hadn't seen myself in a mirror in a long while – Granny didn't bother with such nonsense – and I could have turned absolutely hideous during the time I'd been in Connemara. I felt my face carefully with my fingers, but I had no idea if it had got worse. And I daren't ask Will. That would just be inviting trouble. So I stood there, feeling revolting, like the things I'd seen in jars in Will's form room when Mother had dragged me along to his parents' evening at the end of term. He'd been as horrified at seeing me in the Science lab as I'd been at seeing those creatures. He'd told me later, in his showing-off voice, they were called 'specimens'. That's what I felt like now in Roundmore, a strange specimen in a jar, so I kept my head tilted downwards and tried to hide my face.

It turned out Michael had chosen to spend all of his time in town at Grogan's. When Granny emerged from the hallway, she sent Will in to tell him we were ready to leave. She would not be setting a foot inside the bar herself, she told us sternly. Michael took a long time to come out.

'Did you give Rónán a ring there?' she asked him, when he'd folded his huge body into the back of the van. He smelled like Dad did on Saturday nights when I used to hang around on the landing, pretending to need the bathroom. I loved the smell of the pub on him and I always tried to stay awake until he got home. It wasn't such a wonderful perfume on Michael.

'What are you wanting of me now, woman?' he said.

Granny glared at him in the rear-view mirror. 'Your Rónán. It's time you gave him a telephone call.'

Michael snorted. 'Him and Shirley are on the pig's back in Dublin. What will they want with me?' Granny shook her head and Michael threw himself into 'Whiskey in the Jar'. With his lopsided mouth, he couldn't sing as well as Jack, but for an old man he was entertaining enough.

* * *

38

Trips into town were a rare treat, and for most of that summer, Will and I spent the days exploring the garden of Granny's cottage. It wasn't really a garden at all, just a handful of small fields trapped inside ancient stone walls and windswept hedges. There wasn't anything else to do, since the lake remained off-limits. I'd been excited to discover that Michael kept his cows in a field up the lane. They were white, slow and sad-looking, and I was certain I could ride one if only I could get close enough. But they were in a field we weren't allowed near, because the one between us and them was planted with Michael's vegetables. We weren't allowed to walk over it, so I admired the cows from a distance, and dreamt of patting them and brushing their tails and riding them along the lane.

The ground in Granny's fields had huge bumps everywhere, and Will was convinced treasure was buried under the rough grass.

'I might even find a bog man,' he told me. I had no idea what he meant and he refused to explain.

He began carefully mapping the area, which I found incredibly boring – digging for treasure would be much more fun. Eventually he gave in to my pestering, and we borrowed a spade from the barn and began digging.

Michael came to watch our efforts. 'You can dig for me in my fields,' he laughed, 'if you want to use a spade.'

'Don't you go finding any bodies,' Granny called. She'd come outside for a smoke. She shouted across the field to Michael, 'You remember the year Finbar dug up something ungodly? He swore it was half a human skull.'

Michael nodded. 'I do. 'Twas in the top field. He made a right song and dance about it.'

'Maybe we should try up there,' I hissed at Will from the corner of my mouth.

'And before you think of moving your digging,' Granny said, annoyingly reading my thoughts, 'there's more rock than earth in that field. And what your grandfather found,' she sucked on her cigarette and blew out the smoke slowly, 'turned out 'twas only a piece of sheep's head.'

'I bet she's just saying that,' I told Will, after Granny and Michael got fed up of watching us and went in for a cup of tea. 'That field's probably full of skeletons.'

'She's right about the rocks up there, though,' Will said, and carried on digging.

My brother had no sense of adventure.

Chapter 4

Glancing through the window to the city streets beyond my office, that summer seems the simplest of times. The truth, however, is that I was terribly lonely. I was already aware of a void in my life – a gap Emmet would fill, but our meeting was yet to happen.

* * *

Will and I spent endless days digging. We had a collection of animal bones, broken china and one ancient penny to show for our efforts. My brother made a display of our findings, carefully placing them on a board in the barn. I wasn't allowed to help. He said I'd make a mess of it, like I always did with everything, so I left him to it and went to watch the cows.

Being outdoors suited us both. Will looked healthier than he ever had, and his wind-whipped skin made his green eyes sparkle. My arms were tanned, and strong from digging. Louis's rosy cheeks, though, had become pale. He wasn't allowed out much, on account of having just turned three, and of the lake, and Granny not having eyes in the back of her head. He had to play in the kitchen because Granny didn't completely trust the chicken wire, or Jack's skill at making fences. She had a point – Jack's fencing wasn't the best. I'd found a place where I could squeeze under when Granny wasn't looking. It meant I could search the rock pools at low tide with one of the pond-dipping nets I'd found tucked away in the barn, and hunt for tiny sparkling fish. Louis would look longingly at me as I ran out of the kitchen door. He was tied to the table leg with a long length of rope attached to his rein harness. Sometimes he'd stamp his foot and yell '*Dere 'ma nawr!*' just like Mother used to when Will and I would dash off to dodge a row she was itching to give.

But mostly, Louis just sat and watched Granny's clogs and played in the dust on the floor, with only his teddy for company. I'd asked Granny for an old saucepan and spoon he could use as a drum but she had looked horrified. 'A drum?' she'd said. Then she'd sent Will off to find a small block of wood in the barn to sand smooth. 'That will be his toy,' Granny had told us when she was finally happy with Will's handiwork. And to be fair, Louis took to his block of wood like it was the best toy ever, pushing it around under the table and up the chair legs with vroom-vroom sound effects. It didn't look like much to me but it seemed to make him very happy.

* * *

One of the things that fascinated me about our new surroundings was the goings-on in the lake. Often with a new tide came seals. Their slick black heads would bob just above the surface of the water, and sometimes they'd heave their bodies onto the jagged rocks in the centre of the lake. We wouldn't have known the seals were there if Granny hadn't pointed them out.

'There'll always be a few about,' she said, after showing us how to adjust her binoculars so we could see the animals up close. I was waiting for my turn with the spyglasses, as she liked to call them, and Will was taking forever.

'Hand them over to your sister now, Patrick,' she said. I was surprised she'd actually noticed what was going on between us. Mostly she just left us to ourselves, and often we fought things out within her hearing without her paying the slightest notice. It made a change from what happened at home. Mother interfered in everything we did, and the tiniest hint of a raised voice made her promise to knock our heads together.

I was glad that Granny had stuck up for me. Will was growing a bit too full of himself. I quickly took the binoculars from him –

Mother would have said, 'It's rude to snatch,' but Granny didn't comment – and looked in amazement at what a moment ago I was sure was simply a rock. There, a seal was sunning itself. It was a beautiful sight, and when I got tired of digging for gold with Will, or watching the cows dreamily, I could be found with the binoculars fixed to my face, my arms aching from the weight of them, searching for seals, spotting their heads dipping in and out of the lake. I'd watch them twist round and around, their noses breaking the water as they played. I loved seeing them that way best of all. It was more of a challenge if you didn't know where they'd pop up next. It was far easier to find them balanced on rocks, like little boats stranded as the tide went out, but it wasn't half as much fun.

When Jack had left to go back to Cardiff, the days stretched out in front of us gloomily. But now, somehow, the weeks had piled up behind us and soon the beginning of September was in sight. We knew what that meant – school. Just thinking about being back in a classroom after the freedom of Granny's fields made my stomach churn. But at least it meant going home to Dad, and I was missing him very badly. And even though Tracey Hopkins would make my life miserable in class, I could depend on Karen to keep me company.

Will and I had had the odd letter from home during the summer – a couple of notes in Dad's stumpy handwriting, and most recently of all, a postcard of Barry that had arrived from Jack. It had the Pleasure Park shouting at us from one half of the picture and a donkey smiling from the other. It made me homesick for ice creams and candy-floss, and for the kind of outing Jack could turn into something amazing. Digging in Granny's field and even spotting seals was no competition for Barry Island. Will and I hoped Jack was sending news of how Mother was so much better now, after her ranting, raving and plate-flinging, that we could go home at once. We'd had enough of digging for treasure.

But we were to be disappointed. Jack's postcard had started with 'Eleri still in London, children will need to stay longer'. Surely we'd stayed long enough already? Mother couldn't possibly be taking all this time to get well, even if we had actually shattered her. I was beginning to wonder if we'd ever be able to go home again. Maybe we'd made such a good job of breaking Mother, she was now beyond repair. The thought made me terribly guilty. But there was some good news on Jack's postcard too. He'd be visiting again soon.

'He'll be bringing some messages,' Granny said.

'What kind of messages?' I asked her. I was thinking of telegrams, like I'd seen on that new programme *How*. Or maybe another letter, this time from Mother, informing us of her amazing recovery.

'Things we need from Roundmore,' Granny said. She turned her head away from me and began rummaging on the mantelpiece. 'He'll be bringing shoes, too,' she muttered, speaking to the fire rather than to me. 'And school uniform.'

'School uniform? Why do we need our school uniforms here?'

But Granny wasn't really listening. She'd found what she was looking for – her tobacco tin – and was heading out of the door. I tried again. 'Why do I need my school uniform, Grandma?'

She waved a hand over her shoulder and rattled the tin at me. 'September and the nuns.'

September and the nuns? What kind of an answer was that? I decided I must have misheard, so I asked her to repeat herself. But for all of that day, and the next and the next, Granny refused to say anything more on the subject. She was a stubborn old woman.

* * *

It was a wonderful evening when Jack arrived at Granny's again. Louis and I couldn't help dancing around the Cortina as it slowed to a stop at the barn. Even Will jigged a bit. We'd heard the car turning into the top of the boreen, as we now called the little lane that ran past Granny's cottage and came to a sudden end at Michael's home. Very few vehicles came down our way, and we had become alert to every noise within a mile, so we were able to provide a welcoming party for our uncle.

'Okay, okay,' he said through the car window, trying and failing to calm us. 'I'm glad to be seeing you too.'

'Have you brought everything?' I asked, excitedly. He'd not even had a chance to open his door yet. 'Have you brought the messages?'

'I have, sure enough,' Jack laughed. 'There's tea, cocoa and butter. And some of that minty chocolate you like from back home.' He slammed the car door. 'I've the things you need for next week, too. I'm surprised you're so excited. Glad, though,' he added quickly. 'It's a big thing, a new school.'

My stomach dropped to the floor. I'd had my two minutes of happiness at seeing Jack but now the truth had dawned on me. We weren't going home. Instead we'd be going to school here. How could our parents do that to us?

Jack opened the boot of the car. Only Louis was still dancing now. I looked at Will and saw he felt as bad as I did about the situation. Worse, maybe. I could see tears in his eyes. He pushed past me and rushed into the cottage.

'What's the matter with your brother?' Jack asked. He'd begun taking parcels wrapped in brown paper out of the boot and was stacking them on my outstretched arms. 'We could do with his help here.'

'He forgot something important,' I said, wiping my cheek quickly with a hunched shoulder and wishing I'd had the sense to run off, too.

Jack and I emptied the car as Louis twirled excitedly around us. We heaped all the parcels on the kitchen table.

'They've accepted them, then,' Granny said, seeing the packages as she turned from the pan she was stirring on the stove. 'And what lies did you tell?'

'Only that they're Catholic-raised and you'll do your best to get them to Sunday Mass.'

Granny snorted. 'You promised they'd go to *Mass*?'

'Only on weekends you get the van started.' Jack put the shoe boxes on the floor. 'I told them it's very unreliable.'

Granny nodded. 'It is, so.' She waved her spoon at the table. 'This lot must have cost a month's wages.'

'Children need the right clothes and shoes, Ma,' Jack said. 'We want them to fit in at school, don't we? We want them to be happy.' He seemed suddenly cross with Granny, even though it was the first time he'd seen her since the start of summer. Granny looked at him with a sad expression and the frown on his face disappeared at once. 'Eleri's parents paid for it all and the change is yours. A bit extra for you this month.' He took a bundle of notes from his pocket and put it on the table.

'Mmm,' Granny said. She didn't seem impressed. She began untying the string and opening the parcels. Louis snatched at the brown paper hanging down from the table and scrunched it noisily in his fists.

'That's Claire's, for St Brid's,' Jack said, as Granny lifted up a green checked dress.

'Well, I wasn't thinking it was Patrick's now, was I?' She opened another parcel. It had a pair of grey shorts inside and a grey jacket.

'Is Will, I mean Patrick, going to the Money School?' I asked.

'What's a money school?' Granny said, shaking the jacket and placing it carefully on the back of a chair. She brushed the shoulders with her hand. 'Do you have those in Cardiff or are you talking nonsense again, Claire?' *Talking nonsense again* – it was a phrase I'd heard often enough in the last couple of months.

But I knew it wasn't nonsense this time – although I did accept that quite a lot of what I said was tosh, on account of the overactive imagination which everyone said I had – because I could vaguely remember the old woman's words in the café we'd stopped at on our way down here. That day seemed years ago now, and I couldn't quite remember what she'd called the school, but seeing the money Jack had placed on the table had somehow jogged my memory.

'It's a school for boys here in Ireland,' I insisted, hoping Jack would help me out. He was keeping his head down though and saying nothing. No matter, it was all coming back to me now. 'It was the Pound Note School, or the Penny School.' I looked at my uncle again. 'You remember, Jack, don't you?'

He finally raised his eyes and I thought that maybe he was giving me a warning look, but I only realised just as the words came spilling out. 'I remember now, it's the bad boys' school. "Cash-something".'

Granny glared at me. 'Who's been filling your head with that nonsense?' She looked accusingly at Jack.

'Well, it wouldn't be me now, would it? Or Conor,' he said, in a voice so suddenly cold that I thought something terrible must have happened and he hadn't had a chance to tell us yet. He'd been pretending to be jolly but something really bad had happened. Someone must have died. Maybe Mother was dead. Or worst of all, Dad. Maybe both of them, and Jack hadn't had the chance to say. I felt the blood draining into my feet and I must have gone very pale because Jack grabbed my arm. He sat me in a chair and told Granny to bring a cup of water.

'It's all right,' he said. 'I wasn't cross with you. I'm not angry.'

Louis noticed the change of atmosphere in the room and clambered onto my lap, curling himself under my arm. I held him tightly and sipped the water. Finally, I found my voice. 'Is everyone okay?' I asked. 'Is someone...' I sipped again. 'Has someone died at home?'

'What?' Jack's voice filled the tiny kitchen, but his tone wasn't unkind. 'What gave you that idea? No one's dead. How did you get from Cash Hill School to death?'

'Like I said,' Granny told him, 'someone's filled her head with nonsense. She's too much imagination as it is.' And she went back to stirring her pot on the stove.

I was so relieved to hear that Dad was still very much alive, and Mother too, that I downed the rest of the water in one go. 'It was your voice, Jack,' I whispered behind my grandmother's back. 'And your face. You looked so serious when you spoke to Granny.'

'Sorry to scare you,' Jack whispered. 'I didn't mean to. Maybe your grandmother's got a point about your imagination.' Then he looked

47

me straight in the eye. 'Don't go mentioning that school again, Claire. Not ever.'

* * *

As we ate our tea that evening, we found out Will would be going to St Vincent's School for Older Boys in Roundmore, which was across the town from St Brigid's Primary School for Girls, where I was being sent. Neither of us wanted to go to school in Connemara. We wanted to go home instead, but Will refused to speak about it and he slunk off to our room straight after our meal was finished.

My approach was different. 'Please, Jack,' I pleaded as I cleared away the dishes. Even I could hear the whine in my voice. 'Take us home. We don't need Mother. We can look after ourselves now.'

It was true. My red knuckles were proof of how well I could scrub the armpits of shirts and blouses with carbolic soap. The mud on our jeans stood no chance against me and the washboard. I'd never done so much housework, and Granny believed boys ought to help too. At home it was always me who had to lay the table, sort the colours from the whites and hand Mother pegs on laundry day. I hated doing household chores while Will was free to study his atlases, stare at the clouds or just sit and watch me. It was one of the very many things I found annoying about being a girl.

'It's impossible, Claire. I'm sorry,' Jack said. I knew by the look in his eyes that he really was, but his apology made me feel no better. 'I can't bring you home. Your mother's still not back and your dad can't look after you and work too. And neither can I. Your dad's very grateful to Granny for taking all three of you in. Don't go making a fuss, now. You'll make her think you're not happy here.'

We could see Granny's back out of the kitchen window. She was taking the peelings to the chickens, a job she liked to do herself because it gave her the chance to smoke out of view of us children. She fed the chickens in the mornings too, and sometimes in the middle of the day. I watched her in the yard, with her top knot coming undone and her shoulders slumped, the way they always were in the evening. The sight of her made my heart lurch. Not only had she trained me in housework over the past couple of months, but she'd actually made me love her.

'I like Granny,' I said, knowing it wasn't quite the full truth, but no one spoke of love in our family, 'and I've liked staying with her, but school is scary, Jack. It's not fair to make me go to a new one. How would you like it?' I found my voice cracking.

'Now, don't start with the tears,' Jack said, pulling me onto his knee and jigging me as if I were a baby. 'It'll be fine, so. Won't you be the new girl that all the others want to be friends with?'

'No, I won't. They'll hate me and call me names and throw mud at me.' That's what happened to me at school back home. One day Tracey Hopkins had said, 'Claire O'Connell talks funny,' and then all the other girls in my class started saying the same, and before I knew what was happening, no one would let me join in their games anymore, only Karen. And the reason Karen liked me, so Tracey said, was because no one else was allowed to play with her on account of her mother running away with the vicar. My parents couldn't care less about vicars and I was glad – Karen was the prettiest girl I knew, and I hoped and hoped some of her prettiness might magically rub off on me. One of the names Tracey called me was 'Ogre O'Connell' because, as she said, I was very ugly. Tracey's name-calling made me miserable and she even let her Alsatian chase me in the park once. I'd had a terror of dogs ever since. But at least I knew exactly what to expect when I went back to my old school. Here in Connemara I could only imagine what horrors lay ahead. I wasn't foolish enough to believe I'd be welcomed warmly in Ireland, where I really did 'talk funny'. And I hadn't had a chance to check my face in a mirror for months.

'What's up with the girl?' Granny had come back into the kitchen trailing a curl of smoke from the hand that had just thrown down the last of her cigarette.

'School,' Jack said.

I clambered off his knee, feeling silly to have been caught sitting on it now Granny's eyes were boring into me. I wondered how I'd ever felt that stab of love earlier.

'You've got to go,' she said, 'and that's the end of it. Don't be upsetting Jack. He's had to do all the arranging himself. He deserves a thank you, so.'

A thank you? I couldn't believe my ears! 'I don't care,' I spat. 'I hate your school.'

'St Brigid's is the best school in the county,' Granny said, calmly ignoring my outburst as had become her way. 'Sure, Jack and your father went to St Matthew's, the boys' school next door. Won't you be following in their footsteps.'

'Not exactly, though,' Jack added quickly. 'You don't want to be having anything to do with the boys in the school next door to yours, or the nuns will be on you like a ton of bricks.'

'I'm sure Claire knows she's not to mix with boys,' Granny said. 'Isn't that the way back in Cardiff, too?'

I shook my head miserably. 'There are boys and girls in my school at home.'

Granny raised her eyebrows. 'Sure, there'll be a big wall between you and the boys here.'

'You'll like St Brid's,' Jack said. 'Believe me, there are worse schools I can think of.' He squeezed my shoulder. 'You're better off than Will. I couldn't get him out of Irish lessons.'

'What?' Will appeared at the door, and I realised he must have been standing in the bedroom, listening all the time. 'I'll have to learn Irish?' The colour had drained from his face and he looked more frightened than I'd ever seen him.

'You learn Welsh at home, don't you?' Granny said. 'That Irish class will be no problem for you.'

'Irish is nothing like Welsh,' Will said, his voice shaking. It might have simply been with fear but I was sure there was anger in it too. His knuckles were white where he clutched the door frame.

'Sure, you'll be fine,' Jack said, reaching out a hand that Will shrugged away. 'They're giving you extra lessons after school, Will.'

'For the last time, his name is Patrick,' Granny growled. 'I hope that's the name you registered at school.'

'Of course,' Jack said.

'Well, thank you,' Will snapped. 'So, I have to learn Irish, stay behind after school *and* be called by that awful name.' He kicked the door frame hard.

'There's nothing wrong with Patrick.' Granny was angry now. 'There'll be plenty of them in your class. If it's good enough for Our Saint, it'll certainly do for you.'

Will made a sound that clearly showed he didn't care one jot for 'Our Saint'.

'You'll just be called O'Connell,' Jack said, 'in a class full of Patricks.'

'In that case,' Will grumbled, 'I might as well keep my proper name.'

Jack took Will's chin in his hand, but gently, just so they had to look each other in the eye. 'Believe me, boy,' he said, kindly, 'you don't want to be having a name like William at a school like St Vince's.'

Chapter 5

The morning of our first day at school came too soon. Jack had stayed for a few days, saying it was slack at the dockyard and half the men had been given the week off. He'd volunteered himself in place of our dad, whose rent money was more essential due to us needing a house to go back to when Mother was home again.

My school uniform was far prettier than the one I wore to my old school. Jack had let the shop-lady in Roundmore choose my socks, petticoats and underwear, and if I hadn't been feeling so grumpy, I'd have given her fair credit for her choices. There was a froth of lace I could only dream my mother would buy for me, and bows or butterflies on the knickers that helped tell which way round to put them on. I even had a little lace hanky to place in the top pocket of my dress. When I'd watched Granny in the kitchen on Sunday night, laying my uniform out on the back of a chair, I'd dared to dream that such a lovely outfit might actually make me beautiful. And maybe the girls at my new school would be friendly, like Jack had said, because I would be the new girl. But in the morning as I dressed, it felt like everything I dragged on was sneering at me.

I especially hated my new shoes. Jack had bought them at the Start-rite shop in the Hayes because that was where we always went with Mother for our shoes. They had a few circles cut out on the toes but mainly they were sensible – brown and buckled. But that was not why I hated them. Jack had guessed my size and Will's, and got them about right, which was just as well, he said, as he couldn't 'nip back to change them'. He laughed as he told us this, which I thought very unfeeling of him under the circumstances. If Will and I could only 'nip back home' none of this school horror would be happening. The fact that my shoes had come all the way from Cardiff seemed to mock me for being stuck in Connemara.

'I've cooked some rashers,' Granny said, as I came sulkily into the kitchen. 'You'll be wanting a good hot meal in you for your first day at St Brid's.'

She put down a plate in front me and the smell of bacon made me gag. My mouth was so very dry I couldn't imagine taking one bite of that breakfast, even though bacon and egg would have been a real treat on any other morning. My eyes filled with tears. It was all so unfair.

'Don't you look smart?' Jack had been outside to the privy and was pulling up his braces as he came into the kitchen. Louis ran to him – Granny had been too busy cooking breakfast to tether him to the table leg. Jack swung him up into the air.

How I wished I was three again. Louis didn't need to go to school. He could stay at home with Granny and the chickens, and play in the dust under the table all day long. Louis had all the luck.

'I was thinking,' Granny began, as she dished up a plate for Jack, 'it might be better if Claire dropped her eye.'

'What?' I turned my head sharply and looked at her. Dropped my eye? How could I do that? I'd woken up with the beginnings of a sty on my left eyelid – I could tell by the throbbing. They somehow managed to appear when I already had too much on my plate. Not only was I being flung into a school full of strange children, but in a couple of hours, just in time to meet my new classmates, my eye would look absolutely hideous. If I could leave it at the cottage while the rest of me went to school, I'd have one less worry. But I couldn't do that, so what on earth was Granny talking about?

'Ah, hold on now,' Jack said, 'hasn't she enough to worry about without you messing with her name.'

Oh, I'd got it, then – not my 'eye', my 'i'. Jack was right, I did have enough to worry about without having to relearn how to spell Claire.

''Twould make her seem more Irish without that "i"', Granny insisted. 'Help her fit in, what with her English accent and all.'

'The way Claire spells her name is perfectly normal in Ireland,' Jack said. 'And it's a Welsh accent she's got, not English. Leave her be. She'll fit in just fine.' He turned to me. 'Do you remember what to say if you need the toilet?' We'd been going over this for the past two days and I still hadn't got the hang of it.

'Anwill kadd a-gum dull...' The words fizzled out, along with any chance of me getting to the school privy. My brain had seized again.

'*An bhfuil cead agam dul go dti an leithreas,*' Will announced, as he slouched into the kitchen and slammed his satchel onto the table, making my breakfast wobble in its grease.

'Show-off,' I said. 'You didn't need to learn it, anyway. You won't be excused to use the toilet in the big school. You'll have to pee your pants.'

I'd overheard Granny telling Jack the night before that it was pointless for Will to learn the phrase. At St Vincent's, the Brothers were known for not letting boys out of lessons, even if they begged to go to the toilet. They had to wait and hope they didn't disgrace themselves. I'd heard Jack say, 'Don't be telling him that now, Mammy, or he'll be terrified before he gets there.' But how I enjoyed passing on that nugget of information. I knew he had a habit of needing a wee during classes, and he'd just shown me up, after all, with his superior knowledge of Irish.

'Is that true?' Will asked Jack, his face turning a sickly grey around the edges.

'No, no. Now, Claire, what are you up to?' Jack said, widening his eyes at me.

I ignored his hint. 'I heard Granny telling you about the teachers,' I told Jack. 'She said they're so strict it doesn't matter even if you do ask in Irish. They won't let you go.' And I showed Will my tongue.

But he wasn't looking at me anymore. He was staring out of the window. 'Where's Louis?' he asked. There was a note of panic in his voice. Granny, Jack and I looked under the table, but Louis wasn't there.

Jack was suddenly on his feet but Will was already out of the door and yelling over his shoulder.

'Quick! Quick, Jack! He's in the bay,' he shouted. 'I can see his head in the water.'

* * *

The three of us were quiet as we stood at the wooden bus stop on the big lane. Jack had spared Will the shame of having to spend his first day at St Vincent's in wet shoes by getting to Louis first. Louis hadn't made it as far into the water as we'd feared, just up to his knees. He was beaming when he turned to look at us, so pleased that at last after months of longing, he'd finally managed to get past the chicken wire and reach the water, and he didn't seem to care about how cold it was on his bare legs. Jack kicked off his boots and had only to paddle to him.

'I thought he was floating,' Will said, scuffing a stone round and round the upright post of the bus stop. He still seemed to be in a daze, but whether that was because of Louis or the fear of school I couldn't tell. 'I thought I could see his hair in the water...'

'Bending over, more like, playing,' Jack said, looking at his watch for the tenth time. 'The bus is late. They said it'd be here at five past, sharp.'

I buttoned my school cardigan against the morning chill and shoved my hands into the pockets. Mother hated pockets. She said they made a person slouch. I'd been secretly pleased to find good, deep ones hidden in the cardigan's seams and I intended to slouch to my heart's content.

I was miffed that we hadn't been allowed to stay back at the cottage. We'd had a terrible fright after all – for an awful moment we'd all thought Louis had drowned – but Granny and Jack would hear none of my excuses. There'd been a strange atmosphere when Jack had carried Louis back to the warmth of the fire. Granny, it turned out, hadn't rushed with us to the water. Instead she'd lit one of Jack's cigarettes. She was still smoking it when we got to the kitchen door.

'Tie him to the table leg,' was all she'd said, but her voice and the fingers holding her cigarette trembled terribly. Jack had promised to fix the loose bit of wire Louis had managed to find, and his voice shook too. And then we'd had to grab our sandwich boxes and rush for the bus stop. Jack had said he'd drive us up the boreen, since we were running late.

Just as I was beginning to believe the bus wouldn't arrive and by some incredibly lucky stroke – maybe the same one that had saved Louis from drowning – I'd be spared school after all, an old wreck of a bus appeared around the corner.

'Okay,' Jack said, sounding as nervous as I felt, 'just keep your heads down in class and don't say too much. That's my best advice to you. Don't worry, they won't kill you.'

And my imaginings that perhaps the girls at St Brigid's might be friendly after all, that tiniest hope I'd somehow desperately held onto, vanished in an instant.

* * *

Will wouldn't sit with me on the bus. I didn't care. There were quite a few empty seats so I chose one next to a window.

I'd spotted horses in some of the fields when we'd travelled into Roundmore with Granny in the summer. There was one I'd secretly named Star. It wasn't white, like my imaginary pony, but it did have a pale patch on its nose that stood out against the grey of its coat. All the ponies were grey, small and sweet looking. If you squinted, they blended in almost completely with the big rocks in the fields. It made them hard to spot when they were far away, and I wondered whether Granny would notice if I took her binoculars from their hook in the kitchen and brought them with me to school. Spotting horses would be fun. It would certainly make the long journey go by more quickly. The bus seemed to be going around in circles, driving up each and every tiny lane to pick up one child here and another there. I pictured myself armed with Granny's spyglasses, identifying the ponies in their fields and making a record of them in my notebook. It made me feel important, until I thought about how heavy those spyglasses were. I realised I wouldn't want to carry them to school and back every day, and my role as official horse counter for Connemara lost all of its glamour.

* * *

My new school was confusing. Granny had drilled into me that I was to call the nuns 'Sister', apart from the headmistress who was 'Head Nun'. I was, on no account, to refer to them as 'Miss', as I was used to doing in Wales. I was to say please and thank you using the Irish words Granny had taught me, and I was not to mutter in Welsh. I promised her I wouldn't, but I didn't swear to it on the Bible, so I felt I had a little leeway.

My teacher was called Sister John the Baptist – Sister John for short. How could a woman have a man's name? It seemed all wrong. When Dad had taken me to see *The Sound of Music* in the Odeon, I'd asked him if nuns were real and he'd laughed, which I thought very unfair. Adults always told you to ask if you didn't understand something, so he could have tried harder to hide his amusement. He'd said, yes, they were real enough, and wasn't I the lucky one to have never come across them. He added that nuns like Julie Andrews were few and far between, in his experience, although old boilers like the film's Mother Superior were two a penny. Standing in front of Sister John's desk now, I wished I'd forced my eyelids open in the cinema and paid more attention to the film.

'You'll be the new girl, then,' she said, with no trace of a welcoming smile.

'Yes, Sister. I'm Claire O'Connell,' I said, as Granny had trained me to. I hoped the nun couldn't tell my name had an 'i' in it.

'Well, stand over there until I can find a desk for you,' she said, and she sent me to stand in the corner at the very front of the class where the other girls stared open-mouthed at me. My sty was throbbing from all the attention, and I felt just as I had in Roundmore during the summer – like a specimen in a jar.

There were prayers first which I was supposed to join in with, except I couldn't because I didn't know the words. I moved my mouth in a way that I hoped looked convincing, like I did in the bits of the seven times table I was patchy on. Everyone's heads were bowed anyway and Sister John's back was to me, so it didn't matter much. It gave me a great opportunity to look around the room. The desks were like the ones we had in my other school but older – wooden, with chairs attached by metal runners. There were inkwells sunk into the desks which filled me with dread as I hated using a fountain pen. I was considered far too messy for ink back in Cardiff.

The walls of the classroom had pictures of Jesus and Mary on them. I recognised them from Sunday School back home. It was very unfair we had to go because Mother never went to chapel herself, and Dad growled each time he passed a church. But we were forced to attend every single week so Mother could have Sunday afternoons to herself. The pictures on the walls here were far fancier than the ones in chapel. I'd never seen Jesus with a glowing red heart before. Normally he was just nailed to a cross and staring up at the ceiling. And Mary had never seemed so lifelike in Cardiff. There were other men and women too, wearing halos and with their eyes turned upwards. A list of numbers ran along the top of the walls, with words next to them I couldn't understand, and a long line of fancy letters. I recognised it as the alphabet, but the curls and flicks terrified me. My own handwriting was nothing like that. My knees trembled even more.

The tops of the heads of the girls in front of me mostly looked quite neat. There were lots of straight centre partings giving way to bunches and plaits, tied with green ribbons. I had a green ribbon in my own hair, the only colour the school allowed, and Granny had tied it as securely as she could. At home, Mother plaited my hair tightly in two bunches for school, which reshaped my eyelids painfully. It was, she said, the only way to keep me tidy until home time. I was more than a little worried the ponytail Granny had created wouldn't last the morning.

Running my eyes over the bowed heads before me, I saw that only one head was without a ribbon. That head belonged to a girl who sat at the front of the class, and her hair was coarse and black. Back home my mother would threaten me with the pudding bowl each time I screeched as she combed out the tangles in my long hair. 'I'll put that bowl on your head and cut round it,' she used to say, 'and we won't be hearing your *sgrechian* anymore.' From the blunt cut that girl was wearing, it looked as though her mother had actually carried out the threat. Her clothes seemed new, though, and under the desk her shoes shone.

My eyes travelled once more over the heads bowed in prayer until, at the very back of the class, I noticed two girls who seemed less well cared for. They wore ribbons in their hair but theirs were grubby white and frayed at the ends, and not only were their ribbons a banned colour but their dresses were all wrong too. The girls wore pinafores made of rough, woollen material, not the cotton the rest of us had. We were all in green but these girls were dressed in grey, and though their shoes were well polished, the style of them looked ancient. There was a desk free in front of the girls, and I wondered if that was where Sister John would send me to sit. It would mean being near the back, which normally I'd give my right hand for, but I guessed that sitting near those two girls might make me even less popular than I expected to be. I quickly looked around for another free desk. There was only one other, next to a girl with very blonde hair and fancy ribbons. As I stared at her, the prayer ended and the girl lifted her head. I found myself staring into her huge blue eyes. She stared back, a small smile creeping along her pink lips. I thought she might be even prettier than Karen.

'Iseult,' Sister John said, and the girl's eyes slid from mine to the nun's.

'Yes, Sister,' those pink lips said, and her voice was so sweet.

'You've an empty seat there next to you.'

My heart leapt. I was going to be sent to sit next to this beautiful girl.

'It's for Siobhán,' the girl said. 'She has the dentist this morning.'

'Of course she has,' the nun said, rummaging on her desk, 'don't I have the note you brought from her mother right here. Claire O'Connell, to the back with you, in front of the House girls.'

And my hopes were shattered.

* * *

There was a peculiar smell in my corner of the class. It was woody and sickly and reminded me of long, boring afternoons at Sunday School back home. I couldn't wait to get outside and fill my lungs with clean air. But before that pleasure, I had to survive the morning. To my horror, the first lesson was handwriting, or 'penmanship', as Sister John called it. That passed in a blaze of embarrassment and endless muddle. I just didn't know what I should have been doing, and the teacher nun made no allowances for me. It was clear I was a bother she could do without. I hadn't even filled my pen with ink before she told us to put away our copy books. Next was mathematics, and the House girls did their best to help me find the right pages in my text book, quietly pointing when the Sister's back was turned. Iseult seemed to know the answer to most of the questions Sister John asked the class, but it was the girl with the basin haircut who put up her hand at every possible chance. The nun barely noticed her, except when everyone else was stuck on how to finish the long division sum on the black board.

'Yes, Theresa?' Sister John said finally, after scanning the classroom for the tiniest hint of understanding, and Theresa helpfully told us all where we'd been going wrong.

When it came to dinner time the House girls waited by my desk. I knew I should be grateful for their help and reward them with my friendship but I already had my sights set on a beautiful prize. From watching the back of Iseult's head all morning as she worked away at the tasks Sister John set us, I'd decided that we would be the best of friends. She was clearly very popular with the other girls – they were all gathering around her now while I was hemmed in by the House girls – but I could be special to her, I was certain, just like I was special to Karen. All I had to do was prove it.

'Sorry,' I said to the two girls in the weird grey frocks in front of me, cutting short the explanation one of them was giving me of how dinner time worked, 'I can't stop here.' Iseult was leaving the room and I needed to follow her.

Iseult. I'd never heard such a beautiful name. Why hadn't my mother chosen a wonderful name like that for me? There were three Claires in my class back home and I'd heard Sister John shout at one in my new class. But Iseult? Surely, there was no other person in the world with that name.

I caught up with her in the cloakroom where we'd put our sandwich boxes. She was still surrounded by the group of girls.

'Siobhán won't be back until after dinner,' I heard her say, 'so I think today I'll let...' She gazed around her and caught my eye. My heart soared. She'd seen it. She'd recognised that thing in me I'd seen in her. We were meant to be best friends and she knew it too. 'Dolores,' she said, and the beaming Dolores rushed to her as my heart was squished. 'I know we should all be kind to the new girl,' Iseult added, cupping a hand around her mouth as she spoke to the others, 'but her eye looks so disgusting, it would put me off my food.' And she and Dolores swept out of the cloakroom.

I fetched my box of sandwiches and when I turned, the House girls were standing behind me. The sickly scent that reminded me of Sunday School had followed them out of the classroom.

'You can sit with us if you want,' one of them said. She smiled hopefully then quickly pressed her hand to mouth. She wasn't fast enough, though – I'd already caught a glimpse of her brown teeth.

'Not with us, exactly,' the other corrected. 'You can sit *near* us.' Her teeth were terrible too.

They seemed kind enough but I sensed, from the way the rest of the children treated them, it wouldn't be the best idea to throw in my lot with the House girls. I wasn't that desperate for friends, and the smell that hung around them would put me off my sandwiches.

'Thanks,' I said, 'I'll be fine.' And I rushed off, leaving their odd perfume behind and taking my disgusting eye with me.

Chapter 6

Adults like to believe that children are quick to adapt. It's a neat way to ease the conscience, but I'm not sure it's always the case.

* * *

My first week of school was painfully slow. Just as Monday had begun with the terrible ordeal that was penmanship, so did Tuesday, Wednesday and Thursday. And every day brought a new embarrassment – a prayer I didn't know, or an Irish phrase I hadn't learned. My sty got bigger and bigger and as the week went on, it grew a huge yellow lump that, according to Iseult's friend, Siobhán, was sure to explode. I felt thoroughly revolting.

My shame was so great that every day I kept my head down and ate my sandwiches quickly, saving my apple to eat in the yard. As soon as the bell rang to dismiss us from the hall, I dashed off to a hiding place I'd found – the narrow space between the shelter and toilet block. I'd been tucking myself in there all week, feeling ugly and desperately lonely, as I listened to the chatter of girls in the yard beside me and the shouts of boys in the one next door. It wasn't until Friday that I noticed an even better place to hide. Behind the toilet block there was a small gap in the branches of the hedge that grew around the sides of the yard. I checked no one was watching, then carefully squeezed myself though it. The gap, it turned out, led to a rough patch of grass which gently sloped to become the hill I could see from the classroom window. I was surprised to find a boy sitting on the grass with his back against the toilet block wall.

He waved cheerfully when he saw me. 'Hello, how are ya?' he called.

His smile was so welcoming that the disappointment I felt at finding my brilliant hiding place already taken completely disappeared.

I couldn't help but lift my hand to wave back. 'I'm fine,' I said. 'I'm just,' I nodded towards the yard, 'you know.'

'Taking a break,' he said. 'Me too. I've a spare spot in the sun for you, if you're interested.' And he shuffled up a bit and tapped the grass.

Sister John had warned us about the dangers of mixing with boys and she'd made them sound like the worst villains in the world. But in that instant, I forgot every word of her warnings, and without a second thought I sat down next to him. I'd spent the first week at my new school feeling miserable, and I wasn't about to turn down such a friendly invitation.

'Emmet... From the boys' school,' he said, with a nod in the direction of the building next door.

'I'm Claire ... from the girls' school.'

He offered me an extremely dirty hand. 'Pleased to meet you, Claire-from-the-girls'-school.' We shook, despite the dirt. 'You're not from round here, are you?'

I looked at him carefully. 'How can you tell?'

'Ah, it was the way you said "Claire".'

'I'm from Wales,' I said. 'I'm only here for a while.'

'Are you? Me too.'

'You're Welsh?'

'No. I'm only here for a while. I'm waiting for my mother. She's in New York, marrying a millionaire. Howard's his name. He's a hotel tycoon and when they're married,' he slapped his thighs to make a drumroll, 'she's coming back to Ireland to get me.'

'Wow! That's brilliant. My mother's gone away to London. She went a bit mad. My uncle's going to come and get us once she's feeling better.'

Emmet rubbed his dirty palms together. 'Who's us?'

'Will, he's my brother. And Louis, he's my other brother. He's only three. Will is twelve.'

Emmet chewed his thumbnail. There wasn't much left to chew. 'Will's a Proddy name.'

'Is it?' I had no idea what he meant. 'Maybe that's why Granny doesn't like it. I'm supposed to call him Patrick here, but I always forget.' I stretched out my legs and squashed down the blades of rough grass. 'I've got an "i" in my name. Can you tell? Is that why you thought I said Claire in a funny way?'

'I don't think so,' he said. 'You just don't sound very Irish.'

'That's because I'm half Welsh. Granny doesn't like me having an "i", but Emmet's a nice name.'

'Thank you. I'm named after my da. Wales, now that's on the side of Britain that faces Ireland, isn't it?' He peered at the sun and stuck out his arm. 'In that direction. You have a language of your own there, don't you? I read that in a book of facts.'

I nodded. 'My mother speaks it properly and I can speak it a bit, too.'

'Say something,' Emmet said.

'In Welsh? Like what?'

'What's the word for hello?'

'*Helo.*'

'No, say it in Welsh,' Emmet said.

I shrugged. 'I did.'

'What's thank you?'

'*Diolch.*'

'Deee-olch,' he repeated. 'What's jacks?'

'Jack's what?'

'I mean, what's toilet?'

'Oh, *tŷ bach.*'

'What's shite?'

'*Cachu,*' I said.

Emmet smiled. 'I like that,' he said. 'Cack-hee. Did the cruelty men come and get you when your mother went mad?'

'Jack rescued us.' I tapped the toes of my shoes together. I'd only been wearing them a week but they were already quite scuffed. Mother would have said she wasn't surprised.

'Are you in the House now?' Emmet asked.

'Yes, our granny's house.'

'That's a proper home, that is, your granny's. Is it nice being there?'

'Quite nice, but it's not like being in our real home.'

'Real home is best,' Emmet said. 'You can't beat it.'

I remembered, with a dart of delight, the shiny red apple in my pocket. I took it out and started working my way around it in tiny bites, the way I liked to do.

Emmet was watching me. 'Nice apple?'

'Mmm.'

'Juicy, is it?'

I nodded and wiped a hand across my chin. 'Who are those men you asked me about?'

'What, the cruelty men?' He laced his fingers together and cracked them loudly. 'They're trouble, so.' He touched my thumb. It was sticky with juice from the apple. 'You've a lot of ink on your hand there.' He rubbed my thumb then popped his finger in his mouth.

'Penmanship,' I said. 'I hate it. I'm too messy for ink, everyone says so.' I lifted up both hands so he could better see the stains. I nodded at him. 'Your hands are filthy.'

'Dirt,' he said, pointing to a bare patch in the grass. 'I've been making a model with it. And with spit too. Do you want to see?' He held up a roughly shaped form. 'Buddy,' he said. 'He's my horse.'

'You mean, he's a model of a horse.'

'I mean, he's a model of my horse called Buddy. My friend's going to carve me a wooden one. He can carve anything you want for a sweet or two.' He scratched his head enthusiastically. 'I think a horse will more than likely be two.'

'You've got a horse?' I was truly impressed. 'Like Champion?' How I wished I owned a horse. I was desperate to go bareback riding and gallop over the fields, but since I wasn't allowed near Michael's cows, I was forced to make do with the mop. It wasn't such a bad game, riding a mop up and down the boreen, as long as the mop-head had dried out after Granny'd cleaned the floors. But a real horse would be amazing.

'Champion? Who's that?'

I took a deep breath then burst into song, 'Champion, the Wonder Horse,' but Emmet just stared at me. 'Haven't you seen it?' I asked. 'It's the best programme on telly by miles and miles.' I jumped to my feet and sang him the whole song. When I came to my favourite line, I belted it out and added arm actions. 'Like a mighty cannonball he seems to fly, you hear about him everywhere you go, the name of,' I spun round and around, 'Champion the Wonder Horse!'

Emmet was standing beside me now. His face was red from laughing and he had both hands clamped over his mouth. 'Shush yourself, Claire,' he told me through his fingers, 'or you'll have us caught.'

'Oh!' I said, and covered my own mouth. My eyes popped wide as I realised how noisy I'd been. That made Emmet laugh even more.

'It's a great song, so,' he gasped. 'Sing it again, just not so loud that they're joining in in Wales.'

I laughed then, and sang it over. Emmet chipped in where he could. 'It's brilliant,' I told him, when I'd got my breath back. 'Ricky – he's the boy – he rides Champion and he holds his mane, and they go really fast and he never falls off...' My breath had run out again.

'I wish I could see it.' Emmet sighed.

'So do I. Nothing beats horses.'

'Nothing,' he agreed. We flopped down onto the grass.

'Horses in books are good too.' There were a few daisies nearby, and I plucked some and started making a chain. 'My favourite is *Black Beauty*. I've read it six times.' I was exaggerating, but only a bit.

'Books are great.'

'They are.' I laid the daisy chain on my knee. I'd flung down my apple in all the excitement about Champion, and I picked it off the grass and studied it for bugs.

'My favourite is *Treasure Island*,' he said. 'Do you know that one?'

I nodded. 'Will's got a copy but he left it back at home.' The apple seemed clean enough. I took a big bite. 'He doesn't like reading much,' I said as I chewed. 'He likes maps more.'

'Sure, maps can take your legs to places.' Emmet turned to me and tapped his head. 'But stories take your mind on travels.'

My mouth dropped open and bits of apple fell onto my cardigan. 'I think so too!' This was amazing – someone who liked stories as much as I did. Karen tried to look interested whenever I talked about books but I knew she was just pretending. 'Last night I read about Beauty going to his new—' I gasped. 'Wait a minute!' In all my excitement, I'd actually forgotten what Emmet had told me earlier. 'Tell me about *your* horse.'

'Buddy? He's in the field over there.' Emmet pointed to the hill ahead of us.

'You're so lucky,' I said, although I was feeling pretty lucky myself to have found a gap in the hedge that led to a boy who loved books and had his own horse too.

'Lucky? That's me for sure.' He gave his head another good scratch.

'What colour is Buddy? If I had a horse it would be white with a bit of grey and I'd call it Star.' I was thinking of the ponies I'd seen every day that week from the bus on the way to school. They just stood around in the rocky fields and didn't seem to belong to anyone. Granny had land next to the cottage. Maybe I could persuade her to put one of those horses in a field there. Maybe Will would side with me for once, even though he didn't like animals. Maybe, if we pestered enough, she'd give in.

'Buddy's golden brown,' he said. 'He's not like the Connemara ponies round here. He's special.'

'Like Champion, then,' I said. 'He's brown with a white nose.' Emmet watched as I collected all the fallen pieces of apple from my cardigan and popped them back into my mouth.

'Tell me about your book. You said Beauty went somewhere.'

'To Birtwick Hall, and he met Ginger and Merrylegs. They're horses too.'

'Is it all horses in your book?' he asked.

'There are people as well. Some of them are kind but some are horrible. There's a boy who pulls wings off flies.'

'Does he, so? And what happens to this boy?'

'He gets told off. There are people who beat horses, too. They get sent to the magistrate.'

'The magistrate, is it?'

'He's someone who decides on punishments. I looked it up in my dictionary. I like looking up words. "Tormentor", that's a good one. It's what they called the boy who was cruel to flies. I like "man's laughter", too. That's when you kill someone but didn't mean to.'

'"Man's laughter"?' Emmet raised an eyebrow.

'I know. It's strange, isn't it? What's murder got to do with laughing? And "unmercifully". That's how men flog horses.'

'Sure, that's a lot of cruel words you've looked up. I like long ones.' He cracked his knuckles. 'Consubstantial. Only-begotten. Proceedeth. They're the good words from prayers this morning.'

I tried repeating them and liked the way they rolled around my mouth. 'What do they mean?'

He shrugged. 'Ah, who knows, but don't they feel great on your tongue?'

I could hardly believe what I was hearing. 'Yes,' I said, blinking hard because of the sparkly feeling in my eyes. 'Do you like writing your own stories?' My voice was barely a whisper and my fingers were firmly crossed in my pocket. Karen hated writing stories.

'I make them up.' He tapped his head. 'I keep them all in here.'

I grabbed his hands. 'I love making up stories too! I have lots of them in my head all the time. That's why teachers call me a daydreamer.'

Emmet laughed. 'Sure, teachers, they have no imagination. I've made up stories since I was tiny and I tell them to myself over and over.'

'Me too! But I try to write the best ones in my notebook now, just in case I forget them.'

'Ah, a notebook.' He shook his head. 'Wouldn't that be grand.'

'I have to hide mine under my mattress. If I don't, Will finds it and makes fun of me.'

'That's a shame,' Emmet said. 'A brother shouldn't treat his sister like that.' And he looked at me so kindly and held my hands so gently, I knew I'd found a real friend.

The bells were ringing in the yards behind us.

'Time to go,' he said.

'Will you be in school on Monday?' I asked.

'I will.' He squeezed my fingers. 'Will you meet me here?'

I nodded eagerly. Until I'd pushed through the gap in the hedge, I'd been secretly hoping to be struck down dead with some horrible disease over the weekend – anything would have beaten more penmanship – but if I could spend dinner time with Emmet, then my new school didn't seem half as bad.

'I will,' I promised, and we shook on it. We stood up. I'd managed to get a grass stain on my dress and Emmet's shorts and jumper were covered in dirt.

He pointed to the half-eaten apple in my hand. 'Are you eating any more of that? Only, Buddy, he loves cores.'

'He can have it.' I handed it over and rubbed at the grass stain.

'Thanks. I'll bring it to him after school.' Emmet slipped the apple into his pocket. 'Better be getting back now. Quick.'

I dashed for the hedge. 'See you Monday,' I called over my shoulder, but quietly. I'd learned my lesson.

'Sure, and bring another apple if you have one,' Emmet said. 'You know, for Buddy.'

'I will,' I promised. We grinned and held up our thumbs – mine inky and his muddy.

And as I slipped back through the hedge, I realised he hadn't mentioned my revolting eye once.

Chapter 7

It was raining when I woke on Saturday, a steady miserable drizzle. Granny's mood was as grey as the sky.

'Go fetch the eggs, will you Claire?' she said as soon as I appeared at the kitchen door. Will was already up and sitting at the table, which was very unusual. He'd started sleeping in at weekends, and Granny had taken to badgering me to get him up – a thankless task that just made both of them angry with me instead of each other.

'Put the sack on,' she told me when I went to step outside. 'We don't want you getting soaked now, do we?'

I pulled the sack off its hook and draped it over my head. I was glad Tracey Hopkins couldn't see me. Or Iseult. I was certain they'd never put a foot outside, so ridiculously dressed. But the sack kept my hair dry, and I was glad of that. It always got into a right tangle when it was wet, and I hated combing it. And after all, there was no one to notice me here – apart from Michael from up the boreen, and I'd never seen the baggy jumpers and drab trousers he wore advertised in the copies of *Vogue* Mother left lying around her bedroom. I was willing to bet a sixpence that in Michael's view, wearing a sack on your head was the height of fashion.

The chickens were squabbling amongst themselves when I opened the coop door. They bustled past my legs and over my shoes, still grumbling at each other, until they got outside and banded together to scold the rain instead.

'You'd think they were used to it, being Connemara chickens,' I muttered. It was one of Granny's sayings, and it took me by surprise when it escaped from my lips. She was training me up as her granddaughter, right enough.

There were four eggs – the china ones didn't fool me anymore –

and I placed them carefully into the basket of straw. I turned from the coop and saw the tide was out in the lake. The rock pools looked very tempting. If it stopped raining later, I'd try to sneak under the chicken wire when Granny wasn't watching and see if I could spot some of those tiny darting fish.

As I neared the cottage, through the crack in the door, I heard Will's voice. It sounded angry, or scared, or maybe both. He'd got up early on a Saturday and now he was talking weirdly to Granny. Something was going on, but if I walked into the kitchen right now he was bound to shut up and I'd never find out what it was. I peeped through the gap in the door instead. His chair was facing me but he was so wound up by what he was telling Granny that he didn't notice me looking in. I took a step back and hid at the side of the doorway to listen.

Granny was talking now. Her voice wasn't very clear, as her back was to the door, but I got the feeling she was trying to soothe Will. It wasn't working.

'I don't *want* the extra lessons at school,' he said. 'Aiden's happy to teach me if I help him with geography. It's all arranged. I just need you to tell the Brothers.'

'But you've only been at the school a week, and surely if the Brothers think—'

'What they think doesn't matter. I *can't* have another lesson with that Brother. *Please*, Grandma.'

'You're worrying me now, Patrick,' Granny said. 'Has the Brother—?'

'I just want to stop the lessons,' Will told her. His voice sounded very odd, like it was twisting in his throat. 'It's important.'

'Yes, I can see,' Granny said. 'We'll have to tell them something, maybe that we've found you other lessons.'

'Yes, exactly! I promise you I'll pass the exam, but I'll never learn with that ... that...' I heard someone bang the table. 'With Brother Dominic teaching me. I'll go to Aiden's on Wednesdays and Saturdays. I'll help him with his geography homework and he'll teach me Irish.'

So it was Irish lessons that were making him talk like that. Pah! I'd had a decent mark in my Irish classwork the day before, with a little help from the House girls, and even Sister John couldn't fault me, try as she might. I clutched the basket of eggs closer as a wide smile spread across my face. I didn't even mind the drizzle dripping off the sack and running down my nose.

'This Brother Dominic,' I heard Granny say. 'What age is he?'

'Old,' Will said. 'Older than you.'

'Has he a mark on his face? A red birthmark?'

'Yes,' Will said grumpily. 'Please say I don't have to have lessons with him anymore.'

'Well,' Granny said. 'I can see you feel strongly about it, so I'll write a letter for you to give Brother Dominic on Monday. That man can't have everything his own way.'

'Thank you,' Will said, his voice full of relief. 'Can I go to Aiden's today? There's a bus to Roundmore in half an hour.'

'Ah sure, why not?' Granny said. 'But work hard at your Irish, mind. And while you're there, if Mrs Maloney could find a bit of liver for our tea, that would be grand.' There was a tinkle of coins being tipped out onto the table.

'Thank you, Grandma.' Will's chair scraped on the flagstones and I heard his quick steps as he dashed off to our bedroom.

'Bloody Brother Dominic,' Granny said. And just as I was about to bound innocently into the kitchen, she called, 'Claire, are you determined to catch your death outside that door?'

There was just nothing that passed my grandmother by.

* * *

Will went off to get his bus and I had the bedroom to myself for a change. It wasn't the best room, of course – it was small and empty of toys – but I did have Sindy, my favourite doll. Granny Costa Del had given her to me and I knew I'd been the envy of all the other girls in my class in Cardiff, even if they had sworn they preferred Barbie.

It was still raining, so I couldn't explore the rock pools or ride the mop around the field, but it was a perfect day to invent more of Sindy's life. Granny was sitting by the fire, knitting a green jumper for Louis, and he was napping under the table again. All he ever seemed to do was sleep, but at least he wasn't nagging me to play with him. I pulled the bedroom door to, leaving it just a little open to let in some extra light, then Sindy and I climbed to the top bunk – I refused to think of it as Will's – and I began to tell her all about a boy she would meet when she started her new school, about how he loved stories and books and horses, and about how wonderfully they'd get on.

I'd been totally caught up in Sindy's story when I noticed Granny's voice coming from the kitchen. 'That woman,' she said. I could hear her sawing through the fresh loaf Fergus the Grocer had brought that morning. 'How could she swan off? I know Conor's no saint, but still.' Saw, saw. I could hear the crust cracking and my stomach rumbled at the thought of the soft bread. 'Aren't I the eejit, now? Stuck here with these three. Poor divils or not, they're a lot of work.'

She was talking about Mother again. We were used to Granny complaining about her. She'd made it very clear we'd outstayed our welcome long ago, and her anger at our mother kept bursting out. I didn't realise at first that she was talking to anyone but herself, until I heard Michael's slurred voice. He must have arrived while I was wrapped up in my game.

'She's taking advantage, so. I'll be happy to eat that crust off the pan, if you haven't a use for it.'

I'd had my eye on the crust. I began to climb down from the bunk. If I popped my head into the kitchen maybe Granny would remember that crusts were meant to be *my* treat.

Michael's voice began again, 'You need to put your foot down, Bernie. You're not of an age to be doing this. It's not younger you're getting. And you can't be keeping that maneen under the table forever.'

I heard Granny snort. 'Not of an age, you say? I've the energy of a woman half my age, but that's not the point.'

'Sure you have. I wasn't after saying you were old, now, Bernie. That's not what I meant at all. Would you have any jam for that crust there?'

'I save the crusts for Claire,' I heard Granny say, and she was my loyal grandmother again, whether she was annoyed with Mother or not.

I hid in the shadows and peeped through the gap in the door, breathing in the peaty smell of the kitchen. If I showed myself now, Granny was bound to find something for me to do and I hadn't finished my game with Sindy. Michael was at the kitchen table. He'd peeled off his brown jacket and it was sitting in a heap at his feet, like an old well-trained dog.

'Was a miserable day to go across the water, right enough, but I like to bring flowers for her birthday.' His good hand shook as he took the cup of tea from Granny. 'She'd have been fifty-seven today.'

'Would she now?' Granny said. 'I'm grateful to you for putting flowers on his grave, too. I never get over that way myself.' I saw her reach into the press beside the window to fetch herself a cup but she stopped short and looked out across the lake instead.

'Wasn't flowers I put for him,' Michael told her. 'I put some shells, you know, the ones the children used to like finding. Do you remember? The beach is still full of them over there.'

'Is it, so?' Granny was still staring out of the window. Her knuckles were as white as the edge of the sink she was clutching. 'He liked shells.'

Michael poured some tea from his cup into the saucer and took a long slurp. Dad did that too, sometimes, when Mother wasn't looking. It used to make me laugh. But I didn't like seeing Michael do it. He reminded me of an animal, the way his shaggy moustache dipped into the tea and came out dripping.

'I put five,' Michael said. 'That was his age, wasn't it?' I saw Granny nod. He placed his saucer on the table and pulled a stained handkerchief from his pocket. I watched as he rubbed it over his face. I was relieved that it accidentally mopped up the drops of tea left on his moustache. His eyes looked quite pink when he eventually folded up the hanky again.

'Oh, Bernie, I should never have brought her here.' He whispered it so quietly I wasn't sure I'd heard him at all. But he must have spoken, because Granny turned from the window and looked at him with such a stern expression that I shrank deeper into the shadows of the bedroom.

'Now listen, Michael,' Granny said, sitting down opposite him at the table. 'Don't go back over all that again. It's nonsense, so, and you know it.'

'It's not, though. She was happy enough in Roundmore. She was a townie. I shouldn't have forced her out here into the wilds. That's what she used to call it, you remember, don't you? The wilds.'

'What else could you have done, after your stroke?'

'I know I couldn't have gone back to the trawler, but I could have tried an apprenticeship, been a cobbler maybe?'

'With one working arm?' Granny said.

'Well, I didn't need to dig my heels in and go all out for the sheep.'

Granny shook her head. 'It does no good talking like this.' She reached across the table and patted Michael's hand. It felt strange, seeing their hands touch but I couldn't turn my eyes away. I held my breath. I hoped they wouldn't notice me peeping through the gap. It would be embarrassing.

'I've the guilt, though, Bernie. It won't go away.' Michael's voice was even more wobbly than usual. 'All those tiny babies, one after the other, laid out there behind the cottage. I've *such* a guilt.'

'No good will come of thinking about that,' Granny said, a little sharply.

'I worked her too hard on the farm.'

Granny squeezed his fingers. 'She enjoyed the farm ... well, in the beginning. They were her sheep as much as yours. I remember the lambs she'd bring here, tiny scraps she'd kept alive.'

Michael nodded. 'She was great with the lambing. She could turn them if they were stuck. She had two good hands, not like me.' A sob broke from his lips.

'Oh Michael, you're only after coming from the cemetery. Isn't this the way you're bound to feel? You're a braver soul than me. It's the most I can do to look across the water. Even doing that is too much some days.' She glanced up at the window. 'Why do we stay here?'

'I couldn't leave,' Michael said. 'It would be like leaving Mairead behind.'

'I know. Sure, I'd feel the same about Declan.' Granny squeezed his hand again. 'Why not phone Rónán, patch things up? That would make you feel better.'

Michael shrugged. His eyes were wide now. All his tears had escaped down his cheeks. His one good hand clutched Granny's. 'Ah Bernie, that day with Declan. It plays on my mind.'

'Now, Michael.' She shook her head.

'I should have done something.'

Granny pushed his hand away from hers and straightened in her chair. 'Whisht your nonsense.'

He stood up and held the edge of the table. 'I should have saved him.'

'Time to go, Michael.'

He didn't move. 'When Rónán came to me and said, "They're after robbing the currach," I just thought,' he took a huge breath. 'I thought let them get their own supper tonight, I've had enough of sharing mine.'

'Now.' Granny got to her feet. 'Off home, Michael.'

'I was desperate for drink, Bernie, when Mairead was gone. I wanted to drown it all, like you.' He grabbed Granny's arm. 'But one of us had to stay sober...'

'You weren't a saint. Don't go making out you were, so.'

'Not a saint, no, but didn't one of us have to keep the children fed after Finbar went? Three years you'd been that way...'

'You had your poitín too. I know you did. But no matter.' She picked up his cup and saucer and turned to the sink. 'That's long ago now.'

'The day of the accident, begod I was angry with you, Bernie.'

Granny glared at him. 'Quiet now, Michael. Quiet.' I could see Louis beginning to stir under the table.

Michael shook his head. 'I was sick of doing the right thing.' His words were tumbling out, more slurred now than ever. 'I hated Finbar for leaving you and the children. And I hated that slut from Grogan's—'

'Don't!' Granny's hand came crashing down onto the draining board, and Louis sat up and grumbled sleepily.

'I should have stopped the boys, Bernie.' Michael's words were piling into each other. 'If I'd called them back when Rónán told me he was after seeing—'

Granny's hand flew through the air and she slapped Michael's cheek hard. 'Enough! Go now.'

Michael picked up his jacket. 'I need to talk about it.'

'So you always say, and what good does it do you? Or me?' Louis's grumbling threatened to turn into a wail and Granny swung him up onto her hip. The rope tangled around his legs.

Michael clutched his jacket to his chest. Both sides of his face looked crumpled now and his slapped cheek was red. 'I'm sorry, Bernie.' He dipped his head and left.

I was sure I hadn't taken a breath since Granny first touched Michael's hand, and my lungs felt like they might explode. I breathed out as quietly as I could. Granny was staring at the lake again, her arms wrapped around Louis's body. He tucked his head into her neck and even though I couldn't see his face I knew he was sucking his thumb. Granny stood like that for a long time. Then she half turned her head.

'I'm going for a lie down, Claire,' she called. So, she'd finally remembered I was in my bedroom. Maybe she'd never forgotten.

I paused before I replied. I wanted her to think I was still playing and hadn't listened to their argument. Then I said brightly, 'Okay. Shall I watch Louis?'

'Yes.' She put him back under the table. 'Don't let the fire go out.'

I opened the door wide and showed myself in the doorway. 'I won't,' I told her.

I watched her cross the kitchen. She seemed so old as she steered herself slowly towards her bedroom. The way she was hunched over reminded me of Father O'Reilly.

'Sister John says we have to go to Mass tomorrow,' I said. 'Everyone in class is meant to go.'

Granny sighed loudly. 'And did you tell her we've a problem with the van?'

I shook my head. I'd been too terrified to even look at the nun when she'd cornered me at home time, let alone tell her a fib.

'Well, you can tell her Monday. If the van won't start, we can't be at Mass, can we?'

'Okay,' I said, although I dreaded the thought of having to explain that to Sister John. I'd only been in her class a week but I knew that nun wouldn't swallow a lie, no matter how believable.

'And tell her we've not the money to get it repaired,' Granny added over her shoulder. She stopped at the open doorway to her room and glanced at the photograph that hung there, the one of the laughing boys. 'Mass. And with Father O'Reilly, no doubt. What did that man ever do for us?' She reached out her fingers and unhooked the string of beads from the frame.

And as she moved her hand away, she gently brushed the cheek of the littlest boy of all, the one that looked just like Louis.

Chapter 8

I'd like to believe our grandmother was oblivious to the pain she inflicted by refusing to take us to Mass. I suspect, however, that she was well aware of our dreadful predicament. I spent that Sunday terrifying myself with thoughts of how Sister John would react the next morning when I told her the lie about Granny's van. My stomach flipped each time I thought of the leather strap hanging by the nun's desk, and I dashed to the toilet so many times I used almost all of the sawdust. I should have explained to my grandmother how frightened I was, and perhaps she would have relented sooner. But she'd been in a dark mood since slapping Michael's face, and that made her as scary as my teacher.

* * *

I tried to distract myself from my terror by thinking of Emmet and the dinner time we'd spend together, but the weather on Monday was against us. We weren't allowed outside after eating our sandwiches and I was disappointed. The windows in the dining hall were steamed up and there was a terrible stink of sick. I'd heard Iseult say it was Theresa's fault. She'd had pickle in her corned beef sandwich and it had turned her stomach, and now it had turned everyone else's too. One hundred little girls silently cursed Theresa Maloney's mother and her fancy ways.

It would have been extremely boring in the dining hall if I hadn't had a great imagination. I used the time to invent a witch who loved tormenting nuns and I was looking forward to writing about her in my notebook that evening. I enjoyed the story so much that I couldn't help smiling to myself and chuckling a little, too. I forgot where I was for a while, until I saw Siobhán watching me. She had a smirk on her lips. I sighed. The sty had finally cleared from my eye and I'd hoped the other girls might be friendly now. But instead, Siobhán had started making fun of the way I spoke. I was already used to people saying in Wales that I sounded Irish. Just as I'd feared, here in Ireland I sounded Welsh. How impossibly unfair. Now she'd seen me smiling at my own thoughts, I could only imagine what names Siobhán would call me. I couldn't imagine why Iseult was so friendly with such a horrible girl.

I fiddled with the apple core in my pocket, hoping the rain would clear. I was having a truly miserable day. I was still burning from the telling off Sister John had given me. She'd shouted, in front of all the class, that Granny's broken van was 'not a valid reason for non-attendance at Mass', and she'd waved the strap at me. She hadn't used it, though, and when I'd finally got back to my seat, the House girls looked at me so kindly that I'd almost burst into tears. How I hoped and hoped the rain would stop. But it didn't, and we went back to class for more dreaded penmanship.

Tuesday, thankfully, was dry. Sister John had picked on me in the English lesson and asked me to read aloud from *The Children's Oliver Twist*. It wasn't an easy paragraph, but I thought I'd made a reasonable job of it. I'd been surprised by the way Theresa had lumbered through the half a page she'd read. She was a good reader and could work out even the hardest words, but the way she read made the story sound completely boring. When it was the House girls' turn, they read like star entertainers, and I was disappointed when Sister John stopped them after only one line each. I could have listened to them all morning. Instead, Sister chose Iseult to read to the end of the chapter, and even though she tried to copy the House girls' style, she skipped over so many words the story made no sense at all. I was quietly proud of my offering, even if it wasn't as good as the House girls'.

'I'm so hungry. I need more food,' I heard a voice behind me say in some sort of strange accent, as I ate my sandwiches at dinner time. I turned around and there was Siobhán. 'Poor me,' she said, rubbing her stomach and making a face like she was dying. 'Give me more food.'

The girls sitting with her were turning bright red in an effort to keep their giggles silent. We weren't allowed to talk in the dinner hall, let alone laugh. I was sure the nuns would have stopped us from breathing if only they could.

I glared at Siobhán. She had obviously not been listening in class because what I'd actually read was 'Please, sir, I want some more,' and I was just about to tell her so when Iseult sat down next to me. She was late to dinner because she'd been helping Sister John choose library books for our class. I was a little disappointed not to have that honour myself but I hoped Iseult had found some really exciting ones. The bookshelf in our classroom was full of boring titles and there was never anything interesting to look at in wet play.

'Now, Siobhán,' Iseult said, and she actually placed her hand on my shoulder. 'You know Claire is new and from England.'

'Wales,' I said, but I was so shocked at being singled out by the prettiest girl in class that my voice was barely a whisper.

'Now go and sit over there,' she told me, waving a finger at the end of the table, 'and then Siobhán can come and sit next to me.'

'But I was here fir—' I began, but Iseult had turned her back on me and was unwrapping her sandwiches.

Siobhán was already trying to shoulder me off my seat. 'Move before Head Nun sees us,' she hissed.

I grabbed what was left of my food and before the nun could turn around, I dashed to an empty seat at the end of the table. I kept my head down and tried to eat my sandwiches as quickly as I could, but I'd lost my appetite. I stuffed the crusts into my cardigan pockets. Buddy would probably enjoy them as much as apple cores.

It was easy to slip away from the other children in the yard. Iseult had gone back to class to help Sister John, and Siobhán and her giggly friends had turned their laughter onto someone else – the girl in the class below who had a metal frame on her leg to stop her falling over.

Emmet was behind the toilet block already. He jumped to his feet when he saw me. 'Jaysus,' he said 'I thought you'd forgotten me. I waited here for you yesterday.'

'It was raining,' I said. 'We weren't allowed out. I've brought some cores.' I took them from my pockets. 'And some crusts. They're a bit fluffy.' I pulled a sprinkling of green wool off them.

'Crusts, too,' Emmet said. He stared at my cupped hands.

'Does he like them?'

'Who?'

'Buddy.'

Emmet blinked at me for a moment, then he took a deep breath. 'Ah, sure he does,' he said, taking the crusts. He held them under his nose. 'Egg?'

'Yes, is that okay? I tried not to leave too much on them. Can horses eat eggs?'

'Sure they can,' he said. 'Leave all the egg you want on the crusts. It'll be grand.' He stuffed them into the pockets of his shorts and sat down on the grass.

'How's Buddy?' The September sun was warm and I was so glad to be outside. I turned a few cartwheels.

Emmet watched me. 'You're good at that,' he said, but he didn't get up to try himself. 'Have you been writing any stories?'

'I wrote one about a witch,' I said, pausing my twirling to catch my breath. 'She gives nuns the runs.'

Emmet laughed out loud. 'I like the sound of that witch.'

I laughed with him, then I frowned. The witch I'd drawn to illustrate my story wore a bun and looked quite a lot like Granny. I hoped she wasn't studying my notebook while I was at school.

'I wrote a story in my head,' Emmet said, 'on the way to school this morning. About pirates, just like *Treasure Island*.' He picked a dandelion stalk and put the end in his mouth. 'I looked out for you at the weekend.'

'What do you mean?'

'On Sunday. At Mass.'

83

'Oh,' I said. 'We don't go to Mass.' I was beginning to feel annoyed with Granny's attitude to church. Surely, a service wouldn't be so bad. If Emmet could put up with it, then so could I. 'My grandmother doesn't like Father O'Reilly.'

Emmet snorted. 'She sounds like a fine woman.'

I sighed. 'Tell me about your story.'

'There's a pirate with a parrot on his shoulder.' Emmet sucked on the stalk and blew imaginary smoke rings.

'Like Long John Silver has?' I'd started turning cartwheels again.

'That's the one. It's on the cover of the book. And there's a boy.'

'Jim Hawkins,' I said. My voice came out weirdly while I was upside down. I landed on my feet. 'What happens to them?'

'They sail off and find an island with treasure.'

I plonked myself down beside him. 'And then what?'

'I haven't decided yet.' He tapped the end of the dandelion stalk and I was almost certain I saw ash fall from it.

'Picking dandelions makes you wee the bed,' I told him.

'Urgh,' he said, and threw the stalk onto the grass. He rubbed his hands hard on his jumper. 'Is that a fact?'

'Mmm,' I said. 'Will used to wee his bed. It was because of dandelions, so Mother said. I think your pirate and the boy will sell their treasure and buy a huge house with fields and horses. Oh, and chickens. And there'll be seals in the lake and everyone will live happily ever after.' Emmet was spitting on his hands now. 'That's horrible,' I told him.

'Just making certain,' he said. He rubbed his palms together hard and wiped them down his shorts. 'Did you read any more of your book? What's happening with Beauty?'

'He's escaped from a fire.' I pushed my socks down and let the sun warm my legs.

Emmet shuddered. 'Fire is bad. Francis was in a fire. His face, it's ruined.'

'Urgh, that's horrible.' I touched my own cheeks. 'Beauty was afraid to leave the stable but his groom led him out just in time.'

'Francis didn't want to leave his cottage. His baby sister was in the back.'

'Did he get her out?'

Emmet shook his head. 'It's a sorry tale.' He studied his hands. 'He's in the orphanage now.'

'His parents died, too?'

'No, but they've no home.'

'We've been reading about an orphanage in *The Children's Oliver Twist*,' I said. 'It's our class reader. Do you have one?'

'We're doing our catechism,' Emmet said. 'Does that count?'

I frowned. 'I don't know what "Our Catta"...whatever you said, is.'

'Sure, aren't you the lucky thing?' He shoved my shoulder. 'The catechism is a lot of questions about God and stuff, and if you don't answer right, you go to hell.' He picked a blade of grass and chewed on it. '*Oliver Twist*, that's by Charles Dickens, isn't it?' He scratched his chin. 'Born 1821, died 1870. That's in the book of facts. My teacher has *Oliver Twist* on his shelf. Good, is it?'

'Quite good. It's about a boy who's hasn't got enough to eat and he's always asking for more food. Wait a minute,' I suddenly turned to face Emmet. 'You actually go to *hell* if you get your answers wrong?' I squinted at him to see if he was telling the truth.

He shrugged. 'That's what the Brothers say.' He wrapped his arms around himself. 'Is Oliver in an orphanage?'

'Yes. Well, he lives in a workhouse but Sister John says they're the same thing.'

'Does he live there for always?'

'He gets out soon.' I'd started reading ahead while the other girls read aloud in class. Some of them took *ages*.

Emmet nodded. 'Like me, then,' he said. 'I'll be getting out once my mother comes back from New York. She's catching her ship soon, with Howard.'

'Getting out of where?'

'The orphanage. I'm living there while my mother's away.'

I'd never been to an orphanage but I'd heard about them in stories. I didn't like the sound of the one in *Oliver Twist*. Sometimes, in my other school, the teachers gave us little books with pictures of orphans in them. We had to tear out the pictures and sell them to our friends. Everyone wanted pictures of the girls with curls and the boys with slicked-back hair. No one wanted the children with glasses or buck teeth. I was glad my photograph wasn't in those books. I didn't think anyone would want to buy a picture of me. Mother claimed I had a sulky look, just like Dad. It gave men an air of mystery, she said, but it was downright unattractive on a girl. I was certain those little books would be sent back to the people who made them, and my photo would be stuck fast in all of them.

'I thought orphanages are where children go when their parents die,' I said, remembering what Sister John had told us. She'd pointed to the back of the class as she'd said that, and I'd felt duty bound to put up my hand and explain that my mother wasn't dead, just in London. 'Isn't she the fancy one?' Sister had muttered. 'Your mother's only gone to America,' I told Emmet.

'I know,' he said, 'but it's not all orphans in the orphanage. Loads of us have parents alive. My mother's paying the Brothers to look after me. It costs a mint but she doesn't mind.'

'What's it like,' I asked, 'in the orphanage?'

'Ah sure, it's fine enough. It's better now I can come to school. I'm only allowed to be here because Brother Thomas – he was our English teacher – he broke his neck when the bull went at him, and I have to get good grades in my examinations so it looks well for the orphanage.'

'A bull?'

'Franco. He couldn't have charged a more deserving Brother.'

'There are bulls at your orphanage?'

'Just the one. He isn't ours, he's brought in when he's needed. But we've cows and sheep and goats and chickens and all that.'

'Your orphanage is a farm?' This wasn't how I'd imagined orphanages to be, with lots of animals, and children with parents that were very much alive. I was beginning to feel that Will, Louis and I were missing out by living at Granny's.

'It's all sorts. There's a tailor's, a bootmaker's, a laundry. The Brothers teach us trades. Cash Hill Industrial School, that's the proper name for our orphanage—'

'But you've got animals?' I was kneeling up now, my eyes fixed on Emmet.

'Lots of them. They're bloody hard work.'

'Is that where Buddy is, on your farm?'

'Buddy? No, not him. He's in the fields over there. He's free to roam, so he is. I'll show you one day.'

'One day this week?' I clasped my hands under my chin and pleaded with him. Will would have called me over-dramatic but he couldn't see me so I didn't care.

'If you like.'

The bell was ringing in the yard behind me. I jumped to my feet. The punishment for being late to line up was missing play for the rest of the week. I couldn't have that. I might miss seeing Buddy.

'How about tomorrow?' I said, running for the gap in the hedge. 'We could go and see him then.' This was so exciting.

'Okay,' Emmet called as he ran in the opposite direction. He sounded excited too. 'We'll go tomorrow.'

Chapter 9

When Will and I got home from school, Granny swore she'd been pulling her hair out all day. It could have been true, I supposed, but it looked to me like she still had plenty enough. Her top knot *was* rather untidy, though. Louis was driving her mad, she said. He'd escaped from the table leg that afternoon because she'd tied the leash too loosely. He'd taken two hours to wriggle free but when he'd finally managed it, he'd dragged his rope behind him almost all the way to Michael's cottage while Granny had been checking on the chickens.

'Halfway up the boreen, he was, running for all he was worth.'

He'd got into more trouble after she'd caught him and tied him up again. He'd discovered he was strong enough to drag the table, just a bit, just enough to get to the pile of turf next to the fire. He enjoyed licking it. Granny couldn't turn her back for a minute. I wondered if the turf tasted as good as it smelt, although I wasn't tempted enough to find out. Maybe it was giving him extra strength, like spinach gave Popeye. The table was certainly a heavy piece of furniture to be dragging around, and when Granny shortened his rope, he'd just pulled the table further. Mother had always described Louis as 'nothing if not persistent'.

'He's a bold one, that Louis,' Granny said, 'just like your father was. Always looking for mischief. I'll be writing to your Uncle Jack and telling him to bring you home to Wales. I'm too old for this. Those grandparents of yours in Spain can move their arses and do a turn. It'll give them a break from sunning themselves and spending their ill-gotten gains.'

Jack taking us home? My prayers were going to be answered. 'Shall I post the letter for you, Grandma?' I knew where the little green post box was out on the big lane and I didn't mind a walk.

Granny looked at me sharply. 'Don't you be coming here with your cheek,' she said. 'You're a bold one too. Like your mother, I've no doubt.'

Oh, the injustice. Will had gone off to our bedroom and had closed the door. He was never around to back me up. He didn't say much to me anymore. He still ignored me on the school bus, too, which was a shame as I had no one else to talk to. He had no one either, but even that didn't make me interesting company in his eyes.

'I'll write to Jack when I've a moment,' Granny said, flopping into the chair by the fire, 'and pray he won't be too long in coming for you.'

'You could put us in the orphanage while we wait,' I suggested, quite proud of my idea. I could live there with Emmet, I thought with a surge of happiness, and help on the farm.

Granny's face turned murderous. 'It's the orphanage you're talking about now, is it? The orphanage! Who's saying what at that school of yours?'

I shrank in my seat. 'Only Emmet,' I mumbled, shocked into replying before I'd had time to think.

'What, Emmet you say? A boy? Sure, there are no boys at your school. What rubbish are you talking now, child?' She glared at me. 'Are there boys at your school?' I shook my head. 'So is it an Eimear you're talking of? Is there a girl called Eimear in your class?'

I was suddenly desperate to shout that I knew the difference between Emmet and Eimear and yes there were two Eimears in my class but it was Emmet I'd been talking to. Thankfully I had a bit of sense among my headful of rubbish, and I thought better of it and bit my tongue. I nodded instead.

'Well, she's no right to be filling your head with nonsense. Now go and play with your little brother under the table or it's the orphanage I'll be sending you to, right enough.' And she grabbed her tin of tobacco from the mantelpiece and stormed from the kitchen, even though it wasn't anywhere near time to feed the chickens.

'Louis,' I said, untangling his rope and lifting him onto my lap, 'why are you being so much trouble for Granny?' He was quite heavy now and already filling out the little green jumper Granny had knitted for him. His face was pale and podgy. In fact, while Will and I were even healthier now we were at Granny's, Louis just looked worse. Back home he'd had gorgeous pink cheeks you couldn't help but pinch and strong little legs from running around. Now, I noticed as he sat on my lap, his legs seemed thinner and his tummy fatter and his face had the washed-out look of someone who'd been ill for a very long time.

'Grandma,' I called, 'can I take Louis out for a bit?'

I couldn't see her anywhere outside but her voice came from behind a bush near the lake and I spotted a puff of smoke circling above it. 'You can go along the boreen with him, but keep him on his tether.'

So off we went. I pretended Louis was my pony called Star and he was pulling a cart up and down the lane. It was a good game. I was thinking, too, about Emmet and imagining going to see Buddy. It made my heart beat faster. And then the rain started. It never seemed far away in this place. I reined in Louis. We'd spent at least half an hour running up and down the lane so I didn't feel too bad about dragging him inside.

Surely I'd given him enough fresh air and sunlight to cancel out the months he'd been kept under the table.

* * *

The next day at school was surprisingly wonderful and I was excited to be there. Not only was I going to see Buddy, but the head nun had set us older girls a competition. What's more, it was one I thought I could win – I couldn't believe luck was smiling on me at last. The competition was to write a story. My heart sank briefly when I realised it had to be written in pen, but still I hoped my great use of imagination would make up for the splodges. Even Sister John couldn't help noticing my talent, and she didn't really approve of imagination at all. 'Keep that mind of yours under control, Claire O'Connell,' she told me nearly every day. 'We don't want any flights of your fancy now, do we?' You couldn't have too many flights of fancy as far as I was concerned, but I always replied, 'No, Sister,' and kept my thoughts to myself.

But here was licence to fly off with my fancy, and I was going to grab the opportunity with both of my inky hands. This was my moment to shine. This was what I was famous for at my school in Cardiff – Claire O'Connell and her amazing stories. Now I'd show my new class what I could do, and even Sister John would have to be impressed.

The only problem, besides the ink, of course, was the title Head Nun had chosen – 'My Best Friend'. How boring. Surely she could have picked something like 'The Magic Potion'. I'd written a fantastic story with that title during my last term in Wales, and Miss Pryce had said it was the most wonderful story she'd read in a long while – at least the most wonderful written by a nine-year-old. And I was ten now, so I was bound to have improved. But I didn't have a best friend anymore, and the thought of writing about Karen in Cardiff made me sad. I didn't want to spend the rest of the week covered with ink and in tears, to boot. In a moment of madness, I put my hand up and asked Sister John if we could pick our own title. Her glare was answer enough.

'My bloomin' best friend, indeed,' I muttered as we packed up to go to dinner. 'Just my luck when I haven't got one.'

'You could write about us,' a voice behind me said. I turned to see the House girls smiling at me shyly, their hands half covering their mouths.

'But I don't know anything about you,' I said, a bit too sharply.

'You could make up whatever you wanted,' the one with the red hair said. 'We won't mind.'

'Okay, thanks,' I told them, finally remembering my manners. But I was quite sure I wouldn't end up writing about the House girls, even if I had to cry my way through the rest of the week.

91

Emmet was waiting for me in our usual place, pacing back and fore on the grass. 'Why is it that you're always so late? I thought you weren't coming.'

'I wouldn't miss going to see Buddy,' I said. 'There was a queue for the toilet.' I'd had to wait for ages, and the smell of poo and carbolic soap was still stuck in my nose.

'There's not enough time to go there now.' He sat down heavily and I thought he might be about to cry. 'You need to run straight from the dinner hall, and then we'll have a chance of being there and back before the bells go.'

'Oh.' Now I regretted stopping at the toilet first, but climbing a hill while desperate for a wee seemed an impossible challenge. 'I'll come straight away tomorrow.'

'We can't go tomorrow. Tomorrow's Thursday. Buddy's in a different field on Thursdays. It's too far away.'

'What about Friday?'

He shook his head. 'We'll have to go next week.'

'Okay.' I mumbled. Next week seemed an age away. I sat down next to him and took my apple from my pocket. I nibbled it disappointedly.

'A sweet one, is it?' he asked eventually.

I nodded and took a few more sad nibbles. 'Buddy can have the core. I saved my crusts for him too.'

'Thanks,' Emmet said. He seemed in a better mood. 'Sure, he'll be grateful.'

I was happy he wasn't cross with me anymore. 'We've got a competition in class,' I told him. 'A story-writing one.'

'That's a great competition to have. We have competitions at the orphanage, but they're just polishing floors and stuff.'

'Polishing floors?' I blurted, spraying bits of apple onto Emmet's jumper.

'Ah sure, it's grand.' He chuckled. 'We see who can go the fastest, and I win most times, unless my knees are giving out, you know?'

I didn't really but I nodded anyway. I was so glad he'd forgiven me for being late. 'The title for our competition is "My Best Friend",' I said. 'I hate it. I don't have one to write about.'

'Ah, that's too bad.'

'I did have a best friend. Karen.' My heart gave a little jolt as I said her name, and I realised I missed winding her curls around my fingers. 'She's in Cardiff. There's a girl here I want to be friends with, but she doesn't like me.'

'Then she's a fool, so.'

I was only half listening. 'All the other girls like her, too.' I wasn't certain that was true, though. Some of them seemed to avoid Iseult.

Emmet nudged my arm. 'Look.' I watched as he found a bit of sprayed apple on his jumper and popped it into his mouth.

'Urgh,' I said. 'That's got my spit on it.'

He grinned and showed me the tiny piece of apple on his tongue. 'What's a bit of spit, eh?'

'Spit's revolting,' I said, struggling to my feet to get away from him.

He stood up too. 'I'll show you revolting.' He pushed his finger right up his nose. 'Delicious,' he said, licking it clean and trying to grab me with his free hand.

I dodged away from his grasp. '*You're* revolting,' I told him, although I couldn't help but laugh.

'Yeah,' he said, chasing after me. 'But revolting or not, I'm still your friend.'

I ran circles around him, laughing. 'Emmet, my revolting friend.'

'Exactly,' he said. His eyes were full of mischief. 'So you can write your story about me.'

I stopped running and stared at him. 'You're right.' My problem was solved!

'You could write about my mother and Howard and the ship.'

'And that they're on their way to get you?'

'Sure.'

'And about the bull and polishing floors in the orphanage.'

'If you want,' he said, with a shrug. 'But if it's a good story you're

93

wanting,' he picked another bit of apple from his jumper, 'you could write about Buddy.'

'Yes!' Why hadn't I thought of that myself? We sat down together, our backs against the wall. 'I could say he lives in the field over the hill and that I save my crusts for him.' I bit my lip. 'Oh no, I can't say that in case Granny reads it. I'm supposed to eat the crusts from my sandwiches. She says they'll make my hair curl.'

'Ah, doesn't that explain it. I wondered why Buddy's tail was having these big fat ringlets. It's your crusts, so.'

I stared at him. 'What, eating crusts really works?'

He turned his face to mine, his eyes practically popping from his head. Then a laugh burst from his mouth. 'No, I'm codding you. You should have seen your face.'

'That's not fair,' I said, punching his arm, as Will liked to do to me.

Emmet flinched.

'Wimp,' I said. 'Can't take a punch, eh?' And I did it again, harder.

His face turned white. 'Go easy there Claire, won't you?' he said, rubbing his arm gently. 'That's the one that got broke in the summer.'

'You broke your arm?' I was seriously impressed. I'd never broken a bone and I was envious of Will because he'd broken his wrist playing cricket. 'How did you do it?'

'Oh, just a fall.' He bit his thumbnail. 'It was nothing.'

'Were you riding Buddy?'

He lowered his thumb from his lips and blinked at me. A smile spread slowly across his face. 'I was. We were galloping out over there, and didn't he find a bog hole that his hoof went down into. He threw me clear and I hit the ground and it just snapped, my arm, snapped like a twig.'

'How did you get back home?'

He grinned. 'Buddy saved me. He ran off at first – he had a fright, falling down and all that – but when he saw me in trouble, with my arm just hanging limp, didn't he turn round. And he came back across the bog and he knelt down next to me, like those horses do in the films, you know, the cowboy ones? And I got my foot into the stirrup and I heaved myself up onto his saddle with my one good arm. Then he brought me to the orphanage and he neighed and neighed outside the gate, until a Brother came to fetch me in.'

'Wow.' This really was something I could write about. I was already composing the story in my head – 'My Best Friend Emmet and Buddy's Daring Rescue.' I was going to win this competition, I was absolutely certain. 'That story is even more exciting than *Black Beauty*,' I said.

Emmet smiled. 'Ah, sure, it was a great adventure. Aren't you the lucky one, though, having books to read.'

I shrugged. 'Everyone has books. School is full of them.'

'Exciting ones aren't for the likes of me. That's what my teacher says, anyhows.' He bent his knees and rested his chin on them. 'Like *Treasure Island*. It's on his desk.'

'And he won't let you read it? That's so mean.'

'I looked at the cover again this morning.' He held out his hand and showed me his palm. 'And didn't he catch me.'

I touched the red stripe. His skin was raised and hot under my fingertips. Sister John was forever threatening us with the leather strap. I hadn't seen her use it on anyone yet, only the House girls, but it hung on the wall, a constant threat to the rest of us.

'I wish Will had brought his copy,' I said. 'You could have borrowed it.' Although, as I said the words, I knew that would have been impossible. Will guarded everything he owned and he'd never lend anything to me.

'Ah, that's kind of you, Claire.' He smiled sadly.

'Perhaps your mother will bring you books.'

'My mother?'

'From New York.'

He shrugged. 'She might.'

We could hear the bells ringing in the playgrounds. I handed Emmet the core I'd been nibbling on. 'I hope Buddy enjoys this,' I said. 'He deserves it. He's a real hero. I can't wait to meet him.' I got up and dusted myself down. 'Sorry I hurt your bad arm.'

'It's okay,' Emmet said. He still looked a bit pale but he gave me another smile before examining what was left of my apple. 'See you tomorrow, Claire.'

* * *

We weren't allowed to take our pens out of class, Sister John told us. Some girls cried because they didn't have pens at home, but Sister wouldn't relent.

'No one is to rob the school's pens,' she said. 'Do I make myself clear?'

And we all chanted, 'Yes, Sister,' like twenty little puppets.

I was lucky because I knew Will had a spare pen and some ink. I just needed to sneak it out of his pencil case. He'd be mad if he caught me but I had no choice.

I couldn't wait to get started when I got back to Granny's that afternoon, but chance would have been a fine thing.

'Come play with your brother, Claire,' she said as soon as I walked in through the door. 'He's in a desperate mood again today.' And she went out to catch a breath of air.

I didn't blame Louis one bit. Even I'd come to realise that being on a length of rope attached to a table leg was no picnic. But I couldn't afford to feel sorry for him that day – I had a prize-winning story to write. I went into the pantry and found the crust that Granny had saved for me. It was strange how I hated them around the edge of my sandwiches but I loved the end of a pan. I dolloped some jam onto the crust and tore it into two very unequal pieces. I gave the smallest to Louis.

'Eat this and I'll play with you in a minute.'

Will hadn't come home at the same time as me. He'd gone to Aiden's to practise his Irish. I'd forgotten this wonderful fact until I climbed the steps of the bus after school and saw a space where he usually sat. Fantastic. I could find his spare pen while he was out. Then I remembered he'd have his pencil case with him. I decided I'd start my story in pencil instead. It would probably be for the best anyway. Chances were, I wouldn't be able to read what I'd written if I started off in pen. As well as being messy, I was well known for crossing out words for better ones I found in my dictionary. I wasn't great at spelling, either. Pencil would be my best bet. I could write up the finished story in ink later, and I imagined a beautiful page, the handwriting a fine example of penmanship, without a single blot in sight.

I dashed off to find a pencil and my dictionary. My notebook was hidden under my mattress, as usual. No matter how wonderful Miss Pryce said my compositions were, Will could always find fault and never failed to let me know how I should have written the thing. He was a very annoying brother, and I sincerely hoped he was hating every second of his extra Irish lessons with Aiden. He had an exam the very next month. Sister John, in just over a week, had terrified me into taking up the act of prayer, as she called it, but I'd put it to good use. Each night I prayed that Will would fail. I told him so after a particularly nasty argument, and he'd said that was all he needed. God was already on the side of the Brothers – the Almighty didn't need any extra encouragement to hang him out to dry in his Irish exam. I prayed extra hard after that.

I took my notebook, pencil and dictionary to the kitchen, where Louis was still munching on his piece of crust. He was very jammy. He looked like he'd wiped the bread all over his face on a mission to find his mouth. There was a large lump of strawberry in his hair. I made a mental note to dig it out before Granny saw him. I had plenty of time – she hardly ever looked at him, just a glance now and again to see that he was still attached to his rope.

I took up my pencil and began to write.

Chapter 10

My stomach still flutters when I think of that story-writing competition. The feeling it excited in me as a child, I recognise as the kind of nervous anticipation I experience at the start of a case. Writing brought joy to me then, just as the law is my all-encompassing passion now.

* * *

In school the next morning, while Sister John popped out of the classroom, the talk was all of stories. Everyone had started one – except the House girls, who couldn't seem to find paper and pens at home – and all the girls whispered over each other as loudly as they dared, knowing Sister John would be back at any moment to shout, 'Will you stop with your fussing!' But when Iseult stood up and began to tell us her story, everyone fell silent and listened in awe.

The story she was writing was about the best friend she had in Dublin, the one she saw every time she went to stay with her aunty there. The friend's name was Carlotta and she was beautiful and a ballerina, and her family had a huge house in Ballsbridge with a red front door, four flights of stairs, and a maid, a butler and a chauffeur for their Rolls. She had yellow hair, just like Iseult, and they spent lots of time winding curls into their beautiful locks and swapping dresses because they had the same exquisite taste and one day—

Sister John came back into class. We'd been so absorbed in Iseult's story that none of us had heard the nun's beads clattering on her belt as she strode down the corridor – the usual warning to us that she was on her way. She saw Iseult standing at the front commanding our attention and smiled. 'Well done for keeping the class quiet, Iseult. Aren't you the girl I can depend on. Here, give out these copy books, will you?'

Iseult moved gracefully around the class, handing out the open English exercise books. I thought about her and Carlotta, sharing clothes and brushing each other's hair, and I hated the girl from Dublin with all my heart. When Iseult came to me, she glanced at my work. 'You have an A minus,' she said. 'That's almost as good as my A.' She handed me my book and began to move away, then she turned back with a smile. 'Poor Claire,' she said. 'You must be finding the story writing competition very hard because you don't have a best friend to write about, do you? Everyone knows new children don't have any friends.'

For a moment, I didn't know what to say. Just the fact that she was speaking to me stunned me into silence. Then I suddenly remembered the pages I'd written the night before.

'Well...' I stammered.

Iseult held up her hand. 'I'll be your friend.'

I heard the House girls gasp behind me. I looked at Iseult in amazement. Had she really said those words? 'You'll be my friend?'

'Of course,' she said, and beamed at me. 'That way, you can write your story about me.'

Then I had to duck as she flung the House girls' books right over my head.

* * *

Emmet was waiting for me after dinner. 'Have you the crusts for Buddy?' he asked, holding out his hands. I noticed his fingers were stained purple. There were purple stains around his mouth, too.

'Not many today,' I said, handing them over. 'I ate most of them. I was hungry. Granny says I must be growing because I'm eating like a horse.' I laughed. I was bubbling over with happiness. 'That must be why I like Buddy's crusts all of a sudden.'

Emmet didn't laugh. He was sniffing the few crusts he held in his hand. 'Were they fish paste?' he asked. 'Buddy likes fish paste ones best of all. It's good if there's a lot of paste round the edges. Buddy likes that.'

'Mmm,' I said, feeling suddenly guilty that Buddy was missing out on his treat. 'I'll ask Granny to make extra tomorrow, shall I?'

'That would be fine,' Emmet said, 'if she wouldn't mind.'

'I've got some news,' I said, almost bursting with excitement. I ran along the grass and turned a spectacular cartwheel. I landed with a flounce. 'Iseult wants to be my friend.'

'Iseult?' Emmet said. 'Who's that?'

'The girl in my class I told you about.'

'Oh, you mean the stupid one.'

'Stupid? I didn't say she was stupid.'

'No? What's she like then, this Iseult?' He was leaning against the wall, watching me spin.

'She's *so* pretty. She's got blonde hair and blue eyes. And curls, too.' I wondered if she'd let me brush them, like Carlotta in Dublin did. I hoped she would.

'She doesn't sound too special to me,' Emmet said. 'Sure, there are thousands of girls with blonde hair and blue eyes.'

'You're a boy so you don't understand.' I cartwheeled again and my apple fell from my pocket and landed in the dirt. Emmet ran to pick it up. 'Buddy can have the rest of that,' I told him. 'It's sour.' I'd had one bite and found it didn't suit my sweet tooth, growth spurt or not.

He rubbed it on his jumper and took a bite to see for himself. 'Right enough,' he said, 'but Buddy won't mind. He'll think it's his birthday when I give him this.' He tucked it into his pocket.

'When *is* his birthday?'

'It was in the summer,' he said. 'He was ten.'

'Like me, then. I was ten in June. How old are you, Emmet?'

'I'm ten, too.'

'When's your birthday?'

'Christmas time.'

'Do you get double presents?' I knelt on the grass and tried a forward roll, but the ground was too bumpy and it hurt my back.

'Presents?'

'For your birthday and Christmas, all in one go?'

'Ah, sure I do.'

'You lucky thing. Can you do this?' I showed him how I could walk a tiny bit on my hands.

He shook his head. 'It's my arm, you know. It would buckle under me, so.'

'Oh,' I said. 'I hadn't thought of that. Will can't do handstands either, since he broke his wrist.'

We sat down together, our backs against the toilet block wall. There was still a little warmth in the midday sun and the stones had soaked it up.

'I love the sun,' Emmet said. 'It's like sitting in front of your own roaring fire. Warms you through to your bones.' He lifted his chin to the sky. 'The sun's a star, really. Its surface is six thousand degrees centigrade.'

'Did you get that from your book of facts?'

'*The Children's Guide to Knowledge*. That's the book on the shelf in class I'm allowed to read.'

'The only one?'

Emmet nodded.

A man was out on the hillside with his dog, too far away to bother us, a couple of children hiding from the rest of the school. We watched as he walked slowly up the hill then disappeared over the top.

'That's where Buddy lives, isn't it, over the hill?' It didn't seem fair that the man out walking might see Emmet's horse before I did. 'I can't wait until you take me there.'

'We'll go soon enough,' he promised. 'Do you know the words to "Happy Birthday"?'

'Of course I do,' I said. 'I can sing it in Welsh too. *Penblwydd hapus i—*'

'Can you sing it the normal way?'

'That is the normal way in Wales,' I told him, although the truth was we only ever sang it in Welsh on Mother's and Louis's birthdays.

'I know, but I mean in English.' He gave me a small smile. 'Please?'

So I sang it for him, and when I came to the bit where I needed to put in a name he pointed to himself. 'To Emmet,' I sang. 'Happy birthday to you.' And then I sang it right through in Welsh, just to prove I could.

'Thank you,' Emmet said. 'Deee-olch.'

'You remembered!' In a strange way, it was a comfort to hear my mother's language in Connemara, and on Emmet's lips, too.

We sat there, enjoying the sunshine. From the corner of my eye, I saw Emmet take something from his pocket and pop it in his mouth. It looked like a sweet. 'Are you eating?' I asked and he shook his head. 'You are! You've got sweets and you're not sharing. That's not fair.' I pulled his hand out of his pocket and bent his fingers back. There was a squashed blackberry in his palm. 'Where did you get that?'

'I don't want to be telling you,' he said, but his eyes gave the game away. I got up and went over to the bush covered in berries and picked some of my own.

'Oh, don't be taking them all, now Claire,' Emmet said. 'I've enough competition with this one.' He pointed to a bush like the ones with little red flowers that grew around Granny's cottage. The flowers reminded me of tiny ballerinas.

'That bush is a problem?'

'Not the fuchsia, the bird in it. It's helping itself to all the good ones. Once you move away it'll be back at them.'

'What bird?'

'There, in the middle.'

I looked and looked. I shook my head. 'I can't see it.'

'Your eyes need to go blurry, then you'll see it move. They're fine things to watch, birds. There are thousands of species on the Earth. This one's a blackbird. It's got great camouflage. The robin now, you'd spot that one dashing around in a second.'

I stared at the leaves and eventually I saw what he was talking about – a bird that was watching us from the bush. 'Oh, yes,' I said. 'But you said it was a blackbird. It's not black at all.'

'It's a female, so it's brown and it's a pain in the arse. It eats all the best berries in the morning before I can get out here.'

'You're just greedy,' I said. 'That poor bird can't get food anywhere else except off the bushes.' I popped a large ripe berry into my mouth. 'They're better in tarts,' I said, 'but I quite like them when they're sweet like this.' I found another and studied it carefully. 'You have to check for maggots, though.'

Emmet shrugged. 'The maggots are a bonus for the blackbird, so. Leave that bush alone, now. Did you write your story for the competition – the one about Buddy and me?'

'Mmm.' I felt myself going red. I'd forgotten about that story already. In my head, I'd written a new one with Iseult as the main character, the shining star, my brilliant best friend. Like Karen, but even better. 'I started it but I don't think I'm any good at writing about horses.' I shoved four blackberries into my mouth and sat down.

Emmet fired a gob of spit at a dandelion head. 'Horses are the easiest thing in the world to write about. What have you written so far?'

I took the pages from my pocket. I was ashamed of them now, even though I'd been delighted with my efforts the night before. Iseult was a far more wonderful topic. I could write a masterpiece about her. I handed over the story.

He turned the papers round and around. 'You'll have to read it to me,' he said. 'Your writing's wojus, so it is.'

I snatched the papers back and stuffed them into my pocket. I didn't know what Emmet meant but I could tell it was nothing good. I was used to being criticised, especially for my handwriting, but it still hurt. 'I'm not reading it if you're going to be horrible.'

'Ah Jaysus, don't be like that,' he said. 'I was only teasing. Your writing's not that bad. Give it here.'

'No,' I said. 'You probably can't read, anyhow. That's why you're not allowed proper books.' I could be horrible too.

'Oh, can I not?' He grabbed the papers back. '"My Best Friend,"' he read. '"My best friend is Emmet."' I squirmed at those words. Iseult was my best friend now, even if she hadn't let me sit with her at dinner. 'See,' Emmet said, 'I can read fine. I just wanted to hear *you* reading, that's all. Go on, read it quick, the bell's going to go soon.' He shaded his eyes and looked up at the sky. 'I can tell the time by the sun.'

'Can you? Can you teach me?' Will would be so jealous.

'Sure I can, but another time. I want to hear the story now.'

He sounded so keen that I took the papers from him, smoothed them flat against my leg and began. '"My best friend is Emmet who has a chestnut-coloured horse—"'

'"Chestnut". I like that.'

I smiled. 'There's a chestnut pony in my compendium.' I carried on, '"Chestnut-coloured horse named Buddy. One beautifully sunny day they went for a speedy gallop across the windswept meadows..."'

I liked the story again now that I was reading it aloud. I especially liked the bit where Buddy came back to rescue Emmet and his broken arm. I could tell by his smiles and nods that Emmet was enjoying it too. By the time I came to the end, I was a little sorry I wouldn't be entering it into the competition after all.

'That's brilliant,' he said. 'Sure, it should be in a book.'

I thought my chest would explode with pride. No one had ever listened to me read one of my stories so eagerly. Karen was particularly bad at listening. She usually got confused in the middle and I had to stop and explain what was going on. But Emmet, he'd followed every word carefully and he'd understood it all.

'I bet you'll win first prize with that,' he said, and he gave me a huge smile. 'I'm proud of you Claire, my best friend.'

Chapter 11

It seemed every day while we were at school, our grandmother struggled with Louis.

'Take him out to the field,' Granny said that afternoon when we got home. 'He's had enough of being inside. You too, Patrick.'

Will scowled. 'I've got homework,' he told her, but when he saw the look Granny gave him, he sighed. 'I can do it later.'

'Good man,' Granny said, untying Louis's leash. 'Keep eyes in the backs of your head, mind, or he'll escape in a flash.' But Louis didn't make a bid for freedom, he was very well behaved. It made me smile to see him running around on the grass. He'd got used to living under the table and now he seemed to love the feeling of sunshine on his face.

'Is he singing "*Gee ceffyl bach*"?' I asked Will.

We listened hard. 'It's a sort of version of it,' Will said. 'It must be ages ago that he heard it.'

I could tell now that Louis was pretending to gallop around the field just like the little horse in the Welsh song. It was a game I used to play with him on the lawn back at home sometimes. I chased him, joining in with the song and reminding him of the words. He laughed and cantered away.

Soon he was out of breath and he flopped down in a heap next to Will who was being very quiet, as usual. I sat down next to them both.

'What's wrong with you, Mr Moody?' I gave Will a dig in the ribs I instantly regretted. I'd get one back much harder.

But he kept his hands to himself. 'I want to go home,' he said. 'I hate my new school. Everyone calls me William of Orange.'

'That's a weird nickname.' I tickled Louis and he giggled, rolling round and round on my lap. 'Why do they call you that?'

'Why do you think?' He pointed to his hair. 'William was a king and everyone here hates him. He did a whole load of horrible things to Irish people.'

'I thought you were supposed to be Patrick at school.'

'I am.' He sighed. 'Someone overheard Aiden calling me Will.'

'At least you've got Aiden. In class today, Iseult said she'd be my friend.' I smiled as I remembered. Then I thought about Emmet. He'd called me his best friend, and in my story, I'd called him mine, but I knew I couldn't tell Will about him. At home, my brother had a habit of carrying tales about me to Mother, and I wouldn't put it past him to run to Granny with news about my secret friend. I knew she wouldn't like me mixing with boys. 'Some of the other girls are nasty. I get called names too.'

'Do they take your sandwiches and throw them all over the field?' Will asked, suddenly loud. 'Do they hit you behind your knees with a hurling stick? Do they shove your head down a poo-filled toilet?'

I looked at Will with horror. 'They don't do that at your school, do they?'

'Yes, and worse things, too,' he said. 'The Brothers don't do a thing about it. They're as bad as the boys.'

'You have to tell Granny. Tell Jack. They can't make you stay there.'

'What's the point?' Will said angrily. 'There isn't another school I could go to for miles and miles, at least not a proper school that isn't for orphans. And we won't be going home any time soon. Mother can't look after us if she's in London, and Dad can't work as well as take care of us. That's why we're here in the first place.'

'It's not fair,' I said. 'I hate Mother.'

'You can't hate Mother,' Will said. 'It's not her fault. It's Dad's.'

'How is it?' I was shocked that Will could side with our mother.

'You wouldn't understand. You're too young.'

'I'm only two years younger than you.' It was my turn to be angry. I hated it when Will brought up the matter of age.

'No, you're nearly three years younger than me,' he said. 'And it's grown-up things. Things they don't tell us.'

'How do you know, then?'

'I listen at doors.'

I decided to give him a taste of his own medicine. 'You're not supposed to do that,' I said. 'I'm telling.'

Will surprised me by laughing. 'Who are you going to tell? Granny? She wouldn't care.'

I bit my lip. I'd heard Granny telling Michael that Dad was no saint, so maybe Will was right, after all. It hurt me to admit it. 'What did he do?'

'What he usually does,' Will said. 'Except this time, it was with Yvonne.'

'Mother's friend?' I liked Yvonne. Granny Costa Del had called her 'very glamorous' at Mother's birthday party the year before. Granny came over especially because it was Mother's thirtieth, but Grandpa Costa Del couldn't come, on account of work, which Mother said was telling people where best to save their money – although Jack told us he didn't come because he'd be picked up straight away at the airport. I didn't understand why that was a problem. Granny Costa Del had been picked up when *she* arrived at the airport, and she'd ordered the taxi herself. 'What did Dad do with Yvonne?'

'What do you think?' I shrugged. I couldn't imagine. Will got to his feet. 'We'd better get back.'

I tried to pull Louis up, then realised he was fast asleep. 'I'll carry him,' Will offered to my surprise.

We made our way back to the cottage, slowly. Louis wasn't as light as he used to be and Will was puffing by the time we reached the barn. He leant against the wall for a breather.

'So, are you moody just because you don't like school?' I said. 'Or don't you like living at Granny's?'

'I don't mind it too much,' he said. 'But I know things about her you don't.'

'What? What do you know?' He shrugged so I dug him in the ribs again. It was a bit unfair as he was holding Louis and he already had a stitch from carrying him, but it was so annoying to have an older brother who wouldn't share what he knew. 'Tell me!'

'Okay, okay,' he said. 'There's a Brother at my school who knows her.'

'And what did he say?'

'That she's unreliable.'

'What does that mean?'

Will shifted Louis onto his other hip. 'That we can't depend on her.'

'That's not true,' I said. 'I think we *can* depend on her. She's not like Mother, after all. Mother's someone you can't rely on but Granny seems very—'

'Dependable,' Will said. 'I think so too. But a long time ago, according to Brother Dominic...' He looked at me. 'You're not going to tell her any of this, are you?'

'Who?' I asked. 'Granny? Of course not. Scout's honour.' Not that I'd ever actually been a Scout, and I'd only lasted two months as a Brownie. I'd been thrown out for snorting with laughter every time I had to call Mrs Davies from the newsagent's 'Brown Owl'.

'Okay, then. Brother Dominic said she was an alcoholic. He said, "Once an alcoholic, always an alcoholic".'

I had a hazy idea about what an alcoholic was. Mother used to say Dad would turn into one if he spent too much time with Jack down the pub. 'Is that really bad?'

'Well, if she *was* an alcoholic, she wouldn't be a good person to be looking after us, but I haven't seen her drunk since we've been here,' Will said. 'And alcoholics are usually drunk all the time.'

'So he's wrong then.' I turned my face hopefully towards Will and he nodded.

'I think so,' he said. 'But maybe she used to drink, a long time ago, when Dad and Jack were children. He told me stuff about them, too. Horrible stuff.'

I swallowed hard. I desperately wanted my brother to share what he knew, although part of me was frightened. Did I really want to know horrible stuff about Dad and Jack? But Will had already begun to speak so I didn't stop him. He had decided to tell me the secrets he knew, and I might never get a chance to hear them again.

'Brother Dominic used to be a teacher at the industrial school. That's how he knew them, and Granny too. Dad and Jack went there.'

I'd an idea that Emmet had mentioned something to me about an industrial school, but I couldn't remember what. Will hadn't spoken for a long time so I decided to risk a question. 'The industrial school. What's that?'

'It's where they put boys who've been bad. That's what Brother Dominic told me. He said Dad and Jack were bad boys.'

That didn't surprise me one bit. Mother always said they could start a riot on a Sunday School picnic. If that's all there was to the secret Will had been told, then I wasn't worried in the least. 'I bet they got into trouble all the time,' I said. 'I bet they were really naughty.'

Will took a breath and held it a good while. Then he slowly let it go. 'Look, I can't go into details,' he said, 'so don't ask me any more questions.' And normally I would have made fun of him for trying to sound so grown up, but his voice was very quiet and it scared me. 'Brother Dominic told me what they did, and it was really, *really* bad.'

* * *

That night I sat in front of the fire while Granny combed the tangles from my hair. I was deep in thought about what Will had said. Was it possible that Dad and Jack had been so naughty they'd had to go to a school for bad boys? Although I didn't really believe it, I couldn't help wondering what they might have done. Had they stolen something? Maybe they'd been in a fight? Boys were always ganging up against each other back on our old street, and I could imagine Jack swinging a punch right enough. But Dad? He always told us hitting was wrong, and I'd lost count of the times he'd dashed in front of Mother's wooden spatula to spare my leg a smack. It was true he had bad moods sometimes and he did scowl a lot. And on Saturday nights he got drunk and made a lot of noise, but he wouldn't hurt anyone, would he? Even though Will had warned me not to, I'd pestered him all the way back to the cottage, but he wouldn't say more about what he'd heard. He'd become very quiet again at tea time.

'Patrick's in a world of his own lately,' Granny said, as if reading my thoughts. That terrified me. Had she been able to read the ones about Dad and Jack too? I shuddered. 'Someone walk over your grave?' she asked. She gave the fire a fierce poke and the turf sparked. 'Here, wrap this round your shoulders.'

I took the old sheep's fleece she was offering, the one she kept on the back of the chair by the fire. She swore it kept the draught from bothering the rheumatism in her neck.

'He doesn't like his school,' I said quietly, even though I was quite certain Will would have been furious I'd told her. I was worried about him. I'd have laughed at the thought of his head stuck down a poo-filled toilet at home, but it didn't seem a laughing matter here.

'No one likes school,' Granny said.

'I liked my school back in Wales,' I told her, although I wasn't certain that was the truth. 'I like my school here a bit too.' It was only as I said the words that I realised they were true, despite what I'd told Will earlier – Iseult wanted to be my friend and I loved meeting Emmet at dinner time. I couldn't tell Granny about him, though. 'If I get stuck,' I said, keeping to safe ground, 'the House girls help me.'

'House girls?' Granny said. 'You're friends with the House girls?'

'Sort of,' I said. I'd never have admitted to anyone at school that they were my friends – I'd been there long enough to know everyone else stayed away from them – but the House girls were certainly useful to sit near.

'Well, fair play to you.' Granny carried on working at the knots in my hair. 'There are all sorts in this world.'

'Where did Dad and Jack go to school? Uncle Jack, I mean.'

'Sure, you know where they went – to the boys' school,' she said. 'St Matthew's, next door to yours in Roundmore.'

Like Emmet then, I thought but I didn't say it. We were told often enough at school that boys and girls mustn't mix. 'And where did they go afterwards, after they got their Primary Certs?' I had never heard of Primary Certs before I started at St Brids but now the words were stamped on my brain. They were what we were working towards, like the 11-plus at home. I'd been fed up of hearing about that, too.

Granny stopped mid yank. 'Now, why would you be asking me that?'

'Did they go to the same school as Will? I mean, Patrick.'

'Not Patrick's school,' she said. 'Somewhere else.'

'Why?' I asked. The question slipped out before I had time to think about it.

'Why? Why not? Not all boys go to the same school.' And with that she tugged my hair one last time and sent me off to bed.

Chapter 12

The next day before class began, Iseult was keen to hear what I'd written about her.

'I didn't have time to write anything,' I said. 'My granny was cross with my little brother again so I had to look after him.' That was true but there was another reason why I hadn't started my story about Iseult – guilt had stopped my hand and my imagination too. I had a perfectly good story already written about Emmet and Buddy, one I knew stood a great chance of winning the head nun's competition. All I needed to do was write it up in ink, as tidily as I could, and hand it in. But how could I turn down the chance of being Iseult's friend? She'd offered me that beautiful prize, one I dreamt of, one I had wonderful imaginings about, and I would be a fool not to bite her hand off before she changed her mind. The only problem was Emmet. I hadn't been able to write a word about Iseult when I'd picked up my pencil with a clean sheet of paper spread before me. Emmet's wide smile had stopped me in my tracks.

'Well, you'd better make a start,' Iseult said, 'you've only got 'til Monday. I've finished mine.' She held out pages of beautifully formed writing. There were no splodges of ink, I noticed, and no crossings out. If I managed something half as beautiful, it would be a miracle. I'd heard a lot about miracles since I'd started at St Brid's, but I doubted one would ever waste its magic on me. 'And it's my birthday next month,' she added.

'Your birthday? What date is it?' Maybe she wanted me to mention it in my composition.

'Fourth of October. I'm inviting a friend for birthday cake, and it might be you.'

'Oh.' A tiny spark of hope flickered in my chest.

'I'm running a competition of my own, between Siobhán, Dolores and you. Whoever writes the best story about me will be my friend forever, and they'll come to my house for birthday cake.'

'I'm going to write your story tonight,' I promised. I knew, without a doubt, if I put my mind to it, I could do a better job than either Dolores or Siobhán, any day of the week. The best friend title was mine, and so was that slice of cake.

'Good.' She nodded. 'I've won Head Nun's story writing competition for the last three years. You can put that in your composition. Now, what else can you write?' She bit the corner of her lovely lip. 'I'm Roundmore's junior champion for dancing and my sister was nearly Rose of Tralee last year. She'll win next time. If you want to know anything else, just ask my friends.' And with a flounce of her curls, off she skipped, beating a loud rhythm with her feet, and her arms tucked tightly at her sides.

* * *

It was raining at dinner time and we were herded into the shelter in the yard. An angry nun from one of the younger children's classes guarded us fiercely. I stayed in a corner near the little children, hoping no one would notice me so I could daydream until we went back into class. Iseult was standing in the middle with her gang of friends, whispering from time to time with Dolores and Siobhán. Each time she cupped her hand to their ears, she glanced towards me and my face burned with frustration. I'd show her I was better than those girls. I'd outshine them with my composition and I'd be Iseult's best friend forever – well, at least until Mother came back from London and I went home to Cardiff. I didn't like being on my own like this, avoiding Iseult until I'd proved myself in her competition, and staying away from the House girls. I knew I wouldn't stand a chance of ever being Iseult's friend if I accepted *their* offer of friendship, brilliant story or not. Everyone in class avoided them.

I was miserable on my own but I was glad of the rain. It gave me an excuse not to see Emmet. I didn't think I could bear to hear him ask about the competition. Maybe he'd want to hear my story again. How could I read it to him, now I'd decided I wouldn't be entering it into the competition after all? Sister John was forever talking about how we should all feel guilty for something or other, and if I had to read that story to Emmet, I would definitely feel very, very guilty. So I crouched in the corner with the tiny children, and I tried to disappear.

By the time classes started again, though, the sun had come out and the classroom was sweltering-hot. The lessons dragged on and I stared longingly out of the window every time Sister's back was turned. The thought of being with Emmet, turning handstands on the grass and rolling on the cool ground, seemed like the best thing in the world – guilt or not.

I couldn't wait to file out of class at the sound of the bell. The sun was losing its warmth as I walked along the little lane that led to the bus stop but it still felt good to be outside. I hung back as Iseult and her friends pushed their way to the head of the lane. They lived in town and could walk home from school every single day. How I envied them. They'd be drinking milk and eating jam sandwiches while I was still stuck on the bus as it chugged its way along each and every narrow lane. It wouldn't arrive at the bus stop for a little while yet. It always collected the older children first, which seemed incredibly unfair because surely, they had bigger legs for standing on and they had a shelter too, so Will said, where they could wait in the rain. All we had – the tiny twins from the next village, the snotty boy who seemed to be crying all the time, and me – was a rock to stand next to. It was a low one at that, so it wasn't even fun to play on.

When I got to the boring rock, the twins were there already, holding hands, as they always did. They turned their matching faces to me and I nodded. This had become our routine. There was no sign of the boy. I had no routine with him, except for totally ignoring his existence.

'Oh no,' I said suddenly, and the twins looked at me and raised their identical eyebrows. I had not actually spoken to them before, not ever. I hadn't meant to now, but in for a penny. 'My cardigan,' I told them. 'I've left it on the back of my chair. And it's Friday.'

They blinked their understanding. I could just imagine what Granny would say if I came home without it. She'd complain all weekend that we hadn't had the chance to wash it for Monday. 'Being poor is no excuse for being dirty' she always liked to say. I hadn't known we were poor until she'd said that.

'I'd better go and get it. Tell the bus driver I won't be long.'

I ran up the lane as fast as I could and through the school door. Thankfully there weren't any nuns about. I dashed into our classroom and skidded on a wet patch of floor.

One of the House girls grabbed my arm to save me from falling.

'Watch yourself, Claire,' the other one said. She was kneeling on the floor.

I looked at them in amazement. 'What on earth are you doing?' The girls had a big metal bucket full of soapy water standing between them, and a rag each in their hands.

The girl with dark hair put her head on one side with a look that said, surely, what they were doing was obvious. 'Cleaning,' she told me, and wrung out her rag in the bucket.

'I can see that.' Then I had a terrible realisation. 'Do we all have to take a turn?' It was bad enough having to help clean at home. I didn't want to do it at school too.

They laughed.

'No, of course not,' the redhead said, kneeling down too.

I shrugged. 'Why are you doing it, then?'

The girls looked up at me and smiled patiently, their lips tightly closed. 'Because we're House girls, of course.'

I stared incredulously at them. 'Just because you're called "House" you have to do the housework?' Although as I said the words, there did seem to be some sense to that arrangement.

They glanced at each other before the dark-haired one said, 'No, it's because we're *from* the—'

'Claire O'Connell, what are you doing still here?' Sister John's wide body blocked the doorway.

'I forgot my cardi, Sister.' I ran to snatch it from my desk, suddenly remembering the bus.

As I turned back towards the nun, she waved a finger in my face. 'You're to be at Mass on Sunday, do you hear? And if your grandmother's vehicle isn't fixed, a neighbour is to bring you.'

I couldn't imagine Michael being persuaded to give me a lift to church, so I avoided her eyes as I mumbled, 'Yes, Sister.' I'd need a brilliant excuse on Monday morning.

'Right, well, off with you now. Haven't you a home to go to? And you two girls, get a move on. The school won't clean itself, will it? And make a proper job of polishing the floor in Head Nun's office this time.' I heard her still scolding the girls as I dashed away. 'You know she won't be accepting your shoddy work. It'll be the Good Shepherds for you, if you don't pull your socks up soon.'

'Yes, Sister,' I heard the girls say over the slop of water in their bucket.

I sprinted out of the school gates and off along the lane, hoping the twins had managed to hold the bus for me and feeling very glad that my surname wasn't 'House'.

* * *

There was great excitement when we got home from school – Jack had sent a letter.

'Your mother's better,' Granny said, and Will and I looked at each other in shocked joy. At last, the news we'd been waiting for. We could escape this place. We were free, and I wouldn't have to choose between Emmet and Iseult's story. We jumped up and down with happiness. 'Stop that,' Granny said, 'you haven't heard the half of it yet. Jack won't be coming for you.' She gave a heartfelt sigh.

'Your mother's gone to her parents in Spain. She's left Conor right in it, so.'

Disappointment hit us like a thump to the belly. Will threw his satchel across the table, just missing the butter dish but sending the bread knife skittering to the floor. Thankfully, it didn't slice through Louis. Granny snatched it up before his chubby hands could grab it, and Will stormed off to our bedroom. I slumped into the nearest chair and gave a whimper.

'It's disappointing for me too, Claire. I'm too old for all this. Look at your brother there. He's missing his mother. It's not me he's wanting. It's no life tied to a table leg all day.'

I couldn't argue with that. Poor Louis. Poor me. I even felt sorry for Will. He wouldn't be getting out of his Irish exam, after all. If Mother had gone to Spain, we might never get home to Wales. We might be here forever. How could she? 'Dad can get another wife,' I said, 'if Mother wants to live in Spain. His other wife can look after us.'

Granny laughed bitterly. 'Sure, aren't you the loyal one? No sooner is your mother out of the way than you're looking to replace her.' She started to scowl at me but then her eyes softened. 'Maybe that's no more than she deserves, is it now?' She reached out and stroked my cheek with a rough thumb. She was wiping away the tears from my face but I'd hardly known I was crying. She sighed. 'Maybe that's no more than any mother deserves who's abandoned her children.'

She rubbed her own cheeks and I realised she'd been crying too. Then she smiled at me sadly, before throwing Jack's letter onto the fire. She grabbed her tobacco tin from the mantelpiece. 'Going to feed the chickens,' she said, shaking her box of matches at me. 'Don't let Louis lick the turf.'

* * *

I had to put my disappointment at Jack's news to one side that evening – I was running out of time to write my story, and if I was

117

going to be stuck in Connemara for a few weeks more, I needed to win Iseult's competition. I had no time to waste. I had to write in pencil first, with all the crossings out I'd be bound to make, and then I'd have to carefully write up the story using Will's pen. I'd sneaked it out of his pencil case along with some ink the night before while he was in the privy. He always took ages in the toilet, even though he hated spiders, and I'd had plenty of time to find the pen and ink and hide the loot under my mattress.

The September evenings were chilly now, but the fire kept Granny's kitchen cosy. As I slipped off my cardigan, I felt the pages I'd written about Emmet and Buddy crinkling in my pocket. I took them out and reread them. It was quite a good story, I thought, but now I was reading it again I saw that maybe it was a little childish. Back home, Tracey Hopkins was always calling me childish. I hated her and I hated the names she called me even more, but maybe she had a point. Perhaps I ought to grow up a bit. The story Iseult had told the class about Carlotta had been very grown-up. Mother would have called it 'sophisticated'. Maybe I could write about Iseult like that. Maybe I, too, could write a sophisticated story. I tucked the one about Emmet and Buddy back into my pocket and took up my pencil.

Chapter 13

I was just putting a final full stop to my composition when there was a sudden clatter, and Michael stood in the doorway. He'd flung the door open so hard that all the cups in the press behind it rattled. In his good hand, he was clutching the sack he usually wore over his head, and the rain was running off it onto his trousers. Louis gasped and pointed to the puddle that was forming on the flagstones while Granny launched herself at Michael, flapping a towel.

'You're soaking yourself there,' she said, trying to dab at his legs.

Michael waved her away with the sack, making it rain inside the kitchen. 'I've had a letter, Bernie.' The words were tumbling over his wobbly lips. 'From Rónán in Dublin.' He dropped his sack onto the floor and fumbled in his pocket. 'Look!'

He held out a crumpled envelope. Granny took it and turned it over in her hands. 'What does he say?'

'Read it,' Michael said.

I watched as Granny slid the letter out of the envelope. I wasn't really interested in a letter from Michael's son, but nothing much happened out at the lake and Granny seemed to be quite excited, so I sat up and took note.

The back of the paper was blank, which meant Rónán couldn't have had much to say, even though I knew he hadn't spoken to his father for years. Annoyingly, Granny read the letter to herself, taking an age, her mouth working away at the words. I quite fancied myself as a lip-reader – I thought it a very handy skill to learn – but try as I might, I couldn't make out the words on Granny's thin lips.

'Sure,' she said eventually, folding the letter back into the tidy creases Rónán had made for it at his desk in Dublin, 'there's a turnaround, right enough.'

'What does he say?' I asked, my interest suddenly stirred by my lack of lip-reading skills.

'He says next Saturday,' Michael told me excitedly, 'all three of them,' as if his words made perfect sense.

'Now.' Granny was giving him the look that was her way of smiling. 'I knew a phone call would put it right.' She handed back the letter and patted his arm. 'That's wonderful news, Michael. Wonderful. Will you stop for some bread and cheese?'

'No, you're grand, Bernie.'

'A cup of tea?'

'No, but thank you.'

'Half a cup in your hand?'

'No, no. I've the sheep to be seeing to. I came because of the letter, you know.'

Granny patted his arm again. 'I'm glad you did, so,' she said quietly, and I realised it was the first time I'd seen Michael since the day Granny had slapped him.

He dipped his head. 'Thank you, Bernie. Thank you.' He stuffed the letter back into his pocket, picked up the sack and draped it over his head. 'Terrible weather,' he said, waving a thumb over his shoulder at the rain.

But despite the steady drizzle he was about to head into, he was smiling. One eye drooped and so did a corner of his mouth, but the rest of his face most definitely glowed.

* * *

I was coming out of the privy the next morning with the brush hoisted against my shoulder like a guardsman's rifle, when Granny called, 'Ah, that's where the broom is. Quick, Claire, bring it! We've a job to do.'

She was marching across the yard in the direction of the lane, pulling Louis behind her on his leash. In her other hand, Granny held the metal bucket and mop. The mop head was dry and since, for once, it wasn't raining I'd been planning to take it to the field for a gallop.

I ran to catch up with Granny. 'Where are we going, Grandma?'

'To Michael's,' she called over her shoulder, keeping up the same pace. She was on a mission, I could tell. I ran after her and grabbed Louis's arm. He was tottering along, stumbling on the stone path.

'We're going to Michael's cottage?' I could hardly believe it. Will and I had been up the lane as far as the walls around Michael's fields but we'd never been inside his home. His yard was a real mess and we enjoyed imagining how bad things were inside his cottage. Will liked to say there were rats in the kitchen and dead sheep in the cupboards. I suggested that he kept pigs in his bedroom – I'd heard Granny say his place was a pigsty, so that made sense to me. Will had sneered. 'He's a sheep farmer,' he'd said. 'He doesn't keep pigs anywhere.' Well, I was about to find out, once and for all, what Michael *did* keep in his cottage, and while Will was at Aiden's, at that.

'He's a man, of course. He hasn't a clue what visitors will be wanting,' Granny said. She was getting out of breath with all the marching. 'But we've got today and tomorrow, and if we start now, that should be enough. We don't want them turning back as soon as they set foot in the place.'

Michael was bent over, digging in the field beside his cottage. As we rounded the corner, he straightened up and stretched his back, then mopped his face with a handkerchief. Even from a long way away, I could see it was extremely grubby.

When he noticed Granny, Louis and me, he waved his hanky and looked surprised. 'Hello?'

Granny finally halted her march and dumped down her bucket and mop. She tied Louis's leash to the washing-line post and he plonked himself onto the grass with a sigh. Rushing up the lane had taken it out of him.

'We've come to give you a hand.' Granny raised her palm. 'And don't say you don't want our help, I won't be hearing it. We've two days. We can make all your rooms fit for guests in that time.' If Michael had been about to argue, he didn't get the chance, because Granny turned her back on him and picked up the mop. 'Bring the pail, will you, Claire?' she said, opening the door and striding inside.

I was about to follow her into the cottage when I saw the state of the kitchen, and my feet stopped dead on the step.

'Now,' Granny muttered, 'we'll get some fresh air in here.' She made her way carefully to the window.

Even with the door open, it seemed very dark in the kitchen. There was rubbish and dirty dishes everywhere. Cardboard packets and cans of food lay emptied and discarded on the table – and on the draining board, the chair seats and in the sink. There were half-full sacks of animal feed leaning against the walls, spilling their insides across the floor, and empty sacks slung everywhere like weird, greasy rugs.

But far worse than the way it looked, was the way the kitchen smelt – of mouldy cabbage and rotting meat. The smell was just like how the bin of our neighbour – Mr Harries, back in Cardiff – smelt. I used to hate passing his gate on bin day. The dustbin's lid was broken and he hadn't got round to asking the council for a new one. Mother said it would attract rats, and a drop of Jeyes Fluid wouldn't go amiss. I could well believe that rats lived in Michael's kitchen. I was backing out, horrified – and covering my nose with a hand that I'd just remembered hadn't been washed after using the toilet, but still smelt a thousand times fresher than Michael's house – when Michael came up behind me and tapped my shoulder.

'Sorry,' he said. 'I'm not the neatest.'

Granny's head appeared next to us as she finally managed to wrestle open the window. She waved a hand at me. 'Get in here, girl. You've no time to be standing around out there.'

I took a huge gulp of clean air and headed into the kitchen. I was still holding the brush, which was just as well, as I was convinced I was going to need it to tackle an army of spiders. Will and I had failed to mention *them* while we'd been imagining Michael's revolting mess.

'Will you be wanting your bunk beds back?' Granny asked him, as if the terrible state of the room was no shock at all to her. He'd followed me into the kitchen and Granny had pulled her head back from the window. 'You know, for Rónán's boy?'

'Oh no,' Michael said. 'I've a single for him. I only got the bunks when Shirley was expecting the second.' He shook his head. 'Poor girl. Shirley and Mairead would have had plenty to talk about, wouldn't they?'

'They would,' Granny said. 'Mairead would have been a comfort to Shirley, right enough.'

'She would, she would.' Michael said. 'You know, Bernie, I've been wondering, do you think it's the kind of thing that runs in families?'

'What, the poor babies?' Granny said. 'Maybe.'

'Would it run on the male side?'

She shrugged. 'Who knows?'

Michael sighed. 'I'd better go back outside. I'll leave you women to it. I don't want to be getting under your feet,' and he headed off again, leaving two muddy footprints behind him on the kitchen step, along with the thousands of others he'd been collecting there over the years.

* * *

It turned out that Michael had been digging a pit when we'd arrived that morning. He'd already dug one, he told us proudly, filled it with rubbish and covered it over. He'd had the same idea about tidying the cottage as Granny.

I couldn't help myself. 'You mean there was even more rubbish than this?' I swept my arm dramatically around the room.

Michael shrugged. 'It builds up,' he said.

'Sure, it does if you drop it where you stand and leave it there,' Granny said, her hands firmly on her hips, but she didn't say anymore after that, and I could see Michael was relieved. 'Right,

Claire,' she said, taking some thick woollen socks from the pocket in her apron, 'put these on your hands. We don't want you cutting yourself on the metal. Get the tins rounded up into those empty sacks, and don't be minding the maggots now.'

That was easy for her to say. I'd never seen so many of the horrible creatures. They squirmed in the corners of corned beef tins and swam in the orange gloop left at the bottom of cans of baked beans. Michael had clearly been living on canned meat sandwiches, cabbage and beans on toast for months. My stomach suddenly lurched and I dashed outside.

'Don't retch on the steps,' Granny warned, as my breakfast splattered onto the grass. Then she added, 'Stay out there with your brother if you're not up to the job.'

She was challenging me, I knew, and I wouldn't be beaten. With my stomach thoroughly emptied, I strode back inside, fighting down the heaving that threatened to turn me into a coward. I pulled the socks over my hands and reached out for a can. The maggots reared their hideous black heads at me and I almost vomited again. But I was determined they would not beat me, although I *was* extremely glad of the woolly layer between them and my fingers. I placed the can in the sack, taking care not to tip the revolting contents onto my feet and, swallowing hard, I turned to pick up the next one. I'd show Granny I was up to the job, even if I gagged my way through the morning.

At last, all the tins had been dropped into sacks, along with the rest of the rubbish, and Michael took them outside to bury in the ditch. I rounded up the final few plates and stacked them on the table ready to wash.

'I could do with a good strong cup of tea,' Granny said, resting herself in one of the newly cleared chairs. I shuddered at the thought of drinking anything in Michael's kitchen. Even without the rubbish, it was still filthy. I was glad when Granny said, 'We'll take Louis home and put the kettle on, then we'll come back after our dinner.'

I was strangely happy as we walked up the boreen after our fried eggs and soda bread, and glad to have something solid in my stomach again. I'd remembered to bring Louis's wooden block so he'd have a toy to play with in the grass. He'd enjoyed being tied up outside, to start off with – I supposed it made a change from being under the table – but when it began to drizzle, he'd got fed up and started shouting 'Ganneee'. When he'd yelled 'Claaa', I felt like the worst sister in Ireland, but Michael's mucky cottage was no place for Louis, and Granny and I still had stacks of cleaning to do. I was hoping the block would keep him happy for the afternoon, even if it did rain a bit. He could drive it up and down the rocks that stuck out of the grass. Now the maggots were banished, I was looking forward to washing up at Michael's sink, and stacking the dishes back into his presses exactly where they belonged. I surprised myself at how eager I was to get the task done. I normally hated helping with housework, but Michael had created a terrible mess and I could do something to help. I liked order, I realised with a smile. I liked putting things right, making things better. It was a simple pleasure, a satisfying job, and one I reckoned I could be brilliant at.

But I was put off as soon as I stood at the sink with Granny's dishcloth in my hand. The window in front of me had a curtain of curly papers, and each paper was black with dead and dying flies. Granny must have stuck her head right through them when she'd called to Michael and me out of the window that morning. That was typical – nothing got in *her* way. I wondered why I hadn't noticed them earlier, and then I remembered the maggots. They had demanded all my attention.

'Grandma,' I said. 'Can we take these down?'

She stopped rubbing the table top and looked up. The smell of her beeswax polish reminded me of school and of something else I couldn't place. 'Ah, the fly papers,' she said. 'Didn't I mean to clear them this morning. Disgusting things.' She snatched at a handful of the papers, crunching the flies in her palm, and yanked the strips from above the window, sending drawing pins firing angrily around the room.

Suddenly I remembered where I'd seen papers like that before. They'd been hanging from the window in the room where Jack lived. There'd only been half a dozen flies stuck to his papers, but that was no doubt because Michael's had trapped every other fly in the world.

'Do you think Jack is happy living with the preacher man?' I asked Granny. I hadn't meant to say the question out loud, the thought had just floated into my head then out of my mouth.

'He's living with a preacher?' Granny said. She shoved the fly papers into the sack we were using for the last bits of rubbish then stood back and squinted at me.

I remembered the preacher from our Sunday School. He was old and doddery. 'Not a real preacher. Jack just called him that, I think.' I studied my feet. 'It wasn't a nice room.'

'Was it as bad as this?'

'No,' I said. 'It wasn't as dirty. But it smelt of onions and it was very small. And four men lived there. They had to share the bed.'

Granny sat down hard in one of Michael's wooden chairs. I could see dried tea stains running down the back of it and stains on the other chairs too. Michael wasn't exactly precise when it came to slurping tea from his saucer. We'd have to clean those stains off later.

'I'll have to tell him to stop sending me money,' Granny said, more to herself than to me, then she looked up. 'He's a good boy, your uncle, but he needs to live his own life now. I've been his responsibility for long enough. And your grandparents in Spain are paying me plenty to keep you and your brothers here, so I won't starve, will I?' She stood up and took hold of her cloth again. 'We'll have a drive over to Grogan's when Patrick gets back from Aiden's, and I'll ring Jack to say he's to get himself somewhere better. He doesn't deserve a slum.' She began polishing again. 'And we'll maybe let old Grogan wrap us some chips for our tea.'

'Chips for tea?' It was hard to believe I'd heard her properly – we never had chips for tea.

'Why not? We'll have earned them by then,' she said, polishing for all she was worth and giving me the first warm smile ever. It was a grin mostly made up of gums.

And suddenly I realised what the scent of furniture polish reminded me of – Granny's terrible teeth had jogged my memory. It was the smell of the House girls.

Chapter 14

We cleaned Michael's cottage all day, and once the kitchen was spotless, we moved Louis inside and tied his leash to the table leg. He was glad to get out of the rain and he seemed quite taken with Michael's table and chairs. He drove his wooden block up and down the legs, and he was no bother at all to Granny and me as we worked away on the bedrooms. Michael went into Roundmore for supplies. 'I saw Father O'Reilly when I stopped off at Grogan's,' he told us when he got back with his bag of groceries. Michael had bought rashers, two tins of steak pudding and a box of dried peas. There didn't seem to be any cans of beans or corned beef in his string bag. I imagined Rónán and his wife would be relieved. 'He threatened to call with us.'

Granny stopped polishing Michael's cutlery and lifted her chin sharply. 'And why in all that's holy would he be doing that? Has he ever bothered with us before?' She threw a fork into the drawer so hard the prongs dug into the wood. 'If that priest shows his face, he won't be having a welcome with me.'

By late Sunday afternoon, the cottage sparkled like a new sixpence. I'd found a couple of old ones under Michael's spare bed and he'd told me I could keep them. Before we left for the evening, Granny made him promise to have a bath next Friday, and change his clothes. She'd cut his hair and trimmed his moustache in his kitchen. It was a strange scene, my grandmother waving scissors and telling Michael to move his head this way and that. She might have seemed almost gentle if it hadn't been for her shouting – Michael was just hopeless at following her instructions, and he was quite deaf, too.

Louis had found Granny's hairdressing most entertaining. He picked up the long strands of hair as they fell onto the sheets of newspaper she'd placed on the floor to catch them, then he draped them over his own curls, making a disgustingly greasy wig. I didn't have the energy to stop him, even though the sight of him wearing Michael's hair made my stomach roll. I was exhausted after all the mopping and polishing. I hoped Michael's visitors would appreciate the effort we'd gone to – by the end of that weekend, I'd had enough of cleaning to last me a lifetime.

* * *

My fingers were very inky as I handed in my composition on Monday morning. Before I'd flopped into bed, I'd spent two hours carefully writing up my description of Iseult, in the best handwriting I could manage. I knew my presentation would be nowhere near the standard of the other girls – children in the classes below could write more gracefully than me – and after all the cleaning, my hand had been terribly shaky. But I'd tried my very best not to make many mistakes, and I was reasonably proud of my attempt.

Everyone had entered – even the House girls had added a very small page each to the pile on Sister John's desk – and there was a lot of chatter in the classroom. Iseult's voice soared above everyone else's. 'It's the perfect title for me,' she was telling Siobhán, Dolores and the other girls that had gathered around her. 'Carlotta is the most wonderful and beautiful best friend anyone could have in the whole world. It was just so easy to write about her.'

Sister John arrived in class and we rushed to our seats. 'Well, isn't it grand to see the effort you've put in,' she said, picking up the stories from her desk and flicking through them. 'Three pages from you, Iseult. Wonderfully presented too.' Iseult was beaming – I could tell just by looking at the back of her head. 'I'd expect no less from you, of course. And yours, Siobhán.' Sister John smiled at the girl sitting next to Iseult. 'Two-and-a-half pages, and the script so flowing. Don't you have the most magnificent penmanship?' Then the look on the nun's face changed. 'What are these?' She pulled out two yellowing pages from the middle of the stack. 'Would you look at the state on this paper? And these stories are written in pencil and in the tiniest writing. Sure, I can barely make out a word. Who do they belong to?' She waved them in the air.

'They're ours, Sister,' a voice from behind me said. It was one of the House girls.

There was a ripple of laughter around the classroom. Everyone was turning round and staring towards the back of the class. Not to be outdone, I turned around too.

'But of course they are. What are you doing handing in this rubbish?' Sister John asked. 'You know the rule about pen and ink.'

'We do, Sister,' the House girl who sat directly behind me said, 'but we don't have pens.'

Everyone laughed at that, and the nun joined in too.

'Well, you'll be having your compositions back, then.' She strode to my desk and flung the pages over my head at the House girls. They fluttered to the floor. 'The rules say "pen".'

'But, Sister—' one of the girls began, and Sister John held up her hand.

'Arguing now, is it? Hold your tongue, girl. We can't be making exceptions for the likes of you, can we? If you come to our school, you stick to our rules. And our rules say entries must be in pen, do they not?'

'Yes, Sister.'

'Then, there's no more to say, is there?'

'No, Sister.'

I saw Iseult's eyes flash with something; relief, maybe, and I wondered if the House girls were quietly very good at writing stories. I would never have imagined it – they looked so ragged and downtrodden. But now I thought about it, they usually finished their work well before me, and when I got in a muddle with Sister John's deliberately confusing instructions, they were always able to help me out. Maybe there was more to them than worn-out clothes, bad teeth and the smell of furniture polish.

'I'll be handing these to the head nun,' Sister John said, tapping the slightly shorter stack of compositions, 'and won't she be pleased with you all. She'll read them this week, and we'll have our winner and runner-up next Monday.'

Next Monday? We had to wait a whole week for the results? I sighed. The head nun must be an incredibly slow reader. Sister John went back to her desk and I bent down to pick up the compositions she'd thrown onto the floor. The handwriting on both pages was beautiful, and the small papers were crammed with words. One title said, 'My Best Friend, Caroline' and the other, 'My Best Friend, Paula'. I handed them to the dark-haired girl.

'Sorry,' I whispered, although I wasn't sure what I was apologising for. It might have been for the nun's horrible behaviour. Or because the girls had no pens. Or for the fact that my story now had a better chance of winning.

'Thank you,' the girl whispered back, as she took the papers from me. And even though her eyes were sad, her lips still managed a smile.

* * *

At dinner time, I rushed out to the playground. I was looking forward to seeing Emmet, and I hoped and hoped we would visit Buddy. I'd pushed to the back of my mind the guilty feelings at handing in the story about Iseult. I imagined the head nun might have enjoyed an exciting tale of a boy and his horse, but it wasn't her I had to impress. I needed a best friend in class, and I had to beat Siobhán and Dolores. I was sure Emmet would understand, although I wouldn't explain, in case he didn't – after all, I would hate to lose his friendship. And I was really looking forward to seeing Buddy. As I ran across the yard, I comforted myself with the thought that if I didn't tell him, Emmet would never find out which story I had entered.

I was almost at the toilet block when Iseult ran up behind me.

She grabbed my arm and spun me around to face her. 'Did you write your story about me?' she asked. She'd been running and her flushed cheeks made her even prettier. Her eyes weren't actually blue, I realised staring hard into them, but violet. Violet was one of my favourite colours.

'Yes,' I said, turning a little pink at the attention she was giving me.

'Good,' she said. 'When Sister John gives it back, I want to see it. And then I'll decide who's won my competition.'

'Okay.' I turned even pinker at the thought of her reading my story, but she didn't see. She was already heading off towards Siobhán and Dolores. I nipped through the gap in the hedge.

I'd forgotten to ask Granny for an extra round of sandwiches, like I'd promised Emmet the week before, but I had remembered not to eat my crusts – I'd been feeling quite peckish after morning lessons and it had taken quite an effort to stuff them in my pocket instead of my mouth. But Emmet didn't seem to care about the sandwiches, he just looked thoroughly pleased to see me. I handed over my crusts. 'They're egg,' I said. 'Granny was out of fish paste.'

'No matter. Have you an apple today?'

'Yes,' I said. 'It was a sweet one.' Fergus's grocery van had had new stock in. He'd had a few complaints, he told Granny, about the last batch of apples.

Emmet looked a bit disappointed as I handed over my core. I'd nibbled it right down to the pips, it had been so lovely and juicy. I had thought about putting it in the bin instead of my pocket, but then I'd reminded myself that horses had tough teeth and could eat the hard middle bits. 'Can I give this to him myself today?'

Emmet shook his head. 'I saw him this morning and he was high-spirited. It would be dangerous to go in a field with him like that.'

'Oh.' I hadn't realised Buddy was such an excitable horse.

'But sure, we'll go another day.' He pocketed the core with the crusts and we sat on the grass and stretched out our legs. 'Ah, a fine spot in the sun,' he said, lifting his face to the sky. He tapped the toes of his boots together happily. 'That'll warm us up.'

'No wonder you're cold.' I pointed to his legs sticking out like twigs from his grubby grey shorts. 'You're not wearing any socks.'

'Am I not?' He glanced at his legs. 'I must have forgotten to put them on this morning.'

'Don't your feet feel funny in your boots?' I wriggled my toes. I couldn't imagine wearing shoes without socks. It would feel horrible.

Emmet shook his head. 'They're grand. The boots are a bit big, you know, but they're giving my feet room to grow.'

Now he'd come to mention it, his boots did look huge, and there was a brown elastic band wrapped tightly round one of them. How could anyone forget to put socks on in the morning? I admired the patterns on mine. Granny cooked my socks in a big old saucepan on the fire every Saturday. She said it kept them white.

'Did you hand in our story?' Emmet asked.

I felt the blood rush to my cheeks and I hoped he wouldn't turn to look at me. 'Mmm,' I said. I wasn't actually fibbing because I hadn't said the word 'yes'.

'When will you know the winner?'

'Next Monday.' Still not lying.

'It's sure to be you. It's a brilliant story you've written there.'

'Mmm.' Somehow, even though I wasn't strictly telling a lie, it didn't feel right. I put my hand in my pocket and the story about Emmet and Buddy crinkled between my fingers. I'd rescued the papers just in time before Granny had dunked my cardigan in the sink on Saturday morning. The relief I'd felt at saving the story surprised me. I could sense my cheeks glowing red now, and I turned my face away from Emmet to make certain he wouldn't see. I scanned the hillside, determined to change the subject. 'No walkers out there today.'

'Not a person in sight.' He leant his head back against the wall and closed his eyes. 'How's Beauty these days?'

'He's with Jim, but the sad part's next. It's my favourite bit.'

'Tell me it.'

'Jim gets ill and he gives up driving his cab. He has to sell Beauty.'
I loved the way that chapter made my eyes prickle.

'Is that the end of the book?'

'Almost. I'll finish it tonight. I already know the ending, I've read it so many times.' And then a wonderful idea struck me. 'Emmet,' I said, shaking his shoulder. 'You can borrow it!' How I'd longed to share my favourite book with someone who'd love it as much as I did. Karen had badly disappointed me when she'd borrowed *Black Beauty*. I'd spent ages persuading her to take it home and then, when I'd asked her to tell me the part she liked best, she'd said it was when Beauty won her first show-jumping competition. *Her!* I could have cried. She only had to read to chapter three to know Beauty was a boy. And he'd never, ever been a show jumper. 'I'll bring it for you tomorrow,' I promised Emmet. Suddenly, the guilt I'd been feeling about the story competition was lifted from my shoulders.

He looked at me in surprise. 'You'd bring me your book?'

'Yes,' I said. 'Of course. You can read it to Buddy. He'll enjoy hearing about Beauty and Ginger and all the other horses. I know you wanted to read *Treasure Island*...'

'Never mind that now. Reading *Black Beauty* would be just as good.' His face was absolutely glowing.

'Brilliant,' I said, and I began telling him about all the good and bad characters he'd meet in the book. He listened carefully to every single word and when the bells rang, we almost didn't hear, we were so wrapped up in Beauty's world.

* * *

I'd hoped that, with all the fuss over handing in our compositions on Monday morning, Sister John would have forgotten I hadn't shown up at Mass the day before. But my hopes came to nothing, and I'd trembled behind my desk at the end of the day as the nun scolded me and made me promise never to miss it again.

'Please, Grandma,' I begged when I got back to the cottage that evening, 'can Michael take us to Mass next Sunday?' Will had told me, as we walked up the lane, that he'd been warned about missing it, too, but annoyingly he refused to make any effort to change Granny's mind. It was a battle I had to fight on my own.

'And why would Michael be doing that?' she asked. She was on her hands and knees with her head in the cupboard under the sink so her voice was very muffled.

Louis waved his block of wood at me. His cheeks were streaked with dried tears and his nose was snotty. I picked him up and wiped his face on the bit of rag Granny kept for that purpose. I balanced him on my hip. 'Sister John is being horrible to me. She says if I miss it for the third week in a row, I'm to have the strap.'

'The strap, is it?' Granny's head emerged from the cupboard and she scowled up at me. 'I had the strap many a time in school.' I got the distinct impression there was a mocking tone to her voice. 'And what about you, Patrick? Are you all for Mass, too?'

'No,' he said, and he slunk off to our room.

'Coward,' I muttered after him.

'He's a coward, is he?' She shook her hand at me. In it was a battered box of soap flakes that looked like it had been trapped under the sink for at least a hundred years. 'You think standing up to the Brothers is a coward's way?'

I shrugged. Will had been threatened with the strap, too, and I couldn't understand why he wasn't backing me up. Changing our grandmother's mind wasn't something I could do on my own, and my arguments were running thin. 'It's not fair.' I sighed. 'Everyone else goes.'

Granny hung her head in despair. Clearly, I had disappointed her yet again. She put the packet of soap on the draining board and reached for the kettle. 'We'll make tea.'

'I don't want any,' I said, and I dumped Louis back under the table and stormed out to the yard. If Granny wouldn't ask Michael, I'd have to do it myself.

I found him in the field furthest from his cottage struggling with

135

a sheep, his back to me. When I called his name, my voice came out all raspy – I was out of breath from marching up the lane, and from the anger still bubbling in my chest because of Granny. He lifted his head suddenly, and looked into the lake. I called his name again and he turned very slowly, as if he were terrified of me. One side of his mouth had dropped right open and the eye that wasn't always half-closed was wide with shock. He pressed his good hand to his chest and the sheep saw its chance. It leapt away from between Michael's knees like something demented. 'Mairead?' he stammered. 'Is it you?'

'No, it's me.' I put my hands on my sides and bent over to get my breath back, then I raised my chin. 'Will you give us,' I took a big gasp, 'a lift to Mass,' and another big gasp, 'on Sunday?' He was quite deaf so I had an excuse to yell.

'Claire?' His shoulders slumped as he staggered backwards and sat heavily on the wall.

'Yes. Claire,' I bellowed. He seemed to be in a world of his own. 'Mass. Will you take us next Sunday?' And then I added, '*Please,*' as loudly as I could, because I really needed him to say yes.

'Sunday?' He took a hanky from his pocket and mopped his face. 'I'm sorry, Claire.' He shook his head. 'Rónán's here Sunday.'

Rónán. Of course. After all that cleaning, how could I have forgotten?

'Aaargh!' I roared as Michael sat and watched, and I clenched my fists at the sky. Was there no one to save me from Sister John?

Chapter 15

I finished *Black Beauty* that evening, hoping that the final chapters would distract me from my terrible predicament but even with another five nights before Mass came around again, I couldn't stop worrying about it.

Emmet was waiting for me at dinner time the next day. 'Hello!' he called as I poked my head through the gap. He was bouncing on his toes and grinning.

I'd made a great show of telling Granny that morning, as I'd left to catch the bus, that Sister John had insisted we take a book to school. 'I'm taking *Black Beauty*,' I'd told her. 'That's grand,' she'd said, without as much as a glance, and she dismissed me and my book with a wave of her dishcloth. All morning, while the book was hiding beneath my cardigan, I'd been planning to tease Emmet. I wanted him to think I'd forgotten to bring it. It would be fun, I thought, to make him wait. But when I saw how excited he was, I forgot all about teasing. I reached under my cardigan and produced the book with a flourish.

His eyes opened wide and I was glad I hadn't teased him. 'You remembered!' I placed it in his outstretched hands and he held it gently as he studied the spine. 'Gold letters,' he breathed.

'Open it,' I told him.

I thought he was going to stand there forever, just holding it, but at last he turned to the front page where the nameplate was. I'd given up trying to pull it off ages ago because the glue was too strong, but its corners were ripped where I'd scratched at the paper. 'Ignore that,' I said, waving a hand over the page. 'It was my mother's book. See, her name's there.' I pointed. 'Eleri Jenkins.' I'd tried to cross it out and write my own above hers but the nameplate was too shiny and the ink from Will's pen just slid off.

'This book belonged to *your mother*?'

'Yes, but it's mine now.' He seemed afraid to turn to the next page so I snatched it from him and found the first illustration. It was of Beauty jumping over a ditch with a rider on his back. 'This is like you and Buddy.'

'There are pictures?' His voice was a whisper.

'Only a few.' I flicked through the pages. 'I quite like this one, even though it's rainy.' I showed him Beauty hooked up to his cab.

I put it back in his hands. 'It's...' he began. His face had turned suddenly serious.

'It's what?' I asked, my excitement vanishing. 'What's wrong with it?' I shook his shoulder. 'What's wrong with it, Emmet?'

He rubbed a hand across his eyes. 'Nothing, Claire,' he said. 'It's perfect. It's just...' He looked at me and I saw he was about to cry. He put his head down again. 'I thought you didn't mean it.'

I frowned. 'You thought I wouldn't bring it?' He nodded and a tear dripped off his nose. 'But I said I would, Emmet.' I gave him another shake. 'I said I would.'

'I know.' He sniffed. 'Thank you, Claire.' He pressed the book to his chest.

'Come on,' I told him. I grabbed his sleeve and dragged him towards the wall. I sat on the grass and pulled him down beside me. 'Shall I read the start to you?' He found the first page and handed the book to me. I began reading. '"Chapter One, My Early Home. The first place that I can well remember, was a large, pleasant meadow..."' I could see, in my mind, the field where Beauty lived, and as we sat behind the toilet block, with the sun warming our faces, I imagined that Beauty was Buddy, just over the hill, waiting for us to visit.

'His mother is kind,' Emmet said, when I paused for a breather after a few pages. 'Duchess. That's a fancy name.'

'Duchess is lovely,' I said, 'but she's not in the story much.'

'Is she not?'

'Beauty gets taken away.' I flicked ahead and showed him a page. 'In this chapter.'

'Chapter Four,' Emmet said, before I could impress him with my own knowledge of Roman numerals. 'I'll read up to that one on the way back to the orphanage later.'

'On the bus? I can't read on the bus. It makes me sick.'

Emmet gave a short laugh. 'A bus? Where would I have money for a bus? No, I'll be walking. It's a good few miles across the hill and the bog, so I've plenty of time for reading.'

'Won't you fall over?'

'I'll be careful, so.' He tapped the page. 'Carry on.' I took up the book again and we sat in the sunshine, reading, until the end of dinner time.

And when I handed *Black Beauty* to Emmet, as the bells rang in the yards behind us, there were tears in his eyes again, and I knew he would treasure my book just as much as I did.

* * *

That week was the happiest ever. The sun shone every day, which Granny claimed to be a miracle in Connemara, and each dinner time, Emmet and I read more of *Black Beauty*. With Emmet reading it on his walk to and from school, too, we flew through the chapters.

'It's sad his new owner changed Beauty's name,' Emmet said. We were flopped on the ground and panting, after chasing each other this way and that around the grass. We'd been pretending to be Beauty and Buddy. It was our favourite game. 'Black Auster. What sort of name is that? It's not a patch on his real one.'

'I know,' I said. 'It gets changed again, to Jack this time.'

'Jack? That's a man's name.'

'Exactly. Like my uncle's. It's not right for a horse. Beauty's real name is best.' I picked two fat blades of grass and poked one between Emmet's lips and the other between mine. I longed for a packet of sweet cigarettes to share. 'Granny tried to take the "i" out of my name and that made me really angry.' I puffed on the grass and Emmet did the same.

'I wish I knew my real name,' he said.

'What?' I pushed myself onto my elbows and stared down at him. His eyes were closed as he soaked up the sunshine. 'But Emmet *is* your real name,' I said. 'You're named after your father.'

'I'm named after *someone*'s father.' He let out a long sigh and it rattled the blade of grass between his teeth. 'Emmet is a name I chose for myself,' he said. 'I went to stay with a family once, just for a week in the summer. Lots of people do that ... have in the orphans for a holiday, you know? The father's name was Emmet. I thought it a great name to have, so I robbed it.'

'But you must have had a name before that. What did everyone call you before your holiday?'

Emmet chewed hard on the blade of grass. '551.'

'551? What on earth do you mean?'

He sat up slowly. 'I didn't have a name, just a number.'

'No, that can't be right. Everyone has a name.' I grabbed his shoulders and turned him to look at me but his eyes wouldn't fix on mine.

He shook his head sadly. 'Not in our place, Claire. Everyone has a number instead. Most people have names as well. The boys who were older when they were sent away can remember their names.' He stared out to the hillside. 'But wasn't I only a baby when I was brought to the nuns. Sure, I must have had a name of my own to start with.' He rubbed his face hard. 'But the nuns change babies' names, and real ones get forgotten. Just like Beauty. And then they handed me over to the Brothers. The Brothers like numbers, so.'

'What does your mother call you?'

'My mother?' He blinked at me. 'Ah, I don't remember. I haven't seen her in a while.'

'Oh.' I frowned. 'Well, what do they call you in school?'

'The boy from the orphanage.'

'That can't be right.' I thought about my first day in school and how I trembled telling Sister John my name. 'The teachers must call you something in class.'

Emmet nodded. '"You".'

'"You"?'

'Yes. "You, stand up". Or, "Put your hand out, you," for a leathering, like.'

'Well, you're Emmet to me.' I folded my arms tightly. 'I'll always call you Emmet, and it's a grand name to have.'

'Listen to yourself.' He was laughing. 'You're Irish right enough, now.'

'I'm half Irish and half Welsh,' I said, annoyed but not sure who I was most angry with, the nuns or the Brothers.

He rubbed my arm. He'd got me all worked up, and, from the look on his face, he was sorry. 'Come on, let's have another gallop,' he said. 'The bell will be going soon.' He jumped up and held his hand out to me.

I sighed as he tried to pull me up. My body felt a hundred times heavier than when I'd sat down, and I couldn't figure out why.

* * *

'Read that page again, *please*,' Emmet begged, as we sat together on Friday. 'It's my favourite.' I laughed and started the page over. I could tell how much he'd enjoyed the chapter, by the way he'd held his breath as he'd listened. It was the bit where Beauty arrived at Jerry's home and was given bran mash for supper. Polly, Jerry's wife, had a lovely meal ready for the family, too.

'"Sausage dumpling and apple turnover",' Emmet shouted before I could read the words. '"A capital supper".' He rubbed his stomach and made a show of licking his lips.

I laughed. 'I've never tried sausage dumpling, have you?'

Emmet shook his head. 'I haven't, no. Jim's family sound great, don't they? Polly, Dolly and Harry.'

'Dolly is Dorothy, really,' I told him.

'Your brothers, they're Will and Louis, right?' He thought for a moment. 'Claire, Will and Louis.' He repeated our names as if each of them was special. 'Tell me about the rest of your family.'

141

'There's Dad,' I said. 'He grew up here. He went to your school. Oh!' I scrambled to my knees. 'Perhaps the desk you sit at was his.'

'Did he sit right at the back?' Emmet asked. 'That's where I sit.'

'I don't know.'

'What's his name?'

'Conor O'Connell,' I said. 'Do you think he wrote it inside his desk?' People often did that in my old school. There were only a couple of names in my desk here, though, and they were so faint they were barely worth the ink.

'Only if he was a brave one and didn't mind a leathering.' Emmet picked up *Black Beauty* and opened it at the dry leaf he was using as a bookmark. 'Is he a good da?'

I nodded. 'The best in the world. He sticks up for me and Will when Mother gets angry. And he takes us to the cinema and buys us ice cream in the interval.'

'Were there any good ones?'

'Good what?'

'Films.'

'Oh yes, loads. I saw *Dumbo* and *Peter Pan*.' I bit my tongue. Those sounded very childish. 'And *Kidnapped* and *Tarzan*.' Dad had taken Will to those. Adventure films weren't for girls, my brother had said, and I might embarrass him by screaming in them. So I'd reminded him that he had a louder scream than me, and to prove it I'd kicked him hard in the shin. 'What films have you seen, Emmet?'

'Films?'

'You said Buddy was like the horses in cowboy films – you know, when he rescued you. Have you seen many adventure ones? Have you seen *The Lone Ranger*?' That was another film Will had been treated to while I had to traipse round the shops with Mother. That film was completely wasted on him – Will didn't even like horses.

'Ah.' Emmet bit his thumbnail. 'It's Francis goes to the cinema with his da. He tells me about the films.'

'You should go yourself. You'd like it. I miss the cinema and I miss telly too. What programmes do you watch?'

'I don't get a chance to watch television. The older boys see a bit...'

'That's a shame. You'd love *Champion the Wonder Horse* and *Animal Magic*.'

Emmet was nodding. 'I would.'

'Dad lets me stay up to watch the start of *Panorama* sometimes. That's on really late.'

'*Panorama*? What's that?'

'It's about,' I waved a hand in the air, 'things going on in the world.'

'You and your da watch television together, then?'

I nodded. I didn't want to mention the fact that Will watched *Panorama* too, and that *he* was allowed to stay up until the end.

'What about your mammy?'

'You mean Mother. Will and I aren't allowed to call her Mammy. Louis can, of course, but according to her, "Mother" shows more respect. She doesn't like *Panorama*.'

'Does she not?'

'She's just a nuisance, mainly. She shouts a lot and makes me do the washing up and she hates pegging out socks, so I always have to do that.'

'I like the sound of Jerry's wife.' Emmet was scanning the page we'd just read. 'She makes apple turnover,' he said dreamily.

'Mother doesn't cook.'

'Does she tuck you into bed?'

'No. Dad does that, and he sings me lullabies.'

'Lullabies?'

'This is my favourite.' I squashed my chin into my neck. '"Ol' man river",' I sang, '"that ol' man river, he must know something, but don't say nothing..."'

Emmet laughed. 'That's a fierce deep voice you've got there, Claire.'

I poked him in the side. 'I was trying to sound like the man who sings it on Dad's record.' I took *Black Beauty* from his lap and tried to remember the pages that had my favourite long words. I found the picture of Beauty and his rider and it reminded me of how much I longed to meet Buddy. His high spirits had carried on all week and Emmet said it was better to wait until he'd calmed down before we visited him. 'We *will* go and see Buddy next week,' I asked, 'won't we?'

'Sure,' Emmet said. 'He'll be great by then.' He'd been making a daisy chain and he wrapped it round my wrist and fixed the last flower in place. 'Have you any aunties?'

'There's Aunty Rhian,' I said. 'Mother calls her a jet setter because she lives in London.'

'And have you uncles and cousins?'

'Only Jack, but he's as good as a hundred uncles.' I held out my hand and admired my bracelet. 'He went to your school, too. We don't have any cousins. What about you? What's your father like? Do you look like him? My mother says I look like my dad.'

'I don't know my dad,' he said.

'Oh.' I swallowed hard, remembering what he'd told me about his name the day before. I felt ashamed I hadn't been more thoughtful. 'Sorry.'

'It's grand,' he said. 'My mother says I've the same hair and knobbly knees as him. My eyes are from her, though.'

'Is she very pretty?' I remembered the time I overheard Granny Costa Del telling Mother I'd need to turn from an ugly duckling into a swan if I was going to catch myself a rich husband. 'She must look like a film star if she's marrying a millionaire.'

'She's beautiful,' Emmet said. 'She has this gorgeous smile,' he closed his eyes, 'and when she tucks me into bed at night, she strokes my hair and her hands are soft. And she sings me a lulla ... lulla...'

'Lullaby,' I suggested, helpfully.

'And she smells of flowers and candy and cake.'

I thought that was probably how Mother must seem to Louis. 'You can remember her from when you were really small, can you?' Emmet nodded. 'She sounds lovely. You're lucky. When's she coming back?'

144

'Soon,' he said, opening his eyes again. 'Any day now.'

I tapped *Black Beauty*. 'Shall I read another page? We can start the next chapter.' I hoped my voice sounded cheerful. I was trying to hide how ashamed I felt. I was truly glad Emmet's mother was coming back after all this time, but I didn't want her turning up and taking him away too soon. It would spoil our plans to visit Buddy. The thought made me feel terrible because I could tell from the way he trembled when he talked about her, how desperate he was to see her again.

'Go on, read it,' Emmet said, resting his chin on my shoulder so he could see the pages, 'then I can finish that chapter and start the next on the walk back from school.'

'I'm sure I'd fall flat on my face,' I said, 'if I tried to read as I walked.' I turned to the right page.

'A person gets used to it,' he told me. 'And sure, when else would I have time for reading?' He nudged my shoulder with his chin. 'Come on, start now or the bell will go.'

And we sat there, with the September sun shining down on us, and began chapter thirty-three.

Chapter 16

The next morning, Granny couldn't sit still for a minute. When she wasn't trying to improve my appearance – by finding me whiter socks or retying my ponytail – she kept popping her head out of the door to squint up the boreen. She was looking for Rónán's car in the little dip near Michael's cottage. How it would miraculously arrive there without us hearing it go past in the lane was beyond me, but she kept on putting her head out of the door and muttering, 'Not there yet,' under her breath. I supposed that after all the effort we'd put into cleaning the cottage, she was worried Michael's family wouldn't turn up to admire our handiwork.

Just as Will was leaving to go and catch his bus to visit Aiden, we heard the sound of a car bumping along the lane.

'It's them,' Granny shouted, and pulled Will back into the kitchen. 'Wait a minute, Patrick. Let them have the boreen to themselves. Sure, we don't want to be giving Rónán an obstacle to drive around.'

Will rolled his eyes. 'You'd think the Queen was coming.'

Granny snorted. 'And sure, if she was, I wouldn't be baking a cake for her.'

We heard the car trundle past, and Granny let go of Will's arm and shoved him out of the door. 'Off with you now, don't miss the bus.' Then she called after him, 'And thank Mrs Maloney for the rashers she sent home with you on Wednesday.'

I sat at the table and put the finishing touches to a story I'd been writing. Louis rested his head in my lap. It felt heavy and I guessed he was sleeping standing up again. He always seemed to be doing that these days. My story was about a girl who found so much money under the beds when she cleaned people's homes, she could buy a palace and have a stable filled with horses. One of the horses was called Star and another Buddy, and a boy named Emmet lived in a wonderful cottage near the palace and looked after the animals. I'd enjoyed writing the story very much. Writing always made me happy, and I was even looking forward to the week ahead, with Head Nun's decision about the competition, and my trip with Emmet to see Buddy. Sister John had cornered me as I was leaving class on Friday and asked if I'd arranged a lift to Mass. I'd somehow found the courage to tell her that Michael couldn't drive me this weekend but he'd promised he would the weekend after. It was a lie, of course, and lies sent you to hell according to Sister, but if it saved me from a leathering here on earth, I didn't care. She'd nodded and said, 'We'll see, won't we?'

'Now, Claire,' Granny said, 'we'll get that cake from the oven and have a think about decorating it.' She was chewing her lip. 'Sure, we'll let them say their hellos and have their food, then we'll go and check they're getting along.'

'Okay,' I said, filling the margins of my story with daisies and stars.

'The thing with Michael, you see,' she said, mostly to herself, 'is he doesn't know when to keep his mouth shut.'

It suddenly occurred to me that maybe Michael's son might argue with his father, just like Dad and Mother argued. I'd been looking forward to meeting Michael's family and I was proud of all the work we'd put into getting his cottage ready, but if they were going to be in a bad mood, I wasn't sure I wanted to be there after all. They might be throwing the china, like Mother did. I went back to writing my story, and I made sure the people in it were getting along beautifully.

* * *

Shirley was all smiles as Granny and I took our seats at Michael's freshly polished table, so I guessed no one had argued yet.

147

'The men have gone out, I'm afraid,' she said, 'and Gerard too. They decided to have a walk across the fields.'

'No matter,' Granny said, pulling Louis onto her lap. ''Tis great to meet you, so.'

'It's very kind of you to help Michael get ready for our visit, Mrs O'Connell,' Shirley said. 'Especially when you've enough to do yourself.' She reached out as if to stroke Louis's curls then pulled her hand back and sat on it firmly.

'He told you?' Granny said. 'I wasn't going to breathe a word, and there wasn't so much that needed doing.' I looked around at the sparkling floor and windows, at the cleared counter tops and table. What on earth was Granny talking about? If only Shirley had seen it a week ago, she'd have understood the huge effort we'd gone to. I opened my mouth to tell her so, but Granny managed to jump in first. 'And of course, Claire helped.'

'Yes, we've heard a lot about you, Claire,' Shirley said, shifting her gaze from Louis to me. 'Michael says you're a grand little worker.'

I liked the word grand, so I decided to ignore the little. And to be fair to Michael, he was a huge man, so everyone was little to him. I'd enjoyed helping Granny, and I'd been pleased with the two sixpences I'd found. As Jack would say, I was quids in. 'My pleasure,' I said.

'So charming, too.' Shirley smiled at me. 'Will you cut the cake, Claire? Did you help your grandmother make this?' I'd only arranged the Smarties we'd bought from Fergus the Grocer's van on top of the icing but I found myself nodding, and Granny generously nodded too. 'I'm sure it'll be delicious.' Shirley handed me the knife.

'Dainty slices now, Claire,' my grandmother warned. 'We'll not be wanting doorstops.'

I wasn't sure I was the best person to tell the difference between a dainty slice and a doorstop, and I certainly didn't want the job of attacking the cake, but it seemed rude not to accept the challenge. Shirley clearly believed in me, although she hadn't seen the mess I'd made of slicing a fresh pan. The very first time I'd attempted it, Granny had banned me from using the bread knife ever again. I took a deep breath and stabbed the cake right in the middle. I wasn't sure what to do next.

'Cut it in half,' Granny told me, taking charge before we had a disaster like the bread incident all over again. 'I'll do the rest.' And I was relieved to hand over the responsibility.

* * *

Shirley and Granny had a lot to talk about, although really it was Shirley who spoke the most, while Granny nodded or shook her head. Shirley stared a lot at Louis, too. He'd eaten a chunk of cake and smeared half the icing down his jumper. Then he'd fallen asleep on Granny's lap. I played with the Smarties I'd saved from my slice of cake, arranging them into teams on my plate and pretending they were arguing with each other about who got to sit on the pink flower and who preferred the yellow one.

'Yes,' Granny was nodding. 'A terrible shame.'

I was sorely tempted to eat the red Smartie. I kept popping it in my mouth and spitting it out into my fist without Granny seeing. It had turned pale pink, and I knew the next time I put the Smartie in my mouth, I'd be hard pushed not to crunch it. Then I'd be down to three sweets. I couldn't make two teams with three sweets, it would be lopsided.

'How many were there?' Shirley asked.

'Five, if I remember right,' Granny said, and I almost interrupted her to say there were only four sweets on my slice of cake, before I realised she was talking to Shirley about something completely different. I put my head down again.

'And the last one was just too much.' I could see Shirley shaking her head out of the corner of my eye. I shuffled the sweets around on my plate, trying not to pick up the sucked one. If I did, it would be the end of it.

'She just waded out,' Granny said. 'It was the final straw, that last baby.'

I wondered if the birthday cake Iseult's mother would make for our tea would be as delicious as Granny's. I hoped so. I didn't get many chances to eat homemade cakes. Mother always said she didn't go in for that sort of thing. She proved it, too. The only birthday cake we ever got at home was shop bought. Those cakes looked fancy enough, but the vanilla buttercream was so sugary I always ended up feeling sick after two bites. I took the brown sweet from my plate and popped it into my mouth. I wouldn't crunch it, just suck. I was thinking ahead to when I won Iseult's competition and she'd cut me a huge slice of chocolate cake. Chocolate was the kind of cake I could only dream about having for my own birthdays.

'Did you know...?' Out of the corner of my eye, I saw Shirley look in my direction before she whispered, 'I had a miscarriage too.'

I glanced up to check Granny wasn't looking at me as I pressed my fist to my mouth and spat the Smartie out into it. I'd got the hang of it now and Granny hadn't noticed a thing.

'Michael did tell me. I'm so sorry for your loss.'

'It was very sad,' Shirley said. She was drawing invisible circles on the table top with her fingers. They had red painted nails, like Mother's, and the skin on her hands was smooth, not cracked like Granny's. 'But well, we still have Gerard. Mairead already had Rónán, didn't she, before she lost the others?'

'Rónán had just turned three when they moved here,' Granny said. She ruffled Louis's sleeping head. 'The same as this one.'

I put the two sucked Smarties into one team and gave them the yellow flower to sit on. I named that team Emmet and Buddy. The other one would be me and Star.

'I've often wondered,' Shirley said. And then she stopped talking, so I looked up and accidentally caught her eye. She smiled at me and looked a little sad, so I smiled back and made mine sad too, and then I looked down again at my sweets.

She took a breath. 'I wondered if it was the lambs,' she said. 'My mother's family had a farm and they were very superstitious around lambing time.'

'Sure, Mairead did work really hard and she was only a slip of a woman but she was used to hard work, of course. She'd been brought up in the—' Granny put a hand to her mouth.

'It's fine,' Shirley said, reaching for my grandmother's arm. 'I know she was an orphan. Rónán told me. She worked in a laundry, didn't she, when she was a teenager?'

'Oh,' Granny sighed. 'I thought I was after putting my foot in it. Yes, she came from the big house in town and all those girls worked in the laundries. She did until she was twenty. I think that's right. That's when Michael married her. He got her out, I suppose.'

'Still, she must have had a miserable life as a child. And then the babies. It's no surprise she took to the water with rocks in her pock—'

I hadn't rearranged my Smarties for a while – I'd been keeping my head down and listening to the conversation going on around me – but when Shirley stopped talking, I looked up from my plate and both she and Granny were staring at me. They had sad eyes. I gave them a little smile and popped the pink Smartie that had once been red into my mouth and crunched it. That was the end of team Emmet and Buddy.

'Enjoying your sweets, Claire?' Granny asked. I nodded. 'Time we went home. That brother of yours will be getting back from Roundmore soon enough.'

I put the last of the sweets into my mouth and handed the plate to Shirley. 'Thank you,' I said with a mouthful of chocolate.

'It's thank *you*, really,' she said. 'You were the ones who brought the cake.'

Granny and I waited politely for Shirley to open the door, even though, only a week before, we'd been coming in and out of it like we owned the place. 'It's a shame you missed them, but you know yourself what men are like once they get talking about fields.'

'I do,' Granny said. 'Safe home tomorrow.' And we stepped out into the sunshine.

'Thank you,' Shirley said. She ran a hand gently down Louis's back and he stirred a little in Granny's arms. 'And Rónán and I are really grateful to you for helping Michael.'

'Sure, it made a change,' Granny said. 'He's been a great help to me over the years. I'd have starved long ago if not for him.'

And just as we turned to begin walking away, I saw Granny reach back and grip Shirley's hand.

'Would you do a favour for me?' she asked. 'Don't be mentioning to Michael what you said about the lambing and the babies.' She squeezed Shirley's fingers. 'Keep that to yourself, would you? If he thought the lambs were the cause of all Mairead's pain,' she shook her head, 'sure, 'twould break his heart.'

Chapter 17

While we were sitting around the table having tea the next afternoon, there was a knock on the door. We all looked up in surprise.

'See who it is, Patrick,' Granny said. Then she added in a low voice, 'And please God it's not the priest.'

My heart leapt to my mouth. Sister John hadn't sent Father O'Reilly to track me down and scold me for missing Mass, had she? I held my breath and was so relieved to see, when Will opened the door, a boy about his own age standing on the step instead of the old priest. The boy was holding three small stripy bags.

'Hello,' he said, 'I'm Gerard, and if you're Patrick this is for you.' He held out the blue bag.

I got up from the table and went to stand behind Will. I was hoping one of the others might be for me. I wasn't disappointed.

'This is yours, Claire,' Gerard said, and handed over the red one.

'What are you doing leaving our visitor on the doorstep?' Granny asked. 'Bring him in, will you?' And we stepped aside and let him come into the kitchen.

'So, you're Rónán's boy?' Granny said, making him sit at the table and pouring him a cup of tea whether he wanted it or not. 'For a terrible moment there, we thought you must be Father O'Reilly.'

Gerard looked surprised and Will said quickly, 'No one ever knocks the door. Everyone usually comes straight in.'

'Oh,' Gerard said. 'Sorry.'

'Not to worry,' Granny said. 'We were glad it was you, that's all. Have you enjoyed visiting your grandfather?'

'Yes, thank you,' Gerard said, although his voice sounded a bit uncertain. He sipped his tea and looked at us all nervously. To be fair, we were rather treating him like an animal at the zoo. I think it was because of his white shirt and black tie, and his suit and slicked back hair. He had round glasses balanced near the end of his nose. They made his eyes look like an owl's.

'That's wonderful, so. Have you been to Mass today?' Granny asked, and when Gerard nodded, she said, 'Sure, that's a grand thing.'

I snorted. She didn't fool me. And if Gerard had managed to get to church, then surely Michael could have offered me a lift, too, and saved me from Sister John's nasty remarks in the morning.

I fiddled crossly with the paper bag Gerard had given me. I was desperate to look inside, but the top was rolled down on itself. Will hadn't opened his, so I decided I'd better not open mine, either. I guessed we'd have to wait until Gerard told us to look inside, or maybe we'd have to hang on even longer until after he left. With a flourish, I put the bag next to my cup and saucer on the table. I hoped it might jog him into mentioning it. Sadly, my plan failed.

'This one is for Louis,' Gerard said, holding up the green bag. He was taking small sips from his cup and after each one, his top lip curled. 'Shall I give it to him?'

'Just put it under the table,' I said.

Gerard raised his eyebrows and looked at Granny. She nodded, so he dropped the bag onto the floor. It made a strange clank as it hit the flagstones, and Louis very nearly woke up.

'Now,' Granny said, after Gerard had managed to finish his tea, 'why don't you three children go play outside?'

'I've got homework to do,' Will said, rather too quickly, I thought.

'Claire will play with our guest, then.' Granny gave me a look that dared me to complain. 'Show him the fields.' And she stood and began clearing the table.

I stroked the paper bag one last time before I left it on the table, and led Gerard outside. I hadn't a clue what game to play with a boy who was older than me and dressed in a suit. 'We can try and spot seals in the lake,' I suggested.

154

'My grandfather showed me some this morning.' I could tell he wasn't impressed by our seals, and I was very glad I'd found those sixpences under Michael's spare bed before Gerard got to them.

'I can show you where we've been digging for treasure,' I tried. I thought the word 'treasure' might prick up his ears.

He put a hand to his mouth and yawned. 'Okay.'

We went round to the other side of the cottage, past the barn and towards the corner of the field. 'Our excavation site is over there.' It was the name Will had given it, back in the summer when we'd first started digging and it had seemed so full of promise.

I led him over. 'We used an old riddle from the barn to sieve the soil.' I was quite pleased I'd remembered the correct terms. I was only sorry Will wasn't with us to witness my moment of glory.

Gerard didn't look impressed. 'Did you find anything?'

'We've made an exhibition in the barn. It's mainly bones and china.'

'The barn?'

I pointed. 'What Granny calls the shed.'

He nodded. 'Were they human bones?'

'Perhaps,' I said, although I knew Will had decided they belonged to sheep and birds and some other not-human beings. He'd rubbished my theory that a murder had taken place in that very spot. He said the bones were probably from animals killed on the farm, that's all. To be fair, late at night when the wind was howling around the cottage, I preferred Will's theory to my own, too. 'Do you want to see them?'

Gerard shrugged.

I took him into the barn anyway. There were cobwebs everywhere inside and I hoped he would get covered in them. He'd brought me a gift so I should have been kinder to him, but he wasn't interested in our dig and besides, I didn't know what was in the paper bag yet.

He poked at the bones with a finger, pushing them round on the board and ruining the careful display Will had made during the summer. I thought I ought to tell him to stop but I couldn't be bothered. Will had run off to our bedroom, so he obviously didn't care.

I noticed Gerard's nails had been chewed right down until the skin around them bled, and they reminded me of Emmet's. In that moment, I wished it was Emmet with me at Granny's cottage instead of Gerard. Emmet would love to see the seals in the lake and the display we'd made from the dig. I wished with all my heart that he could come and visit me, but I knew Granny would never agree. Her attitude towards boys and girls mixing was as strict as the nuns'. She'd say having Michael's grandson round to play wasn't the same as inviting someone from the boy's school.

'Why are you staring at my hands?' Gerard pulled down the sleeves of his jacket. 'Didn't your mother tell you it's rude to stare?'

'Didn't *your* mother tell you it's rude to be rude?' I snapped. 'Look.' I pointed to the ruined display. 'You've spoilt all Will's hard work. I'll go and tell Granny.'

'No, don't,' he said, quickly, and I realised proudly that he'd already worked out my grandmother wasn't to be messed with – just in the time it took to drink a cup of tea. He shuffled the bits of bone around as though he could remember where they went. I let him try for a while so I could watch him suffer.

'Don't worry,' I said when I was bored with his efforts. 'My brother'll put them back the way they should be.' I knew, though, that Will had lost interest in the display long ago. He wouldn't have cared if I took our findings back out to the field and scattered them to its four corners.

I led him out of the barn by the most cobwebby exit. 'They're not human, those bones,' Gerard said, as if he were an expert. 'They're not important.'

And in that instant, I decided on a plan. 'Wait,' I told him, and I dashed back into the barn and took down the old pond-dipping nets from their hook.

'Here,' I said, handing him one. 'Do you like rock pools?' I didn't wait for an answer, I was already running off to the other side of the cottage, dragging him by his sleeve. 'There are loads of pools in the lake when the tide's out.' I checked that Granny wasn't watching from the window before I bent down and pulled up the chicken wire. The kitchen door was open and Louis was peeping at us from under the table.

'It's not a lake,' Gerard told me, expertly. 'It's a bay.'

'Okay,' I said, 'just be quick.' I flattened down the grass and held the wire high over his back as he crawled under. Then I squeezed underneath myself. The tide hadn't long gone out and the rocks were slippery. I was going to enjoy watching this ridiculously dressed boy try to avoid clumps of seaweed and knee-deep rockpools. I decided to keep him out there for hours and hours.

But once he'd slipped a few times and soaked the seat of his trousers, the novelty wore off. I lifted the wire and let him escape but as he bent low, he snagged the back of his jacket on a rusty end of the fence. My work was complete. I led him into the kitchen, hoping Granny wouldn't look too closely at him and see how grubby he'd become. She never really looked at Will, Louis or me, so I felt I was on safe ground. The paper bags were still on the table. Will's seemed untouched. He had more willpower than me. Louis's was ripped to shreds under the table and some sort of metal thing was in bits on the floor. There was no sign of him, though. Granny's bedroom door was open. She wasn't in there with Louis. I poked my head through the other door. Will was on the top bunk looking at an atlas.

'Where's Granny and Louis?'

'Must be in the privy, I suppose,' he said.

Gerard was staring at the photograph just inside Granny's bedroom. 'My grandfather's got this picture too,' he said. 'It's in the bedroom I slept in last night.'

'I know.' I'd wiped a thick layer of dust from it, and I'd cleaned off the black sticky dots Granny said flies had made on the glass.

'My father told me who's in it. That's him.' He pointed to the boy with the short hair. 'And that's my grandmother. She's dead now.'

I looked at the woman closely for the first time. She was thin with a sad smile. She had her arm around the boy Gerard said was his dad. Now that I was looking carefully at the photo, I could see she was holding onto him tightly.

He pointed again. 'That's your grandmother.'

I'd suspected that was her. The missing smile and crinkly eyes gave her away. She looked younger but still old, and she looked thin and sad, but not as thin and sad as Gerard's grandmother.

'And that's your father. Cormac, isn't it?'

'Conor,' I said. Gerard was pointing at the tallest boy. His dark hair was longish and curly, and his smile was just like Dad's. It took me a few moments to grasp that that's exactly who he was. Dad. It seemed so unlikely – the photograph looked like it had been taken a hundred years ago – but how stupid of me not to have realised sooner.

Gerard put his chewed fingertip to the face of the littlest boy, the one that looked like Louis. He pressed hard, as if he were squashing a wasp against the window. 'This one's dead,' he said.

Granny appeared at the door with Louis on her hip. 'You'll be wanting to get back now, Gerard,' she said. 'Your parents are leaving for Dublin soon, no doubt.' She nodded at the little paper bags on the table. 'Claire, thank Gerard for his kindness.'

'Thank you,' I said, trying my best to sound as ungrateful as possible.

'You've got chalks from Clerys,' he told me, ruining the moment of surprise I'd been looking forward to. 'Patrick has pencils. And Louis...' He stared at the scattered bits on the floor. 'He had a car.'

'From that great big shop in Dublin?' Granny said. 'Sure, your parents are very kind. Be thanking them for us, won't you?' And she herded him gently out of the door and closed it behind him.

I dashed to the table, grabbed the red bag and unrolled the top. He was right. I had chalks. They were coloured ones, too. Not a bad gift, really. I tipped the packet out and opened it. The smell of the chalk sticks rushed up my nose and took me straight back to the classroom. I shuddered.

'Sure, that's a grand present to have,' Granny said. 'Don't you be tempted to use them on the cottage walls, and I know chalk rubs out, but,' she held my gaze for a moment, 'no rude drawings, Claire.'

I snorted. 'Of course not, Grandma.' Honestly, did she really think I'd do that sort of thing?

Chapter 18

I'd have had a lot of fun with those chalks after Gerard left, if it hadn't been so damp in Connemara. As it was, a cloud filled with drizzle came and hung over Granny's little cottage for the evening and smudged all my artwork. In the end, I gave up drawing on the rocks and put away my chalks. I found my notebook and wrote a story instead, about a rude boy whose head got turned into a toad by a witch. The witch had a bun and crinkly eyes and lived in a house like Granny's. I drew little fish around the edges of my paper, like the ones I'd found in the rock pools earlier that afternoon with Gerard, when the tide had been low and there was still a trace of sun in the sky. The tide was high now, and the sky was heavy with rainclouds that had turned the lake dark grey.

Will was in our bedroom. He was always shutting himself in there with his atlases. I could hear the springs creaking as he moved on the bunk. Earlier, I'd lined up with Louis and Granny on the boreen to wave goodbye to Michael's family. Shirley had smiled and waved and waved, and we'd even had a nod from Gerard. But Rónán couldn't get away fast enough, and the wheels of his car sprayed us with gravel as he drove, his eyes fixed straight ahead, past our cheery little gang.

As I drew at the kitchen table, Louis began grumbling and I freed him from his leash. I lifted him onto my lap and cuddled him. '*Bachgen da,*' I whispered into his hair. I surprised myself by remembering the words Mother used to say to soothe him. '*Bachgen da*. Good boy.' He snuggled closer and I rested my head on his mop of curls and closed my eyes. It wasn't far off bedtime and I was sleepy.

I heard Granny's clogs clattering into the kitchen. She'd been sheltering in the barn to enjoy a cigarette. I caught the thin whiff of smoke that she usually brought back inside with her. It seemed stronger with my eyes shut, even though the door to the yard was open. I knew, because I could hear very clearly the birds that called sadly to each other across the lake every evening.

'I've a note for you to bring your teacher tomorrow,' Granny told me. 'About the van. It says I'll be doing my best to get it repaired for Mass next week.'

'Thank you, Grandma.' I gave her a smile then closed my eyes again. I suddenly felt much lighter.

I heard her clatter off in the direction of the pantry and Louis slipped down from my lap back under the table. The kitchen was very quiet as I sat with my eyes shut, listening to the birds calling outside. I remembered the one Emmet had said ate lots of blackberries on the bush behind school – the female blackbird, with brown feathers that made it hard to spot.

The breeze coming in through the back door had turned cold. I stood up, pulled the sheepskin from Granny's chair and wrapped it tightly around my shoulders. I went to stand at the window. I wanted to try to spot the birds. Emmet had said I should stare blankly until I saw a movement, then my eyes could home in and find the bird easily. I couldn't see any birds in the bushes, but I could definitely hear a few somewhere nearby.

Granny came back from the pantry. I heard her putting a saucepan on the fire behind me. 'Milk will be warm enough for your cocoa in a minute,' she said.

I still couldn't see any birds in the bushes. I willed one to appear. I stared and stared and gradually a brown shape came into view. It was between the branches, among the leaves. As I tried to focus on it, I realised it wasn't in the bush at all but behind, in the lake. There was something in the water, too big to be a bird. Was it a seal?

Next to me, Granny was mixing the cocoa powder and sugar together. I could hear the scrape of her spoon against the cup and smell the chocolatey powder. I'd never seen a seal so close to the shore and so near to the cottage. I moved my head to get a better look.

161

My stomach flipped.

Where was Louis? I turned to look under the table. The rope was fixed to nothing but the table leg. I ran to the door. From there I had a good view of the lake. I tried to call, to shout out to him but no sound came.

'What's wrong, Claire?' Granny asked. 'What is it?'

I forced the words to my lips. 'Louis,' I managed. 'In the lake.'

'Holy Mary, Mother—' I heard the shattering of the cup my grandmother had been holding as I ran from the cottage. She was close behind me.

'Will!' She was screaming it, Proddy name or not. 'Will, come quick! Louis's in the water.'

We tore towards the lake, with Granny screaming and screaming to Will for help, but he wasn't answering.

'Will, get out here. Get out here now!'

And suddenly Michael was there, his huge shape charging down the boreen, his feet skidding over the gravel. He overtook us, struggling out of his coat, throwing it to the ground and kicking off his boots. Louis was floating in the lake, twelve feet out, face down in the water.

Granny held me tightly as Michael ripped back the chicken wire and dived in. A few strokes with his good arm and he was alongside Louis. He grabbed him, lifting his little body and shaking it, but it was limp. He shook him and shook him again.

'Bring him here,' Granny shouted.

Michael pulled Louis onto his chest and kicked his feet hard. He forced his way headfirst back to the rocks. Granny waded into the water and grabbed Louis, her strong arms lifting him up and shaking him for all she was worth.

'No,' she said through clenched teeth. 'No.'

She staggered with him out of the water, taking him away from the rocks, and laid him on the grass. She pressed his chest, one, two, three times. 'You will not die,' she told Louis angrily. The look on her face terrified me. 'You will not.' She pressed and pressed and pressed.

Michael stood at the edge of the lake. He was shaking and shaking. I slumped onto the grass, my legs collapsing beneath me. Michael's wind-burnt face had turned grey. Water was dripping off his shirt sleeves. It was dripping off his chin and his nose and his shaggy moustache. A laugh bubbled up in my throat and escaped from my lips, like a strange shriek. I looked at Louis's body and I felt I had died with him. I wanted to crawl into my bed, pull the blankets right over my head and never get up again.

Granny was still pushing away at Louis's chest. I wondered why she was doing it. 'Don't die on me,' she said. 'Do not die.'

Michael shook his head. 'Leave him. The water's had him.'

Granny didn't look up, she just kept thumping. 'No,' she gasped, 'please, no.' Then she hung her head and brought her hands to her mouth. 'Oh, Declan,' she whispered. 'Not again,' and she softly stroked Louis's face.

Michael touched her shoulder. 'I was in the top field,' he mumbled. 'Saw him crawl under the wire there.' He pointed to the gap, the gap I had made to get to the rock pools.

'What's happening?' Will called from the door. He'd finally realised something was wrong.

We turned to look at him and his face went pale at the sight of ours.

'Your brother...' Granny's words disappeared.

'No,' Will cried. 'No.' He took a step towards us but his legs folded under him and we watched as he fell.

There was a sudden splutter then loud gurgling, and we turned to see water spurting from Louis's mouth, like seawater from a whale's blowhole. It soaked Granny's knees and pooled in her apron. She grabbed his shoulders and turned him onto his side as fast as she could, hitting his back over and over, all her gentleness gone now. Louis coughed and more water poured from his mouth.

'Good boy,' Granny said. 'Good boy.' She pulled him onto her lap and squeezed him tight. 'You're fine now. You're fine now, child.'

I hugged my knees and rocked. Granny dragged the sheepskin

from my shoulders and wrapped it around Louis. Will raised himself from the ground, one hand gripping the door frame and the other clutching his chest.

'Get a blanket for Michael, Patrick,' Granny shouted. 'Go now, quick.' Michael had slumped against a rock and his face was buried in his arm. He was shaking and shaking. He seemed to be sobbing, too.

Granny struggled to her feet, holding Louis tightly. 'I'll get the kettle on and make us some tea. Then we'll drive to Grogan's and ring your uncle. It's time he brought you away from here.' She bent a little so she could speak into Michael's ear. 'We've all had enough of this water now.'

* * *

Granny rang our house in Wales from the little hatch by the front door of the pub – three rings to show it was her – and then she waited for Dad to get hold of Jack, and for Jack to ring her back. It was a long wait. Finally, the telephone rang and she explained to Jack about the accident. He said he'd tell Dad then phone her back, and we began another long wait.

Louis was in dry clothes now but he was still wrapped in the sheepskin. He was getting very heavy, even though Will and I took turns to hold him. Loud chatter was coming from a room off the hallway, and I was jealous of the people inside, and the chairs they had to sit on.

'Grandma,' I began. I was almost too tired to speak. 'Can we go into that room and sit down, please? We could put Louis on a chair.'

Granny looked at me sternly. 'I'll not be stepping a foot in the bar,' she said. Then her eyes softened a little and she patted my head. 'You've had a terrible shock, so. Go in, just by the door. Your uncle's taking a desperate long time to have that word with your father.' And she turned back to the telephone.

Will and I slipped into the noisy bar and the smell of beer and cigarettes welcomed us as I plonked Louis with great relief onto a seat near the door. I longed to be at home, with Dad carrying me to bed and singing me his songs. I closed my eyes and breathed in, sucking the comforting smell of the pub and my father, deep into my lungs.

After a while, I noticed strange sounds among the voices in the bar – a toot of a whistle and a ping of a violin string. I opened my eyes. Through the fog of smoke, I could make out a crowd sitting in the farthest corner. Every one of them was holding an instrument – a violin, a whistle or a small drum. As I watched, they settled down and began playing a tune. It was very jolly, and for a moment I forgot how tired I felt. A man was playing the bagpipes, but he hadn't really got the hang of them. I'd once seen a man wearing a kilt standing outside Howells in Cardiff – Mother's favourite shop – and he'd been playing the bagpipes. Mother had taken ages to choose a new frock, so I'd watched the man for a very long time and he'd been blowing into his bagpipe for all he was worth. But this man in Grogan's didn't realise he had to blow – he just squeezed the bag with his elbow. He still somehow managed to play the song, even if it wasn't in tune, exactly.

The group was playing a lively song and banging the floor with their heels, and despite all the panic of Louis's accident, and how exhausted I felt, I couldn't help jigging along. The music seemed to get right inside me and made me want to move. I could see Will felt the same, although he did a better job of reining in the bouncing. Louis was far too tired to be interested in the music – he just curled up on the chair and sucked his thumb, but at least he was comfortable and the seat was saving our aching arms.

The tune stopped with a flourish and I clapped loudly. I was surprised no one else joined in. The man playing the bagpipes smiled across at me and I felt my face flush. I could have sworn he'd read my thoughts. The musicians put down their instruments and, laughing and chatting, went off to get more drinks.

'Why doesn't Granny want to come in here?' I asked Will. It was such a lovely, friendly place that I couldn't imagine why she'd chosen to miss out on being part of it.

'She can't go near the bar.'

'She's standing in the hallway,' I said. 'That's pretty near.'

'There's no booze in the hallway. She won't come in here because she doesn't want to be tempted. It might be the start of a slippery slope.'

'Oh, okay,' I said, although I wasn't completely certain I understood what he was talking about.

A woman had begun to sing quietly. She had a beautiful, sad voice. I couldn't spot where the sound was coming from at first, but my eyes searched the faces until they found the singer – an old woman in the smokiest corner with her eyes closed and just her lips moving. I thought I recognised one or two of the Irish words she was singing.

Slowly, a hush came over the room and her voice seemed to lift up and float above us. Then an amazing thing happened – the other people in the bar began to join in. They sang very quietly at first, and the music crept all around us until it swelled and swelled, then it faded away again to just the woman's voice. Shivers ran up and down my spine and I leant on Louis's chair. My legs felt like they might give way as the voices rose again and again, until finally the song rolled away as gently as it had come. I swallowed hard – the music had made my throat feel tight. In the middle of all its beauty, I'd suddenly remembered the gap under the chicken wire, and how lucky it was that Louis hadn't drowned. I'd realised, too, how lucky I was that I hadn't, after all, murdered my brother.

I clutched Will's hand. 'What are you doing?' he asked, and he scratched my fingers away from his.

Granny put her head in through the door just as the musicians were taking up their instruments again. She looked cross and so before she could speak I said, 'It's all right, Grandma, we'll come out.' I would have loved to hear more of the music but I didn't want Granny making a sudden dash for the bar. I picked up Louis, then

Will and I followed her outside. She'd spoken to Jack, she explained. He'd be coming over next Saturday. We piled into the van as quickly as we could and she started the engine. And we were away from Grogan's in no time at all.

Chapter 19

Louis's accident, and my role in causing it, should have tormented me for the rest of my days. And in times of stress – when I fear I'm about to lose a case, or throughout my painful divorce from Daniel – my dreams do take me back to the lake, and to my little brother floating face down in the water. When I wake, I sense shadows of that evening hovering around me, but when I try to catch them, they pull away like gossamer threads. It's the music at Grogan's I most vividly remember about that day, and I'm grateful to those musicians for the balm they gave my shocked ten-year-old mind.

* * *

Monday at St Brid's was just the distraction I needed. It was competition results day, and I was bursting with hope. All thoughts of Louis's near-death experience had been firmly pushed to the dark corners inside my head.

The excitement in class before morning prayers would have been uncontainable had Sister John not been sitting at her desk, giving us all the evil eye.

'I've no need to tell you, girls,' she said, in as bored a tone as she could muster, 'that today is the day we'll be knowing the result of the competition. But that is no excuse for silliness. The head nun has a meeting and won't be in school until this afternoon. You'll have to wait until then to find out who the winner is, so.' There was a groan around the classroom and Sister John banged the desk with her board duster. A cloud of chalk rose to smother her furious face, and it would have been funny, if it weren't for the disappointment we were all feeling. 'Be quiet,' she spluttered, swiping an angry hand at the dust. 'This morning, we'll be concentrating on our mathematics, as usual. Now, prayers.' And we bowed our heads with a heartfelt sigh.

Emmet wasn't around the back of the toilet block at dinner time. Everyone else was squashed into the shelter because of the rain but I had managed to sneak off. No one had taken any notice of me except the House girls – and Theresa, who always seemed to be watching me. I didn't think any of them would tell on me, though. They spent all their time at school trying not to be noticed, too. It was strange finding the grass empty. I wondered if it was because of the rain that he hadn't turned up. It wasn't heavy, just drizzle, what Mother called 'picking'. Even so, I didn't want to stand in it on my own. As I turned to go, I saw a face appear at the gap on the boys' side of the school – Emmet's. We ran to each other.

'Have you news about our story? Did you win?'

I felt my cheeks colouring up. What would Emmet say if he knew *our story* was still in my pocket? 'We won't know until later,' I said. 'Head Nun wasn't in school this morning.' The rain was getting heavier. We wouldn't be able to read *Black Beauty* today – the pages would be ruined. I took the crusts from my pocket very carefully so the story hidden there wouldn't make an appearance.

'Ah, crusts,' Emmet said. 'Buddy loved the ones he had last. He neighed, you know, when I brought them to him. I told him it was Claire he had to thank. I think he's getting to know your name. He neighs when I mention you.'

'He knows my name!' I danced on the spot. 'How are his spirits? Is he better?'

Emmet took the crusts from me and jammed them into his pockets. 'He is. We could go see him tomorrow. Would you like that?'

'Yes, yes! That would be fantastic.' I skipped around him. 'But hang on.' That was one of Will's favourite sayings. Mother didn't like it. 'I can't miss afternoon lessons.' I'd dodged the strap so far, and now with Jack coming to get us on Saturday, I wouldn't need to make any more excuses about why I kept missing Mass. But I was pretty sure running away from school would be a great excuse for Sister John to leather me, after all.

'Sure, I told you, if you come here straight from the dinner hall, we'll be back before the bell.'

'Okay,' I said, pulling my cardigan over my head to keep off the worst of the rain. 'Let's do it tomorrow.' I spat on my hand and offered it to Emmet. 'Pact.'

He spat on his and we shook. 'Pact. We'll go and see Buddy tomorrow.' Then the rain became torrential, so we gave each other a thumbs-up and ran our different ways.

* * *

I was last in line, as usual, when the bell sounded to tell us to queue in the shelter before we went back into class. The House girls let me slip in before them as they normally did. They were always at the back of everything, the back of the class, the back of the dining hall, the back of any queue we formed. They didn't seem to mind, though.

They smiled at me as they let me pass. 'It's exciting, isn't it?' the one with red hair said.

I stared at her. How did she know? Had she been spying on me and Emmet? Had she been listening in on our plans to see Buddy? How dare she? 'What do you mean?'

She blinked at my cross voice. 'The results,' she said. 'Sister John will be announcing them when we go back in.'

My heart did a little flip. Of course, the competition. In all the excitement about Buddy, I'd totally forgotten. I could hear the rest of the girls talking about it now. 'Oh, yes,' I said, a little sorry for snapping at her. And then I remembered that the House girls had been disqualified. 'But you're not even entered in it.'

They smiled at me. 'Sure, it's still exciting,' the dark-haired one said, and to be fair, she did look really excited.

'I wonder if Iseult will win again this year,' the redhead said, rubbing her hands together. The sores on her knuckles had been bleeding again. The other House girl had sores on her hands, too, just like Emmet. I'd been meaning to ask him about them. I made a mental note to bring it up on our way to see Buddy the next day.

The bell rang again and we all became silent. And I turned my back on the House girls without a second thought, leaving them to their usual place – the very last in the line.

* * *

Sister John was always asking us to be so quiet in class that she could hear a pin drop, and that afternoon she had her wish. She could have dropped the tiniest pin, and it would have startled us all half to death. She clutched in her hand the result of the competition, given to her by Head Nun. What a spell that paper cast over us.

Sister John wasn't about to give up her power easily. 'Now,' she said, waving the results high above our heads, 'don't I have here what you've all been waiting for. And aren't you the well-behaved ones this afternoon?' She gave us a sneer that stretched into a kind of smile. It was strained around the edges, I guessed from lack of use. 'I've a mind to save this until it's time to go home.' She put the paper on her desk.

We knew better than to groan. It would be easy to accidentally prod Sister John into keeping the results from us for a day or longer – even I realised that, and I'd only been in her class a handful of weeks.

She glared towards the back of the class, and for a moment, I thought she was looking at me. Then thankfully she said, 'What do you think, House girls?'

I was so relieved she hadn't picked me for such a horrible question that I forgot to feel sorry for the girls behind me. But they were up to the challenge.

'You're the best judge, Sister, to be sure,' one of them said, while the other added, 'God is good,' which seemed to be the right answer to every question in the world.

'He is, so,' Sister John agreed heartily, picking up the precious piece of paper again and unfolding it. 'He is, so.'

We sat up straight. Was she about to share the results? We held our breath.

'Now, what has the head nun been writing here?' She slowly mouthed the words to herself, nodding and frowning in turn. 'Well, isn't this a turn-up for the books. In first place is...' She stretched out her arm as though she couldn't quite focus on the name. We held our breath. 'Theresa.' Sister John raised an eyebrow. 'Well *done*, Theresa.' She glared at the girl in the front row. 'Aren't you the lucky one?' Theresa shrugged. 'In second place is,' Sister John did the stretchy arm thing again, 'Iseult.' Iseult's head had slumped at the news she'd failed to get first place and it didn't rise when she heard she was runner-up. 'And what do we have here? An extra award. Head Nun says she was very impressed with Claire O'Connell's use of punctuation, and she's given her a Highly Commended.' I heard the House girls' tiny round of excited applause behind me. 'Well now, Claire O'Connell,' the nun continued, 'isn't that a surprise? And there was I thinking you had a lazy mind.'

I didn't know what to say to that, so I took a leaf out of the House girls' book. 'God is good,' I offered.

Sister John smirked. 'He is so, and so is Head Nun. Maybe it's both of them you should be thanking. Now, I think we should hear the winning compositions. You other girls will know then what to be setting your sights on. Theresa, read yours first, since you're the winner this year.'

Theresa plodded to Sister's desk. She took the paper the nun held out, cleared her throat and turned to face us. 'My best friend is my dear mammy,' she said, before reeling off a long and extremely boring list of Mrs Maloney's talents.

'Well, isn't that grand?' Sister John said, yawning into her hand. 'I can certainly see why Head Nun chose your composition, with your dear mammy being on the parish council and all. Sit down, now.' She rolled her eyes behind Theresa's back as she returned to her seat. 'Iseult, come out and read yours.'

Iseult got up slowly and slouched half-heartedly to the front of the class. She very nearly snatched her story from Sister John, but at the last minute she stopped herself.

'Thank you, Sister,' she said, a bit less sweetly than usual. 'My best friend, Carlotta,' she began, her voice cracking, as if she now very much doubted Carlotta deserved her friendship at all. I whispered a thank you prayer.

Iseult managed to read aloud all three pages of her composition but it was clear she was far from happy. Sister John led us in a round of applause when she'd finished reading – we hadn't bothered for Theresa.

'Well done, Iseult,' the nun said, beaming. 'Don't you have the gift for writing stories. Head Nun said you would have won if it weren't for... What was it she wrote at the bottom of your paper?'

Iseult looked again at her papers. 'Better punctuation needed,' she mumbled.

'Ah, punctuation. Don't be minding that, now. Work hard at your commas and paragraphs, and you'll be our winner again.'

Iseult gave the nun a weak smile and went back to slump in her seat.

'And talking of punctuation,' Sister John said, 'Claire O'Connell, you had a special mention for that, did you not? Perhaps we should hear your story, too. Come to the front of class.'

Dread suddenly sprang into my chest. When I wrote my story, I hadn't realised Sister John would ask me to read it to the class. No one had warned me about that, and this wasn't something I wanted to share with the other girls. Iseult had asked to see it and I was pretty certain she'd want to be my best friend after she'd read all the wonderful compliments I'd given her, but I didn't want the whole class to know what I'd written. I could feel my cheeks burning at the very thought of reading those sickly words aloud. It was too

173

awful. I couldn't do it. My voice would come out as a whisper. My knees would buckle. My dinner would reappear.

'Come on, out with you.' The nun hooked a fierce finger in my direction.

'Go, Claire. Go,' one of the House girls whispered from behind me.

I managed to unstick my tongue from the roof of my mouth. 'I don't feel well, Sister.'

'What in Heaven's name is wrong with you? Put out, are you, at not winning?'

'No, Sister.' All those ridiculously wonderful things I'd written about Iseult read aloud? Oh, the shame. 'I feel sick.'

'Sick, is it? And were you feeling sick before you knew you hadn't won?'

'No, but...'

'I don't want to hear the "but". Out you come, now.' She shook my composition at me. 'And if you vomit on my classroom floor, I'll be sending you for the mop.'

Somehow, I made it to the front of class and as I stood, my hands and knees trembling, my eyes landed on the House girls. They were smiling encouragingly at me. Oh no, did they think I'd written my story about them? In that moment, I wished with all my heart I had.

* * *

Most of the girls looked completely bored as I read the first part of my story. I'd simply written what Iseult had told me about her and her sister – the Irish dancing and Rose of Tralee. Sister John had asked me to tell everyone when I was beginning a new paragraph, since that's what I'd been commended on, which made it a little tricky to read. She'd wanted me to mention the commas too, but after the tenth one she held up her hand.

'We can probably manage without those now. Head Nun has asked me to give you all a special lesson on commas and paragraphs later this week.' Everyone groaned slightly.

'Thank you, Claire O'Connell, for that.' She didn't sound very grateful. She added a muttered, 'Aren't you the advanced ones in Wales?'

Had Sister John asked, I'd have told her that my punctuation had improved here in Ireland. In the summer holidays, Will had found my notebook and mocked my writing by saying it was one long mess with a handful of full stops thrown in. I had no idea why he was making fun of me, and I hated not knowing. So I teased him about not being able to write it better himself, and then he showed me where he'd have put in commas and started new paragraphs. It was the exact result I was hoping for. I'd concentrated hard and memorised his instructions. He didn't have a clue how much his showing off had helped me. And now, here I was, highly commended on my punctuation by the head nun. Ha! That showed him.

'New paragraph,' I continued. 'Iseult has beautiful blonde, bouncy hair and her eyes are an exquisite blue colour.' All of the girls had started listening properly now, and there were a few giggles around the classroom. Iseult herself was studying me seriously. 'Do I need to carry on?' I asked Sister. I gave her a pleading look.

'You most certainly do,' she said. 'We want the benefit of your wisdom, don't we girls?'

'Yes, Sister,' my classmates chorused.

I looked at the House girls at the back of the class and saw sympathy on their faces. If only I'd written about them. If only I'd written about Emmet and Buddy. Why did I have to choose Iseult? Why was I so desperate to be her friend? In that moment, I'd have gladly handed over my slice of her birthday cake to Siobhán or Dolores, or anyone else who wanted it.

'Go on,' Sister John commanded.

I took a deep breath. 'She is a wonderful person...'

'Who?' I could tell Sister John was making fun of me, even though there was no hint of a smile on her face.

'Iseult,' I said, my heart sinking even further. 'She is a truly

175

marvellous friend to everyone and she is very kind to animals, beggars and old people.' I had no idea if that was true or not, but when I'd been composing my story, I'd imagined all the compliments Iseult would like, and then I'd foolishly written them down. They were churning my stomach now. 'She is an extremely intelligent girl and there is nothing she cannot turn her hand to.' That was a phrase I'd heard Mother use. She was always saying it about her friends' husbands, especially when Dad had trouble getting the car started, or when the telly had wiggly lines on it. 'She has special gifts...' This was how I'd heard Granny Connemara describe those distant relatives Jack had told us about. Suddenly I realised it was not something I wanted to say out loud. I turned to Sister John once more with pleading eyes. 'Can I stop?'

'No.'

I gulped, not daring to look at the faces before me. 'One of her most amazing gifts is to heal the sick,' I whispered. Granny's granny had been famed for that. 'Another is to...'

'Speak up, girl,' Sister John snarled.

'Talk to wild animals. They, being natural creatures, can tell when bad weather is on the way.' This was supposed to be Granny's great-grandfather's gift. Oh, the shame of saying these things out loud about Iseult.

'And what are we if not natural creatures?' Sister John asked. I shrugged. She had a point. 'Is that the end of it?' I nodded. 'Well, thanks be to God.'

I returned gratefully to my desk and to the House girls, who smiled very kindly and patted me on the back as I flopped into my seat. I'd let them down badly and their kindness made me feel even more ashamed.

'That is how you use paragraphs, so,' Sister John said. 'Isn't Claire a great example to us all?' Then she smirked as she added, 'Iseult, I think you've a wee fan, there.'

* * *

There was a knock on the classroom door later that afternoon and when Sister John barked, 'Come in,' a small, very nervous-looking girl opened it.

'Head Nun is asking can you please come,' the girl said. 'She's a problem with shutting the window again.'

'Has she, so?' Sister John got up and stabbed a finger at us. 'You'll not make a sound while I'm out, do you hear?' and we all nodded silently, as expected.

Once Sister John had left the room, Iseult sprang to her feet. She snatched Theresa's papers from her desk. 'You think you're so clever,' she said, 'with your "winning story". Everyone knows the head nun only thinks you're special because your mother gives her an extra pork chop on a Saturday. That's why you get the best marks in class.'

'That's not true,' Theresa said, 'and anyhow, you're Sister John's favourite. Everyone knows that.' She tried to grab her story, but Iseult had shoved her desk back on its rails and Theresa was trapped in her chair. Her clumsy hands flapped around as Iseult waved the paper at her, turning it this way and that. Then she held it towards the ceiling, which made Theresa try to hurl herself upwards out of her seat. She looked like a giant toddler, and her face was turning bright red with all the effort. Along with the rest of the class, I couldn't help but laugh, although we laughed quietly so as not to alert Sister John to the situation.

I looked around the room, catching the other girls' eyes. For once they smiled back at me, and I treasured the warm glow of belonging. Then my gaze landed on the faces of the House girls and I realised that not everyone, in fact, was laughing, after all. The House girls looked as if they were horrified at what was going on. I felt a stab of shame, and the cruel smile froze on my lips.

'This is what I think of your composition,' Iseult whispered, and the menace in her voice made me turn away from the House girls and back towards the argument. Iseult's mouth was twisted as though she had a foul taste on her tongue. 'Rubbish!' She spat out the word then held the papers in the air and ripped them into tiny pieces. She scattered them like inky confetti over Theresa's pudding-basin haircut. 'There,' she said, walking calmly to her desk and wiping her hands on her skirt, 'bring those bits back to your mammy and she can put them in her sausages.'

Theresa slid her desk away from her chair and stood up. Her face was still bright red. She fixed her eyes on Iseult. 'It's *your* mother that sweeps the sawdust off the floor and tips the dustpan into her sausage mix. Everyone knows that. That's why no one buys O'Dooley's sausages.'

There were a few gasps at that, and some nervous laughs.

Siobhán put her arm around Iseult. 'That's a lie, Theresa,' Siobhán said. 'No one really believes it. And anyway, Theresa, it was an eyeball Mr Tiernan found in his sausage, not sawdust.'

There were groans from the rest of the class.

'It was not,' Iseult said. She shook off Siobhán's arm and shoved her hard in the chest. 'He did not find an eyeball. It was an eyelid ... a cow's eye*lid*, that's all. I told you not to tell anyone.'

'There,' Theresa shouted, 'it's true. Her mother puts all sorts of rubbish in her sausages. *And* she drops her meat on the floor. Mrs Quinn found hairs on her ham.'

In all this excitement, I'd forgotten my embarrassment at reading aloud, and something Theresa had said earlier had got me thinking. If Iseult really was Sister John's favourite, then maybe Sister would like me too, if I was Iseult's best friend. And from the way Iseult was treating Siobhán, I reckoned I was definitely still in the running for that – and for her tea party as well, though I made a mental note not to eat any of the ham sandwiches her mother offered me.

Theresa was still furious. 'That's why your family butcher's shop is going bust, *Eeee*-zolt.' The name didn't sound pretty at all, the way she said it. 'And it's why our shop has got all your customers. So you can write your composition about that next time, and see if you win then!'

Iseult ran back across the classroom and slapped Theresa hard on her cheek just as Sister John walked into the room. We all scurried to our seats, pretending, for all we were worth, that the argument had never taken place. Only Theresa stayed standing. Her mouth hung open and on her cheek was a scarlet handprint.

'Theresa! What in the name of all that is holy are you doing standing there like some kind of eejit?' When Theresa took a breath to reply the nun added sharply, 'I'll not hear your excuses. Sit down.'

But I knew she'd seen what Iseult had done. She'd been staring at her as she walked back into class. She'd seen the slap. So, it was true. Iseult really was Sister John's favourite, whether there were eyeballs in the O'Dooley's sausages or not.

Chapter 20

I could not wait to get home to tell Granny about Iseult and Theresa's argument. I'd tried to tell Will as we walked up the lane together but he just said I shouldn't spread gossip and went back to studying his atlas.

When I burst into the kitchen, shouting the news that there'd been a fight in class, Granny crossed herself dramatically.

'Sure, what is the world coming to?' she asked and I got the distinct impression she was mocking me, but I'd been practising my reporting all the way home on the bus and I wasn't about to give up that easily.

'She said there were eyelids in the sausages,' I said, breathlessly rounding off my dramatic retelling, 'and eyeballs and sawdust and tails. And all sorts of things.' I'd elaborated, of course, as was my way.

'That's what comes of having rival businesses,' Granny said. 'And those girls are distant cousins, too. They ought to know better.'

'Iseult and Theresa are cousins?' That was news to me. I didn't have any cousins and I'd always longed for one.

'If they're the girls from the two butcher shops in town, then yes. Those families have been arguing for years.'

What a waste to have a cousin, even a very distant one – even one you needed binoculars to see – and not make the most of it.

I took the brush from behind the door and headed for the privy. As I was crossing the yard, I suddenly had a horrible thought. 'Grandma,' I said, going back and tapping the glass of the kitchen window. 'Where do we get *our* sausages?'

Granny lifted her head from preparing vegetables at the sink and saw my worried look. 'From the van, of course. From Fergus the Grocer,' she said, and her lip curled. It was very nearly a smile.

* * *

I almost nodded off on the bus to school. I'd hardly slept, the night before. My mind had been racing with all sorts of thoughts about the adventure Emmet and I had planned for the next day. At breakfast, I'd secretly saved the jam sandwich Granny had given me, and I'd wrapped it carefully in a bit of newspaper so that it wouldn't stick to my cardigan pocket. I knew Buddy wouldn't mind the print. Horses ate grass, after all, and there were all sorts of germs on that. I wanted to give Buddy a feast he'd remember. I was even considering not eating my sandwiches at dinner time. They were fish paste – his favourite – but I doubted I'd be able to resist them. My stomach was rumbling after missing breakfast and I didn't think I'd manage a long walk over the hill if I was half-starved.

My suspicions were right. At dinner time, I wolfed down my sandwiches as quickly as I could, saving my crusts as usual, and once we were dismissed, I ran off to find Emmet. Half way across the schoolyard someone grabbed my arm.

'Claire, wait a minute.' It was Iseult. 'I wanted to have a chat with you.'

'Okay,' I said. I looked around for Siobhán and Dolores but there was no one nearby. I had Iseult all to myself.

'I wanted to say thank you for the wonderful story you wrote about me.' I could feel my heart start to pound. She was about to tell me I'd won her competition. 'I'd love to read it for myself, you know, so I can decide who to invite.'

'Oh,' I said, a little disappointed that I hadn't already earned her birthday tea. I felt in my pocket. The story was squashed in there, along with the one about Buddy, and all the crusts and cores. I handed over the paper and she carefully pinched a corner of it and brushed off the crumbs. 'You can give it back later,' I said. If I wasn't going to find out whether I'd won after all, I hoped she'd wander off to find the other girls. I could hardly disappear behind the toilets in front of her. Sadly, she didn't move.

She unfolded the paper. 'So this is where you put the commas,' she said.

'Yes.' I pointed to them. 'Here, here and here.' I glanced over her shoulder to the hedge, and thought about Emmet waiting there.

'And paragraphs, too.' She held the paper close to her face and studied it. She smiled at me again. 'I've always wanted a friend who was good at stories.'

'Have you?'

'Yes.' She narrowed her eyes and whispered behind her hand. 'My other friends are useless at writing.'

I beamed at her. I knew what she was about to say. She was going to tell me that I was the one she'd chosen to go to tea. She'd realised, at long last, what I'd known since the day I first saw her – we would be special friends. Maybe she'd let me play with her ringlets. I could wind them around my fingers, like Siobhán did.

'Do you want to come with me and talk about stories?' she asked. And she took my hand, and I let her lead me over to the low wall outside our classroom, and we sat down there together. All my excitement about Emmet and Buddy disappeared at once.

'So,' she said, 'how do you know where to put the commas?'

'Well,' I began, trying to recall Will's exact words, 'you put them where you need a little rest.'

'And paragraphs?' Our white socks grazed each other as we swung our legs in time.

'You put those where you need a big one.'

'Show me the commas again.'

I held up the paper. 'Here,' I said, pointing.

'So they're a little rest.' She smiled. 'Read your story and show me what you mean.'

I read it to her and somehow the words no longer seemed foolish. All my embarrassment had magically disappeared. I read happily as our legs swung together.

She put her hand on my shoulder. 'Can I bring your composition home? I want to show my mother.'

'Of course,' I said. I handed it to her proudly. I liked the thought of her mother reading it. 'Have you decided yet?'

'Decided?'

'About who's won your competition.' But even as I said the words, I was pretty certain I didn't need to ask.

'Oh, yes. My birthday.' She folded my composition and tucked it into her pocket. 'Well, I liked the part about talking to wild animals, and that bit about healing the sick.' She stood up and brushed down the back of her dress. 'But Dolores and Siobhán wrote much better stories than you. They're the ones coming to tea.'

'What?' I stared at her in shock. 'But I thought...'

She waved across the yard and I saw the other girls were waiting there, ready to run over.

'My mother knew your father,' she said, as the others rushed up to us. 'She was on the same school bus as him. Until they sent him away...' A dark cloud was hovering over us and big drops of rain began to fall.

'Sent him away? Do you mean to Cardiff?'

'No, not there.' Iseult laughed.

'Where, then?' Siobhán and Dolores and all of Iseult's other fans had crowded around us. I felt like I was running out of air.

'Don't you know?' Iseult's eyes opened wide.

I shook my head. I should have realised she was never going to choose me as her best friend. How stupid I'd been. I'd even copied the twenty-seventh of September from the blackboard into my English book that morning. Iseult's birthday wasn't until October. Even if she had chosen me, I'd be back in Wales before her birthday. Suddenly, that horrible, foolish feeling I'd had when I'd read my terrible composition to the class, crept over me once more. And now I'd missed my chance to see Buddy – again.

One of the nuns was ringing the bell to tell us to go into the shelter.

Iseult shook my shoulder. 'Your father got put away in the orphanage,' she said, pulling her cardigan over her head to keep her curls dry. I could feel her sock scratching my knee as her leg swung back and fore. 'They sent him there,' Iseult said, in a sing-song voice, and she stood up and put her arm around Siobhán. 'Because he was bad. Very bad. He killed someone.' She looked at her adoring fan club as they swarmed around her and then she announced, 'Claire's father is a murderer.'

* * *

Emmet was still waiting behind the toilet block when I managed to escape from the girls, and slip through the hedge. He was reading my copy of *Black Beauty*.

'You're too late now,' he said, without looking up. 'We'll never get there and back before the bell.'

'I know.'

He lifted his chin at the sound of my voice and he frowned. 'You're like a ghost, so.' He came over to me and touched my arm gently. 'Bad day, is it?'

I nodded and turned my face from his. The kindness in his eyes stung my heart. I'd made him believe something that wasn't true, and for what? I'd given that awful girl a chance to hurt me, and now I'd be going home in a few days. Because of Iseult, I might never get to see Buddy. I leant against the wall. The shower of rain had gone over but I could feel the wet bricks through my cardigan.

'I didn't win the competition,' I said. I couldn't bear to tell him the real reason I was upset.

'Oh.' He closed *Black Beauty* and pressed it against his chest. 'That's a shame. But still, it was a great story you wrote.'

'Theresa won. Her composition was about her mother.'

'Is that so?'

'It's not fair because surely a story that uses imagination is better, and you don't have to use your imagination to write about your mother.'

'No,' Emmet said, 'you're right.' He gave me a sad smile then, before he took something from his pocket and held it up to show me. 'I made this for you. It's the longest one I've ever managed so far. I've stopped biting my thumbnail, special, like.' He wound the daisy chain around the top of my head. 'I crown you winner of the best imagination.'

I couldn't help smiling. 'Thank you.'

'I bet your story was better than them all, but nuns prefer mothers to horses. I bet that's why the other girl won.'

I nodded, forgetting for a moment that it wasn't even Buddy's story I'd entered. 'I hate this school. I'll be glad when I go.'

'When you go?' Emmet stared at me. 'Are you going somewhere?'

I sighed. I hadn't meant to say anything yet. 'My uncle's coming on Saturday. He's taking us home to Wales.'

'Oh.' Emmet slumped against the wall and slid down until he was sitting.

'I nearly drowned my little brother.' Just saying the words shifted something heavy from inside my chest. 'It was an accident.' But Emmet didn't seem to hear.

'You'll be gone next week?' His voice sounded empty.

'Yes, but we've got the rest of this week.' I sat down next to him, even though the ground was still wet.

He nodded. 'Wednesday, Thursday and Friday.' He bit at his thumbnail.

We were quiet for a while, then. The man that usually walked the hill had reached the brow, and I watched him disappear over the top.

Eventually, Emmet lifted the book from his lap. 'Will I read to you? I'm just after finishing the bit about Jerry getting ill.'

'That's a sad chapter, but I like it.' It suited my mood perfectly. 'Go on.'

He found the page and began to read. I loved listening to him. Each word seemed precious and there wasn't one he stumbled over. By the time he got to the end of the chapter, I didn't feel so sad.

'Emmet,' I said, 'shall we act it out?'

A smile spread across his face and I was glad he was in a better mood now, too. 'That's a great idea. The bigger boys put plays on at the orphanage, and I always think I'd like to do that.'

I grinned. I loved play acting and was forever trying to persuade Karen to act out stories with me. She said it was a daft game.

'Come on.' I pulled him by the hand. 'You be Jerry and I'll be Beauty. We're out in the snow on New Year's Eve.'

'He's called Jack when he's at Jerry's,' Emmet reminded me.

'I know, but let's call him Beauty. That's his real name.' We ran to the grass and stamped our feet to keep out the cold of the frosty night.

Emmet rubbed my back. '"There, Beauty,"' he said. '"Sure, those men won't be much longer at their party."'

'"But they've been ages,"' I complained. 'By the way,' I whispered, 'I'm Polly now. "Oh no, poor, poor Jerry. You've caught a chill."' Emmet bent double and coughed as if he were about to die. I helped him lie down on the grass. '"Oh, Jerry, what will we do?"'

'"I'm sorry, Polly,"' he spluttered through his coughs, '"I can't drive the cab anymore. We'll have to sell our Beauty."'

'"Oh, no. Not Beauty. That's terrible!"' I dabbed my eyes dramatically, then I whispered in his ear, 'You be Polly now. Beauty's sleeping in the stable and she comes to say goodbye.' This was my favourite part of the chapter, the bit that brought real tears to my eyes. 'You need to kiss Beauty's neck, and stroke his mane and say you'll miss him.'

If I hadn't known Emmet so well, I might have half expected him to refuse, the way Will always did when he had to do anything that meant him behaving like a girl. But when I lay on the grass, Emmet didn't hesitate, he just knelt down beside me.

'"Oh, Beauty,"' he whispered. His voice was so gentle, I could almost believe it really was Polly talking to me. '"You can't stay here. I'm sorry, so."' He stroked my hair and tears sprang to my eyes. '"You have to go away."' His voice trembled.

He dipped his head towards mine and his breath was warm on

my cheek. "'Don't cry, Beauty,'" he said, softly wiping my tears with his fingertips. "'You're the best horse a person ever had.'" He bent low and I closed my eyes. I felt his dry lips as they brushed my neck. "'I'll never forget you, Beauty. Never.'"

His voice was so kind and he kissed me so gently that, no matter how hard I tried, I couldn't push down the sobs. He smoothed my hair back from my forehead. "'Good boy, Beauty,'" he said. "'Good boy.'" And I cried and cried.

"'I love you, Beauty,'" he whispered. I felt a tear splash onto my cheek. 'I honestly do. And when you're gone,' his voice cracked, 'won't I miss you with all my heart.'

Chapter 21

If Sister John noticed my red eyes after dinner time, she wasn't concerned enough to ask what troubled me. I imagine she guessed that enquiring about my problems would turn out to be more bother than it was worth. We ploughed on that afternoon with *Oliver Twist*, my shoulders shaking with left-over sobs, and the House girls rubbing my back from time to time, silently acknowledging my pain.

* * *

I couldn't concentrate on my compendium of pony stories in bed that night. My mind was too full of problems to be distracted by horses. I wriggled around and tried to get comfortable.

'Stay still,' Will said. 'The bunks will collapse if you carry on like that, and you'll be crushed underneath.'

Brilliant. All I needed was one more worry. 'We only have to sleep on them for a few more nights,' I said. I was looking forward to being at home again, but I worried about missing Emmet. He was the best friend I'd ever had and it would be just my luck if I went home before I got to see Buddy. I hoped we could go to his field the next day.

My brother yawned. 'We still need somewhere to sleep until then.'

'Will?' I said, carefully. He was rarely in a mood to talk these days, and I didn't want to encourage one of his nasty remarks. He was becoming too good at them lately. 'Do you like being here? Will you miss it when we go?'

'Sort of,' he said, 'although I'm looking forward to watching telly again.' And I was amazed he'd answered me. He amazed me again by asking, 'Will *you* miss it here?'

'A bit,' I said, 'but some of the girls at St Brid's are horrible.' I was dreading going back to class the next day after Iseult's announcement about Dad.

'You're friends with Aiden's sister, aren't you?' he said. 'Theresa.'

'Theresa is Aiden's sister?' I sat upright on my bunk – as upright as I could, without getting my hair snagged in the springs under Will's mattress.

'Yes. Didn't you know? You haven't argued with her, have you?'

'Argued?' I said. 'I never talk to her.'

'That's odd. She's always talking about you.'

'Is she? What does she say?'

'She says you're good at writing, and you're funny.'

'She's strange,' I said, resting my head back on my pillow. 'How does she know I'm funny? I've never, ever told her a joke.'

'You'll have Karen again, back home.'

'Suppose so,' I said. Karen's friendship wasn't a patch on Emmet's. 'Do you miss Graham?'

'Graham?' His voice caught ever so slightly. 'What made you think of him?'

'Well, Aiden is like Graham now. I mean, you used to go round to Graham's house every Saturday and now you go round to Aiden's. Who do you like best, Aiden or Graham?'

'I don't have to like anyone best. Aiden is good at Irish and Graham is good at maths and I'm rubbish at both, so that's why I chose them to be my friends.'

'Wayne in my old class said you were friends with Graham because of something else.' I thought very hard but I couldn't remember the word Wayne had used. 'It was something to do with washing powder.'

'Just read your book, Claire.'

'Are you getting bullied at school these days? Do they still take your sandwiches and throw them round the field?'

Will snorted. 'No. I sorted that.'

'How?'

'Keith McGinty tried to punch me and I caught him under his chin with the end of a rolled-up atlas. He bit his tongue nearly in two. He hasn't come near me, since.'

'Gosh,' I said, 'Mother was right when she said geography would be your saviour.'

Will laughed loudly. 'You *can* be funny sometimes, Claire. Theresa was right.'

I wasn't sure whether he was being nice or not, so I was quiet for a while before I brought up the huge problem that was worrying me. 'Will, did Dad really do a terrible thing?' I couldn't bring myself to ask if Dad was a murderer. I couldn't bear to repeat Iseult's cruel word.

I heard Will sigh and close his atlas. 'I shouldn't have said anything to you. It was all wrong, anyway. Brother Dominic told me and he's just a horrible old man who spreads gossip. Everyone hates him and nobody believes a word he says.'

'Really?' This was fantastic news. It all made sense to me, now. Iseult's mother had probably heard the gossip from that awful man in her butcher's shop. People always gossiped in shops, and gossip spread, according to Mother. And when it was gossip about a murder ... well, that would be around town like wildfire. My face glowed with relief. I was absolutely delighted that my biggest worry had finally disappeared.

'Go to sleep now, Claire,' Will said. 'I'm blowing out the candle.'

'No, don't,' I begged. 'I'm not sleepy, and I've only got two pages left before the end of the chapter.'

'Use your torch, then,' he said, and he leant over the side of the bunk and blew out the candle with one big breath. The air in the room became thick with darkness.

How I wished I could have the top bunk just once and blow out the candle from there. If only he'd let me. 'I don't want to waste the batteries on reading,' I said. 'I'm saving them for going to the toilet.'

I went as little as often after dark and I hated taking a candle to the privy. The first time I had, it had blown out even before I'd got half way down the path. Holding a brush and a lit candle was like doing a juggling act, and Granny didn't trust me with the paraffin lamp. She said I'd burn down the toilet with me in it, and probably most of Connemara too.

'Just go to sleep then.'

'I can't. My brain's too awake. Do you remember the name of the washing powder they called you at school?'

'They didn't call me any names at school.'

'They did. I remember asking Mother why, and she said it must be because you were so neat and clean.'

'Go to sleep, Claire.'

'Will you be glad to be back at your old school?' I dropped the pony compendium on the floor in case it tempted me to waste the battery power in my torch. 'Was there really poo in the toilet? I mean, when they stuck your head down it at St Vincent's?'

'Go to sleep.'

I bit my lip and tried to block out the thought of my own head plunged into a toilet bowl. Instead I concentrated on all the names of washing powders I could remember. It hadn't been Daz they'd called him, or Persil. I thought a bit more. 'It was Omo,' I said. 'That's what it was. Wayne used to call you Omo.'

'Shut up, Claire.'

'You do remember, don't you?'

'No.'

'Can I have the top bunk tomorrow night?' I still hadn't had a turn of sleeping there and soon we'd be going home and I'd never have the chance again.

'Will you shut up if I say you can?'

'Okay.' Then just to check I whispered, 'Can I? Please?'

'We'll see,' Will said, like he was the most annoying adult in the world.

191

I kept my head down all morning in class and avoided everyone's eyes. I'd tried to convince Granny over breakfast that I was too poorly for school, but she was having none of it.

'Sure, you look well enough,' she said, peering at me for a second or two, and then she insisted I get ready.

I was glad, really, that she'd forced me to school – I wanted to see Emmet as much as I could before I left for home, and I hoped, with all my heart, to see Buddy. After all, Will had said that Dad hadn't done anything wrong, so I had nothing to be ashamed of. All the same, I kept myself to myself.

But I couldn't avoid Iseult at dinner time. 'I showed my mother your composition,' she said, as she sat next to me. Siobhán and the others took seats around me, too.

'Okay,' I said, my mouth full of sandwich. I was trying to eat as quickly as possible so I could go and find Emmet once we were dismissed. I didn't lift my eyes. I didn't want to look at her and her friends.

Iseult shoved the composition under my nose. The paper was covered in brown splashes that could have been tea stains, or blood from the butcher's shop. 'My mother says your handwriting is the worst she's ever seen. She asked if you were five years of age.' She laughed, and so did the other girls. I ignored them and carried on chewing. I'd heard worse things said about my writing. 'And she thinks you must be wrong in the head, all that rubbish you wrote.' She knocked me hard on the temple with her knuckle. 'Just like your father.'

Sister John was supervising the hall and I glanced up and caught her eye. I guessed she'd seen what Iseult had done but she didn't come over. When she rang the bell to tell us we could leave, I stood quickly and stuffed what was left of my sandwiches in my pockets. Iseult and her friends got up too, smirking at me and laughing behind their hands. I started for the door.

'You forgot your composition,' Iseult called after me, and she held out the ruined paper.

I turned back to her. 'You know, Iseult,' I said with a sigh, 'I made it up. All that lovely stuff I wrote about you? Well, your mother was right – it's rubbish.' I snatched my composition from her hand, scrunched the paper into a ball and dropped it into the bin. 'But at least I've learnt how to use commas, and that's far more than you'll ever manage.'

* * *

There was no sign of Emmet behind the toilet block. I sat myself down on the grass and waited. I hoped he would come. The dinner time before, I'd forgotten to give him the jam sandwich wrapped in newspaper, and it had got pretty squashed when I lay down and pretended to be Beauty. I'd unwrapped the sandwich on the bus to school and saw that the print had magically moved itself onto the bread, but I reckoned Buddy wouldn't mind.

I'd been waiting a long while when a girl's voice called my name. I turned to see Theresa's head poking through the gap in the hedge.

'Are you spying on me?' I asked angrily.

'What are you doing?'

'Hiding from people like you.' I stuck my tongue out at her. It was childish, I knew, but she deserved it.

'Can I come and sit round there with you?'

'No.' I hoped Emmet wouldn't appear while she was looking through the gap, or I'd be in big trouble. 'Go away, and if you tell anyone I'm here, I'll let everyone in class know you pick your nose and eat it.' It was true. I'd seen her doing it behind the cover of her desk lid. Sometimes the back of the class was the best place to sit – you saw so many useful things.

Her cheeks flushed scarlet. 'I won't tell on you, I promise.' And she disappeared.

I rested my head against the wall. It looked like Emmet wasn't coming. It had started to rain so maybe he thought it wasn't the best day for our adventure, after all. It would be slippery running up and over the hill. And then my heart sank – what if he'd somehow found out I'd been commended on my story, and that it was Iseult I'd written about, not him. Maybe the head nun had visited the boys' school and told them about my great punctuation. She might have repeated those awful, sickly things I'd said about that horrible girl. Maybe that's why he hadn't come. I felt so ashamed. Why, oh why hadn't I just written up Emmet and Buddy's story in pen? I pulled my cardigan over my head and hid, miserably, from the weather and the shame.

The rain was getting heavier but I didn't feel like going to the shelter. Iseult and her friends would annoy me. I'd stay where I was and perhaps Emmet would turn up after all. I hoped I wouldn't seem too drenched when the time came for me to sneak out of my hiding place to line up when the bell sounded. I sat and waited. And for once, I wished I could wear that sack from the back of the kitchen door.

* * *

Granny insisted on combing my hair when I got home from school. I complained, of course.

'You've no choice, girl,' she said. 'Just look at the state of you.'

Chance would be a fine thing, as Mother liked to say, but with Granny's lack of mirrors in the cottage, I had no idea what I looked like. I could tell, though, just by feeling my head, that my hair was a tangled mess. The rain plus the rub of my cardigan had created a grand collection of knots. Sister John had taken one look at me after dinner time and had rolled her eyes towards the ceiling. Up there, thankfully, she'd spotted dripping water, and she'd been far too busy fussing with a bucket to worry about my damp head.

I didn't really mind Granny combing my hair, although I didn't tell her. She was far gentler than Mother, and she didn't threaten me with the pudding bowl.

'Do you still like your school?' Granny asked. There was an odd tone to her voice that I couldn't put my finger on. Will was out, so it was just Granny, Louis and me in the cottage. He'd gone to Aiden's for Irish lessons again. I didn't know why he was bothering – we'd be long gone before his Irish exam.

I sipped my cup of milk. 'We'll be going home soon,' I said, 'so it doesn't matter if I like my school here or not.' My heart leapt whenever I thought of going home, and then I would suddenly feel sad. I hated the thought of not saying goodbye to Emmet, but I had two more chances to see him before I left. I crossed my fingers and made a wish that he'd be behind the toilet block the next day. 'I'm looking forward to being back home with Dad in Cardiff.'

'Mmm,' Granny said. She was definitely in a strange mood. 'But still, you're happy enough at St Brid's. And Will seems settled at St Vince's.'

I nodded. 'He doesn't mind it there so much now.'

'Sure, that's a good thing,' Granny said. ''Tis, 'tis.' And she carried on combing my hair.

I thought of the daisy chain Emmet had put like a crown on my head. I was keeping it safe in my pony compendium. I thought of a goodbye gift for him. I would write up the story about Buddy in pen, and I'd illustrate it too – he'd love that. And if he'd heard from Head Nun that I'd entered the story about Iseult into the competition instead of his, he might forgive me. I hoped he would.

Louis was crying softly under the table, so Granny put down the comb and picked him up. She rocked him gently. 'Sure, you're not yet over your fright in the water.'

Guilt rushed to my throat at the thought of Louis and the chicken wire. I needed a good distraction, so I fetched my notebook and the pen and ink I'd smuggled from Will's pencil case. I'd do my best to make Emmet's gift as perfect as could be.

It was the very least he deserved.

Chapter 22

I can recall, with absolute clarity, my delight and relief when I sneaked behind the toilet block the next day, to see Emmet waiting there for me. His friendship had become the centre of my young life, even though we'd known each other only a matter of weeks. But then, time seemed to pass far more slowly in childhood, and a week for a ten-year-old could stretch until eternity.

* * *

'You've come,' I said, sitting down next to him. 'I was worried when you weren't here yesterday. Was it the rain? It's lovely today, isn't it?'

He was staring out across the hill. 'It is,' he said. 'It's great to see the sun.' His voice was strange, and when he turned his face to me, I gasped.

'What on earth have you done, Emmet?' One side of his lip was cut and bruised, and his cheek was horribly swollen.

His eyes were full of tears. 'Oh, Claire,' he blurted, and the tears streamed down his face.

'What is it? What's happened?'

He put his head in his hands. 'I lost it.'

'What do you mean?'

'Your book.' He couldn't bear to look at me. '*Black Beauty*.'

I gasped. 'You lost *Black Beauty*?'

'I'm so sorry, Claire.'

'How?' I shouted. 'How could you lose it?'

'I just...'

'I lent you my favourite book and you lost it?' I thumped his shoulder hard, then I curled myself into a ball and lay there, my arms covering my head.

'I didn't know how to tell you.' I felt him touch my back. 'That's why I stayed away yesterday. I'm sorry. I really am.'

'Go away,' I mumbled into the grass. 'I should never have lent it to you.' How could I have been daft enough to think he'd care about my book as much as I did? 'I hate you,' I told him. 'I loved that book. It was my favourite. I shouldn't have trusted you.'

'I know, but Claire—' He bent over me just as I lifted my arm to shoo him away and the back of my hand caught his face. He gasped and clutched his mouth. Blood oozed between his fingers.

'Oh, Emmet,' I said. I got to my knees quickly. 'Are you all right? What have I done?'

He took his hand from his mouth and studied the blood. 'It's just the cut on my lip. It's opened up again.'

I sighed. 'I'm sorry. I didn't mean to hit you.'

He dabbed his mouth with a corner of his jumper. 'It'll stop in a minute.'

I slumped onto the grass again. 'How did you hurt your lip in the first place?'

He lay down next to me and sighed. 'A boy at the orphanage – Brendan, he's big, so. The biggest boy in the place and a bully. He was sweeping the yard. He had a fire going there, burning leaves, he was. He saw me walking up to the gates. I was reading your book.' His lips trembled. 'I should have put it away quicker, but it was a good bit, you know. And he—' Emmet sniffed and wiped his nose on his sleeve. 'I tried to stop him but he punched me and he took *Black Beauty*. I tried to fight him but he—' His voice broke into a sob.

'It's okay.' I wrapped an arm around him and he leant his head against my shoulder.

'It was your mother's book, Claire.'

'I don't care about it being Mother's book, but I will miss it. It's not really lost after all though, is it? You can tell someone at the orphanage, and they'll make that bully give it back.'

I heard him take a deep breath.

'They will, won't they? Brendan won't be allowed to keep it, will he?'

Emmet sighed. 'No.'

'There we are, then. Tell the Brothers. But you'll have to tell them tonight because you'll need to bring it tomorrow. It's my last day in school.'

Emmet was quiet for a long while. 'I'll try my best,' he said at last, then he sighed. 'I'd almost read to the end.'

'Well, you can read the last bit tonight when you get it back, can't you?' I emptied my pockets onto his lap. I knew he'd feel better when he saw what I'd brought for Buddy. 'I've got fish paste crusts from the other day,' I said. They'd been quite whiffy by this morning and I even heard the House girls asking each other what the strange smell was. I thought it was a bit rich coming from them, with their weird beeswax smell. 'Egg sandwich crusts, and a whole jam sandwich in the newspaper.'

'Jam, did you say?' My plan had worked – Emmet had perked up at the sight of Buddy's treats and I was glad. He pushed the crusts into his pockets and unwrapped the black and white sandwich. 'Ah now, I know for a fact Buddy can't eat jam.' My face must have been the picture of disappointment because he said, 'But don't I love it? Shame for it to go to waste. And I don't mind a bit of print either. Would you mind, now, if I ate it?'

Why anyone, other than a horse, would want to eat a stale sandwich covered in newspaper print, was beyond me, but I said, 'If you really want to. It was my breakfast from the day before yesterday.' I squirmed as he took a huge bite.

'Grand,' Emmet said, through a mouthful of bread. 'Grand.' He took another big bite. 'It's a shame we didn't go and see Buddy on Tuesday. He was looking forward to meeting you.'

'I really want to see him.'

'I could bring you today,' Emmet said.

I sat up straight. 'Could you?'

'If we leave now and we're fierce fast.' He stuffed the last of the sandwich into his mouth and shoved all the crusts into his pockets.

'But it's Thursday,' I said. 'He'll be in a field we can't get to.'

Emmet frowned and then he smiled. 'Ah no, not this Thursday. He didn't get moved this Thursday.'

'Brilliant.' I jumped up. 'Let's go.' I grabbed his hand – I didn't even care that it was sticky with jam – and we ran for all we were worth, away from school, away from Iseult, away from gossip and murder and bullies, towards the hill, towards the fields.

Towards Buddy.

* * *

The first part of our journey was easy. We laughed all the way. The hill wasn't very high and we soon managed to get up and over it. The person we saw sometimes walking their dog was nowhere around, so it was just us and the sheep. We ran down the other side of the hill holding hands tightly and screaming at the top of our voices. I'd never seen Emmet so lively – just seeing his happiness made me happy too – and as I was busy watching him and grinning for all I was worth, I caught my foot in a dip and tripped over, pulling him down with me. We rolled and rolled until we finally came to a stop. We lay on the springy grass, laughing 'til we had no breath left.

'Bog hole,' Emmet managed eventually. 'Is your foot hurt?'

I circled my ankle this way and that. 'No, it's fine.'

'I lost my boot,' he said, wiggling his naked toes at me. His foot was filthy.

I stretched out and grabbed his boot. It had landed next to me. 'Where's your sock?'

'Looks like I lost that too.'

'Well, it's not in your boot.'

'It'll be under my bed, or someone else's.'

I studied his boot. Part of the sole had come loose. 'Oh no, look.' I held it up to show him.

'Sure, it's always doing that.' He flicked the sole and made it flap, then grabbed it from me and waved it in my face. 'How'ya?' he said in a squeaky voice, turning the sole into a flapping tongue.

I rolled on the grass, laughing and holding my sides, and so he did it some more. Then he slipped his foot back into the broken boot and took an elastic band from his pocket. He stretched the band tightly around it. 'There,' he said, 'that'll be grand 'til I get at the glue in the workshop.'

He'd lifted his foot onto his knee nearest me and I could see the state the sole of his boot was in. 'You've got a big hole there,' I said. I couldn't resist tickling him through it. The skin was grubby but it felt soft.

'Get off.' He swiped my hand away. It was a half-hearted swipe so I knew he liked it, really. 'Better get going or we won't have time to find Buddy.'

We got up and brushed ourselves down. 'Which way now?' I asked.

'This way,' Emmet said, pulling my hand. 'He's the other side of those trees over there.'

We had to pass a farmhouse first. It seemed deserted, apart from a big dog chained up by the front door. It began barking viciously as soon as it saw us.

'Good doggy, doggy,' Emmet called to it. 'Don't worry, we're not going to rob your house.' But the dog only barked harder.

'Don't talk to it,' I pleaded. 'You're just making it more angry.' I was remembering being chased by Tracey's Alsatian in the park in Cardiff. I'd had to climb to the top of the slide and wait to be rescued.

'He can't do anything to us,' Emmet said. 'He's got that big chain on.'

Chain or not, I was glad when we were past the farm and the dog stopped its barking.

'How much further is it?' I was beginning to worry we wouldn't get to school in time for afternoon classes, and I didn't like the thought of having to pass that dog again on the way back. Maybe then he'd be running free.

'Just through the trees,' Emmet said.

I followed him into the little wood. There were only a few thin trees and I could see through to the other side. 'Where's Buddy? I can't see him in the field there.'

'You wouldn't see him from here,' Emmet said. 'We've got to go right through.' We came to a fence made of barbed wire and thick wooden posts. 'We need to get over this,' he said.

'How?' The wire was up to my middle and rusty, and there didn't seem to be a way to cross it. 'How do you usually get over it?'

'Ah, Buddy isn't normally on that side of the fence,' Emmet said.

'Oh.' I was disappointed at how difficult our adventure was becoming. Surely, we'd never get back to school before the bell. I was certain it would start ringing any minute. I couldn't bear to think about what might happen when Sister John realised I wasn't in class. I wished I'd asked for a Timex for Christmas now, like my brother had. Back then, I'd thought Mousetrap was a much better present because who wanted a stuffy old watch?

'Will I help you over here?' Emmet asked. He'd found a bendy bit in the barbed wire and was holding it down with a stick.

I stepped onto a big smooth rock next to the fence and took his hand. I threw my leg over the wire and winced as it snagged my sock, along with the skin underneath.

'No. Put your foot on it and jump,' he said. I pulled my leg back, carefully, this time, and placed my foot where he showed me. Then I launched myself over, putting my hands out to save myself from landing face first in a muddy puddle.

'Out the way now,' he said, getting ready to jump. He stood on the rock, pressed down hard on the wire with one foot and leapt clear over the fence. He landed on both feet in a patch of long grass.

'Ah, feck.' He groaned loudly and fell back on the ground, clutching his foot.

'What is it? What have you done?'

'It's the wire. It's gone into my foot.'

I could see a nest of tangled barbed wire hidden in the grass. 'Are you hurt?'

He held up a hand. It was covered in blood.

I thought I might be sick. I didn't want to see where the blood was coming from but I couldn't stop myself looking. I went over to him and crouched down. I could see the hole in the sole of his boot and the skin through it. A long, rusty piece of wire had gone in through the hole and then into his foot.

'That's horrible,' I stammered.

He gulped. 'That's not the half of it.' He lifted his hand and showed me. The elastic band holding the boot together had snapped and the leather was bent up. I could see the top of his foot. An inch of wire was sticking out of it, and one of the barbs had gone right the way through his foot. The sight of it brought vomit into my mouth, and I turned away and spat it out quickly.

'God, Emmet,' I managed to say, 'that's horrible.' I rubbed my lips hard to try and get rid of the taste. 'What are we going to do? How will we get back to school?' I could imagine the bell ringing in the yard now. I could clearly hear Sister John's voice saying, 'And where is Claire O'Connell, may I ask?'

Emmet's face had gone very pale.

'Can you walk? Try to get up.' I thought I'd help him by grabbing his arm.

He winced. 'Steady, Claire. It doesn't matter if I can stand, I won't be able to walk.' And with that, he was sick too – bread and jam, all over my shoes.

I started to cry. I'd been afraid that would happen, ever since I'd seen the blood. I wasn't good with blood, and I certainly wasn't good with feet stabbed through with wire.

Emmet clutched his foot hard again but the blood was trickling between his fingers, and no matter how much he pressed around the wire, it just wouldn't stop.

'You could give it a tug,' I suggested, 'just pull it out.' But if he did, I certainly wouldn't want to watch. My stomach lurched again.

'I can't,' he said. 'I'd yank that barbed bit back through my foot.' He sighed.

'I'll have to go for help, then,' I said, wiping his sick from my shoes on a clump of grass. The circles of sock showing through the cutouts in the leather had turned yellowy red and the top of my feet felt sticky.

'There was that farm back there,' Emmet said. 'It wasn't too far away.'

'The one with the dog?' I didn't want to go to the one with the dog. 'Isn't there another farm in the other direction?'

'No, they're all far away.' He sounded tired. 'Go to the one we passed.'

But I didn't want to go back the way we'd come. I peered through the trees ahead of us, in search of some other farmhouse he might have forgotten about. Suddenly I had a brilliant idea. 'I could ride Buddy to the orphanage. We'll be really fast.' I imagined myself galloping across the hills on a mission, just like Ricky and Champion.

'Ah Jaysus, Claire.' Emmet rubbed his head with the hand that wasn't holding his foot. 'You can't ride Buddy.' He looked up at me and his eyes were huge, with lines all around them. They made him look like an old man. He suddenly seemed exhausted. 'It's a long story and I won't be telling it you now. Could you just go back to that farm and get help, please?'

'Okay,' I said. The thought of the farm and its vicious dog terrified me, but Emmet's foot was in a terrible way. I had to go. I had to be brave like him. 'But how will I get over the fence?'

Emmet pointed to his left. 'Look. There's a big gap there.' He shook his head. 'We didn't need to climb it after all.'

I sighed. Suddenly our adventure seemed the worst idea in the world. 'I'll be as fast as I can,' I told him.

He reached up suddenly and grabbed my hand. 'You will come back, Claire, won't you?'

'Of course I will,' I promised. I let go of his hand and ran off towards the farm and the vicious child-eating dog. And I didn't turn, but just raised my thumb as I heard Emmet call weakly after me, 'Tell them to bring some wire cutters.'

Chapter 23

It wasn't as far as I'd thought, back to the farmhouse. I could see it as soon as I left the cover of the trees. There was a woman in the garden, pegging washing on the line. I ran even faster.

'Hello!' I shouted, although I knew she was too far away to hear. 'Hello! Hello!'

The dog heard me, though, and it began barking. It sounded far more vicious now that Emmet wasn't with me, but I couldn't let myself be frightened. There was someone here who could help and I had to get to her.

I rounded the edge of the yard wall, and skidded to a halt at the low gate. The dog had stopped barking and now it turned its head and stared at me calmly. It was still chained up. There was an iron ring in the concrete path near the front door, and its chain was attached to that.

'Good dog,' I murmured. Maybe it would be okay, after all. Maybe it was friendly. I put my hand on the gate's latch and tried to work out how to open it. It was very rusty and the latch didn't want to move. I rattled the gate impatiently. I needed to get to the woman around the back of the house.

The dog launched itself at me, its chain scurrying behind it like an angry snake across the cobbled yard. I screamed and tried to go backwards but my feet wouldn't budge, and the dog hurtled towards me. It was huge and black, and the furious look in its eyes reminded me of the angry Alsatian as it circled the slide. I needed to get away, fast, but my feet seemed stuck to the path.

I watched in shock as the dog flung itself at the gate. Its open mouth came rushing towards my face and at last my body moved. My arms flew up to cover my head and I curled into a ball on the ground, waiting for the dog to bite me, to rip into my skin and tear my body to pieces.

But it didn't. It was stopped in mid-air by its chain. With a disappointed yelp, it was yanked to a halt and it landed with a thud on the other side of the gate.

'Dog!' I heard a voice call. 'Come here.' It was the woman who'd been pegging out washing. She pulled the dog to her, reeling in the chain and looping it over a hook. The sad, hopeless expression the dog now had in its eyes reminded me of how Louis looked, tied up on his leash under the table.

'I hope he wasn't after scaring you. He's a nasty one, so.' The woman gave the dog a bit of a kick in the ribs and then rubbed her boot on its back more kindly before looking at me. 'Now, what is it you're wanting?'

* * *

She kept apologising all the way across the field. 'If only himself was here, he'd know what to do.' Her voice was breathless from talking so much, even though we'd walked only half way to the trees. 'I'm no good with this sort of thing. Not with humans, to be sure. Now if it was a sheep, I'd be grand. Anything to do with sheep. But not people. Now if himself was here...'

'Himself' was in hospital. He had a problem with his prostate – whatever that was, but, as she said, I didn't need to know. She'd found the wire cutters in her husband's tool box but she wasn't sure she'd be able to do anything with them. She'd brought a first-aid box too. 'I told him all that barbed wire needed clearing up. I thought the sheep might catch in it, not a boy. If it was a sheep now, I'd be right, wire cutters and all. But a child, that's another matter.' And on she went.

Emmet seemed to have shrunk, by the time we reached him.

'Oh, the poor scrap,' the woman muttered.

He did look sad, hunched over his injured foot.

I knelt down next to him. 'The lady's got cutters.'

Emmet looked up at the woman. 'Thank you,' he said.

The woman flinched when she saw his face. 'Would you look at that lip?' she said. 'You knocked yourself badly when you fell, so you did.'

I shook my head. 'He'd already hurt his face. Let her see the problem, Emmet.'

He took the hand that had been stopping the flow of blood away from his foot and showed her what had happened.

The colour drained from her cheeks but she managed a small smile and said, kindly enough, 'Now, isn't that a grand mess you've got yourself into? What can we do for it?' She rummaged for inspiration in the first-aid box she'd brought.

'You need to cut the wire,' Emmet said, when she hadn't found anything.

'Oh, I don't know if that's the best thing...' She bit her lip.

'It is, so,' Emmet said. 'Cut the wire under my foot, please. Then I can walk back to school.'

'Well,' the woman said, and I could see she was thinking about sheep and what she'd do if it was one of them caught on barbed wire. 'I suppose it does make sense, right enough.' She shuddered. 'Sure, we can't pull the wire out, what with the barbs above and below.' She took the cutter from her apron pocket and knelt down. 'Hold it still.' She reached out quickly and clipped the wire hard. 'There now,' she said.

Emmet and I stared at her in shock. She had certainly cut the wire but she'd left at least a foot of it still attached to Emmet.

'Right so,' she said, standing up and putting the cutters back in her pocket. She handed Emmet some cotton wool from the first-aid box.

'Hold on a minute,' he said. 'I won't be walking anywhere like this.'

The woman shook her head. 'Lookit,' her face was very pale. 'I can't cut it any closer. Don't be asking me to or I'll faint, so I will.'

Emmet sighed and looked up at me. 'What am I to do, Claire?'

'Give me the cutters,' I told the woman, and she only hesitated for a second before she pulled them from her pocket and held them out to me. She turned her face away.

I snatched them from her. 'Hold the wire still,' I told Emmet. 'Pinch it right next to your skin.'

I placed the clipper part as close to Emmet's fingers as I dared. 'Are you ready?' He nodded and I took a deep breath. I closed my eyes and squeezed the handles together as hard as I could. I felt the wire snap.

'Argh, feckin' hell!'

'Sorry, sorry,' I cried, dropping the cutters. I suddenly felt very shaky. 'Have I made it worse?'

Emmet fell onto his back, and let out a huge sigh. 'No,' he said. 'You were brilliant.' He managed a weak smile as he sat up and studied his foot. 'It's just that I could feel the wire moving in me a bit.' He eased off his boot very carefully.

'If you're right now,' the woman said, 'I'll be leaving you to it. I just remembered, I've a ham on the stove. The whole house will be a cinder by the time I get back.' She pulled another big lump of cotton wool from the roll she'd brought and gave it to me. The feel of it between my fingers set my teeth on edge. 'In case the bleeding gets worse when he's walking,' she said. She brushed off her knees and dashed away around the fence.

I grabbed Emmet's arm. 'Come on, we've got to get back to school. Sister John will kill me.'

He stood up slowly, but when he tried to put some weight on his heel, he collapsed to the ground again. 'I can't,' he said. 'I think there's a barbed bit inside my foot.'

I yanked at his arm. 'You've got to walk, Emmet.' I was terrified about the exploding nun waiting for me if I didn't get back to school as soon as possible.

'It's no good, Claire,' he said. 'Go on your own. You'll be leathered if you don't get back. I'm stuck here.' He covered his face with his hands, and his shoulders started to shake.

'I'm not going without you,' I said. It was useless to waste time trying to persuade him to move. He was in pain, I knew. 'Wait,' I yelled after the woman. 'Please, wait. We still need your help.'

She didn't seem to hear so I ran after her. 'Please,' I shouted. 'Please stop!'

At last the woman turned around. 'What is it? Don't be asking me to carry him now, scrap of a thing or not. I've a bad back.'

'Have you got a car?' I asked.

'I've the old one in the shed, but it doesn't always start.'

'Can you come and get us in it?' I was wriggling the way I did when I felt I might wet myself. 'He can't walk to school after all, and if we don't leave soon, I might miss my bus. Can you drive us? Please?'

The woman rubbed the back of her neck and sighed. I could tell she didn't want to help. What she really wanted was to be rid of us. 'I'll do my best to get it going,' she said, 'but I'm not promising anything. If it starts, I'll bring it up there and to that gate.' She bit her lip. 'Now, that ham.' And she hurried off.

* * *

We waited and waited for her to bring the car. I'd given up all hope of getting back in time to avoid being killed by Sister John. I knew there was no escaping that now.

'Is it still hurting?'

Emmet lifted the cotton wool from the top of his foot and we both studied the rusty bit of wire sticking out of his skin. I'd got used to the way it looked and it didn't make me feel sick anymore.

'It doesn't hurt any worse than a flogging.'

My stomach rumbled. It was quite a while since I'd eaten my sandwiches, and now most of them were lying in watery bits in the grass. 'You said you had a story.' I slipped a crust from Emmet's pocket and began nibbling on it. 'You know, when I told you I'd ride Buddy to find help. You said the story was too long.' I found another crust and handed it to Emmet. 'You might as well tell me now.'

He took a small bite of the bread then put the rest back in his pocket. 'It's not a good story.'

'I want to hear it.'

'Claire.' He turned his sad eyes to me.

'Go on,' I said. 'Tell me.'

He sighed. 'I don't have a horse.'

'You don't?'

He shook his head. 'Not a real one. In the next field, there's a tree that came down in the hurricane, a good few years ago now.' He pointed. 'Go and see.'

'Why?' I asked. He wasn't making any sense and I wondered if it was because he was running out of blood. I knew it happened when you lost too much – I'd seen it in the Westerns, when cowboys started rambling before they passed out.

But I got to my feet anyway and went to the gap in the trees. From there, I could see the fallen tree. It was in the middle of the next field and the trunk was curved. The end of it reared up like the head and neck of a horse, and thin branches stuck out at all angles, like a flowing mane. Thicker branches curled away on the ground, like legs. I understood now. That was Buddy. I walked slowly back to Emmet.

'I can see that stump from the window next to my bed,' he said, as I sat down beside him again, 'in the dormitory.' He found more crusts in his pocket and we shared them between us.

'So I didn't need to save these every day after all,' I said.

Emmet chewed thoughtfully. 'In a way they *were* for Buddy. I was giving them to Francis because he was carving a model of Buddy for me. Well, I was giving some of them to him.' He glanced at me guiltily. 'Francis has nearly finished it now. Just one more apple core, he says.'

'An apple core? Is he making the model out of apple cores?'

Emmet gave a short laugh and popped a chunk of bread into his mouth. 'No. He's making it out of a piece of scrap wood from the carpentry workshop.' He turned his face towards the field where the fallen tree was. 'Francis eats the cores.'

I couldn't imagine why anybody would want to eat a core. It was only pips and those horrible bits that got stuck in your teeth. But I rummaged in my cardigan pocket and took out the one I'd saved from dinner. I felt ashamed that I'd chewed it so thoroughly. There wasn't a scrap of proper apple left on it. 'Here.' I held it out to Emmet. 'Will you bring the model to school to show me tomorrow?'

'Sure, I will,' he said, taking the core and studying it. He held it under his nose and breathed in deeply. 'It smells sweet.'

I nodded. 'It was.' So Buddy wasn't real. I suddenly felt exhausted. I wasn't worried anymore about Sister John or even about missing the bus home. I was too tired to care. 'What about your mother?' I asked. 'Is she really in New York?'

He plucked a blade of grass and put it between his teeth. His fingers were covered in dried blood. 'My mother's dead. At least, I think she is. I never knew her.'

I thought about my own mother. She was probably sipping lemonade and eating endless ice creams on a beach in Spain. It would be very odd to have a dead mother.

Emmet's thin legs poked from his school shorts and the red welts on his knees stood out angrily. 'How did you really get these, Emmet?' I rubbed my finger gently over the thick lumps of skin. 'You said you got them when Buddy dragged you.'

'Would you believe me if I said it was from saying Hail Marys?' He raised an eyebrow. 'And walking up and down the aisle in church on my knees?'

'Really?' I knew people actually did that. It was called 'doing penance'. Sister John was always going on about it. It sounded like a hideous thing to me, being made to crawl in front of everybody in church. 'And it hurt your knees?'

'No.' He managed a small smile, before the pain in his foot made

211

him wince. 'Haven't I been scrubbing floors every night since I was four? That's why my knees are ruined.' He rested his chin on my shoulder. 'Claire,' he said quietly, 'I'm sorry I didn't tell you the truth.'

'About doing penance? Or do you mean about Buddy and your mother?'

'All those, yes. I'm sorry.' He swallowed hard. 'But about *Black Beauty*, too.'

'*Black Beauty*? What do you mean?'

'I said I'd try to get it back.' He bit his lip. 'But I can't.'

'What?' I jumped to my feet. I just had to have my book back. I needed to take it home to Wales.

He struggled to lift himself so he could grab my hand. 'Brendan took it from me—'

'You already told me that.' I yanked my fingers away from his. 'Make him give it back.'

'I can't.' He slumped back onto the grass, his eyes full of tears. I glared at him and he buried his face in his hands. 'He burnt it, Claire. He threw it on the fire. That wonderful book. All those words about Beauty. The pictures—' His voice broke into a sob. 'He let it all burn.'

My hands flew to my mouth. My beautiful book thrown onto a fire. I imagined it burning, the flames licking the gold letters on the cover, and raging through its pages.

'I'm sorry, Claire,' I heard him call after me as I ran. I tore through the wood and into the field, and when I came to the fallen tree, I flung myself at it. I beat the trunk with my fists, and I kicked and kicked at it. I didn't stop until the pain in my hands and feet became too much. 'I hate you, Emmet,' I yelled. 'I hate you!' I dropped to my knees and I cried for Beauty. I cried because Buddy wasn't real, and I sobbed and sobbed, until finally I realised my tears weren't just for those lost things, but for Emmet and his injured foot too.

Slowly, I walked back to where I'd left him. He looked as if his heart was broken. Tears made pale trails through the mud and the blood smeared on his cheeks, and his eyes were huge and sad. I sat down next to him, my shoulder pressed against his. 'It's okay,' I whispered. 'I've got another pony book.'

He leant heavily against me, and I felt the sobs as they rattled inside his chest. 'But *Black Beauty* ... it was your mother's, Claire. Your *mother's*.'

It seemed cruel to tell him how little I cared about that fact, when his own mother was dead. 'Never mind,' I said. 'It wasn't your fault. I know you loved Beauty as much as I did.' I wiped his face with my lace hanky. Seeing his bruised cheek, along with his cut lip, made tears prickle my eyes again. 'I don't care about the book – honest, Emmet. Just please don't cry anymore.'

He rested his head on my shoulder. 'I'm sorry,' he whispered. He pointed to his foot. 'For that, and for your book. I should never have tried to be your friend.' He wiped his nose on his sleeve. 'They're right in school. They say orphans shouldn't mix with the others.'

'That's rubbish,' I said. 'I'm glad you wanted to be my friend. I've never had a friend like you, before. Not ever.'

'I've never had one like you, Claire. You're my best friend.'

'And you're my best friend, Emmet,' I told him. 'I'm glad I met you, even if Brendan did burn our book. And even when I'm back in Wales, we'll always be friends, no matter what they say in school. Their rules are stupid.'

He gave me a small smile, then. 'Thank you.'

'Shall I tell you how *Black Beauty* ends? It's a happy ending.'

He nodded. 'Sure, aren't those always the best.'

So I told him about how Beauty was rescued from a terrible life and how he found a happy home with two old ladies. 'Their groom recognised him because he used to work in the stables where Beauty was born,' I said. 'And he told him, "I know you – you're Black Beauty!" So he got his real name back at the end.'

'He was Black Beauty again?' Emmet blinked at me. He sighed. 'Do you think I'll get my real name back one day?'

'I think the name you chose is a brilliant one,' I said. 'And I don't care what the Brothers call you, you'll always be Emmet to me.'

He squeezed my hand. 'Sing something in your language,' he said. 'I'd like to hear some Welsh.'

The sun had gone in and he was shivering, so I took off my cardigan and draped it around his shoulders. I tied the sleeves across his chest. 'I can sing you Louis's favourite song,' I said, 'the one about two children riding a horse over the mountain.'

'Ah, isn't that a grand choice,' he said, managing a smile, 'under the circumstances.'

I began singing softly, '*Gee ceffyl bach yn cario ni'n dau, dros y mynydd i hela cnau...*' and I felt my anger melt away.

Emmet closed his eyes as I sang, and when I came to the end he whispered, 'Carry on,' so I started all over again. And we sat like that for a long, long time.

Chapter 24

The breeze had turned cold, and without my cardigan, I began to shiver. I snuggled into Emmet's side to steal some of his warmth, but he was even colder than me.

'Is she after coming back?' he asked, half waking from the nap he'd drifted into.

'Not yet.' The blood had stopped seeping into the lump of cotton wool covering the top of his foot. I carefully checked the one covering his sole, and found that the same. 'Do you think she'll ever come back? Maybe I should go and find someone else.'

'Don't go,' Emmet said. His eyelids fluttered as he tried to beg me. 'Stay here.'

I rubbed his arm. 'Okay. We'll wait a bit longer.' I didn't like the thought of running back to school and announcing what had happened. I imagined Iseult laughing at me as Sister John took her revenge. They were nothing but bullies.

'I'm sorry Brendan hit you because of Beauty.'

He smiled weakly. 'Didn't I wallop him back, though. Fierce hard. He's got a grand shiner, so.'

'That was really brave of you.' I was pleased Emmet had paid him back for being such a bully. 'Does your cheek hurt a lot?' I touched it gently.

'Brendan didn't do that,' Emmet said. 'One of the Brothers hit my cheek ... because of my bed.'

'Your bed?'

He turned his face away from mine and said quietly, 'I wet it. And I cried when I got ... leathered for it. They don't like you ... crying.'

'Had you been picking dandelions? Is that why you wet the bed?'

He shook his head.

'What about your arm, the one you told me you broke when you fell from Buddy?'

'Brother Joshua ... he threw me down the stairs.' He seemed to be taking lots of breaths.

'He threw you down the stairs? Why?'

'Does he ... need a reason?'

'But what happened when you went to hospital? You must have had an X-ray and a plaster cast.' I was remembering the things I'd been jealous of when Will had broken his wrist. 'Didn't Brother Joshua get into trouble then?'

Emmet sighed. 'The doctor asked me ... how I broke my arm ... and I told him.'

'The truth? You told him the truth?'

'Yes... But nothing happened. I was sent back ... to the orphanage and got a ... beating ... for not lying for the Brothers... They beat you for ... everything.'

'Do they?'

'And worse.'

'What's worse than getting beaten?'

He bent over his injured foot and studied it. 'Sometimes they come for you ... in the night.' His voice was a whisper. 'If you're no one ... if you're a number, like me ... if you've no family ... to tell...' The words caught in his throat.

'What do you mean? What do they do?'

Out on the lane, we could hear an engine rattling. 'That'll be her,' Emmet said, shaking off my questions. 'Help me up, will you?'

He winced as I pulled him upright. 'Can you stand a bit on your bad foot now?'

He tried but failed. 'Maybe you and that woman ... can help me to the car...' He put his arm around my neck as we waited for her to arrive. 'I'm sorry ... I scammed you, Claire,' he said. 'You know ... saying all that ... about Buddy.' Then he looked me in the eyes and smiled. 'But wasn't he great? They were brilliant, weren't they ... our dinner times ... in the sun?'

I nodded. How I wished we were back at school now, waiting for the bells to ring to call us into class.

'Forget what ... I told you,' he said.

He was resting his weight against me. He seemed to weigh nothing. 'About what?'

'Scrubbing floors ... breaking my arm ... and all the rest of that stuff.' He gave my shoulder a squeeze. 'I was messing with you.'

'Were you?' I turned to him and studied his face. It seemed full of pain. 'Were you making it up about being best friends, too?'

He rubbed his eye with his fist. His hand was covered in dried blood. 'No, Claire,' he said. 'That one's the truth.'

* * *

When I first climbed into the woman's car, I didn't think I'd survive the smell. 'I'll drop you with the Brothers first,' she said to Emmet, shouting above the rattle of the engine. She turned to me, 'Then we'll have time enough to get you back, before the school bus leaves.'

The reek of cow poo was overwhelming, even with the windows open. Emmet was shivering on the back seat, lying among bits of hay and old newspapers. When we'd first got into the car, the woman had given me a long strip of fresh cotton wool. 'I can't be looking at that wire,' she'd whispered to me. 'The way it's sticking out of his skin makes me feel sick.'

The feel of the cotton wool had the same effect on me, but I didn't let her know. I hated touching it, and I was sure I'd breathed in some loose bits as I'd wrapped it around Emmet's foot. They were stuck in my throat, and even though I'd swallowed and swallowed, I couldn't seem to budge them.

Emmet looked much too pale, now.

'We should take him to hospital,' I said. 'They'll know how to get the wire out there.'

The woman shuddered at the mention of the wire. 'Sure, it's a long way to the hospital,' she said. 'I don't want to be going over

217

there. I'm not used to driving. My daughter brings me to see himself when it's visiting. It's too far for me to drive.' She glanced at Emmet in the mirror. 'We'll bring him to the orphanage and the Brothers can sort out what they want to do with him.'

'What do you think, Emmet?' I said. I was sure the hospital was the best place for him, and I wasn't ready to give in without a fight.

But he just shrugged. 'They won't want me going there... Bring me to the orphanage... Thank you, Missis.'

It seemed to take a lifetime to get there. The car bumped slowly along the lanes, and Emmet flinched each time the tyres hit a pot hole. The woman gripped the steering wheel tightly and her knuckles were white with the effort. She wasn't the best driver. I couldn't bear to see the pain on Emmet's face as we jolted along, but I couldn't look away from him, either. He seemed so tiny and helpless, with his pale skin and his swollen lip.

'It's okay, Claire,' he said, finally, after I'd been staring over my shoulder at him for what seemed like an age. 'I'm all right. Look out the front ... or sure, you'll be sick again.'

The woman started fussing then, worrying about her husband's car seats. 'We've blood already to be dealing with,' she told me. 'I don't need you adding to the mess.' So I peeled my eyes away from Emmet, and tried to spot his orphanage from the front window, instead.

The woman's car slowed after passing through a crossroads, and she parked outside a pair of huge iron gates. The name 'Cash Hill Industrial School', in giant-sized metal letters, hung above them.

'Is this it?' I asked. It wasn't at all as I'd imagined an orphanage with a farm to be. I'd pictured a cosy cottage with a thatched roof and grazing animals, and geese and ducks and chickens. This building looked more like the old hospital we passed sometimes, back in Cardiff, that Jack said was full of crazy people – huge, dark and scary, with lots of windows that looked out onto the rest of the world like sad, staring eyes.

'This is the place, right enough,' Emmet said weakly.

The woman clambered out of the car and rang a bell next to the gate, then she waited while a boy ran up from the house. He spoke to her through the railings, before running back to the house again. His clothes looked even more worn than Emmet's.

'You live here?' I asked Emmet. 'This is your home?'

He nodded. 'Some of the Brothers are grand, to be fair... Most days, I think ... here's better than nowhere.'

A massive man dressed all in black came striding up the pathway, his anger clear in every step. He opened the gate and the woman seemed to shrink as he spoke to her. She pointed to the car and said something.

'That's Brother Joshua,' Emmet whispered.

'The one who threw you down the stairs?' I shuddered. 'Will you be all right?'

He shrugged off my cardigan and handed it back to me. 'I'll be grand,' he said.

'Don't forget to bring Buddy to school tomorrow,' I told him. 'It'll be our last chance to meet up.' I bit my lip at that thought.

He gave me a thumbs-up. 'I will.' He lifted his broken boot from the seat next to him. 'Francis promised to ... finish it tonight.' He held up the apple core he'd be giving to Francis, and the fear bubbled out of both of us as laughter.

Something crinkled in my dress pocket. I'd completely forgotten about my story. 'Look,' I said, 'here's the story I wrote about Buddy. It's a present for you.' I held it out to him and suddenly felt shy. I'd tried my best not to make any mistakes, but there were still some ink blots on the pages. 'It's a bit messy, but it's yours if you want it.'

'A present ... for me?' His voice seemed very serious. 'Thank you.' He gently lifted the papers from my fingers and held them against his chest.

'I'm glad I wrote it,' I said. 'I know you didn't fall from Buddy,' and I blushed, remembering how I hadn't been honest with Emmet either, how I hadn't told him the truth about the story competition, 'but still, you're the bravest person I've ever met.'

He didn't seem to be listening. 'A present. Can you sing "Happy Birthday" to me again?' I nodded and started singing quietly. Tears filled his eyes as I sang. 'Thank you, Claire,' he whispered, and the sad smile on his face made my heart ache.

I finished singing just as Brother Joshua reached the car, and Emmet hid the story in his pocket.

'What's this?' the man shouted as he yanked open the back door. 'You ran away from school, did you?' He slapped Emmet on the head. 'So that's how you thank us, is it? And you've barbed wire in your foot to show for it. Be sure your sins will find you out.' He dragged Emmet from the back seat.

Emmet screamed as his injured foot hit the ground. 'Stop it!' I cried, trying to open my door to get out, but the handle was rusty and it was stuck shut. I leaned out through the window. 'Leave him alone,' I yelled, as he hit Emmet on his head again and again.

The man shook his fist at me and I flinched back into my seat. 'You'll get your punishment, too.'

It was obvious Emmet couldn't walk all the way to the building, so the man grabbed him roughly and swung him over his shoulder, like a sack of coal.

The woman sat back in the driver's seat. 'Good God, what a place,' she muttered, turning the key in the ignition.

Emmet raised his head a little, and our eyes met for a moment. He looked truly sad, and sorry, too. I'd seen the Brother's cruel treatment, and I knew that fact hurt Emmet. So I shut my eyes as the man carried him down the long driveway towards the grey and miserable-looking building, and I didn't open them again until Emmet was gone.

* * *

The woman had been wrong – school was closed when we got there. Even the House girls had finished their cleaning and gone home.

'I'll have to drive you back myself then,' she grumbled. 'As if I haven't enough to be getting on with.' She started off towards the main road. 'You'll need to direct me, so.'

I showed her with my hand the ways she needed to turn – the words 'left' and 'right' had got muddled in my mind – and we headed off in the general direction of Granny's. And soon I realised I had no idea how to get there. The only way I could imagine was by following the roads the school bus took, and that was hardly the most direct route – even *I* realised that.

'What's your address?' the woman asked in frustration, as I sent her up yet another tiny lane. 'Maybe I'll know how to get there myself.' But she didn't. 'Sure,' she sighed when I told her the address Granny had taught me, 'that could be anywhere over there,' and she waved a hand in the direction of the sea. Unless she dumped me at the side of the road, which I was certain she had half a mind to do, she had no choice but to follow the bus route.

'Why were you with a boy from the orphanage at all?' she asked from the corner of her mouth. She was reversing the car out of a farmyard and along the narrow lane that had turned out to be a dead end. The hedge was scraping the side of her car, and the squeaky sound made my teeth hurt. 'Sure, half the boys at that Cash Hill School are criminals.'

'Emmet's mother's dead,' I managed to whisper. 'He's not a criminal.' But she just rolled her eyes at me and carried on the slow backward crawl, until her car somehow made it out onto the big lane again.

I directed her past landmarks I remembered from my daily journeys – the little house with half its thatch missing, and the small lake with an emerald green pom-pom of an island in it – then up one never-ending boreen and down another. My hand pointed this way and that.

'For the love of God,' she practically yelled, when she had to reverse for the third time, 'not another U-turn! Couldn't you just be keeping us to the main roads?'

But it wasn't any good. I couldn't remember which road to take without including the trips to tiny cottages where the bus dropped off its passengers. There were just too many roads across the bog, and too many massive rocks. And one rock or bog looked very much like another.

She talked and talked as she drove, things she remembered about living in Cork and how much better it was there. She didn't expect me to join in, which was just as well. My throat was full of cotton wool strands and they seemed to be swelling. I stared out of the window at the mountain towering above us, and I felt like I was an ant about to be ground into the dirt under the boot of a giant. And because of the cotton wool, when that giant decided to squash me, I wouldn't even be able to call out for help. There would be nothing I could do to stop it from happening. The thought made me tremble and I pulled my cardigan tightly around me.

We passed ponies in fields where hardly a blade of grass grew. They were like ghost horses, with grey bodies and sad-looking faces. They seemed half-starved. Even my favourite – the one I thought of as Star – I saw, now, was nothing but skin stretched tightly over bones. I'd looked at that horse every day for a month, but I'd only seen what I'd wanted to. That fact made me feel all hollowed out, and as the woman's car jarred over each and every rock on the endless lanes, my insides felt emptier and emptier.

* * *

Granny almost cried when I walked into the kitchen. 'Oh child,' she said, seeing the blood on my hands. She grabbed my arm. 'What's happened?'

The woman wasn't far behind me. 'She's after running away from school. I've had to drive her over from the other side of Roundmore, so. And himself in hospital too. She's not injured. The blood is the boy's.'

'Oh, thank you, thank you.' Granny clutched the woman's coat sleeve. 'We've had the Guards here. The school sent them. Please, please, have a seat.'

Granny pulled out a chair for the woman and led me to the sink. She helped me wash the blood from my hands. 'We've been awful worried. Thank you so much for bringing her home.'

'Well, I won't say it's no bother,' the woman said, ''tis our Christian duty to help those less fortunate, but I could have done without this today, sure I could.'

'I'm sorry for your trouble,' Granny said, patting my hands dry on the towel. 'Can I offer you a cup of tea?'

'I'd sooner have some petrol, if you have it,' the woman said. 'We came here by every back road there is.' She threw me and my navigating skills an angry glance. 'What's in my car won't get me even half way home.'

'Petrol, yes.' Granny lifted her head and shouted, 'Patrick!'

I heard him moving in our bedroom before he appeared in the doorway. 'So, you're back,' he muttered when he saw me.

'Patrick, get a jerry can and syphon off some petrol from the van in the shed,' Granny said.

Will looked at her as if she were mad. 'What on earth do you mean? I don't know how to do that.'

'Oh, for God's sake.' Granny shook her head. 'I'll do it myself. Go back to your homework.' Will left us to it while Granny turned to the woman again. She waved the teapot at her. 'Will I pour you a cup of tea first?'

'Sure, I am parched,' the woman said.

Granny poured three cups of tea. 'So, where've you been, Claire?' she asked. Her voice was quite calm, although her hands shook as she handed us our drinks. 'The Guards said you were gone from school at dinner time. They said a boy was missing too, from the school next door.'

'Emmet,' I said. My voice was very quiet.

'The boy with the wire through his foot,' the woman said. 'From the orphanage. A wee scrap of a thing he was, and the wire went right through and out the other side. Barbs and all. It turned my stomach to see it.' She seemed to enjoy talking about it now, though.

223

I tried to take a sip of tea but the smell reminded me of the blood flowing out of Emmet's foot. I could still feel the bits of cotton wool stuck in my throat and I desperately wanted to rinse them away, but each time I put the cup to my lips, I felt sick.

'There was an accident?' Granny grasped my hand. 'But you're all right, Claire?'

I nodded. I was feeling very cold, now.

'Sure, it would never have happened if they hadn't run away,' the woman added helpfully.

Granny picked up a letter from the table. 'The Guards brought this,' she said. 'It's from the head nun and it says if you turn up alive, you're to be suspended from school until Monday.'

I nodded again. I should have been pleased at that news – a whole day off school. But I didn't feel like smiling. I was still thinking about Emmet, how he'd been thrown like a sack over the huge man's shoulder. I wondered what punishment he would get. Suspension wasn't really a punishment, not for me, and at least it put off being walloped by Sister John. But then I realised I wouldn't get walloped after all – Jack was coming on Saturday to take us home. I wouldn't have to go back to that school again. But that meant I wouldn't get to see Emmet. Not ever, ever again.

'You've gone very pale and look, you're shivering,' Granny told me. 'Drink your tea to warm yourself.'

I took a tiny sip from my cup but the liquid seemed to swell the cotton wool stuck in my throat.

'Ah suspension, now that's a fair punishment,' the woman said. 'Between you and me, I wouldn't like to think what the Brothers are doing to that poor boy. He already had a terrible swollen face.' She shook her head. 'They're fiends they are, right enough.' She finished off her tea and placed the cup with a clatter back on its saucer. The noise made me flinch. 'Everyone knows, but what can you do? I can't imagine what treatment his foot will be having. The Brother said they'd see to it themselves. I would have brought him to the hospital myself if I hadn't been so short of time.'

'Ah sure, the Brothers will see to bringing him there,' Granny said, but her voice didn't sound sure at all.

The woman shrugged and stood up. 'Anyhows,' she said, pulling her coat tightly around herself and throwing me one last angry glare, 'about that petrol.'

Chapter 25

I was far too imaginative a child to cope with such a trauma – it's obvious to me, now.

* * *

I had terrible dreams that night. Some were of my parents arguing, of my mother throwing plates and calling my father a murderer while he did his best to scrub the stairs, endlessly from top to bottom. Some were of Louis floating in the lake, too far out for anyone to reach, his blond hair like a halo around his head. But mostly the dreams were of Emmet. We'd be running away to find Buddy, then riding the horse across the hills, Emmet in charge of the reins and me holding on tightly behind. We'd laugh and laugh and then we'd fall, come crashing to the ground, sharp wire everywhere. We'd be sitting in a field, with huge rusty spikes of metal piercing Emmet's thin body. Blood would ooze from his lips, from his hands, from his feet. In all the dreams I was safe, but I couldn't stop the awful things from happening to him. I cried out, time after time, and Granny came hurrying to me.

'What is it, Claire?' she'd ask, but I couldn't tell her. I was afraid I had caused Emmet's accident. I'd nagged him to take me to see Buddy, after all. I was guilty and ashamed, so I kept my thoughts to myself, and the nightmares dug further into my mind.

Will complained about me waking him up, and finally Granny sent him off to sleep with Louis in her bed. She took the armchair by the fire. 'I'll be close by if you need me,' she said, stroking my hair. Her touch reminded me of Emmet's and the game we played when we pretended to be Beauty and Polly. The memory comforted me until I slept again and found myself sitting with Emmet in that field. When my grandmother rushed to me once more, through my screaming, I decided never to shut my eyes, never to sleep again. And all the time I was awake, Emmet seemed to be at my side, like a blur in the corner of my eye.

* * *

I should have been enjoying my suspension from school on Friday, and the freedom it gave me, but instead I hid in my bed, trying my best to stay awake. I couldn't bear to dream. The rough blankets were pulled up over my head and on top of them was Granny's sheepskin. When she was certain I didn't have a fever, she took away the chamber pot she'd put under my bed and said I had to use the toilet outside as usual. I went as little as possible, creeping like a ghost through the kitchen, and not even bothering to take the brush with me to fight off the spiders. They could have fallen on my head and I wouldn't have cared. I ignored Louis's pleading to come and play under the table. I hated to see the disappointment in his eyes as I crept past him without stopping. He reminded me of the way Emmet had looked as we sat and waited for the woman to come back with her car. He seemed to be giving up.

'Claire,' Granny said, from her chair by the fire. She was preparing carrots, the scrapings of peel dropping into a bowl on her lap. I was trying to slip back from the toilet to my bedroom without her noticing. 'I think it's time you got dressed, now. You've spent almost all day in bed, and you won't feel any better by hiding there.'

I said nothing. My voice seemed to have disappeared. I blamed the woman's cotton wool. It was stuck very far down my throat and there seemed to be no moving it.

'Go on, now. You're shivering in your pyjamas. Get some warm clothes on.'

I did what she asked, although it seemed to take forever to pull on my trousers and jumper. I wrapped myself in the sheepskin, too, but I was still shaking when I went back into the kitchen.

'Claa, Claa!' Louis lifted his hands to me, but my arms were far too heavy to move from my sides.

'Leave your sister alone,' Granny told him. 'She's not herself. Come sit by the fire, Claire. We'll see if we can't get you warm.'

I sat down opposite my grandmother. She'd moved on to peeling potatoes. Her head was bent over the bowl and she looked so very old. Her hair was mostly grey and her skin was grey too. There were lines on her forehead, around her mouth and on her cheeks. There were bags under her eyes. I thought of Sister John's favourite prayer, the one that started 'Hail Mary, full of sorrows'. Granny's face seemed full of sorrows that I was only just noticing. I couldn't take my eyes away from her sad, sad face. It reminded me so much of Emmet's. He was ten years old, like me, but his face was grey and lined like Granny's, and full of sadness, as well. I thought of his ripped skin, how the wire had torn right through his foot, how it had gaped and bled. My stomach churned.

'Will you have a little cocoa?' Granny asked. Her head was still bowed. I didn't answer, so she looked up and asked again. I watched her lips moving, the way the wrinkles around her mouth changed as she spoke. 'Claire,' she said. 'You're to stop this now. You have to talk.'

I tried to speak, to say, 'Yes, I'll have some cocoa,' but it was as if my mouth had forgotten how to shape the words. My lips moved but no sounds came out. The awful dreams about Emmet were terrifying me by day as well as by night. There was so much blood in them.

Granny's look softened and she asked again, 'Would you like some cocoa?' It took all of my strength to nod my head. 'Grand,' she said and got up to make it.

Louis was crying quietly under the table. Granny rubbed his back. 'You want someone to hold you, don't you?' she said. She looked at me. 'Do you think you could do that, Claire? He's a terror for being held since he went in the water.' I nodded slowly and she untied his rope and lifted him onto my lap.

He put his arms around my neck and cried softly into my shoulder. Slowly, I wrapped my arms around him. 'Cwtsh,' he said, remembering a Welsh word I'd almost forgotten. It had been one of my favourites, a word Mother used to whisper as she hugged me. When I'd been as small as Louis.

'Cwtsh,' I whispered back, the word catching in my throat. And I held him closer, as tears flowed down my cheeks and soaked into his blond hair.

* * *

We were still sitting there when Will came home. Louis had fallen asleep on my lap and I'd rested my head on his, my crying all done. Granny hadn't asked me why I was upset, she'd just handed me my cocoa and left me to it. I'd managed to drink a good amount, and I felt a little better for having something in my stomach. Holding Louis's warm little body and sitting so close to the fire was comforting. I wasn't ready to throw off the sheepskin just yet, though.

Will gave me half a smile when he walked into the kitchen. 'You look a bit better,' he said.

Louis stirred at his voice. 'Will,' he mumbled. Granny hadn't managed to train him out of using that name. She'd more or less given up teaching him to say Patrick, and soon we'd be going home. There was no need for him to learn it now.

Louis lifted his arms. Will picked him up and swung him round and around. 'Did you miss me, little brother?'

The light in the kitchen had changed. The sky had become suddenly dark. There was a crack of lightning and a downpour of rain hit the kitchen window as if someone had flung a bucket of pebbles at it. I shivered. With Louis gone from my lap, I was very cold. I pulled the sheepskin more closely around me.

'What's been wrong with you?' Will asked, over the noise of the rain. He plonked Louis onto the floor.

I shrugged.

'Still not talking, then? Are you ill?'

I shrugged again.

'Is it because of that boy?' Will asked. 'There's been a story going round schoo—'

'What are you talking about now, Patrick?' Granny said, emerging from the pantry with a loaf and a pot of jam. 'Shall I cut you a slice of fresh pan? What about you, Claire? You love the crust, don't you?'

The mention of the word crust reminded me of the way I had been untruthful to Granny by not eating the crusts from my sandwiches in school, and the way Emmet had been untruthful to me by saying he'd been giving them to Buddy. I put my head in my hands.

'What's wrong with you now?' Will asked.

'Leave her, Patrick,' Granny said quietly. 'Let her be.'

She put a quarter piece of the buttered crust into my hand. 'Try this, Claire,' she said. 'Things only get worse if you don't eat.'

Thunder rumbled outside. The crust shook in my hand. I couldn't bear to put it near my mouth. I could have helped Emmet. I could have helped feed him, if only I'd been more thoughtful. I didn't care how much he'd lied to me, I just wished now I'd saved all of my sandwiches for Emmet, every single day. He was starving while I had more than I needed. I'd met him nearly every day for three weeks, so why hadn't I realised how thin he was? Why hadn't I looked at him, really looked, before that awful day in the field?

* * *

When Jack arrived the next afternoon, I couldn't have called 'hello' to him if I'd wanted to – my mouth was still stuffed full of threads. I didn't like to think about them. They reminded me of how the woman had tried to help Emmet with her first-aid kit. And of blood and pain. They were thoughts I didn't want in my head but I

230

couldn't shake them out. I hoped the Brothers had taken the wire from Emmet's foot, but I didn't dare think about how. Could he walk now? Was his cut all stitched up and bandaged? I ached to see him one more time. I was desperate to say a proper goodbye, the way Polly had said goodbye to Beauty.

Louis, so Granny said, seemed physically fine after his own accident. But, as she kept muttering, his spirit had taken a terrible knock. At his first glimpse of Jack at the door, my little brother had climbed onto my lap, turned his back to the room and rested his chin on my shoulder. Every now and then, he'd given a heartfelt sob that shuddered through his little body. It was clear he blamed our uncle for leaving us here and for the accident at the lake. I was glad no one had thought to ask about the gap under the chicken wire, and who had made it. What with Emmet's accident, I had more than enough guilt to be getting on with.

Even Will was behaving oddly. Aiden was expecting him at his house that morning, but Will had missed the only bus into town. He'd stomped around the kitchen at breakfast, slamming the doors of the presses, but he hadn't really made much effort to get up in time. He'd turned his alarm clock off when it had rung at eight-thirty and he'd rolled over with a groan. We'd both gone back to sleep until ten.

Jack was surprised to see the three of us huddled around the fire. He couldn't even think of a joke. Granny was stirring a pot on the stove and barely lifted her head.

'I brought someone with me,' he said, when he realised he wasn't going to get the usual fuss. 'He's out by the car.' We didn't move, so he said, 'I'll go bring him in, then.'

When he'd gone, Granny said, 'It'll be your father, no doubt,' and carried on with her cooking.

Even the thought of Dad being in Connemara didn't change our mood. I caught Will's eye. He gave a tiny shrug. Too much had happened, since we last saw our father, to make his visit mean anything special to us.

'Ma,' Dad said from the door. I hadn't ever heard him use the word before.

Granny half lifted her face. 'Son,' she said, and I saw the wooden spoon trembling in her hand. They stared at each other for a moment, then she went back to stirring the pot.

I expected Louis to climb down from my lap and go to Dad, but he stayed where he was. Like Will and me, he was just too worn out to care. It was very quiet in the kitchen. Jack and Dad glanced at each other, not sure how to break the silence.

'Sorry to hear about the accident,' Dad finally managed. He came over to the hearth and reached out to take Louis. But he clung to me, so Dad had to make do with stroking his head. 'How are you, my baby?' Louis buried his face into my neck and Dad gave up on him. He turned instead to Granny and Will. 'You must all have had a terrible shock. I'm sorry we've left the children here so long. It's been difficult...'

I glimpsed tears on Will's cheek before he put his head down and rubbed a hand roughly over his face.

'Difficult, is it?' Granny said, her voice a growl. She turned sharply from the stove and pulled back her shoulders. 'You dare to tell us about difficult? Your wife is sunning herself with her criminal parents and you're telling us it's difficult?'

'She just took off,' Dad said. 'I couldn't stop her.'

'Then make her come back.' Granny waved her spoon. 'She's three children who need her. You've made a bad marriage, son, so.'

'*I* made a bad marriage?' Dad's voice was raised and Louis whimpered. 'Isn't that rich coming from you? At least I've provided for my children. I've stuck around.'

'You packed them off here at the first sign of trouble.'

'I thought you'd like to help. I thought you'd have an interest. Maybe make amends for packing *us* off, since you brought that up. And it was Jack's idea, not mine.'

'Okay, Conor,' Jack said, putting his hand on Dad's arm.

Dad shook him off and pushed his face right next to Granny's.

232

'We've not said a word to each other since I was ten years old, and the first thing you want to tell me is I made a bad marriage? *You* made a bad marriage, Ma. You were the one who got deserted. And you were the one who deserted me and Jack.'

'Enough, Conor,' Jack said, pulling him away.

'I did not desert you,' Granny said.

'Are Louis's things packed?' Dad asked roughly. 'We'll put them in the car and be off.'

'Just like that?' Granny said. 'In through the door one minute and leaving the next?'

'No, no.' Jack was waving his hands at Dad. 'We're not leaving now, Mammy.'

'There's not much point in staying if this is how she's going to be,' Dad snarled. 'She's still the same, isn't she? Are you sober, Ma?'

'I have been sober ten years,' she said right into his face. 'And if you'd bothered visiting, you'd have known that.'

'Is it visiting we're talking now?' Dad said. I'd never properly noticed the Irish sound of his voice back home, but now it was as strong as Jack's. 'Because if it is, I've a bone to pick with you.'

'No, Conor.' Jack's voice for once was stern. 'Just leave it.'

Dad ignored him. 'If *you*'d have bothered visit *us* in that hellhole you packed us off to, Ma, then you'd have known the Brothers were beating the living shite out of us, day after day after day.' There was spit flying from his mouth. 'Because that's what they did to boys with no visitors.' He was really, really loud, now. 'Did you know that, Ma? Did you?'

'If you want to be gone, don't let me stop you,' Granny said with a shrug. 'I've enough to be doing, without you here.' And she wiped Dad's spit from her cheek and went back to stirring her pot.

Dad turned his back on us all and stared out at the lake.

Jack put his hand on Granny's shoulder. 'Sorry, Mammy, we've had a long drive and a sea crossing from hell, and we're out of sorts. Will I make us a cup of tea, settle us down a bit?' He began to whistle as he filled the kettle. He put it on the fire and got out some

233

cups. The sound of them clattering together, along with his cheery whistling, felt much too loud in the crowded kitchen.

'What do you mean "Louis's things"?' Will spoke so quietly, I almost missed the question.

'We'll all have tea in a minute,' Jack said, as if Will hadn't spoken. 'Come sit at the table, Conor.'

Dad didn't move from his place against the door frame. I was used to seeing Will stand like that, and watching my father leaning there now, I realised how much my brother was growing to look like him.

As Jack placed the milk jug on the table, Will grabbed his wrist tightly. 'He said "*Louis's* things". What did my father mean?'

Jack flinched. 'Now, you see, the thing is—'

Granny cut him off. 'The thing is, nothing.' She turned from the stove and gave Jack a glare. 'I have packed for no one. And unless I pack for everyone, that's the way it stays.'

'Mammy,' Jack pleaded, 'don't argue over this. I explained last week on the phone. Conor's only doing what Eleri asked, and it'll be a lot less work for you.'

'Can you not let the man speak for himself?' Granny said. 'Conor?'

Dad was still leaning against the door frame. His face was calm now, sad looking. I was sorry we hadn't made more of a fuss of him when he arrived, and I thought perhaps I should go and put my arms around him, tell him how much I'd missed him, and how much I wanted to go home. But my body wouldn't move. All it wanted was to sit in the chair and hold on to Louis.

Dad took a deep breath. 'She's not well, Ma. You know that, don't you? She can't manage three children.'

'Not well, is she? Is it your prancing around with her friends that's making her "not well"?'

'Mammy,' Jack said, 'I told you not to repeat that.'

'What did that rich, spoilt girl see in you, I wonder?' Granny said. 'Your handsome looks, no doubt.'

234

'Well, it doesn't matter now, does it?' Dad's face was red and angry again.

'Rich and no morals. Just like her parents, living the high life with money robbed from people who trusted them. A thief, that's all her father is, fancy accountant or not.'

'Enough now, Mammy.' Jack shook his head at her.

'Sure, they can have the three children,' Granny said. 'They've money enough to throw at any problem. Or are you telling me they're paupers, now?'

'No, they'll help,' Dad said, 'but—'

'Right then,' Granny told him, 'they can all go, can't they?'

'No, Ma, that's not—'

Without a word, Will leant forward and swept his arm across the table. The cups and milk jug Jack had so cheerfully placed on it flew off, smashing on the floor. The noise in the tiny kitchen shocked us all. Then Will got up, shoved past Dad at the door and walked out to the yard. Dad turned to go after him.

'Leave him,' Granny growled, and Dad took another step, then thought better of it.

The air in the kitchen seemed clogged with words no one had dared to say. Everyone was looking at the floor and at the milk making its way along the grooves between the flagstones. Louis had got excited at the sound of breaking china. He was sitting on my knees and making little gasps as he pointed to the floor. Under the table was his space, and now it was filled with mess.

Granny was the first to speak. 'This is my final word on the matter,' she said. 'They all go or *none* of them go. And I did visit you, every third Sunday, like all the other mothers, but those wicked Brothers turned me away each time. Now, will someone get the mop?'

Chapter 26

I tried to hide under the blankets the next morning, like Will usually did on Sundays, but Granny came in at half-past-eight and told us to get up. Her tone made it clear she was taking no whinging and making no bargains. I sighed, yanked my jumper over my pyjama top and went to help her with breakfast.

From the pair of boots next to the fireside chair, I guessed that Jack had made his bed in the kitchen. That meant Dad must have slept in the car, and when he came in from having his morning smoke, he looked exhausted. His mood hadn't improved one bit since the night before, and the scowl on his face looked set in for the day as he sat down at the table to eat. We were used to his sullen moods at home, of course, but in Connemara he was fierce and angry. He seemed like a different person here, one I didn't recognise.

It was a very quiet mealtime.

'When is the boat?' Granny asked, as she cleared away the dishes. Jack had wiped his plate clean with a piece of bread but Dad had only half-heartedly eaten his breakfast. A cold rasher was stuck to a puddle of grease on his plate. For once, Granny reined in her rant about wasting food.

'We'll need to leave in a few hours,' Jack said, through a mouthful of greasy bread.

It seemed Dad hadn't even noticed them speaking. He was staring at Louis playing with his block of wood under the table. He was driving it up the legs of the chairs and onto our laps and back down again. It was still his favourite game.

'If you want to pass some time,' Granny said, 'go out with the children. It'll do you all good to spend the morning outside instead of moping under my feet. And you'll be saying goodbye to them

236

soon enough.' So, it had been decided, we weren't going home after all, and I was too numb to even care. Granny sighed deeply. 'I'll see about getting ready what we talked about last night.'

Dad nodded. His face was like thunder but at least his eyes had lost that faraway look they'd had over breakfast. 'You're right. It would be good to get out of this place. It's suffocating me.'

'We'll bring them for a spin,' Jack said, snatching up the car keys from the table and throwing them to Dad. 'Claire ...Will, get your coats.'

I was still in my pyjamas, so I ran to our bedroom and searched under my bunk for my jeans, along with my shoes and socks. I pulled them on as fast as I could. When I dashed back into the kitchen, it was empty. I raced outside after everyone, grabbing my coat from the hook behind the door, and struggling to get my arms into the sleeves. I wasn't certain they'd wait for me – I couldn't be certain of anything anymore – but the car was still parked up when I got around to the front of the cottage and I sighed with relief. Dad was in the driving seat. I clambered into the back, nudging Louis out of the way. Once I sat down, he climbed onto my lap and put his arms around my neck.

'Where's Granny gone?' I asked Will.

'She went to see Michael. She said she needed some fresh air.'

Dad suddenly muttered, 'Why is she so friendly with that man?'

Jack shrugged. 'There's just the two of them out here, now. Sure, it's only natural they're friends.'

'There's nothing natural about it at all,' Dad snarled. He started the car. 'Not at their age.'

Jack laughed. 'I don't think they're *that* close.' Then he stopped laughing and his nose crinkled. 'You don't really think...'

'Well, they've both been on their own a long time,' Dad said. We were going quite fast now, almost as fast as Granny had driven the week before, when we'd gone to Grogan's to ring Jack. There were lots of pot holes in the boreen, and Dad wasn't as good at missing them as Granny. I could feel my bones jarring with each bump.

'I don't want to think about it,' Jack said, and he started to whistle. It reminded me of the times we used to ride in the car with him, singing songs and laughing. But I didn't feel like singing today, and I could tell by Will's scowl that he didn't either. And anyway, there was still some cotton wool lodged somewhere in my throat, and it would take a lot more than a song to shift that.

* * *

It was an odd trip out in the car. It felt like none of us wanted to be there, not even Louis. He'd forgotten to bring his block of wood, and every now and then he'd look at me tearfully and hold up his hands. 'Caaa?' he'd ask, and I'd reply, 'It's under the table, Louis.' I thought about the box of colourful Corgi cars he had back home, and I wondered if he remembered it. I felt sorry that I hadn't packed more toys for him all those months ago when we'd fled from Cardiff. All he played with now was that block of wood and whatever fell from the table – a spoon or a bit of crust. I was a bad big sister, and, with a stab of guilt, I realised that I was a bad best friend too. With all the worry Dad's black mood was giving me, I hadn't thought about Emmet's foot once. I remembered it now, though, and the rasher I'd had for breakfast rolled in my stomach. I took a few deep breaths until it settled.

It was just as well I'd stopped feeling sick, as the roads were very bumpy. Jack directed Dad to go this way or that, up that lane or this, and to turn right or left. Dad didn't seem to have a clue where he was going, and Jack even had to warn him to pull over for a truck coming in the opposite direction. Dad was in a world of his own, and if he'd been his old self, I might have said that to him – he used to say it to me, often enough – but he wasn't in a good mood and neither was I, and it didn't feel like a day for teasing.

'We'd better head back,' Jack said, after a while. 'Drop the kids off and have a cup of tea before we're away again.'

There hadn't seemed much point in us going out. We hadn't even stopped for ice cream, although to be fair we hadn't passed much except bog. And the mountains, of course, although you didn't exactly pass them, they just followed you everywhere you went. I remembered how strangely beautiful they had looked, the first time I'd seen them. Now that I saw them every day, their strangeness had worn off, but their beauty was still there. My eyes could tell that, even if my heart didn't flip at the sight of them anymore.

'Turn here,' Jack said, 'and we can loop around and go back a different way.'

Dad turned off the main road and we trundled past yet more bog. We went over a small stone bridge, and the land outside the car window changed into tree-covered hills. The sea was suddenly close to us, and we passed by a little boat bobbing on the water before the road was covered by more trees. And as we drove into the light again, I was sure I saw in the distance the field with the fallen tree trunk in it. The tree trunk that was Buddy.

'Isn't this...?' Dad said suddenly.

A massive building rose up before us, its iron gates shut tight like a pair of folded arms. I recognised it at once – the place where Emmet lived. I searched the windows for a glimpse of him. Maybe he'd be looking at Buddy in the field, like he told me he often did. I desperately scanned the rows and rows of windows, and suddenly I caught a glimpse of a face staring out into the distance. I cupped my hands against the car window. 'Emmet?' I whispered into the glass as our car sped up and flew past the building. 'Emmet?'

'What are you doing?' Will asked, pulling roughly at my sleeve.

'Nothing,' I hissed, twisting my arm away from him.

'Why did you bring us along this road?' Dad snapped.

'Old times' sake,' Jack told him, and he waved two fingers at the building in the rear-view mirror. 'You didn't see me do that, okay, kiddos?'

I swallowed hard. The truth was dawning on me as the car raced along the bumpy road. This was the place Dad and Jack had been sent to when they were boys. It was the place Dad and Granny had been arguing about the night before. Dad and Jack had been at Emmet's orphanage. I thought about the face at the window, the thick red skin on Emmet's knees and his broken arm. His number – 551. I felt anger knotting in my stomach and tears sliding down my cheeks. I rubbed them away hard. 'They still beat children in there,' I said.

But no one seemed to hear me. Maybe I hadn't said the words. Maybe they didn't make it out across my lips.

Maybe they didn't get through all the cotton wool clogging up my throat.

* * *

There was a cardboard box under the table when we got back to the cottage. It was the one Fergus the Grocer had brought our vegetables in, the week before. Louis's clothes were in it now, and his teddy. I put Louis down on the floor and he ran off to play with the box, moving it around between the legs of the chairs like it was a truck. Every now and then, he unloaded a pair of pants or a sock.

Granny appeared at her bedroom door. 'You're back, so.'

'Why are Louis's things packed up?' I asked, but my voice was quiet and Granny didn't trouble me with an answer.

'We'll have to be leaving soon,' Dad said, striding into the kitchen. 'Jack says the boat's always busy on a Sunday and we don't want to be turned away.' He could barely bring himself to look at me. I wasn't sure what I'd done wrong, but I'd become so used to feeling guilty that I reckoned his anger must be fair enough.

Jack came in, all smiles and cheerfulness, determined to ignore the serious faces looking back at him.

Granny put two plates on the table. 'Eat this before you go,' she said. She sounded tired.

'Thanks, Mammy.' Jack sat himself at the table.

'You can have mine, Claire,' Dad said, finally looking me in the eye. Being given his bread and cheese should have felt like a reward, but instead it felt like a test.

240

I shook my head and mumbled, 'No thanks.' My throat was so stuffed with cotton wool, I couldn't have swallowed a crumb.

He turned his face away from me. I'd disappointed him again. 'Your brother can have it, then.'

I wondered where Will was. He'd rushed from the car ahead of me. He wasn't in the privy because the brush was still behind the kitchen door, and he never went to the toilet without that. He must have gone straight to our bedroom. The door was shut tight.

Dad shoved Jack's shoulder, making him spill his tea onto the table. 'Be quick. I want to go.' He nudged the box of clothes with his shoe, and Louis jumped as his new toy suddenly moved all by itself.

'Is this everything?' Dad asked Granny.

'It is,' she said. 'Oh, but there's his coat on the peg.' She went over to the door and found Louis's blue anorak. It was far too small, now, to zip up over his round belly. She folded it and placed it on top of the box.

I coughed, clearing away the threads in my throat just enough to ask, 'What's happening, Grandma?'

She turned to me and put her hand on my arm. 'I've been thinking, Claire. I'm an old woman. I can't manage a toddler and sure, it's no life living under a table. Would you look at how pale he is?' Her voice cracked. ''Tis too dangerous for him, here. Louis will be better off with your mother, and when she's well enough in a month or two, you and Patrick will be joining him. It's for the best, so.' She put her arm around my shoulders. Maybe she thought I would cry but I didn't have the energy.

I looked at Louis, his little blond head bobbing as he steered his box of belongings around Jack's feet, and I felt a rush of love that made my heart pound. Then I looked at Dad. His head was down again. He wasn't going to meet my eye. How could Dad take Louis away from Will and me? How could he think of splitting us up?

'Does he have to go?' I whispered, but the question shamed me. I shouldn't want to keep him here when all Louis longed for was to be with Mother. I loved him and he loved me back, I was certain of that, but I was a poor stand-in for her. Mother had always loved Louis the most, and he adored her. She'd never had that from Will or me.

Granny stroked my hair. 'He does.'

'I'll be coming back for you and Will soon enough,' Dad said impatiently. 'Are you ready now, Jack?' His face was angry, just like it had been the night before when he and Granny had argued. I was afraid he might argue with her again but he only bent down to look under the table. 'Come on out of there,' he said to Louis, but Louis didn't move.

'You can't go without saying goodbye,' Granny told him. 'Go and get Patrick, Claire.'

'Can't go without saying goodbye?' Dad suddenly raised himself up. He seemed to tower over my grandmother. 'That's rich, coming from you.'

As I slipped out to fetch Will from the bedroom, I heard Jack's voice pleading, 'Come on now, Conor. We want to leave on good terms.'

'Leave on good terms?' Dad said. Why was he repeating what everyone else said?

I stood on the bottom bunk and peered over the rail at Will. His back was turned to the room but I didn't think he was asleep. I poked his shoulder. 'They're going,' I whispered, 'and they're taking Louis.'

Will rolled over. 'But you told me Granny said "all of us or none of us".'

'I know.'

'They're actually leaving us behind?'

'For now,' I told him, and as the words slid from my lips, I knew I was a fool to trust Dad to come back for us.

I waited as Will climbed down from the bunk, not wanting to go into the kitchen alone. The voices in there were getting louder and angrier by the second.

'It's time to go, Conor,' Jack urged. 'Time to leave Mammy to it.'

'Leave Mammy to it?' Dad roared. 'Isn't that what we've been doing since we were children? Leave Mammy have some peace. Leave Mammy feel sorry for herself. Leave Mammy to drown her sorrows.'

Will and I were about to walk into the kitchen when Granny hurled her wooden spoon across the room. She was so quick that Dad hardly had time to duck. 'Don't you dare say that word here,' she said.

'What, ashamed, now, are you?' Dad kicked the spoon and sent it scuttling across the flagstones.

'You know what I'm talking about.' Granny's voice was very quiet. She plucked Louis from under the table and hugged him tightly. He clung to her neck.

Dad raised his hands and pretended to look shocked. 'Oh *drown*, is that the word I mustn't say?'

'Quiet now, Conor,' Jack said.

But Dad wouldn't stop. 'Do you think you're the only one hurt by that word?' He pushed his face inches away from Granny's, and Louis buried his head in her shoulder. 'It almost happened again, didn't it? Were you drunk the other day when you should have been looking after my boy? Were you? *Were you?*'

Granny peeled Louis's arms from around her neck and offered him to Dad. 'Just take your child,' she said.

'I will,' Dad told her. He grabbed Louis from her arms. He was crying now and reaching out for Granny. 'We didn't miss you when you sent us away and *he's* not going to miss you, either.' He kicked the box of Louis's things. 'Get that, Jack.' Then he marched out of the kitchen, taking a screaming Louis with him.

Jack sighed and rubbed Granny's shoulder gently. 'He'll calm down and he'll get better about coming back here. It's early days, yet.' He kissed her cheek, softly. 'See you again soon.' He picked up the box and nodded to us. We had stopped just inside our bedroom, afraid to go into the kitchen. 'Claire ... Will ... come and say goodbye outside,' he said, and off he went.

Granny suddenly looked ancient. She sat down heavily and put her head in her hands. I could hear Louis calling from outside, 'Claa. Claa. Gann-eee!' The sound of his voice hurt my heart.

Granny bent over the table and hid her head in her arms. I could hear her crying. I wanted to tell her that if I was Louis, I'd miss her. I'd miss her very much. But my throat was full of threads, so I rested my hand on her back instead.

'Will! Claire!' Dad yelled from outside.

Will slid his feet slowly into his boots and shuffled out into the yard. I realised that if I left it too late, I wouldn't get to say goodbye to Louis, and who knew when I'd see him again? I pressed my cheek to Granny's head and kissed her hair, then I picked up the block of wood and ran outside.

Dad and Jack were already in the car by the time I reached the boreen. I had to lean in through the windows to hug them goodbye. Our hugs felt awkward, as if we'd forgotten how to hold on and we didn't know each other anymore. Giving Louis one last squeeze stole what was left of my energy. I handed him his wooden block, and he stopped crying and gave me a watery smile. Dad started the engine and Jack waved dramatically from the front window, saluting Will and me.

As the car headed along the boreen, Louis banged his pretend toy car against the rear window. I watched as he disappeared down the lane, his face getting smaller and smaller. And I felt as if my old life, and the Claire I used to be, was disappearing with him.

Chapter 27

With my little brother gone, my guilt – over his near drowning, and over Emmet's accident – became even heavier, too heavy for a child so young to carry. It was a weight I continued to bear for many years as an adult. The morning after Louis left, I found a length of green wool under the table. It was caught on a rusty nail at the top of the table leg. I wondered how often my brother had snagged himself on that nail without me noticing, and the thought made me shudder. It reminded me of Emmet and the wire, of blood, and his ripped flesh.

* * *

Granny shoved a plate of eggs and bacon in front of me. 'You'll need a good breakfast on your first day back.' But the smell of food turned my stomach and I had to dash to the privy. I didn't even have time to put on my shoes.

'Claire,' Granny said, 'you're a deep thinker, but don't be upsetting yourself.' She stripped off my muddied socks. 'Just go back to school and get on with your lessons. Everything will be grand again.' She touched the wool I was winding round and around my fingers. 'I know you'll miss your brother, but sure, your father will be coming for you and Patrick soon enough.'

I lifted my head a little and nodded. I wanted to believe she was right. She grabbed a clean pair of socks from the clothes airer next to the fire, then rubbed my feet between her rough hands. Her warmth spread to my frozen toes. 'And won't it be me doing the missing, when you children are gone?'

She thrust her thumbs into one of the socks and gathered it, then she pulled it over my toes and unrolled the sock up my leg. It felt comforting to have someone taking care of me. Mother had stopped doing that the day Louis was born. Granny sorted out the other sock and slipped my feet into my shoes, then she buckled them for me.

'Come on, Patrick,' she called to the bedroom where Will was dawdling as usual. 'You need to give yourselves plenty of time to get to the bus stop.' Her thumb brushed away the tears on my cheek. 'Your sister's a little slow this morning.'

* * *

I had to stand outside the head nun's door while everyone else began their first lesson. Head Nun was deciding what to do with me. I found the piece of wool from Louis's jumper in my pocket and held it to my face. I wanted it to smell of him, to remind me of his blond hair and chubby cheeks, but it just smelt of Granny's kitchen – cooking smells and turf. I sniffed it again and realised sadly that the smell of Granny's kitchen had become Louis's smell too. I crossed my fingers and hoped he'd be happy in the sunshine of Spain.

The wool wasn't long enough to tie into a loop and use for cat's cradle, so I wound it around my fingers, trying to make one-handed patterns. I wasn't very good at it. I thought about Karen, then, all those miles away in Cardiff. She could invent any pattern with a length of wool. She'd have shown me the best ones to make with my sad bit of yarn.

When the head's door finally opened and the nun saw me standing in the corridor, she gave a start. She'd clearly forgotten all about me. 'Sure, I can't be dealing with you now,' she said, 'I'm late for Father O'Reilly.' And she shooed me off to class for Sister John to deal with.

Sister John was nowhere to be seen in the classroom. She'd left Iseult in charge and the door open. I crept inside as quietly as I could but it was no use, every eye turned to me as I made my way to my desk.

'Oh look,' Iseult said, laughing at me meanly, 'that strange English girl is back. My father says now they're after winning the World Cup, England will be getting even more notions. Do you have notions, Claire? Is that why you ran away from our school?'

I quietly snorted. Iseult didn't know the difference between England and Wales. The eejit. She could say what she wanted. I didn't care. I hated her silly blonde curls, and I wondered why I had ever wanted to be friends with such a nasty girl. Face after face sneered at me as I walked to the back of the class, but when I finally reached my seat, the House girls' eyes were shining, and they smiled at me like long-lost friends.

'Welcome back,' the redhead whispered. The dark-haired girl added, 'We missed you.'

Sister John appeared at the door and raised an eyebrow in my direction. 'There she is, now. Claire O'Connell. You deign to grace us with your presence today, I see.'

I wasn't sure of the correct reply to that but I was pretty certain 'God is good' wouldn't hit the mark, so I just nodded.

'Sure, aren't we the honoured ones? Now, are you going to tell us about your little trip?' She took the leather strap from its hook on the wall and flicked it gently against her palm. 'Stand up.'

I felt my knees buckling as I stood. They wouldn't seem to lock. I pressed myself against the desk.

'Stand up straight, child.'

I was shaking, so standing up straight wasn't something I could do.

'Don't worry, we're praying for you,' I heard a voice whisper behind me.

I wasn't sure a prayer could strengthen my knees or take away the pain of the strap, but I was glad of the girls' support. And a prayer couldn't hurt. I wished I knew a good one myself.

'There's someone in this classroom saw you leaving school and running up the hill.' The nun gave half a nod in Theresa's direction. I might have guessed *she* would tell on me. It was just the sort of thing she'd do. 'So, Claire, where did you go?'

I gulped and tried to speak, but the words wouldn't leave my mouth. The cotton wool was still in there. The nun marched towards me, her rosary beads clacking with every step.

'What did you say?' She was very close to me now. I could feel the air swishing around the strap as she slapped it softly against her palm.

I tried again. 'Over the hill,' I managed.

'We know that. On your own, were you?' I shook my head. 'Who were you with?' I didn't want to say Emmet's name – I thought Sister John might mock it, and I wouldn't call him 551 or the boy from the orphanage.

'Someone else,' I said.

'And was that "someone else" a member of the opposite,' she curled her lip, '*sex*?' There were nervous giggles at that. I nodded. 'A boy!' she said, and slammed the strap onto my desk so hard that the whole class jumped. 'A boy from the orphanage who was badly injured by your delinquency.' She was shouting now. 'How dare you come back into this classroom with that sneer on your face? Put out your hand.'

I could hear the House girls whispering their way through the rosary. I held out my palm. I was glad to see it was quite steady now. I wouldn't let this nun know I was afraid of her. In fact, I realised at that moment that I wasn't afraid of her at all. She could hit me as much as she liked. She didn't scare me.

'Not your palm,' she said. 'Turn your hand over.'

The whispering behind me sped up as Sister John brought the strap down onto the back of my hand, viciously, over and over again. I stared at her as she did it, biting my lip hard and forcing my eyes not to cry. There was a glint of pleasure in hers.

'There,' she said when she'd finally finished. 'You won't be so fast to run off now, will you?' I sat down heavily in my seat as she walked back to her desk. I could feel everyone's eyes drilling into me but I was determined not to cry. 'Girls, get out your copy books for mathematics.' She hung the leather strap back on its hook and turned to us all. I'd never before seen such a wide smile on her thin lips. 'Today, we'll be doing long multiplication.'

I coughed and the cotton wool cleared from my throat. '*Ast*,' I murmured under my breath as I took my maths book from my desk. '*Ast, ast, ast.*' I still wasn't sure what the word meant, but I was certain it described that horrible woman perfectly.

* * *

There was no one behind the toilet block at dinner time. I sat down on the grass and felt very sorry for myself. I could have complained to the House girls about my punishment – they'd suffered the strap, often enough – but it was Emmet I wanted to see. I'd tried to push to the back of my mind the things he'd told me, and even though I knew Buddy was only a fallen tree, the horse still seemed real to me. I wanted him to be real more than anything else. I wanted things to go back to the way they were before Emmet trod on the barbed wire. And I wanted to see him. The tears I'd been holding back all morning began to trickle down my cheeks.

The back of my hand was swollen and red from the beating. I rubbed at it but that only made it worse. No teacher had ever been so cruel to me in my old school. Once, Wayne had taken someone's pen and said he hadn't. I could picture his crying face as the headmaster caned him in front of the whole school. It had been horrible. He'd had a line across the palm of his hand for the rest of the day, but Mr Davies hadn't been as vicious as Sister John.

I wondered what it was that made nuns so angry all the time. The ones at school were always hitting someone or other. I wished I was in Cardiff, with Karen and the teachers I knew well. I wished Dad and Jack had taken Will and me away with Louis. And I wished my mother would stop being angry and come back from abroad. Why couldn't she be like other mothers? Why couldn't she be like Granny? We knew exactly where we stood with her. She'd never throw the best china at a wall and flounce off to Spain.

The bell began to ring in the yard. I sighed and got to my feet. Emmet hadn't shown up, and my hand was still very sore. Lessons stretched out before me like a form of torture I had no escape from. With a heavy heart, I squeezed back through the gap in the hedge and headed for a miserable afternoon.

* * *

I could tell Will was in a strange mood when I got on the bus at the end of the day. His cheeks looked flushed and his eyes seemed excited. On the way to school that morning, he'd let me sit near him – not next to him, of course, just in the seat behind – and I slipped into it again on the way home. From there I could hear him humming, so I tapped him on the shoulder and asked why he was so happy. He said I wouldn't understand. It was very annoying. When the bus stopped, to my amazement, he belted up the lane as soon as his feet hit the gravel. I dashed after him. Despite the fact that he was nearly three years older, as he always liked to remind me, I could easily catch up with him.

'Do you need the toilet?' I asked. I couldn't imagine any other reason why someone who hated running would be putting on a spurt.

He shook his head. He didn't have the breath to answer. Why he was running was a mystery to me, but it was the perfect distraction from missing Emmet and Louis, and from my sore hand, too. I'd already decided I wouldn't complain about that to Granny. I'd be brave and keep my punishment to myself.

When he got to the cottage, he flung open the door and the cups rattled in the press.

'Would you not have a care for my china?' Granny turned from the sink and threw her hands in the air, but her own face changed in a second when she saw the look on Will's. 'What is it, Patrick? What's happened?'

Will chucked his satchel onto the floor with such force it skidded on the flagstones and ended up under the table. It was just as well Louis wasn't in his usual place.

'He's had a heart attack.' Will hardly had breath to get the words out.

'Who?' Granny and I asked as one.

Will flung himself down into a chair. 'Brother Dominic.'

'Brother Dominic?' Granny repeated. She dropped into the chair opposite Will. 'When?'

'At dinner time. In the schoolyard,' he said. 'He was trying to grab Keith McGinty to give him a flogging, and he keeled over.' Will gave a drumroll with his hands on the table. 'And he died.'

'He died?' There was an odd tone to Granny's voice. 'He's dead?'

'Absolutely and completely. There in the schoolyard. Dead. Dead. Dead!' And he banged the table with each word.

'Good God!' Granny said. Her lip was curling at the corner. There was a strange glimmer in her eye. 'Brother Dominic is dead.'

I stared at Will, and finally I realised where I'd heard the name before. 'Oh, he's the Brother that told you about Dad and Ja—' I stopped and slapped a hand over my mouth. I'd said too much.

Granny turned her eyes from me to Will. 'Brother Dominic spoke to you about your father? What did he tell you?' When Will didn't answer, she raised her voice. 'Patrick, what was it that man told you?'

'Nothing.' Will shot me a look, and I felt like a six-year-old. He always accused me of being useless at keeping secrets, and I'd just proved him right. I wished, for all I was worth, that he'd never repeated to me what Brother Dominic had told him, even though it was fair to say I had begged him to tell me at the time. I'd given my Scout's honour that I wouldn't repeat it too.

Granny wasn't giving up. 'What did you mean, Claire?' She was examining my face. 'What were you about to say?'

'I wasn't going to say anything.' I hoped my face wasn't giving away the lie. I rubbed my sore hand under the table and pushed it into my pocket.

'Now, that's not true,' Granny said. 'Tell me, what was it that Brother Dominic said to Patrick about your dad and Jack?'

She looked from me to Will and back again. One of us was going to cave, and just as I was about to blurt out 'the bad boys' school', Will said quietly, 'He told me about them stealing the boat.'

That was news to me. Will hadn't mentioned anything about stealing a boat.

Granny sighed and shook her head. 'I'll tell you about the boat,' she said. 'And it'll be the truth, not the pack of lies those Brothers like to spread around.' She sat up straight in her chair and took a deep breath. 'Forget whatever Brother Dominic told you. He'd have you believe my boys were criminals, but that's not true.' She pulled her cardigan tightly around her. 'Conor borrowed Michael's boat, one afternoon. He didn't rob it, he *borrowed* it. He was ten, your dad, just ten years of age, same as you now, Claire.' She took another deep breath and when she let it out her shoulders slumped. 'He went out on the water there.' She nodded towards the window. 'He wanted to catch something for our dinner. I was ill and I wasn't looking after him and his brothers...'

'Brothers?' I repeated. Will glared at me for interrupting. 'Sorry,' I muttered. 'I thought Dad only had one brother and that was Jack.'

'It's all right, Claire,' Granny said patting my hand on the table. 'You wouldn't have known because I doubt your dad and uncle ever talk of him, but they had a little brother, Declan.'

I didn't want to discover the details of this sad story about Dad and Jack. What I wanted was to run out and scatter the chickens in the yard, or gallop around the field on the mop. But I sat there anyway, with my grandmother's rough hand holding mine, and I let the truth trickle into my brain, even though I didn't really want it there.

Granny squeezed my hand again. 'My husband – he'd be your grandfather, of course – he'd gone away, and he wasn't coming back.'

'Did he die?' I asked, ignoring the look Will gave me. Sometimes, grown-ups talked about dead people as if they'd just gone off on a trip somewhere, and I wanted to know whether this grandfather, that I'd never met or heard about before, had gone somewhere or was *gone* gone.

'No, he didn't die. He went to Dublin, on St Bernadette's Feast, of all days, the saint my mother chose to name me after.' She shook her head.

I'd heard about feast days from Sister John. We'd celebrated one, for Our Lady of Seven Sorrows, a couple of weeks before, with special prayers in school. There hadn't been a feast, though, and I'd been disappointed.

'He'd had enough of living here,' Granny went on. 'Sure, people get sick of just rocks and rain.' She waved her free hand. 'This is the cottage your grandfather was born in. He'd only ever lived in these three rooms. At least he left us a roof over our heads. I'm grateful to him for that, so.'

She lowered her face and paused a long while. I glanced at Will and he shook his head, warning me not to speak. I usually saw silence as something I was duty bound to break, but I followed his lead and waited until Granny was ready to go on.

Eventually she lifted her chin. 'That day out on the water, they brought Declan with them in the boat. They were afraid to leave him behind. I wasn't well enough to watch him and he was always wandering off to the water. He was drawn to it, just like your little brother.' She stole a glance under the table, forgetting, as I had for a moment, that Louis was no longer there.

'Brother Dominic said you were an al... an alc...' I blurted. I didn't know what had nudged me to repeat what Will had told me, but thankfully I couldn't remember the right word.

Granny helped me out. 'An alcoholic. Sure, he wasn't wrong about that.' She sucked in her breath and held it a long time. I found I was holding my own breath, too. I was waiting to hear what happened on the lake, but really, I'd already guessed. Bits of conversations were coming together in my mind, what Michael had said he felt guilty about, and what Dad had shouted in the kitchen before he took Louis away. They were all adding up now.

'The weather turned,' she said finally. 'And Conor rescued Jack but he couldn't save Declan.' Her face was so sad, like Mary, full of sorrows.

I thought of Dad struggling to save his little brothers – how terrified he would have been, how afraid of losing them. The guilt he must carry. I remembered the gap I'd made under the chicken wire and hung my head. That gap might have been the end of Louis.

'The Guards came and said I wasn't fit to look after my children,' Granny told us, 'and they sent them to the orphanage.'

'That doesn't make any sense,' Will said. 'They weren't orphans, after all.'

'No, but we were poor,' Granny told him, 'and in need of help. Sure, isn't that a great excuse to take children away. It's what they do, so.'

'But why?' I asked.

She shrugged. 'They like to say it's charity – teach the children a trade, then make them work for nothing, and starve the life out of them.' Granny sighed and I did too. Emmet had been so very hungry, and all I'd given him were crusts and apple cores. 'I couldn't do a thing to stop it,' Granny said. 'Your dad and uncle were sent to Cash Hill Industrial School, and I wasn't allowed to visit. The day of the accident was the last I saw of them.' She shook her head. 'Sure, we didn't even have a chance to say goodbye. Ten and seven they were, no age at all. Those Brothers, they turned me away, every time, at the school gates. Brother Dominic, he was the worst.'

'And now he's dead,' Will said. He made his words sound like the line you draw when you finish writing a story. The End.

'Amen to that,' Granny said. 'And your dad and Jack weren't wicked boys, like that man would have you believe. They were hungry, that's all, and they were trying to help me. Whatever you hear, remember that. And the children in Cash Hill School, they're not criminals, like people round here say.' She blew her nose on her hanky then pushed her shoulders back. 'Claire, will you make us tea, please? We've that cake I was keeping for after our sausages, but

254

I think a piece each would do well, now.' She crinkled her eyes at me. 'And while we're talking of the Brothers, I've an arrangement with the Lynches on the big boreen. They'll be bringing you to Mass every Sunday, so there'll be no more threats of the strap. Right!' She stood up and rubbed her hands together eagerly. 'That cake.'

And we marked the death of Brother Dominic with a feast day of our own.

Chapter 28

Emmet wasn't behind the toilet block the next day. I sat on the grass, eating the sandwiches I'd saved for him, and felt sorry for myself again. When I put the wrapper back into my pocket, my fingers brushed the box of chalks Gerard had given me. I'd found them under my bunk that morning and they'd given me an idea. I began drawing on the toilet block wall, nothing too big, just a small horse in a field, and underneath I wrote the name Buddy. Then I drew two figures – Emmet in his jumper and shorts, and me in my green dress. I stood back. I wasn't a brilliant artist but it was okay. Finally, in Emmet's hand, I drew a book – my copy of *Black Beauty*. Our copy.

I sat down again on the grass. The ground felt damp but I didn't care. I knew the bell would ring in a few minutes and I would have to get up, go to class and begin another afternoon of lessons. I wondered where Emmet was. Was he working on the farm? Was he scrubbing floors? I couldn't shake out of my head what he'd told me about the orphanage that terrible day in the field, even if he had wanted me to forget it all.

The bell rang and I struggled slowly to my feet.

* * *

I waited behind the toilet block for half of dinner time the next day, adding blackberry bushes, sky and a blazing yellow sun to the chalk drawing. I thought of how Emmet loved to warm his thin body in the sunshine, how he loved the feel of it on his face. We were at the start of October now, and the sun had lost almost every scrap of warmth. When Emmet didn't arrive, I went sadly back through the hedge.

Theresa was standing near the gap. 'Hasn't he turned up?' she asked.

I was about to snap at her, to tell her to mind her own business, when I noticed the look on her face. She seemed to care about the answer. I shook my head.

'I didn't tell on you and your friend to be spiteful,' she said. 'I overheard Sister telling Head Nun maybe your dad was after robbing you from school.'

I blinked at her. Surely Sister John hadn't really thought that?

'She called him a thief. "Once a thief, always a thief," she said. I saw you running away with the boy you meet at dinner time, so I told them. I mean,' she put her hand to her mouth, 'I didn't tell them you were meeting him every day.'

'Thanks,' I muttered. I hadn't given a thought to anything but seeing Buddy when I'd run off with Emmet. I hadn't imagined my father might be dragged through the mud because of me. I suddenly felt weighed down again.

'I know he's not,' Theresa said. 'A thief, I mean. Aiden says it's just gossip.'

I nodded. 'He was only borrowing our neighbour's boat.'

'Aiden's my brother,' Theresa said. 'He's friends with your brother.'

'I know.'

'Did you hear Brother Dominic's dead?' she asked. 'Aiden won't mind school so much now he doesn't have to dodge him. Brother Dominic touched Will too, didn't he? I heard Aiden telling our mammy.'

'What?' I squinted at her. 'I don't know what you mean.'

She shrugged. 'Anyhows, do you want to play a game?'

'What game?' I asked. I was exhausted. The disappointment I felt at Emmet not showing had stolen all my energy.

'Chase?'

She might as well have asked me to swim the ocean with her. I shook my head. 'No, thanks.'

'What's that on your dress?' she asked.

I looked at myself. I'd rubbed my chalky hands on my stomach and my green dress was smeared with yellow and blue. 'It's chalk.'

She shrugged. 'Sure, if you've chalk, how about playing hopscotch?'

I sighed and found the box in my pocket. Even if I didn't really want her as a friend, it would be rude to keep putting her off. I held out the chalks with a tired hand. 'Okay, but you draw the squares.'

* * *

We played hopscotch for the rest of the week. I let the House girls borrow some chalk and they drew their squares alongside ours. They weren't allowed to actually play with us, they said, or they'd get into trouble with the nuns, but it was just as much fun playing side by side. I'd even learnt their names – Caroline and Paula.

The four of us made a funny little group – I hopped half-heartedly, all the time wishing I was with Emmet instead, while Theresa thumped the schoolyard with her two flat feet like a jolly carthorse, and the House girls played as though they'd never had so much fun in all their lives. Now I'd started looking at them properly, I could see there was something beautiful about their smiles, despite their ruined teeth, and watching them skip and laugh made me happy and sad at the same time, the way thinking of Emmet did. Their hands were still covered in sores, just like his had been. I'd forgotten to ask him why, but I guessed now it had something to do with all those polished floors.

Iseult's birthday had come and gone, and I hoped her cake had been truly revolting. Out in the yard, she made fun of our game, and along with Siobhán, she said that Theresa and I were no better than girls from the laundry. When they couldn't get us annoyed by name-calling, they played tig around our hopscotch squares and generally got in our way.

'Iseult,' I said quietly one day, when I'd had enough of her making fun of Caroline and Paula's black teeth, 'you think you're pretty, but you have an ugly laugh.'

258

She stopped in her tracks. 'I do not,' she said. 'I most certainly do not.' She laughed a little to check. She looked at Siobhán. 'I don't have an ugly laugh, do I?'

Siobhán took a moment too long to reply, and Iseult's face crumpled.

'And if you keep on being mean,' I added, making hay while the sun shone, 'you'll end up with an ugly face to match.'

'You're all horrible,' Iseult shouted, bursting into tears. 'You're just jealous because I'm the prettiest.' And she belted off to the toilets, with Siobhán running behind, insisting Iseult had the most beautiful laugh she'd ever heard.

Theresa grinned and patted me on the back. 'Sure, that was great,' she said. 'She's much too full of herself.'

But the House girls shook their heads, and looked thoroughly disappointed in me.

'That wasn't a kind thing to say, Claire,' Paula told me, sadly. 'You wouldn't like it if someone said that about you, would you now?'

She was right, I wouldn't. 'Iseult does have a horrible laugh, though,' I said. 'It's because she's always making fun of other people.' She was cruel, and it showed in lots of ways. Why shouldn't she know? And anyway, she had once called my father a murderer to my face. Accusing her of an ugly laugh was very poor revenge.

At the start of each dinner time, for two whole weeks as we headed towards the middle of October, I left Theresa and the House girls to their hopscotch, and I squeezed between the toilet block and hedge. I faithfully waited ten minutes for Emmet, counting to sixty ten times and marking the wall with a line of chalk as each minute passed. He hadn't come back. The drawing of Buddy, Emmet and me was smudged now by the rain, and the book I'd drawn in Emmet's hand had all but disappeared. I'd written a message below it that said I'd been waiting for him and that I'd be back again tomorrow. I had to keep crossing out the day and adding a new one.

And with each day I crossed out, my heart grew heavier and heavier.

There was a postcard propped on the mantelpiece when Will and I got home on Friday, and a scribbled note from Granny next to it that told us she was at Michael's.

Will got to the postcard first. 'It's from Mother,' he said, turning it over and reading the back.

'I know that,' I told him. The picture of a lady in a black lace headdress holding a fan was proof enough that the card had come from Spain. Granny Costa Del had given me a doll dressed like that for my sixth birthday. It was on the window-sill of my bedroom in Cardiff, trapped inside its plastic box to keep out the dust. 'Is she sending for us?' I pushed my head under Will's arm so I could read the card, too.

Mother's large, flowery writing spilled off its edges. 'Dear Claire and Will,' she wrote, 'I hear you are both settled in your new schools and doing well at your lessons.' I didn't know where she'd got that idea from, although I had overheard Granny telling Jack about my commendation in the story competition the weekend he and Dad took Louis away. Granny had mentioned Will's Irish was really coming on, too, with Aiden's help, but that didn't mean we were 'doing well'. 'Louis is having fun in the swimming pool and enjoying the sunshine.' Lucky him. 'Be good for your grandmother and remember not to argue!' That was obviously all she imagined Will and I ever did. 'The family here in Spain send love, Mother.'

Will sat down heavily in the armchair next to the fire and let the postcard flutter to the floor. 'What a boring note,' he said. 'It hasn't told us anything.'

I picked it up and read the card again in case I'd missed something. But there was nothing else to find – no hidden messages or words written between the lines. 'At least Louis is happy,' I said. I thought of him in a swimming pool, splashing about in the sun. I was certain Mother would keep an eye on him so he wouldn't drown, and I was glad his dip in the lake hadn't given him a lasting terror of water. Perhaps I could shake off my guilt about the chicken wire.

'She's obviously enjoying herself,' Will said, 'so I think we have to accept that we won't be going home.'

'What? Not ever?' I dropped into the chair opposite him.

'Probably,' he said. 'If Mother and Louis are having such a good time in Spain, she won't want to go back to Wales, will she?'

'She can't stay out there forever. What about Dad?'

'He'll just carry on the way he always does. Why would he miss Mother when he's got his girlfriends?'

I thought about the way he'd hugged Yvonne at Mother's birthday party and the way he used to look at Karen's mother before she ran away with her vicar, and I realised Will was right about Dad. 'Maybe one of his girlfriends will take care of us,' I said.

Will snorted. 'I doubt they'd want to be bothered with a couple of kids.'

'So we're stuck, then.' I scuffed my heels against the flagstones. 'Do you mind being here?'

He sighed. 'Not really. I'm getting used to it, I suppose.'

'Me too,' I said. 'It's better at school now Theresa and the House girls are my friends.'

'You shouldn't call them "House girls",' Will said. 'It's cruel.'

'What do you mean? That's their name. Everyone calls them "House girls".'

'They call them that because they're from one of the orphanages,' he said. 'It's the big building in the middle of town. The one for girls. The "House". Haven't you learnt anything about this place?'

'They're from an orphanage?' It all made sense now – their worn, odd clothes and the horrible way Sister John treated them in class. They were orphans like Emmet. How stupid of me not to realise. I sighed. 'I don't understand the differences between all the schools and orphanages.'

'Well, it's quite simple, really,' Will said, suddenly sitting up in his chair and sounding for all the world like he was presenting *Blue*

Peter. 'There's the school you go to in Roundmore, and the boys' primary next door. Then there's my secondary, and the girls' secondar—'

'I know all that,' I cut in. His voice was annoying me. 'It's the orphanages that are confusing. There seem to be so many of them.'

'Only two around here,' he told me, expertly. 'There's the "House" for girls in Roundmore, and Cash Hill Industrial School, way out of town, for boys. It's the one we drove past with Dad and Jack, where they were sent after the accident with the boat.'

I shuddered, remembering the miserable building with bog all around it. 'Being sent to that school would be like a punishment.'

Will nodded. 'I bet it's horrible there.' He took a deep breath before carrying on. 'Those orphanages have their own schools inside, but a few children get sent to the normal ones in town, if they do well at exams.' I thought about Caroline and Paula, and how they always managed to quietly get me unstuck when I was in a tangle with classwork. And Emmet had tackled the hardest words in *Black Beauty*, and had barely paused for breath.

'But we're not supposed to mix with orphans,' Will said. 'That's the rule. You shouldn't be friends with those girls from the House. They could get punished for talking to you. Didn't you know?'

I shook my head. I'd known I shouldn't be meeting with Emmet, but that was because he was a boy. I hadn't realised I shouldn't talk to Caroline and Paula. They'd gone against the rules to help me, and I was very lucky they had. I'd never have made it through the first few weeks of St Brid's if they hadn't. They'd taken risks for me, and I'd taken their kindness for granted. I sighed. I remembered their hopeful faces as I'd stood before the class to read my composition. How could I have been so horrible? 'We don't play together,' I mumbled, 'just near each other.'

'You were friends with an orphan boy too, weren't you?' Will said. 'He was from Cash Hill, like Dad and Jack. Everyone at St Vince's was talking about the two of you running away.'

I gulped. So, Will knew about Emmet. *Everyone* in his school knew. 'We weren't running away,' I said. 'We were looking for something.'

'Where did you meet him, anyway?'

'Behind the toilet block. We were both hiding there.'

Will leant towards me. 'Was it true,' he asked, 'about the barbed wire going right through his foot?' And when I nodded, he said, 'Oh Claire, that must have been a horrible thing to see,' and I could hear the concern in his voice.

Tears welled in my eyes. 'He hasn't come back to school,' I said. 'I hope he's okay.'

Will bit his lip. He reached out and squeezed my arm. 'Well,' he said eventually, 'you have Theresa as your friend, now. And it's probably best if you don't play with the orphan girls anymore.'

'I told you,' I said. 'I don't play *with* Caroline and Paula, I play *near* them.'

'Just be careful you don't get into trouble with your teacher. Sister John, is that her name?'

I nodded. '*Ast.*'

Will laughed so hard he snorted. 'Do you even know what that means?'

I shrugged. I liked the way the word hissed through my teeth and I didn't particularly care what it meant.

'You're calling your teacher a bitch.' He was still laughing. 'It's just as well she doesn't understand Welsh.' Then his face became serious again. 'No more going behind the toilet block, Claire. That really will make the nuns furious. Do you promise me?'

'I promise,' I said, although my fingers were firmly crossed behind my back. I had to find Emmet again, and the only way I could do that was to go to our hiding place.

'Good,' Will said in his most serious voice. 'School will be much better if you stick to the rules.'

I wiped my eyes on my sleeve. 'And school will be better for you, now Brother Dominic's dead. Theresa told me he touched you.'

The colour drained from Will's cheeks. 'She shouldn't have said that.'

'Sorry.' I could see I'd upset him but I wasn't sure how. 'I only meant you won't have to worry about him anymore.'

Will leant back in his chair and sighed. 'No, you're right. School *is* much better now he's dead. Everyone was so afraid of him. There are some horrible people in this world, Claire.' He sounded ancient, like Mr Davies, my headmaster back in Cardiff. 'But we cannot let them win.'

I thought about Brother Joshua, and Jack's rude sign as Dad drove us past the orphanage, and I knew exactly what Will meant. 'Do you think we'll see Jack soon? I miss him, and we weren't very nice to him when he was here last.'

'I think he'll definitely be back for visits,' Will said, with so much confidence that I instantly put all my faith in his words. 'He's dependable, just like Grandma.'

'Ha!' I said. 'You called her "Grandma" and she's not even in the room.'

'Well, that's what she wants to be called,' Will said, 'and I think she deserves that, don't you? She's okay, isn't she, our grandmother? And she's our proper family now. You, me and Grandma.'

I smiled. 'You, me and Grandma.'

'The three of us against the world,' Will said, and I believed him absolutely.

Chapter 29

I've often wondered what might have happened if I'd kept my promise to Will. My future, perhaps, would have taken a different turn, and not one towards the law. But I didn't keep my promise.

* * *

The following Monday, I stole behind the toilet block. I was desperate to see Emmet again and to know that he was well. And if he didn't turn up that day, I'd decided I would stop waiting for him. The disappointment was becoming too painful. There was no sign of Emmet, so I sat back against the wall and closed my eyes to count. It was drizzling again. I thought of my mother's voice insisting it was 'only picking with rain' – a saying, no doubt, she'd hardly ever need in Spain – and I damned her for the second time that day. The first had been in morning prayers, when Sister John had noticed my mouth was moving randomly. After almost two months in her class, I still didn't know the words – at least, not in the right order.

I heard a rustle beside me and opened my eyes with a start. 'Emmet?'

A small thin figure was squeezing through the hedge. 'Emmet!' I shouted, seeing the bloodstains on his shorts and jumper where he'd wiped his hands that awful afternoon. I leapt to my feet and ran to him. 'Your uniform didn't wash clean, either.' I held out the sleeve of my cardigan. A grey stain patterned the cuff. 'Granny soaked it in cold water, but she couldn't get it out.' I laughed. What a stupid thing to say to him when I hadn't seen him for so long. 'I don't mind the bloodstain, really. It reminds me of how brave you were.' Emmet hadn't said a word, and so I glanced up from my sleeve and looked at him properly. He wasn't Emmet at all. 'Oh,' I said, suddenly, letting the wall hold me up. 'Who are you?'

'Christy,' the boy said.

Christy? But he looked so much like Emmet. He had Emmet's narrow face and deep eyes. He had Emmet's bony cheeks and thin legs. He was wearing Emmet's uniform, with the holes in the elbows and the hems hanging down on the shorts.

Christy rubbed his palm down the front of the bloodstained jumper then he held his hand out to me. 'Pleased to meet you, Claire. I've heard a lot about you.'

I slowly took his hand in mine. Shaking it reminded me of the priest. We had to shake his hand at the end of Mass. Father O'Reilly's fingers were smooth and soft, and his nails were always neat. Christy's fingers were bony and rough, with red sores, just like Emmet's, and his nails were bitten low.

'Are you from the orphanage?' I asked him.

He nodded and his bottom lip quivered when he said, 'I am.' His voice sounded as sad as I felt. 'It's a long walk from there to here, but it's great to get out of the place.'

'Is your name really Christy?'

He lifted his eyebrows. 'What do you mean?'

I looked down at my inky hands, ashamed to be asking such a horrible question. 'Do you have a number?'

'Ah,' he said. 'Yes, I'm 604.'

'Emmet's 551.'

'Sure, but only the Brothers use numbers.'

'Did you steal your name too?'

He smiled a bit at that. 'No, my mother named me Christy.'

'Do you remember her?'

'Sure, wasn't I after seeing her last Sunday?' His voice had a dry chuckle hidden in it and it reminded me of Emmet's. 'She brought me sweets and a cake and a whole bunch of bananas.'

I studied him. He didn't look like a boy who'd been eating cake and bananas the day before. He didn't look like a boy who'd ever eaten much food in his life. 'Really?'

He shrugged.

'Where's Emmet?' I asked. 'I've been waiting for him for weeks but he hasn't turned up. I got suspended from school. Did he get suspended like me?'

Christy shook his head. 'He got thrown out for good. The school said they didn't want him back, so the orphanage sent me instead. My English and maths are almost as good. Today's my first day.'

'Did they punish him?' I asked it in a whisper. 'What did the Brothers do to him?' I hadn't really wanted to ask that question but it had slipped out. I hoped Christy's answer wouldn't live up to my nightmares.

He took a deep breath. 'The Brothers—' He looked at me. 'Emmet told you how bad they are, did he?'

I nodded. I'd been trying hard to forget what he'd told me, but his words were stuck in my head.

'They shave off your hair if you run away.'

'They shave off your hair?' I touched my own. It would be awful to have my head shaved. It was a horrible, cruel thing to do. But my hair would grow back and Emmet's would too. Maybe that wouldn't be so bad. 'Did they do that to him?'

Christy nodded. 'And they took away some of our food. They stopped our margarine and gave us all dry bread for a week. If one person runs away, everyone gets punished.'

That didn't sound like much of a punishment to me. I hated margarine. If I couldn't have butter on my bread, I'd prefer it dry. I didn't tell Christy that, though. I just said, 'We weren't running away. We were going to find Buddy.' The words suddenly sounded silly on my lips and I felt my face go red.

'Sure, it's all the same to the Brothers,' he said. 'They were really angry. He got skinned. They leathered the hell out of him.'

'I got leathered by Sister John,' I said. I rubbed my hand and showed him. 'Here.' The mark the strap had made was long gone but I could still feel the sting if I remembered hard enough.

267

Christy gave me a small smile. 'It hurts on the back of your hand, doesn't it?' he said. 'More than on your palm.'

I nodded, blinking away tears at the memory of the pain. I'd tried to be so brave at the time. I'd imagined telling Emmet all about it but I was glad Christy understood. I plonked myself down on the grass.

'The nuns, they know what hurts the most, so,' he said. 'The Brothers, though, they're bad, too.'

I wiped my eyes quickly, hoping Christy hadn't seen my tears. Even if you didn't care about margarine or having your head shaved, being beaten was a terrible punishment.

'How's his foot?' I asked. My voice seemed small. 'Granny said they were bound to take him to hospital, but Brother Joshua,' I hated to think of that giant of a man, a monster, with Emmet thrown over his shoulder, 'he told the woman they'd look after Emmet themselves. Did they make him better?'

Christy sat down next to me and studied an ant making its way across the mud between us. He plucked a blade of grass and gently lifted the ant with it. I couldn't bear to look at Christy, with his lip quivering, so I watched the ant instead, marching up and down the blade of grass.

'They didn't bring him to hospital,' he said eventually. 'They never bring anyone there unless they've broken an arm or a leg.' He held up the piece of grass and the ant marched down it. 'When I saw him, he was covered in a rash and he was talking nonsense.' He gave a shaky laugh. 'Sure, wasn't that always the way with Emmet, talking nonsense?'

With his free hand, Christy reached into his pocket. I watched as he pulled out a small model, made from wood. 'Francis finally finished this. I was bringing it to Emmet that last night. Francis had been promising it him for ages. He felt bad he'd taken so long.'

I looked at the model in his hand. It was beautiful – golden brown, a tiny version of the Buddy I'd imagined, with a swishing tail and flowing mane. Francis was an excellent carpenter.

'Emmet said he wanted you to have it.'

I stared at Christy. 'But it's Emmet's. I can't take it from him.'

Christy smiled at me sadly. If I closed my eyes a fraction, I would have sworn the boy with me was Emmet the adventurer, the horse-imaginer, a boy waiting for his mother. My best friend.

The ant was still marching along the blade of grass. It seemed to think it was going somewhere in a hurry. We both watched as Christy turned the grass this way and that. We sat there for a long time in silence, and all the while his other hand offered me the model.

Eventually a bell rang in the schoolyard behind us. I sighed and lifted the horse gently from Christy's palm. I felt its smoothness between my fingers. It was a small carving – I could close my fingers around it and hide it in my hand.

'If he was talking nonsense,' I whispered, 'he might have changed his mind.'

Christy shook his head. 'No, Claire,' he said quietly. He touched my hand and gently folded my fingers around the model.

I held Buddy tightly and made a wish. I wished Emmet was with his mother, safe in her arms on the back seat of Howard the Millionaire's fancy car. I imagined her stroking Emmet's hair and feeding him chunks of fish paste sandwiches as Howard drove them away from the iron gates of the orphanage. Away, away, away.

And as the car zoomed down the road, it was towing a horse box and I heard Buddy neigh loudly as the car and trailer disappeared in the dust.

Both bells were ringing in the yards behind us now.

Christy got up. 'Will you be here tomorrow?'

I thought for a moment. Tomorrow, Theresa and I could play hopscotch again alongside Caroline and Paula. It had been fun of sorts. I looked up at the boy standing beside me. He was thin like Emmet, and just like him his shoulders sagged. I remembered my promise to Will, and how I'd crossed my fingers as I made it.

'I'll be here,' I said, getting to my feet. I would give my chalk to

Caroline and Paula, and ask them to share it with Theresa. Three was plenty to play hopscotch. I felt in my pocket and found the sandwiches I'd hidden there. They'd begun to escape from their greaseproof wrapping. 'Here,' I said, 'I saved these for...'

But it didn't matter who I'd been saving them for.

Christy's eyes opened wide. He took the sandwiches from me gently. He held them up to his face and opened a corner of the paper.

'Egg,' I said.

'Egg,' he repeated quietly, breathing in deeply. 'Egg sandwiches.' I watched him for a moment.

'See you tomorrow,' I said. If we didn't rush now, we were going to be late lining up. 'Here, same time tomorrow. And it'll be fish paste then.'

He still didn't move.

'Put them in your pocket now, Christy,' I said. 'Go line up. You'll get into trouble if you're late.' He looked at me as if he'd woken from a dream. 'You don't want to be late on your first day, do you?'

He shook his head, stuffed the package into his pocket and ran for the hedge.

And then, just before he disappeared, he turned and held up his thumb to me. It was a sign I'd seen Emmet make so many times before, as if everything would always be fine, as if we could be friends forever behind that toilet block. Emmet and me.

The breath caught in my throat and I felt those wisps of cotton wool in my mouth again, but I smiled and held my thumb up high. Then I swallowed hard and I slipped back through the gap in the hedge.

Postscript

The wedding took place on an April afternoon when the world, very suitably, seemed full of promise. The city was jammed with dawdling tourists and fast-paced locals vying for space on too-narrow pavements. We joined the throng, and strolled from Dublin's City Hall to the castle's garden, where Will and Jeff had arranged to have their photographs taken.

I walked arm in arm with Cillian, my son. It was a rare treat to have him with me, as his home now was so far away from Ireland, and I savoured every moment. His two girls skipped ahead of us, disappearing into the crowd and re-emerging again with a grin in our direction. We ignored the annoyed looks they received – it was a day for love and laughter, for wide smiles and fun, for living and letting live.

There were very few other people in the garden when we arrived. Cillian and I found a bench and I sat down with relief. I couldn't remember the last time I'd worn such high heels. It would have been on a night out with my husband, and he'd been my ex for thirty years.

Cillian had only just settled himself when Elsie, his youngest, rushed up, and the two of them dashed off in search of a loo. I checked my phone. The team and I were in the middle of a case, and I wanted to be sure the long-awaited documents we'd been promised from the Sisters of Mercy had safely arrived.

I smiled over at Will and Jeff as they stood, arms around each other, beaming at the camera, and I waited for my new emails to appear. The men looked so handsome in their dark blue suits and floral ties. Even their grey neatly trimmed beards matched. Their joy was infectious. I knew how much this day meant to them,

271

particularly Will, who liked everything to be ordered, signed and official. He'd proposed the moment the result of the referendum had come through. He and Jeff had been together for over forty years by then. They'd met in their final year at Trinity and despite the careful way they'd needed to manage their relationship in public, despite the strain that put on them, they'd stayed together, stayed happy. The wedding felt like a rightful celebration of that achievement.

Mother had come over from Spain – with only a little persuasion from Louis. At eighty years old she still had a fierce kind of beauty I'd long given up yearning for. That sort of attractiveness had never been mine, not even in my prime. Mother hadn't remarried after divorcing Dad all those years ago but she'd always attracted a lot of male interest. Will and I had wondered if she might bring her latest beau to the wedding – a stranger tagging along, we'd schemed, would have provided extra entertainment, and Will had sent her a 'plus one' invitation by way of encouragement. Jeff berated us for being mocking and cruel, but he'd never spent any time in our mother's company, so we dismissed his concerns and carried on regardless. She disappointed us by deciding to come unaccompanied. Louis was glad, he told us – her taste in men was not something he generally approved of. They were usually either expat bores or young Spaniards in need of cash.

Mother had plenty of that. Aunty Rhian had turned out to be not so much a jet setter as someone with a drug dependency. Sadly, she'd died a young woman, and Mother had been the only beneficiary of their parents' estate. Fraud had indeed featured large in their fortune. Will and I had investigated our grandfather's dealings and didn't at all like what we'd discovered. We wouldn't be accepting an inheritance from Mother when the time came. Louis was welcome to the whole of it. It was only fair, after all, as he'd lived with her for most of his life, and that couldn't have been easy – even for him, her favourite. I glanced over at Mother. She was sitting next to Louis's young wife who was nodding patiently as our mother admonished her about her children's behaviour.

'Sure, your mother hasn't changed,' a voice said, and I felt the bench dip as another person joined me on the seat.

I turned and smiled at Jack. 'Never happier than when complaining. Poor Madalena. I don't know how they can live with Mother, I really don't.'

'By all accounts it's a huge house she has, so they'd be well spread out.'

I shrugged. 'Even so, I don't think I could manage it.' I brushed a grain of rice from Jack's shoulder. The City Hall hadn't allowed us confetti. 'You're looking dapper.'

'For a man my age, you mean?' He nodded towards Will and Jeff. 'They look well, don't they?'

'Very handsome,' I agreed. 'They're so happy.'

'Hope for us all, eh?' He cleared his throat loudly.

I smiled. 'On the lookout for someone, then?'

To my knowledge, Jack had never had a long-term partner. It was too often the way with people who'd grown up in the institutions. For them, forming relationships as an adult could be complicated, and that sometimes became part of the evidence the team and I included when seeking redress for clients. Over the years, I'd tried to persuade Jack to allow me to represent him, but he had simply wanted to draw a line under that part of his life. He had made his peace, he said. As for my father, his own experience at Cash Hill Industrial School was a subject I couldn't even broach. Despite the career path I'd taken, he'd never once spoken of it to me.

'Definitely not looking for a partner.' He coughed again. 'How about you?'

'Oh, I'm glad for Will and Jeff,' I said, 'but I'm perfectly fine as I am.' I thumped his back to help him clear his chest. It was a routine we fell into whenever we met up. These days, that was often. He was living in Inchicore now, just a bus ride from my apartment near the canal.

He straightened up with a sigh. 'It's hard to beat our own company, so.'

We laughed, acknowledging how set in our ways we'd become. He wasn't far off eighty and I was heading towards my sixtieth birthday. Being single suited us both. Jack still enjoyed his cigarettes and a pint; work was my addiction. We each had well-practised ways of filling the voids in our lives.

Cillian returned and we shuffled up so he could join us on the bench. He put an arm around my shoulders and I leant into him, breathing in the scent of his aftershave. He and the girls would be returning to the States in a couple of days.

'How was your stay in Connemara?' Jack asked. 'Sure, you had enough rain.'

Cillian laughed. 'Well, it's not like we were expecting sunshine. We had our macs and wellies, so we got out in it.'

Granny's cottage was a favourite place for all of us now – a holiday home, no less. She'd have found it amazing, I'm sure, to think of four generations holidaying in her little cottage. Jack, Will and I, and Cillian and his family, were regular visitors there, and we relished its remote beauty and its position on the bay. On the windowsill in the kitchen stood a tiny wooden horse. I had treasured it for fifty years, the way I'd treasured the memory of dinner times spent with an orphaned boy. The mere handful of weeks I'd shared with him seemed more vivid to me than any of my childhood years, that brief relationship more defining than even those with my brothers – a fleeting friendship that had impacted a lifetime.

'It's a shame Granda couldn't come after all,' Cillian said, watching his girls playing tig with Louis's children. 'He hasn't seen Lily and Elsie since they were babies, and that was on Skype.'

'Mmm,' Jack and I murmured. My father had attempted to tease us with a 'will he, won't he?' situation up until the last minute, but Will, Jack and I weren't fooled. Dad hadn't set foot on Irish soil since the day he drove off from Granny's with Louis in his car. He'd sent a card most Christmases, remembered birthdays on a hit and miss basis but otherwise been totally absent throughout our childhood, and Will and I had got used to it. Like Mother, Dad had become a stranger.

'Poor Marge,' Cillian said, 'getting food poisoning just before they left for the airport.'

'Mmm,' Jack and I agreed.

Yes, poor Marge. To the quiet satisfaction of Will and I, Dad's glamourous second wife, Yvonne, had turned out to be as dependably unfaithful as our father. So he'd played it safe with wife number three and married Marge. She was a sad specimen, forever shouldering the blame for Dad's lack of integrity, and pitifully loyal.

My phone pinged as the emails arrived. I scrolled through them and found the one I'd been waiting for. 'At last.'

'Work?' Cillian asked, but he didn't stay for my reply. Elsie was getting into an argument over a stick with Louis's son, and he rose quickly to intercede. Jack and I watched as Cillian distracted them from their spat, making the children shriek at his monster-like growls and chasing them with outstretched arms.

I unclipped my handbag and took out the memory stick. 'I brought the story for Louis.'

'The summer of '66?' Jack asked.

I nodded. 'I don't know what he'll make of it. Will's read it and given me his blessing.'

My big brother was strolling over to us. 'Time for family photos,' he called, just as Cillian leapt from behind the hedge with a triumphant roar. He ambushed Will, pinning his arms to his sides.

My little granddaughters and niece and nephew circled them, squealing with excitement, while Louis and Jeff ran to Will, laughing and pretending to rescue him. Even Jack rushed to join in, coughing as he went.

I snatched up my phone to capture the scene. The photographer saw his opportunity too, and dashed across.

'Quick!' He motioned to me. 'Get in the group.'

I stood up as Mother teetered over on her stilettos, leaning heavily on Madalena's arm. She held out a hand to me. '*Dere 'ma,*

Claire,' she gasped. We always spoke to each other in Welsh now. I'd relearnt as an adult, using an app on my phone. It made good use of my power walks to work in the mornings, and I had hoped the language would bring us closer together. Those hopes had come to nothing.

My mother needed more support to balance on her heels, that was why she'd reached out. I was under no illusion that it was a gesture of affection. But I decided, in that moment, to imagine it was simply about maternal love, so I took her hand and tucked it into the crook of my arm as she steadied herself against me.

We joined the men and children as the sun shone down on our joyful gang, and I slipped the memory stick into Louis's top pocket. 'What you asked for,' I said, when he looked at me quizzically.

'Get in close,' the photographer called, and we squeezed together, bumping elbows and hips, and laughing at our ineptitude.

* * *

As the others made their way towards the terrace overlooking the castle gardens for champagne, I set off across the river to my office. If I was fast, it would take only twenty minutes to get there and back. Thirty at most. I'd be surprised if Louis could herd Mother and the children to the reception in that time. I was glad I'd had the foresight to slip a pair of pumps into my bag before I'd left home. Despite the celebrations, I knew I wouldn't be able to resist picking up some of the newly arrived documents. I'd sort through the paperwork as quickly as I could, find the information I wanted and scan it with my phone. It would be my reading material before bed.

I crossed the bridge and headed away from the quays, along a quieter road to the rear of the Four Courts. As I slipped through the gate to the tiny garden, I noticed my regular bench was free, the one at the back of the building tucked against the wall. It was where I sat to eat lunch in the sunshine, on days I had time for such a luxury, and where I often brought case notes to read. I stopped for a moment and ran my hand over the plaque, checking the words, as I liked to do. The metal was smooth under my fingertips, and the brass held a hint of the afternoon sun.

'In memory of Emmet,' the script said, 'the bravest of boys and my best friend.'

Author Note

While researching *Emmet and Me*, I read many first-hand accounts of life in Irish industrial schools. There were two sources I returned to time and again.

The first of these was the memoir by Peter Tyrrell, *Founded on Fear*, collated by biographer Diarmuid Whelan from letters discovered after Tyrrell's death. Tyrrell spent his childhood, in the 1920s and early '30s, as an inmate of Letterfrack industrial school. He suffered and witnessed extreme cruelty there and, decades after leaving the school, campaigned to raise awareness of institutional abuse. With the exception of Irish senator Owen Sheehy Skeffington, with whom he regularly corresponded, Tyrrell felt no one in power was listening. He ended his life in 1967.

The second source I returned to many times was *Suffer the Little Children*, published in 1999 by Mary Raftery and Dr Eoin O'Sullivan. This is a shocking and very moving study spanning four decades of survivors' experiences in the industrial school system. In the 1960s, Peter Tyrrell feared little had improved in the years since he'd left the system, and Raftery and O'Sullivan's study showed he was right. Time had moved on, but for the children unfortunate enough to pass through these institutions, conditions were often still extremely harsh.

In survivors' accounts, among the heart-breaking examples of neglect and abuse, there was often mention of one particular cruelty. Former inmates bear witness to its dehumanising effect. It is summarized in *Suffer the Little Children*:

'The practice of assigning a number to each child in an industrial school was almost universal. In several schools, the children were only called by their numbers, with their names never being used. This practice tended to die out in the 1960s.'

ABOUT HONNO

Honno Welsh Women's Press was set up in 1986 by a group of women who felt strongly that women in Wales needed wider opportunities to see their writing in print and to become involved in the publishing process. Our aim is to develop the writing talents of women in Wales, give them new and exciting opportunities to see their work published and often to give them their first 'break' as a writer. Honno is registered as a community co-operative. Any profit that Honno makes is invested in the publishing programme. Women from Wales and around the world have expressed their support for Honno. Each supporter has a vote at the Annual General Meeting. For more information and to buy our publications, please write to Honno at the address below, or visit our website: www.honno.co.uk

Honno, D41 Hugh Owen Building, Penglais Campus,
Aberystwyth University, Aberystwyth, SY23 3DY

Honno Friends
We are very grateful for the support of all our Honno Friends.
For more information on how you
can become a Honno Friend, see:
https://www.honno.co.uk/about/support-honno/

Also by Sara Gethin

"Heart-wrenching, captivating and beautiful...
[an] exceptionally moving and powerful novel."

Caroline Busher, Irish Times bestselling author

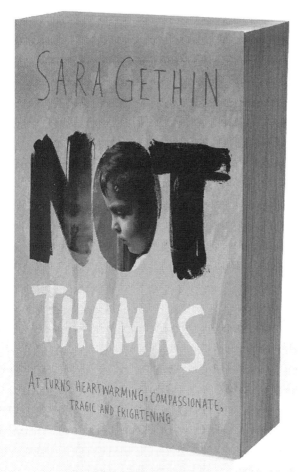

Shortlisted for the *Guardian*'s Not The Booker Prize
Shortlisted for the Waverton Good Read Award
A Waterstones Wales Book of the Month